THE DESCENT OF THE HALO

The Descent of the Halo
Copyright © 2017 Shea Swain

Warning: The Descent of the Halo is for 18 years and older.

ISBN-13: 978-1976212994
ISBN-10: 1976212995

Cover Designed: Sanja Balan of Sanja's Covers
Edited: Pam Howard
Proofreader: D. Swain, Kim Bey, Kelly Bey-Borden
Format: Shea Swain

Other Books Written By:

What Lilly Wants
previously known as Lascivious
An Erotic Novella

INVIDIOUS Betrayal
A Full-Length Paranormal-Sci Romance

ABSOLVE
A Short Romantic New Adult Drama

The Changing of the Seasons
Winter's Icy Heart
A Taste of Spring
Contemporary Romance

Chained to the Devil's Son
A Full-Length Dark Romance

The Binding of the Halo Series
Four Full-Length Paranormal Romance Series
The Binding of the Halo Book I
The Awakening of the Halo Book II
The Descent of the Halo III
The Battle for the Halo IIII
&
The Coesen-Origins

Heaven on Hell Island
A Contemporary Romance with Sci-fi undertones

Dedicated to my inspirations…
Sonserae
Daniel III
Daniel IV
Cianne

There were no palaces made of gold. No harmonious chords sung by

Angels standing near the pearly white gates of Heaven to lead the

way.

Heaven wouldn't have me.

Death abandoned me.

Left barely alive, with the darkness, immeasurable time, and the

memories of her and him. Though, as hard I fought the darkness

their faces were blocked from me. As time slowly crept on, their

presence, their warmth, their love, left me.

In the end, I felt nothing but the pain of my loss and the desire for

revenge.

Caleb

Prologue
The Atlantic Ocean
Late summer, circa 1816

The stench of urine and feces combined with perspiration, other bodily fluids, and filth assailed Jai's senses. It was so terrible that she found it difficult to think of what was happening to them. Or, where they were being taken?

What are they going to do to with us?

All of these questions crossed her mind before she and her ward were thrown down the steep stairs and chained to their countrymen of various tribes. She even thought about what her people would do when they discovered they were missing.

As hopelessness washed over Jai, she could only think of her ward, Marda, who clung tightly to her. The girl's thin arms were wrapped around her neck so tightly that breathing through the stench had become even more difficult.

Jai gently pulled at Marda's arm so she could take in air. Loosening the girl's grip caused Marda to slide a few inches down Jai's torso, settling more into her lap. Awake now, Marda moaned.

Jai sighed. Even if she could focus, even if she could use her ability, there wasn't much she could do to the pale people who held her and many others with dark skin captive on the water vessel that was carrying them. She was just a neophyte, a novice that no matter how well she knew how to wield her power it wasn't an ability that could save them. In truth, Jai's ability was only enough to secure her future as the first wife to the Prince of her tribe and secured her position of handmaiden to his sister, the Princess Marda, until their joining.

A loud cry rising above the continuous sobbing caused young Marda to squeal and tighten her grip again. *Another has passed*, Jai guessed.

Jai understood their language like it was her own. The ability was a gift most Coesen were capable of. So, she understood the pale man when he came down with a pair of clothed men of color to haul off the one who'd passed. They carried the body up the steep stairs and through an opening, which was the only source of light shining into the sunken room, and tossed the body overboard. None with shackles moved.

The light was the way to freedom but only through death.

Jai looked down at Marda who began to shake and cry uncontrollably. She wrapped her arms around the girl, squeezing a little tighter. "Close your eyes little one," Jai whispered in their tongue.

As Marda closed her eyes, Jai gently stroked her cheek. She may not be able to use her ability to escape but she could take Marda away from this place. Not physically, of course, but to Marda the images in her mind, whimsical and amazing, will be as real as the stench of the floating prison they were in.

Jai closed her eyes and called on her ability and almost instantly young Marda fell silent.

With the girl tucked away in a world of sweet dreams, Jai opened her eyes. She looked around the room at the scared, lost faces that were crammed together so closely that there was little space to extend a limb. Her attention settled on the men who were kept separated and who were chained to one another and shackled to the floor. Her gaze landed on one particular male. He was watching her too.

Why?

She was considered a beauty among her people. Her eyes were dark brown, her black lashes were long, and her dark brows were naturally arched. Her chin and nose were long and narrow due to her Egyptian ancestry but they blended perfectly with her warm beige skin, salmon colored lips, and her darker than coal hair. And even though she'd only seen sixteen dry seasons, her intelligence matched her beauty.

Jai still wasn't certain that attraction wasn't his motive.

The man watching her slowly bowed his head while maintaining eye contact with her.

He knows what I am.

Did he think she could save them? There would be no saving them, at least not by her anyway.

She studied the man's features—his comely looks, his build which showed his physical strength, and his quiet reserve that spoke of his patience.

A tear rolled down Jai's cheek when she saw the tribal markings on his chest. He was from the small village where Jai and ten other Coesen representatives were sent on behalf of the Quende King, Garwe.

King Garwe had also sent his daughter, Marda, to show how serious he took the Kepe King's proposal. Talks of joining the two tribes had gone on for two full seasons. King Garwe knew the Kepe wanted to merge due to the raiding of villages by pale men that had consumed the coastal lands, but according to their law, the Coesen people were to remain indifferent to the dealings of Middlings.

It was rumored that King Garwe wanted more power. By joining the two tribes he could gain that power. His youngest daughter Marda, whose beauty at eight dry seasons shamed other Coesen, was to be presented as bride to the Kepe King's son.

No one foresaw that the Kepe village would be raided and the Coesen King's daughter would be taken from their lands.

Jai shook her head at the man who bowed, then lowered her head in a modest bow to him. She'd seen the Kepe warriors fight bravely. Most were killed in the quick raid. In some backward way, Jai considered those who lost their lives to be the fortunate ones.

She let her head fall back against a wooden beam she was leaning against. Somehow, she knew that where they were going, her regal status no longer mattered.

Maiden Hall Plantation
Virginia, Fall of 1816

Marda lifted her head when the wagon stopped. Shaking with fear, she tried not to think of how empty her stomach was as she thought of how far from home she was. She looked up at Jai, who was watching a pale-faced man who stood beside the wagon. He was speaking to a Negro standing next to him. The pale-faced man barked out commands and the Negro just mumbled and nodded, never looking the man in the eyes.

Negro was what the pale-faced people called people with dark skin. She heard them say it many times since her capture. She didn't care for the word. She didn't care for the word Nigger either, another of their words for dark-skinned people. If she had to choose between the names she heard the pale people use for people of color, she preferred colored, but that didn't seem right to her either.

Marda also disliked their way of speaking. Their words sounded harsh, clipped, and forced. Not like her language. Her language sounded like a soothing song. And her people often smiled at one another. Not like this pale man or the others she saw in this land.

Marda eyed the Colored man as he made his way to the wagon where she and four others like her were huddled together. It wasn't long before she felt herself being pulled from Jai's arms and out of the wagon. She tried to tighten her grip around Jai. Marda even clawed at Jai's arms and screamed, but the brown-skinned man yanked her free.

"Simma down here girl," the brown-skinned man said.

Only, Marda kept screaming.

"Ain't nobody gonna hurt ya here, chile. I'm Barkly." He placed her feet on the ground, grabbed her by her arms, and shook her.

Marda looked up at the man's face staring down at her. He had a tired face but his light brown eyes had a gentle look to them. When he let her go, she moved closer to him as he helped Jai down from the wagon.

Marda shuffled to Jai's side and grabbed her arm as the brown-skinned man slapped his hand against the wagon. As the wagon pulled away, Marda watched through hooded eyes as the others in the back huddled closer together.

The brown man spoke to her and Jai but Marda just continued to look at the wagon as it rolled further away, down the dirt path. Marda's eyes searched out the pale man who made some kind of trade for them when they were herded off the boat earlier. He sat in the front of the wagon with ropes that were tied around the others' necks in his hands.

The man was called Shaw, and his pale gray eyes peered back at her as he rode away. Marda cringed when she saw his thin lips turned up into a wicked smile. When Marda felt Jai pull her close, she turned away from Shaw's crooked grin.

"Dis place, 'tis new for y'all but all gone be fine." The brown man smiled as he led them through a field of low cut grass. "The misses, she fair to us."

Ahead, there was a small white dwelling with openings for air and a portal for entering. It was the prettiest thing Marda had ever seen but the man didn't stop there. Marda slowed to appreciate the dwelling as they passed but the brown man continued walking and Jai continued to pull her along. So, Marda quietly followed but was rewarded as they traveled through a maze of hedges and colorful flowers.

In the distance, a large white dwelling came into view. Marda exhaled a breathless sigh. In her eight dry seasons, she had never seen anything so grand, so beautiful as the dwelling that stood before her. For the first time since being thrown into this new world, she thought of something other than home.

She wanted to explore every corner.

As they approached, she saw that the sheer size of the dwelling was magnificent. The paint was so white it was blinding. It had so many air openings and tall white beams that seemed to hold the upper-level up. Her current thought was where the opening for her to go inside would be in such a place.

Marda was so enthralled that she wasn't paying attention to where she was going so she ran into Jai, who had stopped at a white wooden entry on the ground.

Barkly bent down and tapped two times on the wooden entry. "Barkly here, wit dem girls the Missus asked fer."

Jai and Marda looked at one another, then to the entry as it was pushed up and open. Marda felt the urge to back away but relaxed when she felt Jai squeeze her close. A round face woman with a round body popped her head out of the large hole in the ground. She wore a head wrap and was dressed in coverings that made her look like one big mass of fabric.

"Don't just stare at me. C'mon in now," the heavy woman said. She reached for Jai but Jai ripped her hand from the woman's grasp then looked at the man.

"Dey fresh off the boat," Barkly said to the woman. "Don't know our talk much." He pointed to Jai and Marda, then to the heavy woman. "Y'all get on in now."

Jai slowly extended her hand, but held onto Marda tightly with her other. They slowly walked down into the underground space with the round woman's help. When the entry slammed closed above them, they both whipped their heads around.

They were alone with the round woman in a dimly lit room. The woman took Jai by the hand and pulled her over to where light flickered in the room.

"Let me eye ya some," the robust woman said as she stood in front of them. She circled them slowly. Every so often she would touch or move them closer to the light. She inspected them the same way the pale man, Shaw, had. She looked in their mouths and worked her hands through their hair.

"Good," she muttered under her breath. Then she saw the mark behind Jai's ear.

Marda watched as the heavy women licked her thumb then wiped at the mark.

"Hmm," she said when the mark didn't come off. She shrugged. "Seein ya both, I got a mind to guess why Shaw pay fer ya. A fine face don't mean spit if y'all can't learn proper. 'Cause me no never mind if ya can't use words but it gone be hard learning ya'll to." She shook her head. "Don't want ta think what it gonna do to my work load, to learn ya'll and get ya right for Miss Catherine. Goin' be some work fer sure. *Humph*," she rubbed her apron, "well let's get ya' clean."

The large sash windows allowed the sunlight to brighten the entire room. Jai and Marda stood next to each other with their heads lowered but stole glances at the objects in the room. There were so many things that neither of them had ever seen before. Things that Marda wanted to touch but she stood still as the heavy woman, who called herself Tempie, talked to a woman they couldn't see clearly because she sat in a chair facing a window with her back to them.

"Scrub 'em real nice Miss Catherine," Tempie said to the woman.

The woman stood and turned around slowly to look at them. Jai somehow knew not to look at the woman. But Marda couldn't help looking at the beautiful pale skinned woman that walked over to them. Her fair hair looked soft and was pulled up and secured with jeweled ivory combs. Not one single hair was out of place. The light beige dress she wore had short sleeves. A brown satin trimming was tied just under her bosom and the sash stretched down in the front of the long narrow sarong all the way to the hem.

Marda watched the woman with wonder and excitement in her eyes. And when the young woman kneeled down in front of her, she looked into the woman's bright green-blue eyes.

"This child is lovely," Catherine said to Tempie. She placed her finger gently under Marda's chin and moved her head from one side to the other.

"Marked befo' dey come miss," Tempie said as Catherine focused on the pie shaped mark behind Marda's left ear.

"And dey ain't speakin' much. Guessin' dats good."

"Why is she clothed in this attire? It hardly fits."

"Young masta Fredrick's old things' all I find dat's small enough. Ain't never had no small girl in the main house befo'. I speck I can fetch some from de field folk."

"No," Catherine said sweetly. "I'll see what I can find in my trunks that you can make use of."

Marda, mesmerized by young Catherine's eyes and beauty, slowly lifted her hand to touch the woman's face. But before she could touch Catherine, Marda screeched when she felt a burning sting on the back of her hand. She jerked her hand away.

The shock of being touched in anger for the first time was overwhelming. Never had she felt the sting of anyone's aggression. Marda's eyes began to water just as Jai stepped in front of her, giving Tempie a vicious look.

"Tempie!" Catherine yelled as she stood. "You know I don't allow that type of treatment in my home. You will never touch this child in that manner again."

"Miss," Tempie said as she cowered, "she was fixin' ta touch you miss."

"Never you mind that Tempie. In this house, you abide by my rules," Catherine said firmly. Tempie backed away and lowered her head. Catherine then kneeled down in front of Marda again. She looked to Jai and spoke.

"Is she your daughter?"

Jai didn't look at Catherine. She just held a cowering Marda close, eyeing Tempie.

Marda could see how the green-eyed woman would think that. She and Jai shared a common Egyptian ancestor and they did indeed resemble each other but Marda's skin was a darker, a soft sable color.

"Dey don't speak like us, Miss." Tempie slightly raised her head but quickly lowered it again.

"Well," Catherine said, "I suppose we will have to talk more so they can learn." She looked at Jai and smiled. "I am sorry." She then slowly extended her hand.

Marda, sensing the woman's gentleness, slowly walked around Jai and stood face to face with her. Catherine took Marda's hand and lifted it to the side of her face. Marda felt the woman's soft, warm skin under her hand.

Catherine looked to Jai. "You and your daughter will not be treated unkindly as long as you are in my home." Catherine gently pulled Marda's hand away and cupped it to her chest, then she slowly stood. "Tempie, take them to the kitchen and give them something to eat. They look starved."

Chapter One
Wingate University Hospital
Present, October 12th

"**H**e stays!" Cianne yelled. The heavy wooden chair she was sitting in hit the floor hard behind her as she stood.

A few of the Guards flinched, including Cassius, who continued to watch her when all the other Guards lowered their gazes in submission.

Caleb had positioned himself in front of her. He kept his eyes on Cassius and the several Royal Guards who stood behind their commander just inside the doorway.

"Until," she said then softly added as she looked at Cassius, "until I want him to go."

Cianne knew there was no way she could fight them off. The abilities she inherited from Caleb were untried, raw, and unpredictable. He advised her that using them was the only way to learn but she feared that she might seriously hurt someone if she lashed out in anger.

She was also unsure of her Coesen abilities at the moment.

By the way the Guards quickly lowered their eyes, Cianne knew they feared her. Hell, she feared herself, but she would not let them harm Caleb. He was her father, and even though he was an unconscionable killer who didn't look a day over twenty-five, he found her and helped her when no one else could.

She wouldn't make him leave her side. Not now, not ever.

Cianne watched Caleb bend down with his eyes still locked on the eight men who stood by the doorway. His movements were slow and deliberate as he picked up the chair and placed it behind her to sit.

She eased herself down on the chair but kept her eyes on the current threat.

Cassius balled his fist at his side. "You don't know what he's—"

"He stays," Cianne interrupted, relaying a calm in her tone she didn't feel. She had to stay calm, that's what Caleb told her. Though her heart raced and she felt energized.

When she saw the Guards backing away, some out of the room, she thought they finally understood, but her relief faded when she saw Vivian entering the room. The guards only made way for their Sovereign, and not because of her decree.

Vivian walked over to the side of the hospital bed. She regarded Cianne and Caleb, who were on the other side, then she looked to Cassius and his men who remained near the entrance. Statuesque and beautiful, Vivian took in the scene for a few seconds then raised her hand.

Cianne saw Cassius give Vivian a pleading look before slightly lowering his head. The commander of the Royal Guard spun around then stalked through the doorway. His Guard followed him silently.

"They need to take him now," Vivian said softly, looking at Cianne. She gave Caleb a sideways glance but quickly turned her gaze back to Cianne. "I should inform his parents of the situation."

"I don't want them told yet," Cianne said quickly. She stood and walked in a small circle then looked to Vivian. Her nerves were shot. The day's events had almost broken her until… Until Caleb. Her burning eyes found his. Blue-green eyes, eyes the exact shade of her own, stared back at her, unflinching. "I just want to be sure first."

Vivian agreed with a nod of the head. She then turned to leave, only hesitating for a moment before exiting the room.

Cianne turned to face Caleb. "Why can't you heal him completely?"

"I don't know," Caleb said. His tone suggested he couldn't care less but the intensity of his stare told a different story.

Cianne envied the strength Caleb emitted. She liked that about him.

"What about me? Can I heal him?" Even if it killed her, she would do it.

Caleb sighed as if he knew her question and her determination before she even asked it. "Even if you were able, you'd run the risk of killing him. Your abilities have been dormant for many years. It's too risky."

Cianne dragged her hand over her eyes and down her face. "Do you think he'll survive surgery?" she finally asked.

"Tristan is strong," Caleb said, "he's alive only because he is a fighter."

Cianne offered Caleb a half smile then sat back in the chair next to the hospital bed. She laid her head next to Tristan's leg. Taking his cool hand in hers, she closed her eyes and tried to will Tristan to fight harder. To fight for her, the kids, for them.

She didn't look up when she heard the knock on the door or when she heard the footsteps of someone entering the room. She lifted her head only when Caleb touched her shoulder.

"Hello, Soahn." The man stood just inside the room. He said nothing for several long uncomfortable moments as he stared at her. When Caleb cleared his throat, the man dressed as a doctor swung his gaze to Caleb and creased his brows, then began to speak again. "My name is Dr. Kevin Bannerman. I'm Tristan's doctor and I will be performing his procedure." With that, the doctor waved in a team of people who began rearranging wire and tubes that were running from the wall into or on Tristan's body.

Cianne stood when the staff moved the bed to roll Tristan out of the room. She hurried over and kissed Tristan several times on his face and lips.

"Forever," she whispered in his ear. *He heard me. He will listen.*

Cianne reluctantly moved out the way so the bed could be rolled out of the room. She walked aimlessly out into the hallway and watched as Tristan was rolled further away from her.

"Cianne," Caleb said, his tone low but clear.

Cianne turned around. She raised her palms to her cheeks and wiped at the tears as she looked at Caleb and the nurse who stood beside him. It was the same nurse who held her hand in the operating room when she gave birth.

Gave birth, she thought. *Oh God, my babies.*

She'd run out of the operating room and straight to the emergency room when Caleb told her Tristan wasn't dead. That he saved Tristan and was keeping him stable. Now, Tristan was being prepped for surgery after previously being pronounced clinically dead.

Cianne's watery eyes fell on Caleb. The realization that he had saved Tristan brought on more tears. She owed him everything. She would never be able to repay him.

"Would you like to get cleaned up?" the nurse asked.

Cianne sniffed as she glanced down at the hospital gown and lab coat she wore. Her hands moved to her hair and immediately got tangled. Cianne dropped her hands and looked at the nurse. "Yes," she said. "Then I want to see my children."

It was then that Cianne noticed the wheelchair the nurse moved toward her. She didn't want that and started to shake her head no when she glanced over at Vivian's pleading eyes.

Fine. She rolled what she could only assume were red puffy eyes, but sat in the wheelchair anyway.

The nurse wheeled her through a maze of brightly lit hallways until they came to an elevator. She wheeled Cianne through the elevator doors as Caleb held them open. Caleb slid inside the compartment with them and the nurse pressed a button.

"Now, you will be on the floor where we keep our new mothers."

Once off the elevator, the nurse pushed the wheelchair down a hall then into the first open room. It was huge and didn't resemble any hospital room she'd ever seen on television. The bed was huge with shimmery cream sheets and tons of pillows. There were upholstered furnishings and television in the sitting area, a huge window, and a dinette set for eating. The room resembled a motel room but so much nicer.

"I'm sorry about the wheelchair. Keeping up appearances is very important to us," the nurse explained as they stopped beside a closed door inside the room. "I speak for all Coesen here when I say that we are honored to care for you and your family, Soahn." The nurse bent to lift the foot rest then smiled up at Cianne. "Congratulations." The nurse bowed before leaving the room.

Cianne immediately turned to find Caleb giving the room a once over. *"Don't leave me, ok."*

"I won't," Caleb silently sent back to her. He walked over to the window and peered out of it.

Closing her eyes, Cianne took a deep breath. She took another before she opened her eyes and pushed open what she figured was the bathroom door. With a flick of her fingers over the light switch, the room lit up. Cianne moved over to the shower, pulled open the stall door and turned the faucet handle. She expected to feel pain or at least sore when she slipped out of the lab coat and hospital gown but she didn't. In fact, her body felt physically perfect.

Not at all like the victim of a shooting or someone who just had twins.

Inside the shower she didn't register if the water was too warm or too cold as she washed the dried blood from her body and hair as quickly as she could while images of Bianca's vengeance echoed in her mind.

Once clean, Cianne quickly dried off as she glanced at her reflection in the mirror. It was her, yet it wasn't.

Unwilling to deal with what that all meant, Cianne focused on a large designer bag that rested on the floor by the door. *That wasn't there before.* She grabbed up the bag, opened it up, and fingered through the contents inside. Everything inside the bag was new but was similar to her favorite things she used often at home.

Cianne dressed then took a brush from the bag. As she looked at her reflection in the mirror, she made every effort to control the flood of emotions that threatened to overwhelm her while she untangled her hair. She'd learned a lot from Vivian over the past year, a lot about keeping her emotions in check. But she could barely contain her anger over Bianca's choice to take her father from her.

Intense emotions pulsed through Cianne with every beat of her heart. Fear for the man she loved threatened to break her. Hope that Tristan would pull through drove her. Anxiety over the possibility of raising her children without Tristan beside her was the most helpless feeling she'd ever known.

Bottle it up. Bottle it up.

When Cianne exited the bathroom, she walked to the bed, using it as her point of focus. She didn't look at Caleb as she climbed into the hospital bed for fear that she would just lose her mind. Too much had happened. She didn't want to be around anyone but she didn't want to be alone either.

She wanted to scream but the last time she lost control she destroyed an operating room.

After several minutes of silence, Cianne spoke. "I don't know what I should call you. I mean," she looked at Caleb, "do I call you Caleb or…" Her eyes filled with tears again as she thought of her father and how she would never see him again.

Cianne lowered her head as she eyed Caleb. He stood with his back to her as he continued to peer out of the large window. It seemed as if he either hadn't heard her or that he had and just wasn't going to respond.

"I can't remember the pain I felt or if I felt any pain at all when I lost my father. But know that if there was a way that I could have helped Joseph, for you Cianne, I would have." He tilted his head downward and to the side so that she could see his profile. "Caleb…will be fine."

"Alright…Caleb."

Cianne wanted to say more. A million questions swirled around her disjointed mind but the horror of the day kept creeping to the forefront, causing her to break down again. She lifted her head when something appeared in front of her blurred vision. Caleb was handing her a box of tissue. When she looked at him, at his shockingly youthful face, Cianne wanted to tell him that she was happy he was with her. That she dreamed of meeting him but there was a knock on the door.

"*Knock, knock.*" The familiar nurse pushed open the hospital room door. Another nurse followed her.

Cianne braced herself as the two nurses walked into her room, each pushing a newborn bassinet. She couldn't see much from the position she was in so she sat up as the bassinettes were wheeled beside the bed. Just the tops of their heads peaked out of the blankets they were wrapped in. And only a few dark curls were visible under the little hats they wore.

Butterflies somersaulted in Cianne's stomach. Nervous, she looked to Caleb for some sort of…support, but he was staring down at the children with a look of awe on his face.

One of the nurses carefully lifted the baby who was wrapped in a blue blanket and wore the blue hat. "This is your baby boy," the nurse smiled.

Cianne opened her arms and the nurse gently placed the baby in them. She cradled the soft bundle close to her and sniffed in his baby scent as she brushed her head over his hat.

Then she slowly pulled down the part of the blanket that covered him. Cianne cooed when she saw his round delicate face. His eyes were closed and he looked peaceful but the red glow of his cheeks was stark against his fair skin tone, suggested that he'd maybe just settled down. Her baby boy grunted then wiggled, causing Cianne to freeze as if she had done something wrong.

She stiffened and shot the nurse closest to her a panicked look.

"It's fine," the nurse said, "he's getting comfortable."

Cianne slowly let her body settle back then touched his little fingers and inspected his tiny nails. When she touched his chin, the baby opened his pink rose petal lips and stuck out his tiny tongue. Cianne laughed as joyful tears slid down her face. She lifted him and rubbed his precious face against hers before kissing him as softly as she could on the cheek.

"*He smells so nice*," she transferred as she looked over at Caleb.

Caleb looked amazed when their eyes met. She looked back to the baby and gently slid his blue hat off his head. A full head of thick black curls stretched straight as Cianne removed the hat, then bounced back to his tiny head. Cianne touched a curl.

"It feels like silk," she chuckled.

"And this is your baby girl," the other nurse said.

Cianne looked at her boy once more before she handed him back to the nurse who initially gave him to her. She then took her baby girl in her arms and laughed. "They look identical."

"For now," the nurse said, "they are fraternal so as they grow they will start to look different."

Cianne inspected her beautiful baby girl just as she did the boy but realized she forgot something. She laid her daughter on her lap, pulled the blanket down and gently tilted her baby's head to look behind the baby's ear. She then looked behind the other baby's ear.

"They have no mark," she said with surprise.

"Neither of them has the mark, Ms. Baxter." The nurse holding the baby boy said.

Cianne almost smiled. Her babies may have escaped her fate.

She lifted her daughter up to her face and kissed her on the cheek. "You are so beautiful Nadia (Nah-di-a)," she said. Cianne placed her little girl on the bed between her legs. Then she reached for her son. When the nurse gave Cianne her son she lifted him up and kissed him again. "And you are my miracle..."

Chapter Two

Ten years earlier
Zoo

"**T**ristan*, a young girl has run off. I am going to look for the girl with these people," Patrick Arlington said to his grandson. "Would you like to come or would you rather stay here with Gordon?"*

Tristan looked up from the zoo pamphlet he held, to his grandfather, then to their driver, Gordon. "I'd rather stay here."

"I'll be back soon."

Tristan nodded. When his grandfather left, he folded the pamphlet then placed it down on the bench and looked around. Gordon was a few feet away, smoking a cigarette. His attention was focused on the information board he stood in front of.

While Tristan watched Gordon, a strange sensation overtook him. Something was calling to him. Not calling his name or anything, but he felt an odd pull. He got to his feet and headed in the opposite direction his grandfather had gone and away from their driver.

Soon he found himself standing in front of a little girl. He thought it odd that he hadn't run into anyone else on the way. He was at a zoo that was crowded just minutes ago.

"Are you the lost girl?" he asked.

He realized two things immediately. The first thing was that the girl looked very unhappy. The second thing, she was the prettiest girl he'd ever seen. Why he smiled at her he wasn't sure. She was crying, yet he couldn't help smiling.

If she thought him weird she didn't let on. She just looked up at him with wide odd-colored eyes.

Tristan handed her his handkerchief then sat down next to her. They sat for several minutes saying nothing to one another. It was as if nothing needed to be said and he was fine with that.

Soon, people found them including his grandfather.

Ashamed that he'd ignored his grandfather's request to stay put, Tristan stood. He didn't see the girl reach for his hand but when he felt her touch, it seemed that everything in the world made sense. Just being near her made sense. But he was only nine years old so what did he know?

Only, when he said goodbye to her, Tristan felt as if he was losing a part of himself.

He wasn't at the zoo anymore. No, this place was cold and it smelled like rubbing alcohol.

God, it's cold.

Suddenly, the chill left him and his body began to shake uncontrollably. Tristan screamed so loud, so long, that his throat was raw.

Someone was holding him down.

Oh god, the pain.

His body was ablaze.

Help...help me, he tried to yell out but his words were nothing more than strangled cries. He was on fire. His bones had to be ashes by now but why was he still conscious?

"God, help my son."

Tristan heard his mother's cries. Another scream ripped from his mouth.

*The girl...*he tried to tell them. The girl with the green-blue eyes can help me.

But no one understood him.

No one but her.

"Oh God!" his mother shrieked.

His screams echoed throughout the hospital wing.

Present Day
October 28th

Tristan opened his eyes as he sprang up to a sitting position. He stared at his hands then ran them over his face. Was it all a dream or maybe it was a memory? Was he still dreaming?

He scanned the room. Nothing about the room seemed familiar until his eyes rested on a guy who sat with his ankle resting over his leg on the window seat, watching him. Tristan's brows wrinkled and his eyes narrowed.

Patton's house, this is the guy who knocked me out.

"Where's Cianne?" Tristan demanded. "Cianne!" he called out.

When the guy didn't respond to his question, Tristan pulled the sheets off his legs but his arm jerked back. Something was restricting his movements. He looked to his arm and saw IV tubing. Tristan traced the length of the cord with his finger then pulled it until the rolling stand crashed into the bed. He then ripped the tubing from his arm, disregarding the slow trickle of blood that dripped out. He then tried to move his legs off the bed but he couldn't get them to move.

Move damn it.

"You should relax," the guy suggested with a shrug.

Tristan looked over at him.

Where is Cianne and why is this guy here...and who the hell is the bastard anyway, with his smug expression and pretty boy looks?

Tristan turned his attention back to his legs. Determined to move them, he slowly slid one leg off the side of the bed, then the other. A searing pain shot up his back but he ignored it.

"Where's Cianne?" he asked again.

An image of Bianca standing over Cianne while holding a gun flashed in front of his eyes. "Oh god," he whispered. His head clouded, he felt sick, his throat felt dry, and his pulse raced.

Tristan didn't think about the pain that coursed through his body when he pushed off the bed and stood. Cianne and their child were all he thought about. They needed to be ok. His eyes glossed over. His breathing became erratic.

"Oh god…they're ok." He repeated it again and again.

He took a step. Even when he began to fall forward, neither his condition nor the pain was a concern. Her eyes were all he saw as his legs gave out.

Something strong caught hold of him before he hit the cold hard floor but his mind was already shredding. His body went limp. Everything in the room became a blur as tears fell from his eyes. He struggled for air as he cried out her name.

"Breathe," the guy told him. He easily lifted Tristan in his arms and placed him back on the bed, "you have to breathe."

Tristan didn't see the door to his room open nor did he feel the soft hands that touched his face. Only when her lips touched his did he try to focus on the person in front of him.

His eye moved over Cianne's face. Reaching up, he let his fingers trace her cheek then her chin. She was so soft, so beautiful. Warm.

Is she real?

Tristan leaned forward and brushed his lips over hers. He tasted her sweetness and his salty tears when his mouth opened over hers. He placed his hand around the back of her neck, pulling her closer, kissing her frantically.

"I'm sorry," he said. "I'm so sorry."

"Don't," Cianne whispered against his lips.

He grimaced and she pulled back.

"Tristan, I don't know what I would have done if you…" She embraced him.

In her tight grasp, Tristan found it easier to breathe.

"*You're* leaving?" Cianne transferred.

Sobbing, crying, and tears were not his thing. Nor were slobbering, sucking, and kissing.

"*Just going to speak to the doctor,*" Caleb transferred back without turning around. He stepped out of Tristan's hospital room and walked down the hallway, passing several empty rooms along his way. He saw Vivian talking to Mrs. Bertram in the waiting room at the end of the hall. He gave her a slight nod but continued walking down the hallway.

Caleb approached Dr. Bannerman. "Tristan's awake." He glanced at Vivian who was walking up, then looked back to Bannerman. "He tried to get out of bed. Moved his legs off the bed and stood. He took a step."

"Doctor?" Vivian asked, her face a barely concealed mask of shock.

To Caleb, the doctor didn't look at all surprised. Bannerman actually smiled, then put his clipboard down and pointed to an empty conference room across the hall. Caleb followed the doctor but let Vivian enter the room first. Vivian walked by him, giving him a suspicious glance, but she went inside the conference room.

Bannerman closed the door; he didn't seem to have any reservations about being closed inside a room with Caleb.

To appear less threatening to Vivian, Caleb moved to the far side of the room then leaned against a wall and placed his hands in his pockets. Not that anything he did would make him less threatening.

"The injuries Tristan sustained damaged his lower spine. By all accounts he should be paralyzed from the waist down. I knew there was a chance… But I had no idea it was going to work this well." Dr. Bannerman smiled big, obviously pleased with himself.

"What was going to work?" Vivian asked.

"I'll explain," Dr. Bannerman said with excitement. "Your daughter, Kayla, gave me the opportunity to treat

Tristan a little over ten years ago, and in return I gave my word that I would keep what he is a secret."

If Caleb hadn't glanced over at Vivian, he would have missed her slight frown of displeasure. He was displeased as well but he refused to show it. Knowing Kayla trusted this man but ran from him…

"For ten years, I have been experimenting with Tristan's original blood and tissue samples that I collected during his Conversion. What I discovered was that if I introduced those samples, slightly altered of course, to dying tissue, that tissue healed at an astonishing rate. I tested his DNA with the dead tissue of an average human. The host tissue showed promising signs but after about a day or two and in some instances sooner, the combination of Tristan's donor sample and the random sample died. Based on my experiments, I reasoned that if I reintroduced his Conversion DNA to him…well, I never imagined it would work on such a grand scale. It seems that his body is repairing itself, as if he is going through the Conversion Cycle again. Just like when Kayla and I found him."

Caleb's gaze moved over the doctor then to several objects around the man. If anyone in the room had his superior hearing they would have heard Caleb's heart rate increase to a staggering rate.

What kind of relationship did this man have with my Kayla? Why would he put his neck out for her and betray the Sovereign's trust?

Caleb blinked, the only outward sign that he was dealing with and reining in an unexpected and unnatural bout of emotions.

"And you decided to keep this information from me?" Vivian hissed.

Caleb looked from the doctor to her. He wondered if she would lose her cool. She didn't have his control. Her emotions danced close to the surface, waiting to explode. He wondered if he would be the lucky recipient. Or would it be the good doctor with all his secrets?

Caleb smiled on the inside… He was thinking, wishing, the crone would lash out. In doing so she may just reveal her mysterious ability. The Council of Four's abilities and their successors' abilities were usually kept secret in the world of Coesen and even to each other. However, it didn't matter. Vivian was still no match for him, but he was a curious man.

Though, not curious enough to breach her mind.

"I didn't know if it was going to work. I just knew that everyone had been through a lot and a miracle, if it worked, was what everyone needed," Dr. Bannerman explained. "I apologize for not informing you," he bowed to Vivian, avoiding her gaze.

"Of this current offense or the one that has been ongoing for over ten years?" Vivian scowled.

Caleb sighed with contempt. *Such drama*. He rolled his eyes. "Is this permanent?"

"The damage to Tristan's spine is normally considered a complete injury. The possibility of locomotion is almost nonexistent in similar cases. Though my research with Tristan's Cycling DNA would suggest that yes, his miraculous recovery is permanent. Tristan moving his toe would have been a positive result now, but he moved both legs and tried to walk." Dr. Bannerman looked down then back to Caleb and Vivian. "To be clear, I'm not saying he will be like he was before the shooting. But if his body continues to repair itself and he is willing to work hard, I don't see why he can't be walking in a year or so." Bannerman sat down on the edge of the long conference table then looked off into space.

The doc sure had that mad scientist thing down. Everything but the look, Caleb admitted to himself. Dr. Bannerman was handsome by anyone's standards Caleb admitted, as the doctor turned his attention on him.

With a glint in his eyes, Dr. Bannerman said, "If you allowed me to examine you, maybe take a few tissue samples…Tristan could benefit from whatever it is that allows you to heal yourself."

"I'm sure Cianne will be happy to volunteer." Caleb pushed off the wall and strolled toward the door.

"She's unstable right now," Bannerman said. Caleb turned the knob but didn't open the door. "Her abilities are slowly manifesting, maybe for years to come. We do know that she can repair her damaged tissue. An apparent trait she gets from you. Not to mention we don't know what *you* are. Honestly, she may combust at any moment."

Caleb turned to look at Bannerman. But not before he reminded himself of the promise he made to Cianne a few days ago. *No killing…no intimidating.* He tilted his head back, wondering how she would feel about him breaking the good doctor's nose.

Bannerman stepped forward. "You on the other hand, have had your abilities in their entirety for…" he paused, "for how many years now?" He smiled when Caleb didn't answer. "Just a little bit of your blood is all I need to get started."

Caleb opened the door and left the room.

Tristan pulled Cianne closer into his side. Her being tucked beside him in the hospital bed wasn't close enough for him. But he was content as he listened intently to her retelling how Caleb brought him back to life before finding her in the operating room and releasing her abilities she inherited from him.

Apparently, he was clinically dead for more than forty minutes. If he wasn't changed by her, and didn't go through the painful Cycling process to become her Protector when he was a kid, her father wouldn't have been able to save him.

All of it was so hard to believe but that was his life. What was even harder to believe was that the blond senior citizen who looked like he was twenty-something was her father. He was *the* Caleb, the Big Bad who was mentioned in Coesen tales meant to scare their young.

Another hard pill to swallow was that just a few days ago Cianne buried the only father she knew up until two weeks ago.

The knowledge that he wasn't there for her during such a trying time tied his stomach into knots. Tristan was grateful for their family and friends being there for her when he couldn't.

Cianne told him that for two weeks she stayed virtually by his side while he lay unconscious. She was so brave.

"So, we can't do the mental talking thing anymore?" Tristan asked. He buried his face in her hair, closed his eyes, and sniffed in her scent.

"For Caleb to help you, to bring you back, our connection had to be severed. You are still my Protector but feeling my fear as well as your pain was too overwhelming for your body to handle while it was trying to heal," she said, as she grimaced.

He felt her finger tracing one of the new scars on his chest.

"The combination was literally killing you. Breaking our bond was necessary."

Tristan wanted to see her face so he leaned back and lifted her chin up with his finger. She was so beautiful, so precious, he knew he would have climbed out of the depths of Hell if he had to. Waking up and seeing her safe, holding her in his arms—it felt so good he didn't want to ever let her go.

He kissed her on the forehead then relaxed back. They lay in silence together but Tristan couldn't relax completely. Cianne didn't say anything about their baby and fear kept him from asking. He tried to focus on everything she told him but thoughts of their daughter kept resurfacing in his mind. He could only assume that if Cianne hadn't brought the baby up yet, then it couldn't be good.

He didn't want to ask. But he had to know. He shifted then rose up on one arm. Cianne adjusted but gave him a questioning look. Tristan opened his mouth to speak but a knock on the hospital room door had him looking over his shoulder.

Dr. Bannerman stuck his head inside the room. "Excuse me, I should have waited for you to tell me to enter."

"Doc!" Tristan sat up. "You came all this way for me?"

"It's fine, Dr. Bannerman. I was just getting him caught up," Cianne said as she slid from his arms and to her feet.

"Ci?" Tristan questioned.

Tristan instantly felt the loss of Cianne when she moved away from him. It was as if his body had iced over with the absence of hers. He quickly turned his head to keep her in his sight.

Cianne smiled at him then did some kind of hand signal he didn't quite understand. Tristan reached for her only for her to gently push his hand away. A soft gesture yes, but his heart throbbed with pain as if she'd smacked it away.

"How are you feeling, Tristan?" Dr, Bannerman asked.

Tristan watched Cianne walk around the foot of the bed. She gave him a smile but he could only offer her a look of confusion as he watched her leave the room. He looked to his doctor, one of his oldest companions, again.

How do I feel?

"Like I went to hell and back," Tristan responded honestly with no humor in his words.

Dr. Bannerman sat on the bed next to him and touched his shoulder. "I need to look you over but I know there are some people here who would really like to see you first. That is, if you're up to it."

Tristan nodded, so Dr. Bannerman turned his head, looked up at what was most likely a security camera in the ceiling and gave a wave of his hand.

The door swung open and Tristan's mother's face came into view. Dr. Bannerman had to stand quickly to move out of her path. His mother was already crying when she took Tristan in her arms. His body ached but he relished the soreness as a gift.

Tristan watched his father enter, walking into the room a little slower than his wife. His father waited and watched him and his mother in silence until Tristan reached out to him with one hand as he held onto his mother with the other. They held each other, as a family, for several minutes. Tristan couldn't remember ever seeing a tear in his father's eyes in all his life, until today.

"This really isn't a good look for you," Brian said. He beamed as he entered the room.

Mr. Bertram released Tristan, pinched at the bridge of his nose, then cleared his throat. Mrs. Bertram stroked Tristan's cheek before backing away from the bed so Brian could move closer.

Assuming they were doing the bro-back-pat, Tristan raised his hand to grab hold of Brian's. Except, his friend bypassed his hand and went in for a tight hug.

"Aren't you supposed to be away at college?" Tristan asked with a smile.

"I've got this friend who has his own jet, so I can pretty much come and go as I please." Brian grinned as he backed away.

"You scared us," Tranae said. She wiped at her tears as she hugged him.

"I'm sorry." Tristan gave her a reassuring squeeze then released her.

He looked around at his family and friends who smiled at him. Then the atmosphere in the room changed and it seemed to Tristan a bit too quiet. Everyone parted and a path was created for Vivian. She walked over to Tristan and took his hand in hers. She bent forward, touching her cheek to his. The act took him by surprise.

"Glad to have you back," Vivian whispered in his ear.

Tristan knew his expression was one of awe and...he wasn't afraid to admit, fear, as Vivian straightened and moved aside. When Vivian moved out of the way, Tristan saw Zeta standing against the wall by the door. She looked uncomfortable but smiled and gave him a halfhearted wave. Tristan shook his head. He wasn't going to let her get away with closing herself off. He held his arms out, motioning her to him.

Tranae pushed Zeta forward.

Zeta held her head low as she reluctantly moved close enough for him to pull her in.

"Don't look so sad." Tristan embraced her. "I will be out of here and training again in no time." Zeta smiled but pulled back. Tristan noted the unshed tears in her eyes before she scurried off to hold up the wall again. He also noticed the look Vivian and Dr. Bannerman shared when he spoke to Zeta.

Before he could ask what the look was about, his father cleared his throat again. "Well everyone, I think we need to give Cianne and Tristan some time alone."

Tristan felt a tinge of sadness seeing his family and friends leave but he had important things to discuss with Cianne. He watched everyone slowly clear the room, each promising or requesting more time with him later, with the exception of Zeta, who didn't say anything or make any promises, which niggled at Tristan.

Was she creeped out by sick people and hospitals? He wondered if Zeta had ever lost anyone close to her. Something had to be responsible for her to close herself off like this. She was probably terrified.

Tristan decided that he would do his best to show her that he was fine.

When the room was cleared, Cianne poked her head in and smiled at him then retreated. Tristan's heart raced and his breath hitched at the mere sight of her, it always had. He wondered if the day would ever come when her effect on him would dim. As he waited for her, he knew that nothing would ever change for him concerning his love for Cianne.

The door opened again and Cianne walked in carrying what looked like a baby. *Our baby*. Everything slowed as he pushed himself up higher in the bed. He blinked. Then blinked again. Tristan raised his hands off his lap then thought better and lowered them. His eyes met Cianne's then moved to the bundle in her arms as she walked over to the bed.

"This is your daughter, Nadia Kayla Bertram." Cianne lowered the baby so he could see her. "Say hello to your daddy, Nadia." The baby made low slurping sounds as she sucked on her little tongue.

Tristan looked at his daughter then up at Cianne. *This is really happening*. "She's…" he paused as he looked at his daughter again, "she's real. This is real?"

"She's real," Cianne whispered then sucked in a breath as she began to cry. "Would you like to hold her?"

Tristan held his palms up. "No," he said quickly. He looked up at Cianne nervously. "What if I hurt her? She's so small and…and beautiful," he said.

"You won't hurt her," Cianne said then sniffed. She slowly placed Nadia in his outstretched arms. Cianne sat down next to him on the bed then looked to the door. "I'm ready," she called out.

Tristan couldn't help tensing when he saw Caleb push the door open but he immediately relaxed when Tranae entered holding a blue bundle. Tristan looked at Tranae then he looked to Cianne with questioning eyes. Tranae, who had tears running from her eyes, smiled as she carefully placed the bundle in Cianne's arms, then she backed away and left the room.

"And this, is your son, Aidan Joseph Arlington Bertram." Cianne held the sleeping baby up so Tristan could see him.

Aidan stirred a bit but didn't wake.

Tristan closed his eyes then opened them slowly. Cianne's expression was guarded, as if she was waiting for him to say something, as tears rolled down her face. But he was speechless. Nothing could or would ever mean more to him than this moment and he had no words to express that.

Nadia made a tiny sound, drawing his attention to her. Tristan then moved his gaze to Aidan who rested in Cianne's arms. They were their children. This was his life. Cianne had given him clarity, a purpose, herself, and two perfect children.

Tristan opened his mouth to speak but was only able to mumble something incoherent as he leaned forward and placed his hand on Cianne's cheek then wrapped his hand around the back of her neck. Pulling her close, he kissed her several times on her mouth and face.

"Thank you," he said as he sucked in a gulp of air. Tristan cried freely, kissing her lips over and over again.

"Thank you for loving me," she sobbed.

Chapter Three

Four Months later,
March,

Cianne opened the car door and stepped onto the graveled ground of the parking lot. She slowly closed the car door and looked around Ridgeview Park. It was early afternoon and the park was already bustling with people.

Good...having people around was good.

She slowly walked along the winding sidewalk until she found the park bench that faced Roland road. She sat down and looked over at the makeshift memorial that sat under a lamp post near the intersection where her father's, the man who raised her, life was taken.

That terrible day played out in her mind again as it had so many times over the past few months. She closed her eyes and turned away. Focusing on a mother who was pushing her child on a swing, Cianne suddenly felt envious. That mother would raise her child with none of the fears, worries, or memories she had when she gave birth to her children. That mother was also totally oblivious to what was going on in the world around her and her family.

Distracted by her thoughts, Cianne was startled when she saw Caleb's hand in front of her holding out a handkerchief. She scanned the park around her but after a moment she realized that Tristan wasn't going to appear, and she wouldn't hear him in her head whenever she was afraid, to ask her if she was alright.

"I wondered if I would see you again," she said then sniffed. Cianne took the handkerchief Caleb handed her and wiped away her tears as she looked over at him. His deep green eyes showed a hint of concern as they looked back at her. "Careful," she said as she half-heartedly laughed. "I may get the impression you care."

"I do," Caleb said looking away. He focused on the memorial in the distance.

"Really?" Cianne said sarcastically. "It's been three months. I thought you would have wanted to see the children, be in their lives, be a grandfather to them." She looked down at the lace handkerchief that she twisted in her hands. It was embroidered with a C and S in fancy script.

"It's not as if I could just walk up to the door and ring the bell."

"Couldn't you?"

"You know I can't."

"Right," Cianne snickered, "you are public enemy number one. Apparently, you did something so bad that every Coesen in the world wants you dead but no one wants to tell me what it was." She pulled her hair back from her face and looked him in the eyes. "What was it? What did you do?"

For a moment, she thought he was going to leave but he didn't. Instead Caleb took her hand in his.

He sighed then said, "Close your eyes and relax."

Cianne gave him a curious look but did what he asked. When she closed her eyes, she heard his voice.

"Don't break the connection. I will when I'm done."

Cianne was about to nod but her head felt fogged and then a weightless sensation surrounded her. A flash of light sparked behind her closed eyes then she saw Caleb as a boy in her mind. Somehow, she knew it was him. He was in a tree watching a little girl swimming in a lake. Cianne felt like she was there with them, but neither he nor the girl noticed her.

She could smell the grass and feel the moisture of the night air on her skin. She found herself watching the girl as intensely as Caleb was until everything suddenly disappeared.

Wait…no, I want to see.

Cianne opened her eyes. She frowned as she looked at Caleb, wanting to know why he stopped the vision. He placed his hand on her shoulder to steady her but at the same time he stood. Without a word, Caleb walked away. Confused by his sudden departure, Cianne was about to call to him when she heard him in her head.

"*I won't be far*," he transferred.

"Good afternoon, Ms. Baxter."

Cianne whipped her head around to see two men approaching. Men she recognized. "Morning Officers," Cianne said.

Det. Malone stopped and stood just to the side of her. Officer Perkins smiled and slightly lowered his head in a slight bow.

Cianne disregarded Perkins' gesture.

"It's uh, hard to get ahold of you," Malone said with a smile, "how have you been?"

Cianne used her hand to try and shade her eyes from the bright sun as she looked up at him. "Good, I suppose," she said.

"May I sit?" Malone asked.

Cianne nodded and he sat down beside her. She looked to Officer Perkins who walked a few feet away and stood with his back to her and Malone. She watched Perkins as he turned slowly from side to side. To her, it looked as if he was looking for someone. Sort of like the way Tristan scanned rooms he entered.

"I've wanted to speak with you about your case," Malone said.

Returning her focus back to the detective, Cianne managed to stay calm. She had honestly forgotten about the kidnapping and the murders. *Is Tristan still a suspect?* She never asked him if he'd done it.

"*Don't panic.*" Caleb's voice inside her head was calming. "*Just relax.*"

Cianne peered past the detective at a few guys on the basketball court. Then she looked at a woman passing with a stroller in front of her. Caleb was close enough to hear her conversation but she couldn't see him.

"We found the ringleader. He's a security guard who was employed at Kennecott University. His name is Edgar Patton. It seems that he and Nicklaus Carter planned to extort money from Tristan and split the take with Peter Walters and Jason Cruz. They didn't count on Peter having a soft spot for you. We figure Edgar killed Jason and Nick because he didn't trust them to keep his identity a secret." Det. Malone pulled out a photo and passed it to Cianne. He tapped the photo. "Patton may also be responsible for the disappearance of Dr. Garrison as well. Evidence found in his home suggests that he may have been worried about what Dr. Garrison found out during your therapy sessions."

Cianne looked at the photo of a white male with short cropped hair and brown eyes. "I've never seen this person before."

"You wouldn't have. This guy is ex-military and very smart." He took the photo. "He made sure there was little to no evidence to connect him. If it wasn't for Dr. Garrison's disappearance and the record of a phone call Patton placed to the doctor's home, we would have never had reason to visit Patton's home to ask a few routine questions. When we saw a high-powered rifle in plain sight through a window, we had a reason to search the home. In that search, we found evidence that connected him to your case."

"So you have him in custody?"

"No," Malone said. "And that's why I wanted to speak with you. It seems that Mr. Patton has left the country. But be assured that we will find him and bring him back," he said with determination.

So much so that Cianne wanted to believe him but somehow, she knew the scenario that the detective laid out was way too neat.

"You and your family shouldn't be in any danger. We know his identity and have all the evidence to prove he murdered three, possibly four people. When these kinds of criminals run, they always have to be dragged back in handcuffs so you have nothing to worry about."

Cianne touched his hand. "I thank you for seeing it through," she said, forcing a smile.

"Well," Malone said, then stood, "I guess we'll leave you then."

Malone walked over to Perkins, who abruptly pulled his cell phone from his ear and stuffed it into his pocket. Officer Perkins looked back at Cianne and lowered his head again before they walked back in the direction they came.

"Caleb," Cianne whispered. She mentally called out his name a few times but he didn't answer. After a few minutes, Cianne stood. She made her way toward the parking lot. Before she reached her car, she made out several of Cassius' Coesen Guards and two large black SUVs blocking in her car.

"Soahn," Cassius said, then bowed. When she was only inches away he opened the door to one of the SUVs.

Cianne narrowed her eyes and sighed with frustration. No wonder Caleb didn't answer. She looked at Cassius then over to the Guardsmen. "I'll drive my car," she said as she moved to go around him.

Cassius blocked her way. "I would much rather you ride with me," he said, holding his hand out toward the back seat of the SUV for her to enter. He bowed again.

Cianne stared at Cassius for a moment before reluctantly climbing inside the truck. Once inside she extended her hand out to Cassius; her car keys dangled from her fingers. Cassius didn't take the offered keys. Instead, Cianne watched him nod to the Guard who stood near her car then he slid inside the truck beside her.

Cianne watched the Guard place his hand on the hood of her car. Seconds later, her car's engine started up then revved. Cianne watched the Guard as he opened her car door, sat down, and adjusted the mirror. She sat back on the leather seat and looked forward. If she wasn't so angry, she would have been impressed with that little car trick.

"You do realize that leaving without telling anyone where you are going is careless." Cassius did some type of hand signal out of the window then he sat back and pushed the button for the windows to roll up.

Cianne noticed as they pulled away that one truck stayed behind. She closed her eyes in an attempt to contain her anger.

"They're looking for you," she told Caleb.

She didn't know if he heard her but she felt she had to warn him. She didn't want him caught. She also didn't know what Caleb was capable of but she could sense the power coming from him. If she was right, Cassius needed a lot more men than a truck full.

The ride back to Vivian's compound was a quick one so Cianne didn't have much time to cool her anger. Once the car stopped she opened the door herself and got out, instead of waiting for the door to be opened for her. She stormed into the house, heading straight for her bathroom. Once inside the bathroom with the door closed, she pulled her hair away from her face and tied it into a tight knot as she stood over the sink. She turned on the cold water and looked at herself in the mirror.

"Calm," she spoke to herself, "calm down."

But she didn't. Cianne's heart was practically beating out of her chest. Her fingers gripped the sides of the sink. The tips and her knuckles were white from the pressure she applied to the marble as the mirror steamed up.

Cianne focused on the water that poured from the tap. The knob was turned to cold and cold water was running from the spigot but it sizzled before it hit the basin and then evaporated.

The heat is coming from me.

Surprised, she backed away from the sink with her hands up. They looked normal. She tapped her wrist with her pointer finger. When she felt nothing, she spread her hand over her wrist. Her hands didn't feel hot but she knew the heat was coming from her. She could feel it coursing through her like her anger.

"Calm down," she repeated over and over.

The steaming water began to cool. Once the steam was gone, Cianne placed just the tips of her fingers under the running water. When she felt comfortable with the temperature she splashed the water over her face. She patted her face dry then unknotted her hair. Her eyes flickered to her reflection in the mirror. Tears slowly began to fall. Only she wasn't sure what it was she was crying about.

Was it the fact that her family of four had been living under Vivian's roof for the past three and a half months? Or perhaps it was that she was discovering new abilities daily and had no idea how to handle them. The idea that she could be a danger to everyone she cared about was always at the forefront of her mind. She had to protect them from herself.

Zeta picked the towel up off the floor and wiped her face. She was worried and it probably showed. "I think you are pushing yourself too hard," she finally told Tristan.

She threw the towel back to the floor and turned around to face him. He looked up at her and smiled. That softened her worry just a bit. She hated that he drove himself this way. Why was he so determined?

"Fine," she said with a twisted mouth, "I will tell him as soon as he gets back that you're ready but I have conditions. You must promise to have a proper rest. Let your muscles get accustomed to the new and improved you. Then you can start your training with Cassius."

"Deal," Tristan said. He walked over to Zeta and grabbed her upper arms. He held her out in front of him and looked at her before pulling her into a hug. "You've been a wonderful instructor."

Zeta allowed her head to rest on Tristan's chest and closed her eyes. In the moment he embraced her, she imagined so much more than just a simple hug between friends. In her mind Tristan kissed her hungrily on the neck. Then he made his way to her lips and kissed them passionately. But the image faded when he released her.

Zeta watched him as he reached for a towel that hung from a hook and wiped his face and neck.

He smiled at her again. "Don't look so worried," he said. "I'm at 100% now and completely healed. I can handle it." Tristan walked over to the open pool house/gym doors. The scars from the shooting moved with every flex of the corded muscles of his back.

Zeta still flinched when she saw them. Knowing that they were a result of fatal injuries still caused her grief. She turned away when the bile began to rise in her throat. She tried not to think of his death and usually she was able to look at his scars without reacting, but today she felt like she was losing him all over again.

"I hope you can," she said as casually as she could. "Cassius is much harder to please."

"Hey," he said as he looked back, "Don't forget it's movie night. Cianne's choice."

Once a week for the past three months, the three of them sat in the theatre room and watched a movie. It was originally something to do to take their minds off all the sadness that surrounded Cianne, but it quickly became a ritual.

"I'll get cleaned up then run to get the food," Zeta offered. When she looked over her shoulder, Tristan was gone.

Zeta sighed as she picked up the towels and closed the double doors. She hated herself for loving him. And what made it worse was the fact that she loved Cianne just as much. Only her feelings for Tristan had morphed from admiration and simple attraction to being in love.

She should have been more careful. It wasn't like she didn't see it coming. From the moment she first laid eyes on him, when she arrived at Cianne's house with Vivian and Whodai, she was smitten. He was the most beautiful man she'd ever seen in her entire life.

She was in so deep it scared her. But what scared Zeta most was that she knew in her heart that she could never deny him. Whatever Tristan wanted, she would give regardless of who got hurt. She knew what she had to do and the only reason she hadn't requested a transfer sooner was because she thought Tristan needed her help in recovering from his injuries. What she didn't expect was that he would prove the doctors wrong and recover fully in only three months.

Her chest felt hollow and she was finding it difficult to breathe. Zeta sat down next to the pool and inhaled deeply. She had to catch her breath. It felt as if her heart was being pulled apart because she just realized it was time for her to leave. She had to leave, because staying would only be torture.

No one can ever know how I feel about Tristan.

She would die before she hurt the woman she loved above all others, the one to whom she owed the utmost loyalty.

Cianne held Aidan against her chest, slowly rocking him back and forth, humming a nursery rhyme. When she finished the song, she opened her eyes. Tristan was in the nursery, standing over her. He'd crossed the entire width of the room without making a sound. It was creepy the way everyone moved around the house so silently. It wasn't natural to not make noise. They should at least announce themselves verbally or make a sound when entering a room.

"Where have you been?" Tristan whispered. He slowly lifted Aidan from her arms. He cradled his son then kissed him on the head before placing him in the crib beside Nadia.

"I went to the park," she said in a hushed tone. She waited for a sign of his disapproval. His face would show nothing, but a shift of his weight from one foot to the other would speak volumes. It was something he began to do after the shooting, when he was fighting his emotions.

He didn't react though.

"Did you find what you were looking for?" he asked. Tristan stood over the crib, rubbing Nadia's back.

"I think so," she lied.

"Good." Tristan smiled.

Cianne wasn't sure if his smile was genuine. He was known to mask his anger with a smile. It kind of raised the hairs on her neck then but now, with him being all "God of War", the smile could be freaking terrifying.

Tristan reached up and turned on the baby monitor sitting on a shelf above the crib, then walked over to Cianne and pulled her up on her feet. He bent down and lifted her in his arms like he had done so many times before the incident that almost crippled him.

"Tristan," she whispered, "your spine—"

"Doc said I'm completely healed when I went to my appointment today." Tristan stepped into the hallway and pulled the nursery door closed. "You know how I felt when he gave me the good news?" he asked. "I'll tell you. I felt numb. Because," he said before she could question him, "all I could think of was the one thing I want most in the entire world. Do you want to know what that one thing is?"

He carried Cianne to their bedroom that was adjacent to the nursery.

"To go to Disneyland," Cianne said playfully as Tristan laid her on the bed.

He laughed as he walked over and locked their bedroom door. He then turned on the baby monitor that sat on their nightstand. "I'd be lying if I didn't admit that Disney World did cross my mind but…" He stepped out of his shoes.

"*Hmm*," Cianne said aloud, pretending to think, "You want to change your cell phone provider."

Tristan took his shirt off and dropped it on the floor. His Royal Guard brand that trailed up his arm, over his shoulder, and onto some of his neck, was in stark contrast to his skin, making it more vivid.

So sexy.

He flexed before he got on the bed and crawled to her. "No," he said as he kissed her collar bone. "The one thing I wanted was to make love to you," he whispered in her ear.

"That's funny because you said the same thing when you left the hospital and I fell for it even though doing so could have hurt you. But you smiled and I agreed. You wanted nothing more than to make love to me again when you woke up that next morning, and I agreed. To celebrate waking up in a bed without rails, I think you said. That celebration almost put you back in the hospital. We celebrated your first home cooked meal and the first time you changed a poopie diaper too."

"What can I say?" His breath caressed her neck. "I like to celebrate."

Cianne put her hand on his chest to stop him from coming closer. "It seems you want to commemorate every moment of our lives by making love."

He moved her hand away. "And that is bad…why?"

Cianne used both hands to push him back now. "You're all sweaty." She wiped one of her hands on his shorts.

"I remember a time when you loved my man scent. Wanted to bottle it and sell it if I recall," he said kissing her neck.

"I do… I did," she moaned out. Her mind stalled for a moment as his lips touched her skin. "But we have to talk."

Tristan frowned, tilted his head, then backed off her. His face was blank when he asked, "What's wrong?"

"I'm ready to go home," Cianne said, then sighed. She looked at him. His expression hadn't changed. She didn't expect it would. With all his training Tristan had become even harder to read.

"Are you sure you want to leave here so soon after—"

"No," she admitted, "but I don't feel like we're in control of our lives here. Like every decision is being made for us."

"I thought I would have more time but if you are ready to leave here, then I'm ready," Tristan said, "but do you really want to return to your house?"

"No," she confessed, "I don't but what choice do we have?"

"I didn't think you would." Tristan said. He sighed. "If it's ok with you, I think my parents would love to have us stay with them for a little while. My room is big enough for the four of us and it's already decorated."

"That would be great," she said, then smiled, "but more time for what?"

"To build our new home," Tristan said plainly. "I planned to surprise you with it when we brought Nadia home but things didn't go according to plan. The construction took a backseat. Not to mention Aidan was a big surprise, so I had to change the design a bit but it will be ready soon. I promise."

She threw her arms around his neck. "Do you always think of everything?"

"According to you, I only think of one thing," he said, frowning playfully. Tristan pulled her arms away and jumped to his feet. "And being as you're locking that thing down, I guess I need to take a cold shower." He raised his eyebrows a few times and turned his head in the direction of the bathroom.

Cianne mouthed the word "later" as she stood. She watched Tristan long enough to see the exaggerated sad face he made as he dragged himself toward the bathroom. She smiled big as she unlocked and opened their bedroom door.

Their life as a regular family was about to begin. She actually bounced down the flight of stairs, her destination…the kitchen. The baby bottles had to be cleaned and tiny clothes needed washing. She asked the staff not to do these things because she was the twins' mother and she took pleasure in taking care of them. But who said she couldn't have a little help every now and then?

Cianne dug her cell phone out of her pocket and dialed. "Hey Tranae, it's movie night my choice, can you hang?" There was no need to reveal her true intentions. Cianne smiled to herself.

When the door slowly opened, Cianne looked up to see Vivian peeking inside. A week had passed since she and Tristan decided to move out. She told Vivian later that evening. As she expected, Vivian didn't make a fuss. Her grandmother accepted the news with the same impassive look Tristan often wore. Though, they hadn't discussed the move since.

Cianne laid Nadia on her blanket that was on the floor and waved Vivian in. Nadia rolled over on her side and grabbed at Aidan. Both babies cooed and babbled.

"Good morning," Vivian said. Both babies strained to look in the direction of Vivian's voice. "Hello, my little darlings." She sat down on the floor across from Cianne so the babies were between them.

"Good morning." Cianne smiled. "Say good morning to mamma Vivian," Cianne told the babies. They both continued to coo and babble.

"Are you all packed up?" Vivian asked.

Cianne wondered when they would have this talk. "Mostly," she said. Cianne dangled a pair of teething keys over the kids. "I want to thank you for all you've done for me and Tristan. I don't know what I would have done if you hadn't been there for us. Letting us stay here so he could heal with proper care and training was a wonderful thing you did."

"You are my grandchild, Cianne. There's nothing I wouldn't do for you," Vivian said. She lifted up Aidan and stood him on his feet. She let him dangle his legs and push to a standing position a few times. Vivian looked around Aidan to get a clear view of Cianne. "Dr. Bannerman called again."

Cianne winced, "I don't see the point."

"He just wants to give you a check-up."

Cianne shook her head. "To see what makes me tick, right?"

"Cianne, he just wants to see why medicine has no effect on you. Even our medicines are useless. Aren't you curious about how you were able to heal yourself and what medicines can help you, if any? Think of what he may uncover for our medical advancements. He also mentioned that you told him you could tell the difference between Coesens and Middlings now."

Cianne looked down at Nadia, ignoring Vivian.

"I'd like to hear how," Vivian said.

Fine, she thought. "Every living animal has a sort of energy they emit. I can sense that energy," Cianne told her. When in the hospital she noticed a difference in the energy that was emitted from the Coesens versus average people but hadn't taken the time to really study it. If she were in a room mixed with both she would have trouble identifying who was who, though she knew it was just a matter of time before she could.

"We can help you control your abilities, Cianne."

Cianne played with Nadia's toes. "I'm really not that interested in opening up Pandora's Box. I just want to live a normal life. I know it sounds dull to you but to me it sounds wonderful. I want to go to college and become something. But mostly I want to see Tristan's wonderful smile each day before he leaves for work and I want to anxiously await his return. I want to walk my children to the park to play each day before dinner and drive them to school when it rains. I know that being normal isn't possible for us and I know I will have to use my abilities at some point," Cianne said then sighed, "but I rather do it on my terms."

"You sound just like your mother did before she ran off with…"

Cianne looked up at Vivian. The disgust in her face told Cianne that Caleb would never be accepted by them. Which reminded her of something else she wanted. She wanted to know more about Caleb. The thought of Caleb brought a memory back to her. Cassius showed up at the park last week.

"Are you having me followed?"

"Is that why you feel you have to leave here, because I have Cassius keeping an eye on you?" Vivian laid Aidan back down on the blanket. "Cianne, Tristan can no longer feel your fear or locate you if you are in danger. You are completely cut off from your Protector and I want you safe. You are vulnerable now. Have you considered that Caleb could have severed the bond between you and Tristan for his own devious plans?"

"Caleb saved Tristan. The connection we shared was killing him. Do you know how awful it must have been for him? The pain Tristan endured that horrible day proved deadly. It was more than any Coesen could handle. I'm grateful to Caleb for severing that connection." Cianne reached behind her leg and grabbed a soft toy for Nadia. "Moreover, why would Caleb do such a thing unless it was necessary?"

"I know Caleb seems harmless to you but believe me he isn't. He is very dangerous Cianne, and has eluded us for years. We didn't even know he still lived. You don't know what he is capable of because you aren't interested in who you are, who your children are." Vivian stood.

"Why would I be? You want me to be a part of a culture that treats the very people who protect them as second-class citizens. A culture that has the technology and medicine that could benefit the people of the world in so many ways but will not share these gifts because of a law that forbids you to get involved. A society that would demand that I give up the only person who has done nothing but love me for who I am, the father of my children, because love means nothing when it comes to duty.

"No Vivian, it's not that I'm not interested in who I am," Cianne said angrily. "I already know who I am. I am destruction, cleverly concealed inside an attractive package. The question is…do you know who I am?" Cianne took a deep breath. "No…how about I show you?"

A sudden wave of heat moved through the room causing Vivian to take a few steps backward. Vivian quickly looked herself over with an exasperated expression. She then looked to the children who were lying on the floor in front of Cianne, who was still sitting.

Cianne saw the concern on Vivian's face but continued anyway. "Don't worry. I would never do anything that would harm them, but to keep your mind at ease…" Nadia and Aidan abruptly rose up from the blanket, hovering in the air. Cianne remained seated on the floor as the children floated away from her. Vivian watched the children hover past her and come to a stop just outside the bedroom's entrance.

Cianne waited until Vivian turned back to face her. The second their eyes met, the large windows in back of Cianne shattered inward into millions of small chunks. Not a single cube-shaped piece hit the floor. Instead they simply froze in midair just behind her.

"Can any of you do this?" she asked.

Vivian looked to the twins who were still hovering several feet in the air behind her. Then she looked back at the cubes of glass behind Cianne. She shook her head. "No. There are some who can move things with their mind but nothing like this. The concentration it must take to hold onto the children, speak to me, and hold each tiny piece of glass without moving is, well it is miraculous." Vivian marveled.

"Miraculous? Then you really don't know what I am," Cianne's voice cracked. Her mouth turned down as she saddened. Just as she spoke the last word all the glass melded back together and was whole again inside the window frame.

The children were back on the rug in front of her, laughing and babbling.

Vivian gasped, most likely because the process to fix the glass and return the children to the floor in front of her took no more time than it would for someone to blink an eye. Cianne looked down at the children then back to Vivian.

"No one knows me," Cianne said quietly.

Vivian seemed to ponder what Cianne had done. Finally, she said, "You're my grandchild."

Cianne closed her eyes and took a deep breath. In a weird way, she was relieved and happy Vivian said those words. "And I'm happy to be just that to you. But I want you to know that I am going to continue to see Caleb. That is, if he wants to see me. If he wanted to harm me he had plenty of opportunities. So, I would appreciate it if you don't use me as bait anymore."

Vivian opened her mouth to speak but said nothing. She rubbed her hands together. "I'm sorry if you felt like you were being used. I can assure you that it will never happen again," she promised. "I am also sorry that you feel the way you do about people who you haven't taken the opportunity to learn more about." Vivian dropped her hands to her side. "I will leave you to your packing now."

Cianne watched Vivian slowly leave the room. She wanted to stop her and apologize but what could she say? When the door closed, she got to her feet and went to the window that overlooked the patio, the one she used for her demonstration. She could see Zeta sitting alone by the pool. From the look on Zeta's face, Cianne could tell that it just wasn't a good day for the women who lived on the property.

Chapter Four

It was virtually pitch black around the borders of the Bertram property. Tristan walked the grounds over a hundred times in the last few weeks. Today he wasn't walking the perimeter to test their security.

In truth, Tristan knew that the security system wouldn't keep out the one person he waited patiently to appear. If Caleb wanted to get through unnoticed, he would.

Tristan heard a noise behind him but didn't turn around. Somehow, he knew that Caleb intentionally alerted him by snapping some twigs that fell from the large cypress trees lining the borders of the property. When Tristan turned around he saw Caleb kneeling about ten feet away. Even with his super sensitive hearing he didn't hear Caleb's approach and that made the anger that was simmering inside him boil.

Caleb stood up.

Eye to eye now, Tristan looked for a sign of humanity or compassion in his father-in-law. He searched in Caleb's eyes for what Cianne saw or what she wanted to see. Cianne and her father had the same eye color, but to Tristan that was where the similarities ended. Cianne's eyes reflected emotions like love, compassion, empathy, and desire. In Caleb's eyes, he saw nothing.

"I don't know what your reasons were for helping me but I wanted to say thank you. That aside, I knew it was just a matter of time before you came here and I don't like it. I think you're a monster and I don't trust you around Ci or my kids. The only reason you're standing here is because I love her and I want her to be happy even if what makes her happy is being around you. And her wanting to be around you, I do have a problem with. I want you to know that if you say or do anything to upset or hurt her in any way, I will not rest until you regret it."

Caleb tilted his head as he stared back at Tristan. The guy his daughter had chosen was definitely something. What, he didn't know just yet.

The kid narrowed his eyes and took a step toward him but with a slight move of his hand, Caleb froze Tristan in place. Caleb then stepped closer, standing shoulder to shoulder with him but facing the opposite direction.

Caleb turned to face Tristan's frozen profile. "The only reason *you* are standing here, as opposed to six feet under, is because I love my daughter and I want her to be happy." Caleb looked toward the house then back to Tristan before he walked slowly away.

He thought about how Tristan found the almost unnoticeable tracks he'd left in the very spot he was frozen in, last week. Caleb couldn't make it easy but had left the tracks to test Tristan. He needed to know if the kid would call Cassius and report his visit.

But Tristan hadn't. It seemed Cianne's happiness was still more important than the hold the Coesen had on Tristan. Their requirement for blind obedience hadn't taken hold of the young man yet which meant there was still hope. Though he wondered how long Tristan's resolve would last.

Caleb entered the home through the patio door. Shortly after, Cianne arrived in the entry way of the room. When she saw Caleb, she gasped and raised her hand to her chest.

"I didn't mean to frighten you," he said. "My apologies."

Cianne whipped her head around. "Tristan," she said, looking at the doorway, "does he know you're here?"

"We've talked." Caleb sat in one of the chairs. "I think we understand each other now."

"Do you?" Cianne sounded concerned as she walked into the hearth room. She placed her book on the table and sat on the sofa that faced him. "Then that means that I am the only one who's confused. Do you think a visit from you every few months is going to help us create some sort of relationship?"

"So, you want a relationship?" Caleb asked.

"Well, yeah," Cianne said, "I don't know." She sighed. "Yes. I do want a relationship with you, Caleb. I don't know what you've done and I don't want to. The only thing I want from you is to be here for us, and the truth from this point on."

"I've always given you the truth and will continue to do so."

"Ok then," Cianne said as if she'd accomplished something. "Alright, so we can start off with a clean slate."

Caleb didn't answer.

"The slate is clean, right?"

He could almost see her mind working.

Cianne frowned. "How long have you been here…in town?"

"I arrived a few days after Tristan rescued you from the abandoned school."

Caleb watched as Cianne bit on her bottom lip. It was something so familiar to him yet foreign at the same time. "Did you…uh, were you involved in what happened to Nick and Jason?" The words came out slow and quiet.

For the first time in decades Caleb was astounded. He was certain, by the way Tristan looked at him earlier, that he knew all about his deeds concerning the Coesen. *Why didn't Tristan tell Cianne yet*? It wasn't like Tristan kept his dislike for him a secret. And Tristan knew for certain that he was the one who killed Patton but still he kept that information to himself.

Apparently, Tristan truly meant to keep Cianne happy.

Caleb wanted nothing more than for her to accept him but he was not in the habit of lying, especially not to her. "And Patton," Caleb said with no emotion.

"Why did you do that?" Cianne gasped. "Are you…they said you are so detached from the world that you kill without a second thought?"

"Contrary to popular belief, I am not detached and I do not kill without carefully thinking it through." He studied her reaction carefully. He thought it odd that she cared enough about those oafs to question his decision to take their miserable lives. It was almost endearing.

"How much time does it take you to decide if you're going to kill another human being?" She frowned.

"Faster than most I suppose," Caleb said, halfheartedly. Cianne looked worried. "I watched each one of those men for weeks. Neither was innocent." Caleb looked to the fireplace. "Especially your friend Nick."

"And that gave you the right to take their lives?" she barked.

He moved to the edge of the seat. "I saw the way Tristan reacted to them in the police station. If I didn't, he would have." Caleb held her gaze. "Would you rather he'd gotten his hands bloody, because killing can change a man, Cianne." Her eyes widened then her expression changed from worry to anger, then shock to doubt. "I want you to know that I hadn't killed anyone in over eighteen years."

"So, you killed them because of me." Her words were clearly not meant for him but more for herself. "What do I say to that?" she asked.

"I didn't tell you for you to feel guilty. I just wanted you to know that I don't take pleasure in killing. I'm not a monster, Cianne. I'm a father."

Cianne kept her eyes on Caleb. His face was smooth, almost perfect, and he didn't look a day over twenty-five. He was very handsome. His bone structure was strong and distinct but gave off a boyish quality. Caleb's eyebrows and thick lashes matched his evenly trimmed dirty blond hair that flipped at the top and lightened at the tips. But it was his brilliant green-blue eyes that drew the most attention, and their eyes were exactly the same.

"How old are you?" she asked.

"I was born Caleb Scott in the year 1806."

"My god, that would make you over two hundred years old," Cianne exclaimed. "You look as young as I do. How is that possible?"

"Would you prefer me to look like a man who has a teenage daughter?"

Right before her eyes, Caleb's face aged twenty years. Cianne wasn't prepared for what just happened. She was a little shaken, and a low cry escaped her before she covered her mouth. Once she was able to speak again, she said, "Okay, that's different." She inspected the lines at the corners of his eyes and the aged skin that now was his face. "But this isn't what you really look like is it?"

"No," Caleb admitted. Just as quickly as he changed to a mature middle aged man, he changed back to the twenty-something Caleb she was familiar with. "This is my true form. I stopped aging in my twenties."

He can change his appearance. It all makes sense now.

"You were the boy at my engagement party, the one who sat with me in the hall." She shook her finger trying to remember the boy's name. "Turner," she said with excitement.

"Turner was my mother's maiden name," Caleb told her. "Which Caleb do you prefer? I can be either."

Cianne's brows wrinkled. "Um, I guess I would rather see you as you really are."

"Then this is it," he said.

Can I change my looks like he can? She wondered about the extent of his ability. *Can he copy another person entirely?*

Cianne looked at him and an alarm went off in her head.

"Did you kill Dr. Garri—" Cianne was just about to finish the sentence when she saw Tristan out of the corner of her eye. He was panting and shivering. She ran to him. "What happened to you?"

"Nothing," Tristan strained. He eyed Caleb as Cianne held him in a partial embrace. He spent the last few minutes using every bit of strength he had to get to the house. He couldn't move any part of his body no matter how hard he tried for several minutes after Caleb did whatever it was he did to him. Each appendage tingled like a small electric charge was running through him. And when he finally regained control, he fell to his knees, gasping for air. It was as if he was a stone statue.

"I wanted to get a work out in before bed." Tristan looked down at Cianne. "To see how fast I could actually run." He pulled her into him, again eying Caleb over her shoulder when he spoke. "I may have overdone it a little. No big deal." Tristan kissed her on the cheek then held her at arm's length. "I'll be upstairs if you need me."

Cianne watched Tristan walk out of the room. "I'll be up in a bit," she said. When Tristan was out of hearing range she swiftly turned to Caleb. "What did you do to him?"

"Nothing really," Caleb said. "As I said, Tristan and I understand one another now. You had a question for me before he interrupted."

Cianne asked, "He's going to be alright, right?"

"He'll be fine." Caleb grinned.

Seeing him smile for the first time almost had her smiling in response but she was too upset. "I promise," he assured her.

Cianne shook her head as she returned to where she was sitting before Tristan came into the room. As far as she knew

Tristan never lied to her before, which meant that she had no way to tell when he was, but somehow, she knew he was lying tonight.

"Did you have anything to do with Dr. Garrison's disappearance?"

"I did," he answered plainly.

"What did you do to him?" Cianne held in her anger, not wanting to lash out.

Caleb stood. "His heart gave out."

Cianne looked up at him. This man, who looked like he could be her brother rather than her father, had no compassion for human life. She wondered if he truly cared for anything or anyone at all. "How could you? He was my friend."

Caleb looked down at her. "Dr. Garrison was never your friend. You only met him once, on your first office visit. He died that weekend, when he took what he thought was an unsuspecting teen by the name of Turner to his home. Dr. Garrison was a perverted child molester. He took advantage of those who brought their children to him for help. He was also responsible for the disappearance and death of two boys from Utah where he once practiced. You can take solace in the fact that he didn't physically die by my hands, and I can promise you his death was more tolerable than he deserved. It was me who you befriended." Caleb walked toward the patio doors. He was gone before she looked up.

Beginning of April
Vivian sat at the large desk in the office. She wrote a few more words on the piece of paper before folding it three times and placing it in an envelope. She sighed as she lay the pen down and looked out of the window. It had been almost a month since Cianne moved out and the Council was still not convinced that her granddaughter wasn't a threat.

Vivian understood their apprehension. She would have concerns too if she were on the outside looking in as they were. There was nothing she could do to ease their worries.

She continued to stare out of the window into the darkness. Something moved out there or she thought she saw something move. Vivian narrowed her eyes and moved her head slightly to the side, narrowly escaping the bullet that came through the window and imbedding itself into the wall behind her.

Vivian spun around in the chair, avoiding the assailant's second and third shot as he dove through the same window and into the office, shattering glass all over the carpet. The assailant landed on his feet behind her. Vivian knocked the gun from his hand.

When the gun dropped to the floor an all-out battle ensued. Her long loose satin robe swung in the air as she avoided his skillful attacks and turned them back on him. Their skills seemed matched but Vivian had something extra on her side. When she finally knocked him to the floor and took two steps back, she was sure that she had broken his leg but the man got to his feet and dove at her again. Vivian wrinkled her brows at this but raised her foot over his other leg and broke it in the same place as the other.

To her amazement, that didn't stop him either. With his eyes fixed on her, the assailant dragged himself across the floor attempting to get his hands on her. Vivian kneeled in front of him, just out of his reach. He extended his arms out trying to get her in his grasp.

"Cassius," Vivian whispered the summons.

Cassius appeared just inside the doorway a moment later. His eyes moved from Vivian, who was still kneeling, to the inching figure of the man who was struggling to get her. With a bolt of speed Cassius stood over the man. He placed his foot on the assailant's back, applying enough pressure to flatten him so that he was face down and unable to move forward.

"Why didn't you summon me sooner?" he asked angrily.

Vivian ignored Cassius and his disheveled appearance. She stood, then slowly walked a few steps to her right and stood still. She stayed there for a few moments before taking few steps to her left.

"Have you noticed how he's tracking me?" she asked Cassius. "He hasn't taken his attention off me for one second."

Cassius lifted his foot off the attacker's back and walked in front of him then kneeled. He waved to Vivian to move again. He kept his eyes on her as she walked around the man who lay on the floor. Vivian stood behind her attacker.

The man strained, arching his back to reach her. Using his arms, he tried to turn his body in her direction. Vivian watched as Cassius brought his fist down hard on the right side of the man's face. That seemed to have no effect and didn't distract the assailant at all.

"Do you know him?" Cassius grabbed the attacker by the jaw and held his face up. They both watched as the man struggled to see her out of the corners of his eyes.

"No." Vivian walked over to the desk where she was sitting before she was interrupted. She picked up the phone receiver and dialed a number. "Yes, I am sorry to wake you. There's been an incident here. I need a window repaired."

Zeta leaned back in a relaxed position over the kitchen counter while Cassius was seated in a chair directly in front of the attacker. Vivian joined Cassius and Zeta in the kitchen. Her attacker was tied up tightly to a wooden chair.

Zeta looked to Vivian. "Should we set John Doe's leg?"

"Cassius," Vivian said. Both Cassius and John Doe, who had been entranced by each other's gaze, turned and looked at Vivian at the same time. Her attacker once again tried to free himself from his bondage when he saw her.

Zeta walked over and steadied the chair so the man didn't fall over. She looked to Cassius who turned his attention back to the man.

"I do think we should have a doctor look at him but not for his legs. Is Bannerman still in town?" Cassius looked back at Vivian.

"I'll give him a call," Vivian said.

Tristan stared at the man everyone was referring to as John Doe. "How long has he been like that?" Tristan asked.

Zeta looked at her watch. "He's been this way since about four this morning," she said then shrugged, "so it's been about seven hours."

Tristan walked over to the John Doe and snapped his fingers in the man's face.

"He won't respond. We've tried everything."

"It's like he's a zombie." Tristan bent down so he and Zombie Doe were eye to eye. Then he slowly backed away. "What are they going to do with him?"

"According to Dr. Bannerman it's not much they can do," Zeta said. She sat on the kitchen counter facing the prisoner.

Tristan walked over and stood next to her. He continued to stare at the man in the chair who kept his eyes on the doorway as if he was waiting for someone. "So," Tristan said to Zeta, "what time is your flight?"

"I'm taking a red eye. I need to be at the airport by eleven pm." She kicked her feet out then back in a rhythmic fashion he often saw little girls do.

"And you're sure you have to return now?" Tristan peered over at her. He didn't understand her urgency. Zeta was still in her three-year service to the Royal Guard.

Zeta didn't face him. "I have no choice," she said sadly.

He never considered that there would come a day that he would enter this house and not see Zeta. He totally understood how his friend Brian was swooped away by life but Zeta…was where she belonged. Tristan never considered them being apart.

"You can't wait until after the wedding?"

Zeta playfully punched him in the shoulder. "I would never miss you guys' special day." Zeta hopped off the counter top as Cassius entered the room. She and Tristan stood up straight as their commanding officer approached.

Cassius looked at Tristan and lowered his head slightly. Tristan returned the nod and relaxed. Zeta had to wait until Cassius made eye contact with her before she could relax.

"Training is canceled today." Cassius informed him as he casually walked over to Zombie Doe. Cassius placed one hand under Doe's chin and the other on the back of his head. With a quick motion, Cassius snapped the man's neck. "Take him to the garage," he ordered.

Tristan nodded as Cassius walked by him and out of the kitchen. Zeta stepped toward the body but stopped. She took a deep breath then moved around the chair and began untying the knots. Seeing how bothered she was, Tristan quickly walked over and helped untie the man.

Neither of them spoke a word as they loosened the ties. Tristan could see her face was losing color so he lifted the limp body over his shoulder before she could.

"You alright?" Tristan asked her as they walked toward the garage. She looked at him with wide eyes and nodded. He knew Zeta had seen death many times before today. She had killed.

What is going on with her?

Tristan glanced her way as they entered the garage where Dr. Bannerman and Officer Perkins were waiting. Dr. Bannerman motioned for Tristan to place the body on a metal table he had set up. Tristan gently placed the body on the table as he looked around the garage that now resembled a makeshift operating room.

"Tristan," Vivian said as she entered the room. Vivian gave him a smile but somehow it wasn't quite right. It was forced and looked uncomfortable versus comforting. Tristan lowered his head. "Has Tristan been brought up to speed?" she asked Perkins.

Tristan looked at Officer Perkins. He was still getting used to the fact that Officer Perkins was a Coesen. Vivian apparently called him in to infiltrate the local Police Department when Cianne was kidnapped.

Tristan gave Perkins his full attention. As Perkins spoke, Tristan found himself looking at the body that lay on the table. When Perkins finished, Tristan was now aware that there was an attempt made on Vivian's life. Apparently, Zombie Doe, whose body was being cut open at present, was also a Coesen. His name was Leroy Fenton and he bore the mark of the Quende tribe.

Quende, as in Cassius' tribe, that was governed by the Royal, Chandra.

Dr. Bannerman also explained what was done to Fenton. Tristan learned about Jzerect, a type of Coesen black magic that is forbidden. Combine this form of science or black magic with the voice of a powerful Wheddler and you have a Zombie on a never-ending mission.

"So, you're saying he's possessed," Tristan asked.

"In a sense, yes." Bannerman nodded. "All his needs and wants have been replaced with one single objective. That is to kill Vivian Harper."

Tristan crossed his arms then looked over at Vivian. "Why would someone want you dead?"

"The same reason why some people want to kill your President," Perkins spoke up.

Zeta told Tristan that Perkins was once a Protector. When his ward was killed, his abilities faded as do any Protector's whose Coesen passes on. Tristan wondered what exactly happened with Perkins and his Coesen but Zeta didn't go into detail.

Tristan turned back to Perkins. "This isn't the first time?"

"Hazard of the job," Vivian answered.

"That's why we're here," Cassius said as he entered the garage. "I'd like to say this attempt was like the others before it, but this is the first time this method was used. Whoever sent him had no regard for this man's life. He had no choice in the matter."

As far as Tristan could tell, Cassius wasn't an emotionless pit but the man also didn't wear his heart on his sleeve. It was clear that this bothered him. The question was what part bothered him the most. Was it because black magic was used? To practice the black arts was a death sentence for Coesen. Or was Cassius feeling some kind of way about Fenton? Killing isn't easy but it must be harder to deal out death to one of your own tribesmen.

"Will they come after Cianne?" Tristan's words came out more calmly than he felt.

"I'm the target," Vivian said.

Her words didn't convince him, and for a brief second Tristan thought he saw a look of fear flash across Vivian's face. She recovered her queenly demeanor so quickly that no one else seemed to notice.

Tristan watched Vivian give the body on the table one last look before going back into the house.

Cassius waited until Vivian was in the house before he spoke again. "I've been investigating these attempts for some time now and I'm no closer to finding out who's behind them." For the first time since Tristan had known him, Cassius looked angry. "Every time I get a step closer to finding something out, I get pushed several steps back."

"So, *these* attempts...you think they are all related?" Tristan asked.

"Yes," Dr. Bannerman answered. He looked up from the corpse that lay on the table. "Each assassin has some similarities. Their finger prints and birthmarks were removed. But this one is different. He was reported missing a month ago. I doubt he was a willing assassin."

"He was programmed," Cassius told them.

"Bannerman is the most gifted Wheddler we have and he wasn't able to get through to Fenton. Killing him was the only way to stop him," Perkins added.

"How is something like this possible? To make a person a killing machine that cannot stop," Zeta asked. She kept her eyes on the dead man.

"It isn't easy," Dr. Bannerman said. He pulled off the plastic gloves and threw them on the table next to the corpse. "The Dark Arts were outlawed for a reason. When paired with a powerful ability, it can be disastrous."

Tristan looked at Cassius. "So, what do we do?"

"You, will do nothing. I am going to shake a few trees." Cassius cracked his neck then said, "And see what falls out."

"I think we should follow up on Fenton. Maybe trace the drug," Perkins said. "Fenton is different from the rest so the person behind this may have made a mistake with him."

"We've already been down this road, Perkins. You think they left us some in-plain-sight evidence. These people are smart and we aren't going to catch them because of some error that only happens on crime television shows," Cassius said angrily. He walked around Zeta and Tristan. Cassius looked back before stepping through the door. "You need to leave this to the professionals Perkins, and stick with solving Middling crimes."

After Cassius disappeared into the house, Perkins placed his police hat on his head, stood up, then placed the stool he sat on back under the work bench. "I'll be back for the body when it gets dark," he said. Perkins didn't wait for a response. He left through the same door as Vivian and Cassius.

What was that about?

Knowing that it wasn't the right time to ask, Tristan decided that it was best to get Zeta away from Fenton's body. By her rigid posture and focus, he could tell she was wired. When he took her by the hand, she turned her wide eyes on him then her shoulders slumped as she visibly relaxed.

He led her to the media room where Vivian and Cassius retired. Tristan entered the room with Zeta and gave her hand a reassuring squeeze. When Tristan noticed Cianne, his body reacted immediately. He knew at least half the room heard the change in his heart rate but he held his head high.

Smiling at Cianne, he kept hold of Zeta's hand. But Zeta pulled her hand from his and sat on the arm of the sofa where Vivian and Cassius were seated. He gave Zeta a questioning look, but went to stand a few feet away from Cianne. No one seemed to notice that he didn't greet Cianne with a kiss like he usually did.

"I was just telling Cianne that postponing the wedding would be foolish," Vivian said. "I wasn't able to see Kayla get married and I regret it. This wedding means a great deal to me."

"Alright," Cianne said with some hesitation.

Over the last few months, eloping sounded better and better but they *did* promise Vivian and his parents that they would let them plan the wedding. All the bride and groom were required to do was attend. In truth, it was a small sacrifice to make for two women they both loved.

"Great!" Vivian said then gave Cianne a curious look. "Where are the children?"

"Tristan's parents are keeping an eye on them for me," Cianne answered.

Tristan glanced around the room, noticing each appeared to show signs of worry on their faces.

"Do you think it wise to leave them unprotected?" Cassius asked.

Tristan smiled as he looked over at Cianne. Cianne looked back at him and gave him a slight nod. Tristan raised his hand and moved it slowly toward her. Heat rippled over his hand and through him as he got closer. Instead of his hand contacting her body, her image dissolved in front of them like a wave of heat. He would have been touching her shoulder if she had actually been in the room.

"She's working on staying visible even when matter goes through her, but it takes an immense amount of concentration," Tristan said.

Everyone was completely silent as they looked at him then the empty space beside him. Zeta's mouth fell open. Cassius stood and moved his hand over the spot where Cianne had stood. And Vivian just sat there. After a few more seconds of silence, Vivian did something Tristan had never seen her do. She began to laugh. Not just a chuckle, but a boisterous all out laugh.

By the way Cassius and Zeta looked at Vivian, Tristan was sure the woman hadn't laughed in years.

Chapter Five

The Council of Four chose blue for the color of their Hall many years ago just for the calming effects. That was why long pale blue and white sheer fabric hung from an invisible ceiling behind four white curved benches that were placed evenly around a circle. In front of the pillowed benches was a sunken floor of light and air.

The misty form of Chandra, the head of the Quende, was already seated upon her Tribal seat. The apparition of Brenna, head of the Gegdi, appeared next, followed by Eldra, of the Bode tribe. Vivian, of the Arkean tribe, was the last to appear in a seated position. Just like the others, her form was made of mist.

"Good day," Brenna said, addressing her peers. "I have no news to report from my region that would need the council's attention." She opened her hands to the council.

"Good day. I have no news that would require the council's attention," Eldra said. She opened her hands to the council as well.

Chandra extended her arms out. "Good day. I have no news that requires your attention."

"Good day all. I have no news to report." Vivian looked at each of the members. She would keep the attack on her life, which occurred earlier in the week, to herself.

Being Sovereign, she didn't need to inform the council of everything. She didn't require their opinions, she chose whether to hear any that they expressed. She also didn't need their approval to pass or reject a decree. Ultimately, the power lay in her hands.

The Council was enacted centuries ago to maintain the peace between the tribes; to inform the head of each tribe of formal decrees impacting all Coesen; to hear grievances from the head of each tribe; and to pass judgment on criminals whose crimes are so heinous that the Sovereign must hear their case.

"The Council is open for discussion," Vivian announced. The process of open discussion was kept civil. If you had nothing to discuss, you looked to the person to your right, giving them the opportunity. Brenna had the floor first, but with nothing to discuss she looked to Eldra.

"Has she decided what she will do?" Eldra asked.

It was clear that the topic on everyone's mind was Cianne.

Vivian looked to Eldra. "My friends, Cianne's will is strong, just as Kayla's was. Only, she sees the Middling world as her world. She doesn't understand our ways and is uncomfortable with the way we govern. It will take time to convince her otherwise."

Eldra nodded. "Has she exhibited any other abilities, and what of the children?"

"Yes, though she chooses to dismiss them. The children have not shown any abilities so far. But they are still young," Vivian lied. To reveal that she senses power from one of the twins already would be foolish. Besides, all royals in line for the Council are not be required to reveal their ability.

"What of Caleb?" Chandra disregarded the fact that Eldra had the floor.

All the women turned to look at her.

"Caleb continues to elude us. Cassius found him once and will find him again. Our only connection to him is Cianne, who does not see him for what he is," Vivian explained.

"She's protecting him?" Chandra's anger was evident and could be heard in her tone.

"There's no reason to believe that she is protecting him. She's only stated that she will not be used as bait." Vivian looked back to the center of the circle. Eldra and Brenna did the same. "In the matter of Tristan, he and Cianne will be married soon. I have given them my blessing."

Chandra's eyes widened. Brenna looked puzzled. They both turned to Eldra.

"I have given my blessing as well," Eldra chimed in.

"But what of the law?" Brenna asked.

Vivian turned to Brenna. "Each of you will have to decide if this law is still practical. In a month's time, I will listen to your arguments and make a decision."

Brenna seemed to think it over for a few moments. "I shall give my blessing now."

Vivian nodded. "I thank you, Brenna."

Their blessings meant no repercussions. Chandra may still be a problem, and considering the circumstances, Vivian wouldn't fault her. If Tristan carried Coesen blood in his veins it would be all too easy to command that Cianne's union to him be upheld by all Coesen. Tristan was safe only under the laws pertaining to a Protector and Royal Guard. Which meant that he could kill a Coesen to protect himself, his ward, all royals and any citizens without judgment. Marriage was an entirely different subject.

Vivian gave Chandra time to respond but after a minute, she spoke, "If there isn't anything else..."

"I want to know what it is that you are doing to capture Caleb," Chandra demanded. "It seems to me that you all have forgotten what he has done to our people. Or are you all willing to forget for the sake of an unreliable teenager who just happens to be his child?" Chandra looked to Eldra then to Brenna. "First we ignore one law to accommodate this...this *Halo*. None of us has actually seen or witnessed her power. And what of the rest of the prophecy? She may just kill us all.

"Yes, I voted to let that abomination you all seemed to be enchanted with, to live. Mainly because I believed that the demon who fathered her was dead. We should have killed her in her mother while she lay defenseless in the womb."

Vivian fisted her hands and bit the inside of her lip but before she could respond, a mushroom cloud of smoke blew out from the center of the room. It looked as if a small bomb had exploded. Inside the center of it a figure began to materialize.

Each woman reacted differently. Eldra smirked. Brenna gasped. Chandra's misty form faded somewhat as she stood. Vivian didn't react at all.

"If you Witches wish to die of old age rather than by my hands, you will leave my daughter and grandchildren in peace," Caleb said with a blank expression as he floated before them.

"The nerve of you, you…you animal!" Chandra barked. "Relish what life you have now," she said angrily before fading away.

"Amazing," Eldra said, clearly impressed. She stared at the solid form of Caleb floating in the center of their circle.

Brenna said nothing but just stared at the twenty-something man who turned his head to look only at Vivian.

Vivian spoke, "I don't know how you are doing this but I promise you I will find you and make you suffer for your disrespect shown here today and the crimes you've committed against my people."

"Kayla saved you nineteen years ago when we met but she's gone, Witch. Who will save you now?" Caleb smiled. "Tell me ladies, have you ever seen a chicken get its head cut off? Me being a farm boy, I can tell you that the fowl runs around in a frenzied state for several minutes after decapitation. Touch one hair on Cianne's lovely head and I will cut off your heads, and the last sight you will see is your body jerking around like a chicken."

Caleb disappeared just as suddenly as he appeared.

"I think I see what Marda and Kayla must have seen in him," Eldra said, then sighed.

"I definitely see what they saw," Brenna said, with a look of awe in her eyes.

"Good day ladies," Vivian said curtly, "I have a manhunt to oversee." Vivian's image dissolved.

April 16th

Cianne stood facing Tristan on a podium between white columns that were draped in calla lilies with shimmering silver satin bows, a theme that echoed throughout the elegant hall.

Tristan pulled her into his arms and looked deeply into her eyes. "Forever, Mrs. Bertram," he said. Then he kissed the bride.

Dressed in a one-piece silver satin A-lined dress with a sweetheart neckline and an asymmetrical panel wrap at the waistline, Cianne leaned into Tristan and returned the kiss with everything she was.

The guests stood and the hall erupted with cheers and applause.

"Forever," Cianne said, grinning. Laughing, she leaned into Tristan when he released her. He kissed her on the forehead then lifted her off her feet and spun her in a circle.

"I present to you, Mr. and Mrs. Tristan Bertram," the minister said joyously over all the loud well-wishes and cheers.

Once Tristan placed Cianne back on her feet, she turned to Tranae who held Aidan in her arms. Her friend's eyes glowed with loving tears as she smiled at back. Cianne then looked at Brian, who stood beside Tristan, holding a sleeping Nadia.

It was all so surreal. An elegant wedding fit for a princess, the man of her dreams, and their children safe and healthy. This was a day she would always remember. Everything was perfect.

Cianne looked to Tristan who took hold of her hand and gave it a gentle squeeze before he turned them to their guests, then descended the stairs. Brian and Tranae, holding the children, followed them down the aisle of standing well-wishers and through the double doors into a world of love and possibilities.

Getting to the honeymoon location was an adventure in itself. Cianne clutched Tristan's hand on several occasions through the flight to their destination. She couldn't remember ever being on a plane before, but with her memory issues, who knew? As it stood now, turbulence wasn't something she was fond of, but who was?

The boat ride wasn't much better. Normally, she had no qualms about boats but to enter one minutes after arriving at the small island airport for the short ride to the five-star private island resort was a bit of bumpy overkill.

Cianne glanced at the Coesen Guard who held out his hand to her as she carefully climbed out of the boat. Accepting Vivian's terms to not only leave her kids in their grandparent's care but to also take a small security detail was a way to keep everyone happy. Though she wasn't sold completely on the idea of a honeymoon without her children, Cianne did like that they had people looking out for them that she did trust.

The island and the overwater bungalow which was attached to land by a hundred-foot dock was beautiful. She and Tristan had five days of relaxing, clear blue water, and white sands. The villas on the main island were so well spaced that if they chose, they didn't have to see any of their entourage throughout their entire stay. Yet, all their needs would be taken care of so they could enjoy each other.

To Cianne, it was the perfect joining of modern seclusion.

Once inside the over-water bungalow set on posts, Cianne took her time admiring the luxurious accommodations. When she noted that Tristan didn't seem too awestruck she started watching him. Having seen his fair share of the finer things in life, Cianne figured he wasn't impressed at all. She forgot her admiration of her surroundings and focused her attention on her husband.

Husband. He was forever hers…and it felt amazing.

Tristan walked over to a large welcome basket on the bedside table and opened one of the bottles of champagne. He poured some of the liquid into a set of glasses then brought the glasses over to her and handed her one.

"To our family," he said then raised his glass.

"To our family." Cianne raised her glass to his then took a sip.

Tristan grabbed hold of her hand and led her to the humongous bed. He took her glass and placed both his and hers on the side table. He sat her on the bed, took off her shoes, then flipped off his shoes and got on the bed. He lay down first then pulled Cianne back so that her head rested on his chest.

"I'm sorry your father wasn't here to see this day." He rubbed her head.

"I am too," she said. "But I'm sure he's looking down on me, happy for us. I've married into a wonderful family." She held her hand out, motioning to their room. "This place is an example of how generous and loving your parents are. It's amazing." Cianne fumbled over a few words then said, "I don't even have the words for what I am feeling right now."

Tristan sat up, forcing her to sit up as well. "Ci, my parents didn't pay for this, Vivian did."

"No," Cianne said as she pushed off the bed and stood, "Vivian had the place and the employees checked out after your mother gave her the details. Your parents had all the paperwork and the tickets."

Tristan got to his feet. "Because it was all sent to the house," he said. "My mom took charge because that's what she does and she knew we've been so bogged down with the kids. She thought she was helping by handling it all."

Confused and a bit on edge, Cianne stood in place as she glanced around the room. When her eyes fell on the welcome basket, she approached it. Her finger grazed over all the gourmet treats inside until she touched the plain white envelope. She pulled it out and read the letter to herself.

Dear Mr. and Mrs. Bertram,

Please forgive my tactics but I felt that if Vivian knew that this island getaway gift was arranged by me, she may have forbidden you to come. I arranged for it because I worried that you two would have delayed this very necessary part of your union. You should never delay your honeymoon. Your mother and I never had one but if we had it would have been here. No harm will come to you here. You have my word.

Yours Truly
Caleb

"Caleb?" Tristan rubbed her neck.

Cianne sighed as she nodded. She held the card to her chest and smiled.

"Should I be concerned?"

She knew Tristan didn't trust Caleb yet, even though he knew she did. For him to know that this was Caleb's doing, yet he wasn't grabbing for their luggage was all she could ask for. The look on his face told her that even with her approval his concerns weren't going to subside. But she tried anyway.

"No," Cianne said calmly. "He means well."

Tristan motioned to the note, so Cianne handed it to him. She watched him read over it and when he was done he handed it back. Tristan said nothing as he walked out of the double bay back doors to the edge of the deck and peered over the hundred-foot dock that connected them to the white sandy beach and island where the staff buildings were hidden by a small forest.

Cianne walked up behind him, wrapped her arms around his waist, then laid her head on his back and said, "Don't make this into more than what it is, Tristan. He just wanted to give us a wedding gift."

Tristan took in a deep breath. "I know." He turned around and lifted her chin with his finger. "You wanted him there, at the wedding."

The unshed tears in her eyes answered for her.

"I wish you could have had that father-daughter dance that every girl dreams of." Tristan kissed her lips then added, "Or at least a brother sister dance." He winked.

They had to tell his family and their friends that the youthful Caleb was Cianne's long lost brother from the father she'd never met. It was the only explanation she could think of when he wouldn't leave her side in the hospital.

"Do you know how hard it was for me to explain to my parents why your only brother wasn't at our wedding?"

Cianne nodded. She squeezed her eyes shut, refusing to let a tear free.

"I'm sorry things are so complicated, Ci."

"I'm happy, Tristan. Being with you and our children makes me very happy." Cianne touched his cheek. "As long as I have you, everything that's complicated is manageable." She kissed him.

Cianne's eyes popped open and she sprang up to a sitting position. Not wanting to wake Tristan, she quietly slipped from the bed, grabbed her robe, and wrapped it around her.

Unsure of what woke her or caused the uneasy feeling coursing through her, she walked out of the open patio and down the long deck toward the island. The sound of the water moving calmed her as she walked. The moonlight also aided in her sense of well-being as she strolled along the dock. Soon the sand of the beach replaced the wood of the dock.

Cianne wiggled her toes in the cool sand as her feet sank in a few inches. As she walked barefoot along the beach she heard someone behind her clear their throat. When she turned around she saw Caleb walking toward her.

Caleb didn't know what to do with his hands when he stopped just in front of Cianne. Like her mother, she was beautiful, smart, and caring. That was the only reason he thought this meeting would work in his favor.

"Congratulations," he said.

"Thank you," Cianne said, smiling. "Thank you for all of this."

Inside, he beamed like a child at her acceptance. "It's the least I can do for my only daughter." *Whom I love very much,* Caleb wanted to say. He'd practiced saying "I love you" for several hours but saying it to her now seemed…forced. Maybe because he never thought he would ever get the chance to say those words to anyone ever again.

Maybe he'd been out of touch so long he'd forgotten what love really was.

Cianne lifted her arms up, moved in, and hugged him. The action took him completely by surprise. Caleb hesitated but eventually he wrapped his arms around her waist.

"I think you owe me a dance," Cianne whispered thickly in his ear.

Choked up by her emotions and her act, Caleb grunted, "I was hoping you would allow me the pleasure."

He held his daughter close as they danced on the cool sand under a clear sky and beautiful moon. He didn't mention to Cianne that they had a spectator as they swayed side to side, using the ocean waves to keep the rhythm.

There were so many things he wanted to say but for now he just held his daughter close and carved this moment into his memory as his new son-in-law turned and quietly left him to his moment.

◉

Cianne loved the island and all it offered but they only had two more days and the five-day honeymoon would be over. The fresh air and tranquil turquoise water will soon be replaced with parking lots, people, and polluted air.

The privacy, the staff who provided every need with nothing but grace, and the way her new husband doted on her was more than any woman could ask. Even still, she wanted to experience the night life on one of the larger islands before leaving.

With their plans for the evening solidified, Cianne felt the need to check on the children. So, when Tristan left to secure transportation to explore the largest neighboring island, she closed the bedroom door. Normally, she would call Tristan's parents to check on the children but she missed their faces. And, it seemed like the perfect opportunity to hone the one ability she rarely used.

Fading was the name Cianne gave her teleporting skill. It was a perfect fit because she basically held her physical form where she was while her spectral form traveled to where she willed, remaining invisible to all around her over the distance. She'd practiced some and was pretty confident about holding herself in a faded state around non-Coesens. If she failed to hold the invisible form, she could appear to those around her in solid form out of thin air. That mistake would be in direct violation of Coesen law.

She had no doubt reached her law-breaking limit with the "powers that be". Plus, if she failed to maintain her faded image, she could definitely give her in-laws a heart attack. *Heck*, heart attacks all around, she thought when she considered that Martha, Ben, and Celia, the Bertram's house staff, may be around.

Then I'd better do it right, she told herself.

Standing in front of the patio window inside their honeymoon suite, Cianne considered the distance. She hadn't attempted a Fade of this magnitude. The distance was vast compared to the few miles she was used to Fading.

If it doesn't work, I'll just call.

There were no known side effects for a failed Fade as far as she knew. Relaxing wasn't necessary and that was a bonus. If there came a time when she was unable to calm herself, she would still be able to teleport. Cianne only had to think of where she wanted to be. With just a mere thought, her body began to fade.

As her image dissolved, the bedroom door to the bungalow burst opened. Cianne yelped as she turned her head just in time to see Tristan flash to her side and grip her arm.

"Where are you going?" he demanded.

Oh god, what have I done?

A panicked whimper escaped her lips as she grabbed his wrist to fling it away. But it was too late to stop the Fade.

With no idea of what her inherited ability from Caleb was doing to Tristan, she used her free hand to hold onto him. The furniture in the bungalow disappeared around them. They stared at each other, Cianne's eyes were just as panicked as his, as his grip on her arm tightened to an almost painful hold.

No…no…no.

The bungalow disappeared around them. Cianne closed her eyes. She tried to brace herself for the worst. Her mind conjured thoughts of Tristan's arm, severed and bloodied at the elbow, with his fingertips still dug into her wrist. But when she opened her eyes she saw Tristan, still gripping her sensitive wrist, and he was a hundred percent intact, though faded.

Freaked, Cianne pulled away from Tristan. He must have had a short lived "freak-isode" as well because he allowed her to step away, both of them forgetting that they were in mid-fade. His image flickered from semi-faded to almost invisible.

Cianne reached out to him and grabbed his wrist while maintaining their semi-faded form. "Are you alright?" she whispered. By the look of him he was more surprised than hurt.

"I don't know," Tristan told her. It was apparent he'd just started breathing again when he answered. "I uh…" he started to say as he looked around their bedroom at his parent's house, "I um, I think so."

Tristan raised his free hand in front of his face and stared at it for a while then dropped it. Then he shook his head in a manner one would, in order to compose themselves.

"So," he said in an accusing yet playful tone, "we're checking on the kids?"

The fact that she'd unintentionally whisked him from their honeymoon suite in a ghost-like state to spy on his parents' babysitting abilities seemed to be of no consequence. The fact that she could have killed him…well no matter now. That was so Tristan. Her cheeks burned with embarrassment.

"It's fine Ci," he said softly," I missed them too. Let's see what they're up to then." He led the way out of their bedroom and down the stairs.

It was dinner time and the Bertram house was filled with happy chatter, an immense transformation from several months ago. Mr. Bertram sat at the head of the table. Beside him in a high chair covered in baby food that was pasted to her skin, was Nadia. Nadia swatted at her laughing grandfather's hand as he tried to spoon some food into her mouth.

"Come on princess," he said as he put the spoon to her lips. When Nadia refused to open her mouth, Mr. Bertram closed his eyes tight and shuddered before trying the mush himself.

Tristan covered his mouth with his free hand but Cianne saw his shoulders shake with laughter. The relationship between Tristan and his father had evolved into something beautiful since the shooting. Death had a way of making a person see what was important.

Cianne turned her attention to Mrs. Bertram who was seated in her usual spot, to the right of her husband. Unlike

Mr. Bertram, whose dinner looked cold, dry, and undisturbed in front of him, Mrs. Bertram's dessert plate sat in front of her. Beside her, in Tristan's usual spot, was Aidan. He sat in his highchair with his hand around a small spoon, apparently feeding himself.

It was a skill that most babies attempted at ten to twelve months but Aidan had mastered it a month ago. And with four teeth fully grown in, he was already on solids. Her six-month-old little boy was developing faster than his sister and most other babies his age. Cianne stopped comparing the two soon after the first few months.

Cianne tried to hide her son's progress from the Bertram's and all her Middling friends as much as she could. Aidan was very perceptive and smart but also strong willed and independent. He refused to allow anyone to feed him.

"Mama, up," Aidan said, then dropped the spoon and raised his hands up.

To Cianne's surprise, Aidan's eyes were pinned on her and Tristan. His words sent the room into a whirlwind of praise from his grandparents. They of course were oblivious to the fact that Aiden somehow saw them.

Aiden's words also alerted Nadia. She raised her eyes and swept her gaze around the room until she saw them too. Before Nadia could reach for them, Cianne lifted her free hand and patted the air to calm them. She then placed her pointer finger over her puckered lips. Aidan dropped his hands immediately and looked down.

My smart sweet little boy, she thought. The little bugger smiled as if he heard her thoughts. *Had he*?

Dismissing the idea with a shake of her head, Cianne focused on Nadia. Instead of calming, Nadia started to cry as she continued to reach for them. Her grandparents tried soothing her with words but it only took one look from Aidan to quiet her. Aidan always had a way with her that neither Cianne nor Tristan understood.

"See." Tristan smiled as he whispered, "Little man has everything under control." He waved goodbye to the children then led Cianne out of the dining room. "With the security Vivian has in place, they are safe. So, I think we can get back to our honeymoon. Don't you?"

Tristan was happy the boat ride from their bungalow to the largest adjacent island didn't take too long. In under thirty minutes, he and Cianne were seated at the bar inside the tranquil but crowded restaurant. He watched Cianne as she took slow sips from her drink and tapped her foot to the island music that played. Her wide-eyed interest and awe brought a grin out of him.

She looked amazing in the open-back, low V-neck, floor sweeping ivory dress. Her skin was brushed with some kind of sheer powder that made her already luminescent tanned tone look even more delectable. Her hair was pulled away from her face in a loose knot but several strands always managed to fall free. She looked at him and smiled, the drink straw perched between her luscious lips. To this day, Cianne was the most beautiful creature he'd ever laid eyes on.

Cianne placed her palm on his white shirt and squeezed her eyes shut. "Is it too strong?" Tristan questioned.

"I could use something fruitier."

Tristan held his hand up to get the bartender's attention as he glanced to his left where two men sat at the opposite end of the bar. Both men gave him a subtle nod, acknowledging him. Tristan returned the gesture.

When the bartender noticed him, Tristan ordered Cianne another drink. When he turned back to Cianne, she was facing the live band that was set up on the stage in the rear of the bar. He wasn't sure if she noticed his interaction with the two Coesen Guards who just nodded at him.

After he gave the establishment another once over, Tristan looked back at Cianne. It seemed she was unaware of all the Guards who mixed in with the locals and tourists tonight.

To be honest, he didn't care if she hadn't taken notice. Cianne was having a good time and that was the only thing that mattered to him. The Guards…they were around to ease Vivian's mind and their presence didn't bother him in the least. Even though he felt that he was capable enough to protect his wife and ward.

"This one has no alcohol in it." Tristan lifted the drink off the bar and handed it to Cianne. As Cianne held her hand out to take the glass, he gave it a gentle caress. She smiled a smile so lovely it took his breath away. She didn't allow him time to recover. Instead she moved toward him and whispered a promise of a blissful night in his ear. When she pulled away, Cianne offered him a seductive smile.

"Excuse me."

Tristan looked at the waitress who stood in front of them. She gave them a pleasant smile as she placed two drinks on the bar behind them.

"Compliments of the patrons at that table there." The waitress pointed to a table located in what seemed to be a private section of the restaurant/bar.

Cianne looked over to the table where a woman and a man sat, before he did. Tristan noted that the woman was between the ages of twenty-five and thirty. She had shoulder length black hair with bright pink tips. She wore a pink shirt and skirt, giving credence that her favorite color just might be pink. Her brown eyes looked soulful, yet sultry.

The man sitting with her was tall and lean. He was dressed in a flowing shirt and a pair of shorts but didn't have anything physically noticeable. What peaked Tristan's interest about the pair was that they were Coesens. He just knew it. Just like he knew that woman was the Protector, even though he couldn't see her mark from this distance.

When the man noticed that Tristan and Cianne were looking their way, he said something to the woman. Without hesitation, the woman rose and started walking toward them. When she was a few feet from them, the woman lowered her head before speaking in her native tongue.

Roughly translated, she said, "My name is Satome of the Bode tribe. My ward's name is Erik," she turned slightly to allow them to see him better. "We would be honored if you would join us for a drink."

Tristan prepared Cianne on what would happen if she was noticed. The Coesen were a clandestine group but their numbers were many. As he studied and learned the culture, he learned that Coesen always spoke their native tongue to those they weren't sure were really Coesen. It was an easy way to weed out tattooed imposters. Apparently, the birthmarks were admired and often replicated.

Tristan and Vivian also warned Cianne that she may be recognized, be it by the awesome power she exuded or by the Coesen who made it their business to know the politics of their people. If they were to come in contact with civilian Coesen, Cianne was to keep that Tristan was her Protector a secret.

He took other precautions as well. He wore a brown loose fitting long sleeve shirt so that his Royal Guard brand was hidden, and he wore a fingerless glove to cover the back of his hand.

"Satome and Erik would like us to join them," Tristan playfully translated in English for his wife.

Satome took a step back, placing her hand over her chest. She looked surprised. Tristan assumed it was because he spoke the Coesen language. He watched Satome as understanding filtered through her mind. Her eyes widened then her body stiffened. She was going to drop into a full out bow but Tristan shook his head.

She relaxed a bit but not much as she regarded Cianne with unrestrained awe. "You are really them?"

"We are...them," Tristan confirmed.

Cianne took a sip of her drink. "You didn't think we were them?"

Satome immediately began to shake her head. "I thought you were Coesen but just tourists. I would have never approached you. Erik would have." She cleared her throat. "There have been a number of imposters. More now that…" She stopped in mid-sentence then looked around. "I cannot apologize enough." Satome glanced at the Guard sitting at the other end of the bar. Her warm brown complexion visibly paled.

Tristan followed her gaze to the Guards who were making their way over to them. He gave them a look that said, "hold off". The Guards halted without question and returned back to their side of the bar. Tristan turned his attention back to Cianne, who was smiling at the woman in front of them.

Cianne raised a brow at Tristan, silently asking what he thought. Missing their telepathy more than ever, all he could do was nod.

"Nonsense, we'd love to join you," Cianne stepped down from the barstool.

When they reached the table, Erik stood. Tristan noticed the subtle look Satome and Erik shared. Understanding immediately, Erik bowed low. He then waited for Cianne and Tristan to take a seat before he and Satome sat.

Erik's eyes moved over Tristan before nervously moving around the bar. "We are delighted that you could join us. I am Erik from the Gedgi tribe," he said. "We would have prepared for your visit if we would have known of your coming. It is an honor to be in your presence."

Though Erik spoke calmly, Tristan still heard an uneasiness that lay beneath the surface of his words. Cianne smiled but Tristan could tell she was a little embarrassed.

"We're happy to be here," Cianne mumbled.

Erik looked confused for a moment but quickly accepted her words with a smile. Tristan knew that it was rare for a Royal to be seen in a place like this, but to also converse with a commoner socially in a place such as this was unheard of. No doubt Erik was wondering if Cianne really meant that they were happy to join him and Satome or was she being sarcastic. The status and class system the Coesen lived by was archaic but some, mainly the Royals, still held on to those old ways with a tight fist.

"Are you enjoying our little slice of paradise? Have you…" Erik glanced at Tristan but returned his gaze to Cianne, "done much yet?"

Most of the Coesen who Tristan came across, other than the Guard, both Royal Guards and Sentry Guards, had no idea how to address or even hold a conversation with him. To them, he was somewhat of a celebrity. Just one interview with Coesen News Today, a Coesen owned and run news show, had propelled him and Cianne into the limelight.

They were the talk of the Coesen and Middling worlds.

America and most of the rest of the world grabbed hold of the story of a normal teen who had no idea she was *the* heir to a throne that most of the world didn't know existed. All people needed to know was that Vivian Harper and her family were as rich as the Catholic church, they had royal titles attached to their names, and utilized security guards.

The fact that Cianne was beautiful and a princess equaled instant stardom, newly-established fan clubs, stalkers, and fake social media pages. The fact that no media outlet except for that Coesen's news show was able to pin them down for an interview made them even more interesting.

For the Coesen, Cianne was a fairy tale come to life, a prophecy foretold that had come to fruition. It was one that fitted Vivian's rather sudden one hundred eighty-degree spin on being more transparent with her people. And by most accounts, her plan for Cianne to be the People's Queen was working. The fact that most of the Coesen world had accepted him and their marriage without his participation in the Tandot, and had virtually made him into a sex symbol was unexpected.

It was assumed that he was a Child of Jai, which carried a stigma of its own, but with The Four backing them and the public's love, they hadn't encountered too many problems. Yet, no one knew he was a Middling or her Protector. He suspected that those omitted pieces of information would not go over well. Tristan wasn't certain when Vivian planned to share this with her people but he was certain she had a plan.

"The island is amazing," Cianne answered Erik. She turned to Satome and said, "It must be so exciting to live in such beauty. How long have you two lived here?"

Satome tried without success to hold back her shock, then delight. She turned to Erik with an anxious look in her eyes. Erik was also holding back a smile as he nodded to her.

Satome met Cianne's gaze, "For several years now." She looked at Erik again. A grin pulled at her lips as she lowered her head.

Tristan became aware of two things after witnessing the exchange. The first, that even though Erik treated Satome, his Protector, like an equal, he was planning to keep things formal while in his and Cianne's presence. The second, there was something that blazed in Erik's and Satome's eyes when they looked at each other.

Tristan wondered if Cianne noticed it too. If she had, she made no attempts to convey it to him.

The conversation continued between Cianne and Erik. Tristan was content to just sit there like a man married to a powerful woman often did. He answered what few questions were sent his way but said nothing more. Eventually Cianne squeezed his leg under the table. Tristan knew it meant she was tired of the formalities.

He commended her for her effort thus far. Coesen life…it was the life he wanted for them. Cianne knew this and was trying to acclimate for him but he would leave it all behind the moment she decided she was done with it all.

Cianne had enough of the formalities. "I have an idea. How about we just forget what my mark means tonight and just act like four regular people," she finally suggested. "Do you think you guys can relax a little so we can get to know each other and have a good time?"

Erik seemed to think over the request while Satome's eyes sparkled with acceptance. Erik looked up at Cianne before looking at each of the eight Guardsmen that were scattered throughout the building.

Tristan watched as she followed Erik's gaze, noting each Guard.

"Do you know of someplace we can go then?" Cianne asked Erik. She wasn't angry by the extra security but this was her honeymoon and she should be able to enjoy herself the way she wanted. When Tristan didn't protest her request, she knew he was on board.

"Yes," Erik said, "but we may not be allowed to leave, and even if we are, they'll surely follow."

Cianne closed her eyes and sent out a simple command. All at once, the eight Guardsmen looked at her while the rest of the patrons appeared oblivious and enjoyed their evening. Tristan moved to get to his feet; no doubt he sensed something was happening. Cianne opened her eyes and took hold of his hand and stood. Erik and Satome, both seeming confused, stood up as well.

"They'll be staying here." That was all Cianne offered as explanation.

Tristan looked down at her for a few moments, as if he was trying to guess what it was she had done, then he shrugged and led them toward the exit. She tried to keep her eyes straight but Tristan, Satome, and Erik focused on a Guardsman they passed who was seated at the bar. When Cianne glanced at the Guard, his eyes seemed determined on a course of action but his body refused to respond.

Erik gave Satome a questioning look but they continued to follow quietly.

"What did you do?" Tristan asked her as Erik led the way to his car.

Her husband didn't whisper the question…so Cianne didn't whisper either. "I sent out a mental message to all Coesen and Protectors inside the building and the surrounding area. I told them that I was leaving and that I would appreciate a little privacy." Every one of them, including Erik and Satome. heard the mental transmission but apparently Tristan hadn't. "Just in case they didn't understand, I made sure none of them except, Erik and Satome, could follow us."

She took away their ability to move with a single thought.

Do you live here with Erik?" Cianne asked Satome as they stood in the small but modern kitchen.

The apartment was absolutely adorable. The living space where they left Eric and Tristan was spacious, nicely decorated.

Satome glanced over her shoulder at Cianne before reaching for glasses inside one of the high cabinets. "Umm…no, I live across the hall. We felt it would be best if we stayed close but not too close." She placed four glasses on the counter and opened the refrigerator. "Is ice tea alright or would you like something stronger?"

Cianne could tell Satome didn't know what to think of her. She also knew that Satome had a secret. The way the woman looked and acted around her ward, Erik, it was clear that she had feelings for the man. If Cianne was right, those feelings ran deep. She considered she may be wrong but Cianne would bet that she was right.

"Tea is fine," Cianne told her. She began to nibble on her bottom lip thinking of how to get Satome to relax. Talking to the woman was like trying to communicate with a nervous child. For over an hour she'd tried to find common ground. At one time, Cianne thought it would be easier to make Coesen friends, being as they were all sort of the same. How wrong she was.

Satome was going to make her work for a connection but once it was made Cianne knew they were going to be friends. She wanted a connection with a Coesen who didn't feel responsible for her like all the others. Plus, Cianne surmised that she and Satome had something in common. Only she just couldn't come out and ask. That would be tactless.

So, she decided to go about it another way. "I imagine it's hard to be as close as you two and still make time to find love. Do you get along with the women Erik dates?"

Satome stiffened, opened her mouth to respond, then closed it. Then she softly said, "I try my best not to interfere in his…private affairs."

Ok, I hit a nerve. "Do you have someone special?"

Satome turned fully around and eyed Cianne for several heartbeats with questioning eyes. If she was suspicious of the line of questioning, she didn't say so. "No, I do not," Satome said turning her attention back to pouring tea.

Cianne realized Satome wasn't going to trust her with her secret. Why would the woman reveal something so personal that could lead to her arrest? *No one would be anxious to tell the Sovereign's granddaughter of their forbidden love.* Cianne decided to change the direction of their conversation and talk about something general.

"It must be really convenient living so close. So, when he needs you, all he has to do is pick up the phone and call," Cianne smiled, "and just like that, you're here."

After another suspicious look Satome spoke, "Well not exactly."

"How then?" Cianne nervously bit her lip. "I'm really interested. I was raised as a Middling and just recently found out what I am. I haven't studied Coesen ways."

"Really?" Satome seemed generally curious now. "That explains the whole being friendly to me thing. You really don't know any better, do you?"

Cianne shrugged.

Satome chuckled. "Erik doesn't call me on the phone or anything like that. If he just wants to talk to me about something, all he has to do is say my name. He can say it in a normal speaking tone or just barely a whisper. I will hear him if he wants me. Somehow, Protectors know the difference between being summoned or if our names are just being spoken in general."

"Just a whisper, you say?"

"The softest," Satome confirmed. "Say your Protector's name as low as you can. It will be heard if it's a summons no matter the distance. It's like a beacon. He or she will leave the bar and come to you."

Satome thinks that one of the Guards at the bar is my Protector. A dangerous idea came to Cianne in that moment. *If I reveal my secret, Satome may trust me with hers.* Cianne was certain Satome was in love with Erik. She just had to get her to admit it.

"Alright." Cianne frowned, knowing what she was about to reveal and hoping she wouldn't regret it. She faced the kitchen entry, tilted her head slightly, then raised her eyebrow before whispering as low as she could, "Tristan."

The last syllable barely made it out of her mouth before Tristan was at her side.

"You are breaking the rules, Mrs. Bertram," he said. Tristan brushed a loose strand of her hair behind her ear as she gazed into his eyes.

"I was just testing you," Cianne said then smiled. She shivered as Tristan lowered his head to kiss her shoulder.

When Tristan straightened, he peered over Cianne's shoulder. Cianne assumed he was looking at a stunned Satome. Over Tristan's shoulder, frozen just inside the entryway, Cianne stared at a wide-eyed, furrow-browed Erik.

"He's...he is your Protector?" Satome asked in disbelief.

"You married your Protector." Erik accused Cianne.

"We can explain," Tristan offered as he gave Cianne a condemning glance.

It only took a few minutes to explain everything regarding Tristan being a Middling turned Protector and not a child of Jai. Erik and Satome were amazed by their story. Satome even made a request to see his brand. She was enamored when Tristan uncovered the Royal Guard/Maatii brand on his right hand and arm.

"How long have you two been a couple?" Cianne finally asked. She posed her question to Satome who sat on a loveseat across from her and Tristan.

Satome turned to Erik, who sat in a single chair to the side of them.

"We aren't a couple," Erik spoke up, "But I won't deny that I'm in love with her," he added, looking down.

It must have been a surprise to Satome because her breath hitched and she stared at him. When she finally spoke, her voice was shaky, "I love him too." Her eyes filled with tears that she was clearly holding back. "But I will not allow him to risk his life and everything he has worked hard for. The punishment for breaking this law is death."

Erik gazed at Satome lovingly from the opposite side of the room. Their eyes reflected a sadness Cianne knew all too well when she remembered longing for what she thought was an untouchable Tristan. It was beyond selfish that she never even considered those affected by the Coesen law she willfully ignored, because she was so wrapped up in her own happiness.

"Death? Tristan, you knew the consequence was death?" She gasped when Tristan nodded. "And you went along with our marriage?"

Tristan took her left hand in his then turned her wedding rings in a full circle around her finger. His eyes spoke the words he didn't say but Cianne translated them to herself. *I'd suffer a thousand deaths for you,* she imagined he meant…or something like that.

"The law is being reviewed." Tristan faced the others.

"Well, there must be something that can be done now." Cianne touched Tristan's face and turned his head back to her, "Right?"

"I'm sure the law will not be on the books much longer but if you want to change it now Cianne, you know what you must do." Tristan grabbed her hand on his cheek then placed it in her lap.

Getting involved with the Coesen and their politics was the last thing Cianne wanted to do. The truth of that fact must have been evident on her face.

"Forgive us," Erik spoke softly. "It's your honeymoon. We didn't mean to upset you with our troubles. We make no demands of you. Both of our situations are complicated and I am confident things will work out the way they should. Just meeting the both of you has given me hope that things are changing for the better."

"I agree," Satome said, sounding hopeful, "You're different from the other Sovereigns. You'll bring about change. Erik is right. We should be celebrating." Satome lifted her glass, "To new friends and a world of possibilities."

Cianne smiled but she didn't feel like celebrating. She relied on her manners and repeated the toast along with everyone else but it was forced and felt wrong. She didn't like a lot of the Coesen laws, just like she didn't like some of the laws she had to abide being a U.S. citizen, but she never got so worked up about them. She had always been content with her simple way of life even if it meant loneliness.

She wanted no parts of Coesen politics but how could she turn a blind eye to a law that she herself broke, but because of who she was, because of who she knew, the law was under review. It wasn't fair but did she have it in her to insist on the change Erik and Satome wanted, needed?

If she did, it would mean adopting the Coesen lifestyle.

Even without their past connection, Tristan must have sensed her unease. He placed his hand on her leg and gently moved his hand up and down. As always, his touch relaxed her. For the rest of their time in Erik's home, Cianne was able to push the matter of Protector/Coesen relationship out of her mind. It was her honeymoon, the only one she'll ever have and she decided she should enjoy it.

Chapter Six

Caleb stepped foot onto the exquisite property and unnaturally green lawn a little after ten in the evening. Three weeks had passed since he last spoke with Cianne. She and the children consumed his thoughts since his time with her on the beach, during her honeymoon. She was who he was thinking about now as he strode across the lawn and past the pool house that was being used as a training area.

He made no effort to avoid the security cameras that were placed throughout the property though he was an expert at avoiding detection if he chose. Caleb walked around the grandiose pool and up the path in full view of the cameras that tracked him. He didn't know if Vivian was watching but he moved slow, he wanted her to see him coming.

It is more warning than she ever gave me, he thought as he pushed open the patio doors to her office.

The next morning
Cianne was suddenly encased in coldness, chilling her to the bone for only a split second before the feeling was gone just as quickly as it came. She felt clammy so she rubbed warmth over her exposed skin with her hands. The feeling lingered.

She closed her eyes but when she opened them she was somewhere else. In front of Cianne was a field of endless green grass as far as her eyes could see. She slowly turned around to see a lake of blue water behind her. In the center of the lake was a stone water feature with four stone angels that doubled as fountains.

A short distance away, her children sat on a blanket. They looked older, but not by much. Cianne took a step toward them but she didn't feel the ground beneath her feet. She took another step…then another…bringing her closer to the kids as they played.

When they noticed her, their happy faces expressed the joy they felt. The kids laughed in unison as they watched her approach. It wasn't long before she realized that she'd taken over thirty steps and still the kids remained out of her reach.

Cianne called for her children but she heard no sound come from her mouth. She brushed her fingers over her throat. Confused, Cianne turned back to the lake. She saw someone on the other side, across the water.

Cook? He stood alone, smiling at her. She tried to scream for him but again, nothing came out. All she could do was watch as Cook turned away from her and began to speak to someone else.

Cianne looked to the person Cook spoke to. When she saw the person, she moved forward, disbelieving her own eyes. Her heart pulsed and one of the beautiful stone angels on the fountain in the lake exploded with such force that the water from it rose high then fell toward her like a tidal wave surrounding her.

A strong hand grabbed her wrist and pulled her from the raging water as she silently screamed for her rescuer to leave her and save Aidan and Nadia.

Cianne found herself on a patch of grass, choking and gasping for air. When her breaths came in and out with ease she sat up. As she moved her legs they brushed something soft.

She peered down at herself and saw that she was not only dry but dressed in her wedding gown.

Pulling her eyes away from her gown took some effort because it made her feel whole and calm but when she did look up, she saw Tristan kneeling beside her. But he wasn't dressed like she was. He wore a regular shirt and a pair of jeans.

Cianne looked around Tristan to see the children still in the grass playing. She looked across the lake where Cook stood with the people he was talking to. Her father, Joseph Baxter gave her a knowing smile as his eyes swept over her, Tristan, and the children. But Vivian's smile was more one of apologetic sorrow.

Confused, Cianne turned her attention back on Tristan. He too was smiling, and as he took her hand in his and turned her rings one full turn, he leaned into her and kissed her shoulder.

Tristan put his cheek to hers and whispered in her ear, "I promised to love you forever, Cianne and I will. Be strong for me buttercup."

"Tristan," Cianne breathed.

Tristan heard the summons and felt the desperation in Cianne's voice. He exited the bedroom and ran down the stairs so fast that his body appeared to be just a blur. He heard the crash as he descended the winding staircase only to find Cianne sitting amongst broken glass.

"Are you alright Mrs. Bertram?" one of the movers asked. The young man from We Haul It moving company sat down the lamp he was carrying and walked toward Cianne but stopped when he noticed Tristan.

Tristan ignored the confused look on the mover's face as the man looked at the winding stairs and up to the second floor. He took Cianne's face in his hands and peered into her eyes. Though he could no longer feel it, he knew from the look on her face that her fear was coming off her in waves.

"I'm fine," Cianne said.

Tristan glanced up at the man, giving him a silent dismissal. The mover picked the lamp back up and continued on his way. Tristan helped Cianne to get to her feet then lifted her in his arms and carried her to the sofa in the foyer; it hadn't been moved to the family room yet.

He hurried to the kitchen, mindful not to use his abilities since moving men filled the new house. Getting a bottle of water meant moving around heavy stacks of boxes. But there was no one in the immediate area so Tristan took his foot and gave the bottom box a slight push. The tower of boxes slid across the room until they hit a wall with a thud.

Not caring if anything was broken, he grabbed a bottle of water from the fridge and quickly returned to Cianne. He watched as she took a few sips from the bottle before speaking.

"What happened?" he asked.

"I don't know," Cianne admitted. "I think I was daydreaming or something."

He knew Cianne was tired. The children were a handful, moving into their new home was taxing, and she'd been extra stressed since meeting Satome and Erik. He still remembered Satome's words, "Maybe you will change things when you become Sovereign." and the pensive look on Cianne's face in response. The words had stuck with him as well.

"You had a nightmare…while you were awake?" Tristan asked calmly, but he didn't feel any sort of calm. Cianne hadn't had a vision in such a long time and he knew that if they started up again she would be devastated.

He was about to ask her about it when his leg began to tingle. He looked at his pocket and took his cell phone out then focused on Cianne. She gave him a nod. "Yes," Tristan answered, "she's here with me. What's going on?"

Cianne stared at him while he listened to Cassius on the phone. He wasn't certain what his face reflected but inside his mind reeled. *It isn't possible*, he told himself as the phone slid from his ear and onto the couch between them.

"Ci…"

Cianne's eyes widened and her mouth fell open.

She knows.

Tristan pulled her to him and wrapped his arms around her, holding her as tight as he could without hurting her. Her arms draped around his neck and she buried her face into his chest. The sounds that surrounded them, men hard at work moving their furniture into their new home, hid her sobs.

"My grandmother, she's dead," Cianne moaned. Her voice sounded so weak when she asked, "isn't she?"

Tristan nodded because he couldn't trust himself to say "yes" without breaking completely down.

The Fasen

Cianne sat rigid in the ostentatious chair that resembled a modern throne. She gripped the intricately carved brushed steel armrest so tightly that her fingers ached. The stark white seating was very comfortable but with the high-back chair positioned on the dais, it gave her the kind of status and attention she hated. But the throne fit perfectly in the Victorian style mansion that sat on a very large and private estate in Canada.

Though the large hall was filled with friendly faces and associates of Vivian, Cianne felt no comfort from them. As she looked around the large crowd, some seated but most standing, she felt chilled by the sheer numbers of Coesen she didn't know and all the pairs of eyes focused on her. Cianne's eyes would meet with those belonging to many strangers but she always felt the sudden need to look away.

Maintain eye contact, Cianne. Always let them look away first.

Cianne remembered Vivian's words and held contact until the woman watching her offered a slight bow before turning her attention to someone else. Released, Cianne sighed as she looked to her cold hands. She slowly rubbed them together in case someone wanted to shake her hand rather than bow the formal acknowledgment. She hated when they bowed.

Alone.

She felt so alone in the crowded Hall. The people here had come from all over the world to pay their respects to Vivian, their fallen Sovereign, and to Cianne, the supposed successor. Sovereign was a title she didn't want and had no intentions of accepting. The Coesen lived by rituals and customs she found disturbing.

One such custom was responsible for why she sat in this room, on this pretentious throne, without the one person who could offer her peace. Protectors weren't allowed inside the throne room. Tristan, Cassius, and Zeta, along with many other Protectors who were present, had to gather in the ready room, a separate area for them to mourn and wait for their wards. The Coesen attending were Vivian's trusted companions and knew the truth regarding Tristan so there was no pretending here.

"Once the representatives from the three families arrive, you may retire, Soahn," Langley spoke quietly.

Cianne looked up at the very handsome Caucasian gentleman who stood to her left. Mr. Kenneth Langley was the name he gave her when he introduced himself as Vivian's lawyer. Apparently, Langley and his ancestors were Coesen and bore the Quende birthmark. Tristan told her that they were ostracized because of their appearance and were often referred to by another name.

It was Langley's mansion that Vivian used in Arizona, though Cianne only saw him on the property a couple of times. The Langley's were regarded as family by the Harpers, and were accepted and had regarded Ark Manor as home since the late nineteenth century.

Cianne was on the verge of another crying spell and she could tell it took strength on Langley's part not to break protocol and hug her. He was clearly a gentleman; a woman's tears did something to him. Cianne could also tell by his demeanor that protocol meant everything to him so he would not be giving her the comfort she most desperately needed.

She watched his jaw tighten before he pulled his gaze away and forced his attention to the two people who approached. Langley bowed his head to them when they stopped in front of her.

"The Royals Raya Tam, first born; and her sibling Whodai Tam," Langley announced.

Cianne barely saw the dark-skinned beauty who bowed in front of her, through her puffy red eyes that filled with tears. Raya's eyes were just as red and it seemed she was having a difficult time standing as she bowed. The woman would have surely fallen over if Whodai hadn't had her arm set in his.

"We extend our deepest sympathies. Our nation has lost a great leader," Whodai said as he bowed his head. His face was sullen but he held himself together.

I want to be that strong.

Cianne sucked in air to speak but Raya's distress only fueled her own. She couldn't find her voice. All she could do was nod as more tears surfaced and fell. Whodai tried to move forward but Raya held him in place.

Can no one offer the slightest comfort?

Cianne screamed inside her head. Why were there so many rules? How were they all so cordial at a time like this? She'd just welcomed her grandmother into her life again.

As comforted as she was by Whodai's words and his sincerity, all Cianne really wanted was Tristan. She watched as Whodai walked away and into the crowd.

A new stream of tears fell from her eyes. *I'm not strong enough for this.* She refused to let another minute go by without him.

"Tristan…" Cianne whispered so low that she didn't hear her own words.

Tristan maneuvered through the room and its occupants with such ease and speed that it was a while before anyone realized he was in the room. At first, the only indication he'd even entered was the cold gust of wind that touched some of the guests as he rushed in from outside, where he waited for Cianne to summon him.

Beside Cianne, on one knee, Tristan took her hand in his and lowered his head like a servant instead of her husband. He heard a few gasps and some whispers but Cianne's grief superseded everything else. Tristan knew Coesen Law, but nothing meant more to him than his wife.

He felt the eyes of everyone in the room as he placed his forehead to Cianne's. When he heard her sigh, he closed his eyes and willed his strength into her. Unfortunately, he lacked the true ability to do such a thing but him just being with her…that would do.

Tristan ignored whispered adorations about his speed and the talk of Cianne's blatant disregard of Coesen law. Because of what he was, a Protector, a lesser to them, and that he was touching the acting Sovereign intimately in front of everyone during the Fasen Ceremony, was against the law of Coesen.

"Uh hum."

Tristan glanced over his shoulder then immediately stood. The entire room was focused on the Royal Eldra, who cleared her throat, and the other Royals, Chandra and Brenna, who stood on either side of her.

Cianne slowly moved her gaze over each of the women's faces. Still holding her hand, Tristan lowered his head so Cianne figured she should do the same in the eerily quiet room. When she raised her head, she looked around at all the faces. Some of the people looked shocked, some looked scared, and others seemed to be waiting for something.

She didn't chance a look at Tristan. She wasn't versed in their laws but she knew the one she was breaking. All because she couldn't keep it together for a few more minutes.

Cianne looked down. She felt the need to explain. "I…"

Eldra raised her hand and placed her finger gently under Cianne's chin, lifting it so that they were eye to eye.

Cianne's tears continued to stream down her face as she looked at the beautiful woman in front of her. She instantly saw the family resemblance and knew that this was indeed Whodai's and Raya's mother.

Eldra wiped a line of tears away then caressed the side of Cianne's face with her hand. Cianne couldn't help leaning into the woman's gentle touch.

"Lovely one," Eldra said sweetly, "you do not bow for anyone." Then Eldra lowered her hand, slowly kneeled to one knee, and bowed her head.

Seconds later, everyone in the room took Eldra's lead and did the same. All Protectors and the Royal Guards who had gathered outside and in the hallway with a clear view inside the room also kneeled. Everyone kneeled except for Chandra, who looked angry as she gazed around the room at all the other Coesen.

"Her ashes will be taken to the center of the globe and released." Langley told Cianne after the ceremony as they sat side by side on a half-round sofa in a large room that Vivian often used for entertaining.

Cianne glanced over at the man. He looked as if he hadn't slept in days. She never witnessed how close he and Vivian had been but seeing the way he looked, she wondered how close.

Her gaze moved around the room to locate Tristan, needing to see his face for comfort. He sat at the bar with Cassius and Zeta.

Eldra, Brenna, and Chandra, the Council of Three as it stood, sat together on another half-round sofa facing Cianne and Langley. Whodai stood quietly behind Raya, who sat in a chair near a wall of windows. His arm draped over her shoulder and her hand gripped his.

"If that's what she wanted," Cianne said quietly. She was exhausted and she just wanted to retire to her room, be with her children, and hold them tight. The "no children allowed at the Fasen" rule was maybe the first Coesen law she was ok with.

Cianne regarded the Council. "Thank you all for coming. I know that you do not usually meet physically in the same place at the same time, but made an exception this day."

"We wanted to show our respect," Brenna told her.

Cianne touched Langley's hand and was about to tell him something more but a disembodied voice sounded in her head asking a question. She turned to face Brenna. "I can, Soahn Brenna," she answered.

It was apparent that the Council was curious about her abilities and Brenna, from the Gedgi tribe, wanted to know if she could speak telepathically to anyone.

"And you can hear me, if I want you to," she transferred to Brenna.

Brenna nodded then smiled.

"We aren't just here to show our respect, Soahn Cianne. We have come together today because we view the Fasen, a day of grief, also as a day of renewal," Eldra said. "It is customary to induct the Sovereign's successor on this day."

Cianne's mouth gaped open and she was sure her face turned stark white. She looked back to Langley. He stiffly agreed with a nod of his head.

"I decline." The words rushed out of Cianne's mouth.

Tristan didn't have to connect to anyone to feel the emotional shift in the room immediately after Cianne spoke. Shock and disbelief covered the faces of all except those who spent time with him and his wife. Those people knew how she felt.

Though, even with the magnitude of Cianne's words everyone in the room seemed virtually calm. That was, everyone except for the Royal Chandra, who'd been watching Cianne with disdain most of the night but now peered at her with utter hatred. Tristan had sensed her dislike of them from the moment she arrived.

"I can't stand this a moment longer!" Chandra yelled, demanding everyone's attention.

"Please Chandra, you were out-voted," Brenna said calmly. "Vivian made the declaration before she passed."

What declaration?

"This isn't the time or the place for this," Eldra said to Chandra.

"This is a perfect time," Chandra said angrily. "Because of you," she pointed to Cianne, "our Sovereign is dead. You, who have no loyalty to your own people but hold murderers and Middlings in high regard." Chandra sneered at Tristan then looked back to Cianne. "Caleb will pay for this."

Tristan watched as Cianne's eyes took on a faraway look. He moved to stand but Cassius placed a hand on his knee, silently ordering him to stay seated.

Tristan's brows creased. There was no way he was going to allow anyone to speak to his wife like that. He shifted again but saw Zeta shaking her head at him. She was also silently begging him to stay seated.

He knew the law. He was well aware of the penalties for raising a hand to a Royal. Tristan had never struck a woman and wasn't about to, so death was off the table. The penalty for challenging a Royal was fifty lashes. He was willing to deal with that.

"Chandra," Eldra called out. Both she and Brenna began to speak to Chandra in hushed tones in their native language.

The vacant look on his wife's face twisted into defeat. Tristan knew losing Vivian had and would continue to affect her deeply. She'd been through so much and he'd be damned if Chandra was going to blame Vivian's death on her too.

He watched as Cianne slowly stood. Oblivious, the three women continued their heated discussion. Cianne focused on him, giving him a weak shake of her head. The pain she felt was clearly etched in those flawless green-blue eyes of hers.

"She says she needs a few minutes alone," Cassius told him.

Since the shooting, she was unable to communicate with Tristan telepathically. He hated that everyone but him could hear her in their head if she wanted them to. He knew Caleb said severing their connection saved his life but he hated it.

Tristan gave Cianne a beseeching look but didn't follow her when she silently left the room. But after he was sure Cianne was gone, he stood up. Tristan didn't know if the Royals were aware that he spoke their language but by her arrogant tone he deduced even if Royal Chandra knew, she wouldn't care.

Enraged by her words, Tristan reconsidered his vow to never hit a woman. Yet, when he spoke he made sure his words and demeanor appeared calm. "You should leave," he said to Chandra, in the Coesen language. He felt everyone's eyes on him.

Cassius jumped to his feet, "Forgive him, Soahn Chandra, he grieves."

Tristan wasn't at all frightened by the wicked smile Chandra gave him. It might intimidate others but he was unfazed, and by the way she narrowed her eyes at him, he would bet she knew it.

When Tristan heard Chandra's quiet call for Victor under her breath, he realized how offended she actually was.

When Victor, Chandra's Protector, appeared at her side looking agile and fit, Tristan readied himself. Victor was a good three inches taller than him, about twenty years older and ripped like an MMA fighter. The beast of a guy gave a questioning look to Chandra but seemed to get his order without her voicing it. He turned and glared at Tristan who stood about thirty feet away, fearlessly glaring back.

In tune to his surroundings, Tristan heard Zeta slide from the barstool behind him. She was planning to back him up. Tristan locked his attention on Victor as he raised his arm a fraction of an inch, motioning Zeta to stand down.

"You can leave on your own, with dignity and grace," Tristan said, with the same calm, "or I *will* assist you."

"You dare threaten me." Chandra stood. Her anger reflected on her face and in her tone. "Victor," she said, "this…Middling needs to be taught what happens to those who dare to be insolent."

What occurred next happened so fast that no one other than a Protector could see it clearly, and even they may have had a little trouble making out the scene. There was movement, then several gushes of air swept through the room before the large window on the far side shattered.

When the movement ceased, Victor lay outside on the cold lawn in the chilly Toronto mid-day air and Whodai was crouched in his fighting stance, guarding Tristan, who hadn't moved.

"What he *was*…isn't my concern and shouldn't be any of yours," Whodai said. His eyes moved over everyone in the room and all the onlookers who'd heard the commotion and had come to investigate. "What you should concern yourselves with is that he *is* the Potentate, the mate of the Halo who *is* our departed Sovereign's successor. I will say this only once." Whodai stood up slowly. He spoke the last words in their language which translated to, "Anyone who moves against the Halo or her Potentate will not get the second chance I've graciously granted Victor." Whodai then turned his attention to Chandra. "I respect your arguments and I mean you no disrespect," he lowered his head but not his eyes, "but you were asked to leave, Soahn Chandra."

Chandra looked as if she had been slapped across the face. Several witnesses in the crowd gasped when she raised her hand in the direction of Whodai and Tristan. Whodai moved so his body blocked Tristan's entirely.

Tristan quickly moved to Whodai's side. He wasn't about to let anyone face an attack for him, even if a small part of him longed to see Whodai flat on his ass.

"Enough," Eldra stood. She positioned herself between her son and Chandra. "This is to be a day of reflection, not a Royal rumble. Chandra, your perspective as always has been reviewed, and you have been out-voted." Eldra glanced over at Cassius. Some silent understanding passed between the two before she looked back to Chandra and said, "You may take your leave."

Tristan watched Chandra glare at Eldra for several tense moments then look to Brenna with disbelief evident on her face. Apparently Eldra was someone Chandra didn't want to mess with, because when Cassius walked over and offered his arm, she reluctantly took it.

Before leaving the room, Chandra looked back. "This day will be known as the day that started it all," she said angrily before leaving. Her entourage quickly followed.

Tristan entered the dark ceremonial room and flicked the light switch, illuminating the round area. He strolled between an aisle of six white columns as he moved toward the center of the room where four identical round upholstered benches surrounded a seven-foot illuminated pedestal where Vivian's urn rested.

The Reflection or Memorial ended hours ago, but here Tristan found Whodai sitting with his head hung and his body relaxed. Tristan approached slowly, and when he reached the center he stood next to the bench Whodai sat on.

"Is she well?" Whodai asked. His elbows rested on his knees while his hands dangled between his legs. He didn't bother looking up.

"She's coping," Tristan said, then sighed. Cassius mentioned that Vivian was very fond of Whodai and was actually like a godmother to him and his sister. "I suppose everyone is trying to handle it the best way they know how."

Whodai didn't respond or look up.

After a few minutes of silence Tristan said, "I wanted to say thank you for what you did earlier, considering how you feel about me."

"May I be candid?" Whodai asked. He sat up straight and looked up at Tristan.

"I prefer it," Tristan told him.

"Under normal circumstances, you and I wouldn't even know each other. I don't have many dealings with Middlings. So, I particularly don't care for your kind," he said plainly. "Saddle that with the reality that you are married to the woman I almost died for. The woman I was told I would marry if I was strong enough and good enough, since I can remember. I don't need to tell you how she affects or rather infects your mind once you've met her." Whodai shrugged. "You, who I generally find inferior in every way, have something I can never have, and because of that Tristan, we will never be BFF's."

Tristan raised a brow at Whodai's candor, yet his reasons were valid. "Then why risk Chandra's ire by defending me?"

"I'm a company man." Whodai shrugged. "I've accepted your union. Accepted that she chose you, and for that reason alone I accept and will honor the title you now carry." Whodai stood. He gazed at the urn, his eyes red as if he was holding back tears. "Besides, I wasn't risking my life," he smirked, "I was risking our lives." Whodai walked away.

Whodai walked down the hallway he spent a good deal of his youth running through. He turned the corner and tensed, realizing too late that he wasn't alone.

"A word Whodai," Eldra said in her customary hushed tone. She stood in the shadows, out of sight of any mourners who straggled.

Whodai tried to mask his surprise that she'd gotten the drop on him, with a relaxed stroll toward her.

Impatient with his unhurried movements, Eldra sighed as she shot her arm out and pulled him into the darkness with her. "What were you thinking?" she demanded, her eyes blazing with anger. It was an anger he hadn't felt from her since he was a boy. "Do you have any idea what you've done?"

"Mother…" Whodai started, but was silenced by the heat of her stare.

"You dare address me with that title," she said as she cringed, "in public."

Eldra's nails dug into his arm, piercing the skin, but he didn't pull away. As if it were possible, Whodai stood up straighter. "Forgive me, Soahn Eldra."

"This situation is very sensitive, and to Chandra it is very personal. It needed to be handled delicately, a trait you have proven time and time again to lack. As a figurehead from my direct line, you are an example and must follow the laws above all others. Yes, the job of protecting our Royals is your responsibility as a Guard, but today you represent royalty. I understand you felt a need to act, but no harm would have befallen Soahn Tristan. Brenna and I would have never allowed it." She stepped closer to him. "Your punishment will be mild. But I won't tolerate disobedience, especially from you."

Mild?

Whodai wanted to laugh. "I apologize for my misconduct, Soahn Eldra," he said impassively. He waited for Eldra to turn and walk away. When she did, he followed. She would want to dish out his punishment right away.

Whodai held in his contempt, always. He held his head high, even knowing that he had an audience.

◉

Tristan watched as Eldra and Whodai walked away. "What was that about?" he asked Zeta as they climbed the stairs.

"He has challenged the will of one of the Four. Something only an equal can do," Zeta told him. She didn't look at him and hadn't really since she arrived two days ago. In truth, she was avoiding him and he wanted to know why.

Later.

For some reason, he was worried about Whodai. Tristan remembered reading something about acceptable punishments in one of the Annals. There were three levels of Royals. The Sovereign, always an Arkean Queen, was at the top and supreme. She held the highest rank, power, and could overrule the Council of Four.

The heads of each of the three tribes made up the remaining Council, were considered first level Royals. Their offspring and descendants were second level. The Council members' siblings and their descendants made up the third level of Royals. Everyone else was just a citizen, Protector, Guard, or Dregan unless they married a Royal and was extended the appropriate title and power.

Those who fueled a Royal's anger were punished. In what way, the Annals did not say.

"What will happen to him?"

"He will be judged," Zeta sighed. "The Bode tribe is immersed in the old ways and traditions. Out of the four tribes they have held on to a lot of customs that most of us feel are barbaric." Zeta stopped at the top of the stairs. Tristan stopped on a step below and looked up at her. "He will be judged," she said again, "and if he is lucky, his punishment will be physical." She continued climbing the stairs, leaving Tristan to wonder.

"Versus," he called out.

"Mental," she said without turning back.

Chapter Seven

Langley's Estate, U.S.
May, a little over a week after the Fasen.

Perkins took a needed deep breath but his temper was rising. "If you'd just listen to me and stop being so damn condescending!" he yelled as he watched Cassius walk by him without a glance.

Cassius put the bag he was carrying in the trunk of the car then turned around to face Perkins. "You listen to me," Cassius said. "We already know who killed the Sovereign. The son of a bitch's image is plastered all over the security tapes. That's all I need."

"So, the dead woman who was found in the room with the Sovereign doesn't interest you at all?" It was just like the Quende to disregard something so important just because the woman found dead with Sovereign Harper was missing a few genetic anomalies, which made her all human. "Not to mention the fact that Caleb has never been caught on any of our security cameras in the past…I don't know…forever, but the night he allegedly comes to kill Sovereign Harper, he somehow couldn't avoid them. Why would he be so careless after all these years?" Perkins pointed out.

Cassius shook his head. "I don't care why. That Middling was just in the wrong place at the wrong time and Caleb killed her for it."

Perkins followed Cassius around the truck. "Who was she then?"

"Who, what, and why is none of our damn business," Cassius said as he got in the back seat of the truck and slammed the door but rolled down the rear window. "Look Perkins, I know that you *police officers* follow a formula, that you've forgotten the way we do things. Me and my men are going to make that son of a bitch pay for what he's done and I'll be damned if you are going to hold me up a minute longer because you feel that I need to convince you of his guilt with clues and evidence. His comeuppance is long overdue. So, if you don't mind *Officer Perkins*, my team has spotted Caleb in San Antonio." Cassius tapped the headrest of the driver's seat. The car moved forward. "Watch your toes."

Perkins cursed. The nerve of that self-righteous prick. He watched the vehicle ride down the driveway in disbelief. Cassius was really going to dismiss the dead human who was found with Sovereign Harper. There was a reason she was there. That girl was the key and Perkins knew it, but it seemed he was the only one who thought so.

Home of Cianne & Tristan

Caleb climbed through the open window on the second floor. Getting into the house unnoticed was difficult but it wasn't impossible. There was little to no cover leading up to the house for a person who didn't want to be seen by anyone or anything except for the night sky. The good thing was that, if he was discovered, the closest neighbors were far enough away that they couldn't see or hear any disorder coming from the people who lived in the home he had just entered.

It was dark in the room but he needed no light. Caleb stepped around the bedroom furniture, making virtually no sound. He walked over to the door that led to the hallway and listened. When he felt comfortable that his path was clear,

Caleb opened the door slowly. He walked casually to the master bedroom and searched for what he came for.

"You're getting careless." Tristan said as he entered the dark room.

"Not careless," Caleb said. With his back to Tristan, he continued to search the jewelry box. "Just not concerned."

Tristan moved exceedingly fast, faster than Caleb would have guessed possible for a human, even with Protector abilities. Caleb was truly impressed, but Tristan wasn't fast enough. Finding what he came for, Caleb turned just as Tristan swung on him. Caleb stepped back, raising his own fist and bringing it down hard onto Tristan's back. Tristan stumbled forward from the impact but didn't fall because Caleb grabbed him by the neck.

Lifting him off the floor with one hand, Caleb looked up at Tristan as he applied pressure to his throat. Tristan struggled to free himself but it was no use. "Even with the great Cassius' instruction you are no match for me, son. I *can* call you son, right?" Caleb smiled. "See, the thing is *son*, none of you are much of a match for me. Even when Cassius had his power he was just my plaything and now your general is reduced to a mere man so…"

Caleb stopped mid-sentence. Yes, he had Tristan by the neck but his hold wasn't what caused the pain that reflected in the boy's face. Suddenly Tristan was pulled from his grasp. Tristan moved through the air like a bullet. Caleb whipped his head around in time to see Tristan land on his feet but quickly fall to his knees in pain.

"Cianne don't—" That was all Caleb was able to say because he was hit with a sudden wave of intense heat. Caleb took a step back, pivoting his body sideways in an attempt to avoid the next invisible energy blast that came toward him. He saw Cianne move into the room. Her eyes were completely red, and the look on her face was pure hatred. That hate was for him and him alone but…

Caleb glanced over at Tristan. The boy was truly impressive because he was now on his feet, speaking to Cianne in a calming manner, and moving toward her. *The fool, what is he doing?* Caleb had only seconds to think. He looked at Cianne again, not long, but his quick examination was enough to make a decision. It was one that he would regret in a minute or sooner.

Caleb raised his hand in Tristan's direction. Tristan launched into the hallway and over the second-floor banister. After the half-second his attention was diverted, Caleb felt an intense blow to his chest. The force of it pushed him onto the six-drawer chest and into the wall. He rebounded forward and stretched his hands out to brace for another impact.

Can't take another one of those.

Caleb glanced at Cianne before jumping to his feet then launching himself out of the second story window. He tucked into a roll when he hit the grass. He pushed to his feet then looked up at the window he just jumped from. He ignored the pain in his chest, but his lungs burned. He coughed, a mixture of blood and vomit spraying from his mouth. He cursed the pain then took off in a dead run.

He ran the length of the large property and four more blocks to his car in less than ten seconds. Once inside his vehicle, he moved his rearview mirror so he could look at his eyes. A redness in his pupils was glowing and growing outward, slowly overcoming the whites of his eyes.

"No," he said. Winded, Caleb squeezed his eyes closed. "No…damn it, please no," Caleb begged as he fought back his anger.

He opened his hand and focused on the ring he took from Cianne's jewelry box and placed it on his finger. *His ring.* Thoughts of Kayla filled his mind, her smiling, eating, and rubbing her pregnant belly. Calmed, the darkness retreated.

Caleb looked at his reflection once more. Satisfied, he straightened his rearview mirror. He put the car in drive and peeled off at full speed.

Tristan held on to the banister tightly with one hand as his feet dangled over the wide open great room below.

"Tristan!" Tranae screamed from the first floor, "what the hell is going on?"

He pulled himself up and over the banister with ease. "Check on the children," he yelled as he ran into his bedroom and jumped out of the window. Cianne and Caleb went through it only a minute before.

A few feet away, he found Cianne standing as still as a statue. Her back was to him so he cautiously took slow, deliberate, steps. "Ci," he said as he moved closer.

Cianne spun around so fast that Tristan stumbled back. Her eyes were soulless and completely red as they stared vacantly back at him. She gave him a look that suggested he was a stranger to her. Anger and aggression poured from her and was directed at him.

This is new.

Undeterred, Tristan took another careful step toward her, but when he put all his weight on his front foot, he sprinted to her. Taking Cianne captive in his arms, he spoke into her ear. "Come back to me, Ci." He felt her tense briefly before her body went limp in his arms. Tristan cradled his wife in his arms, kissing her head as he carried her back to their house.

"It's alright Ci," Tristan said as he got up from the reclining chair he slept in. He walked over to their bed and sat down next to her.

"Caleb?" she asked. Her face was wet with perspiration.

"We searched but weren't able to find him." Tristan pulled a strand of her wet hair away from her eyes. Her gaze fell on his bandaged hand. "It's fine, only two fingers were broken. They're healed, I just forgot to remove the bandage."

Her eyes took on a haunted look. "You have to stay away from him," she said frantically. "Promise me you'll never go after him again, Tristan." She gripped his arm when he didn't respond right away. "Promise me."

Tristan kissed her on the head. Pulling away, he looked at her lovingly. "Relax," he told her. "Look, Cassius and the Guard are downstairs. Everyone has been waiting for you to wake up."

"How long have I been out?"

He grimaced. "A little less than a day," Tristan told her as he kissed her chin. The panic in her eyes flared. He knew exactly what was wrong. "The children are fine." Relief washed over her as she fell back onto her pillows. Tristan crawled up on the bed and lay beside her. He looked up at the ceiling.

"Ci," he said quietly, "I think you should maybe work with someone to learn how to control your powers. You…scared the hell out of me."

"I won't hurt you." She turned to him and sat up on one arm.

Tristan absently rubbed his fingers up her arm. "That's not what scares me. It was like you weren't even you anymore."

She pushed his hand away then pushed off the bed. "What are you talking about?"

Tristan got up too. Cianne didn't seem to remember what happened. If she didn't know then that meant she wasn't conscious when it was happening. "It's happened twice already. I was told that the day you thought I died that your eyes turned red. You destroyed an operating room without lifting a finger."

Cianne backed away from the bed. She pushed away Tristan's hand when he reached for her. "That was different."

He rubbed the back of his neck, avoiding her eyes. "I'm afraid that there's a chance that you won't return from where ever it is you go when that side of you appears. When it takes over you're not…with us."

"I can control it." Determination webbed through each word. "It has only happened twice, right? Both times I was upset." She looked at him pleadingly. "Maybe anger is the trigger. I can handle it."

"I looked into your eyes Ci." He laid his hand on the side of her face. Cianne closed her eyes briefly, seemingly relishing the warmth of his touch. "And I saw nothing of you in there."

"I just need a little more time, Tristan. I promise if I can't get a handle on it, I'll get help. I've come back every time, didn't I?"

Tristan looked into her eyes. Fear, love, and acceptance were all present and it ate at his resolve. He leaned in and kissed her full lips. "My kids need their mother and I need my wife. I want you safe, so consider what I've asked," he said. Then he grimaced. "The kids are asleep. I'll make you something to eat. Join us downstairs when you're ready."

Thirty minutes later Cianne stepped into the kitchen. She shyly rubbed her arm then said, "Hi."

Tristan wondered how someone so beautiful, so amazing as his wife, could still be self-conscious among the people who would lay down their lives for her.

He pulled out a chair for her to sit in. After she was seated he placed a plate in front of her. "Tranae called," he said as he sat next to her. He pushed the plate closer to her when she didn't pick up the fork next to it. "I told her you would call her early tomorrow morning."

Cianne gave him a slight smile that told him she heard him, but still she didn't touch her food. Tristan then turned his attention to Cassius. "So, the tip that Caleb was seen in Texas was a ploy."

"To get us away from the house," Cassius agreed.

Tristan lifted the fork and impaled a piece of cubed chicken and a piece of broccoli. Cianne took the fork from his hand as he waved it in front of her mouth. He waited until she put the food in her mouth before he turned away. "But why go through the trouble?" Tristan said his thought out loud but it was meant only for him.

"He didn't want to be apprehended," Jacobi said. He leaned against the wall behind Cassius, slowly peeling an orange.

Cianne lifted her head. Tristan watched as she peered at Jacobi for a moment. When he saw a hint of recognition smooth over her face, she relaxed, then fear quickly replaced her calm expression. Her gaze whipped to Tristan. He didn't speak but hoped that she read the warning in his eyes.

Tristan also had concerns about his young friend's first rotation into their security team but he had no say, unless Cianne accepted the *crown*. With Caleb on the loose, Eldra and Brenna decided that he, Cianne, and the children needed a full security detail.

He had no doubt that Oloyede and Shane, the men with whom he and Jacobi went through the Maatii challenge, would have volunteered as well, but they were already assigned. Jacobi, a fearless kid who thought he was invincible, was now in harm's way, just like they were. It bothered Tristan just as much as it bothered Cianne.

Perkins looked at the rookie Guard. A smirk twisted one corner of his mouth. Tristan had a feeling Perkins was remembering a time when he had Jacobi's gung-ho attitude.

"He doesn't fear being caught," Cianne interjected. She looked around the table at the men one by one until her eyes met Tristan's. "Caleb is stronger and more powerful than all of us. If he wants us dead," she said, "he'll come for us and none of us will be able to stop him."

"You stopped him," he said to her. "You even hurt him."

Cianne pushed the plate away. "You don't understand. He didn't come here to kill us. If he had, we wouldn't be sitting here." She looked down and moved her fingers slowly over the napkin in front of her. "I don't know why, but I think he came for his ring."

The ring, Tristan thought. *But why?*

"So, what do we do, wait until he feels the urge to kill again? If he can't be tracked or defeated then what are we supposed to do?" Jacobi calmly asked. He popped a slice of orange in his mouth.

"We prepare. So that we are ready for his next appearance," Cassius said confidently. "I'll have more Guards here by Thursday morning."

"No," Tristan said, his eyes meeting Cianne's. They were in agreement. "No more Guards."

"There's no need to risk anyone else. That goes for all of you too." Cianne looked at Jacobi, then Cassius, and Perkins.

Jacobi pushed off the wall and walked over to Cianne. He got down on one knee. "I'm here to protect you and your family of my own free will. It is an honor and I understand fully what that means."

Cianne grimaced. She looked at Tristan, pleading with those sultry eyes of hers. He would give her anything but not this. He couldn't emasculate a warrior, even one so young. "Jacobi will be fine," Tristan promised.

That seemed to appease her.

"Felix and Kim will want to stay as well," Cassius added. The two veteran Guards were outside making rounds, unseen of course.

"Alright," Cianne said, hesitantly.

"Jacobi, Felix, and Kim will stay here on the property if it's alright with you. I will remain at Langley's place," Cassius said.

Cianne waved away the comment. "We have more than enough room."

"I have to be going." Cassius stood. He lowered his head to Cianne then to Tristan. "I'll inform Kim and Felix of the arrangements. I'll be back tomorrow morning."

Jacobi stood, bowed his head, then followed Cassius out of the kitchen before the others stood.

"Sir, if you have a moment?"

Tristan planned to chastise Cianne. Her food sat basically untouched, but he looked at Perkins. "Sure Perkins," Tristan said, then pushed out of his seat. "But only if you stop calling me sir." Tristan kissed Cianne on the forehead before leaving the kitchen with Perkins. They walked toward the front door slowly.

"I want to follow a hunch. Doing so would mean that I won't be here if you need me."

"You don't need my permission, Perkins. Cianne hasn't taken the oath. Any assistance from you guys is strictly appreciated but purely voluntary. If you need to go…then by all means be safe." Tristan extended his hand to Perkins.

Perkins gripped his elbow firmly. "I'll keep in touch."

Tristan watched as Perkins stepped down the porch stairs. Perkins was one of the true good guys in the world. He was a Coesen who Vivian placed in the local police department during the kidnapping investigation. Tristan never even knew the guy was a Coesen then. Even though Tristan still didn't know Perkins all that well and he didn't know his story, he trusted the guy.

Bertram End of the Month Dinner

"If you want I can call Dr. Lawrence. I'm sure he can do home visits, if she's not up to leaving the house yet." Mrs. Bertram said as she watched Aidan put the spoon full of peas to his mouth. Aidan managed to get every pea in.

Tristan saw the amazement in his mother's eyes as she watched Aidan eat. His potatoes and bits of meat were still neatly separated, but almost gone as he dipped his spoon for another bite.

"Oh Nadia," his mother said, amusement on her face. Nadia was putting her hands in her bowl, clutching some peas then smashing them in her mouth. The other food from her bowl was smashed in Nadia's lap or in her hair. Mrs. Bertram took a napkin and wiped Nadia's face and hands. "Good girl," she said, kissing Nadia's fingers.

Tristan looked down at his half-eaten plate of food then shook his head. "No. I'd rather she make the decision for herself." He wasn't going to suggest another therapist. Especially since he went along with her father in encouraging her to see Dr. Garrison, a child molesting murderer who apparently rubbed Caleb the wrong way, which led to his disappearance.

"How is she doing, really?" Mr. Bertram looked at his son.

"Honestly," Tristan said, "she's doing fine. She didn't want to miss this Sunday's dinner but she's been tired lately."

Tristan pushed away from the table then stood. He pulled Nadia out of the highchair.

"*I'll* change her," his father said. He stood up and took the baby from Tristan's arms. Mr. Bertram held her up in the air and looked at her. "Hey baby girl," he said as he smiled at her. Nadia laughed, showing two little teeth that were poking through a thin white layer of her pink gums. Mr. Bertram kissed her dirty face then carried her out of the dining room.

Mrs. Bertram wiped Aidan's mouth with a napkin then picked at his glossy black curly hair with her fingers. She looked over at Tristan. "You look tired. Are you guys getting enough sleep?" she inquired.

Tristan knew it wasn't sleep he lacked or missed. He could go two weeks with only a couple hours of sleep, without feeling the effects of sleep deprivation, thanks to the upgrade from Cianne when Caleb unbound her abilities she inherited from him.

"As much as any couple with twins," he answered, then frowned. *Now, finding time for intimacy…*

"We'd be happy to take them off your hands for a few days," his mother said. She wiggled her brows suggestively.

Tristan frowned again. "That's my cue," he said then stood. He collected some of the used dishes that sat on the table.

"Put those dishes down," his mother told him, "and if you can't trust your parents then who can you trust?"

The agitation in her tone was unmistakable. Tristan put the pile of dishes back on the table. "Mom, the twins are a hand full. They're unique," he told her, "and there's a lot going on right now."

"More reason to let us keep them for a few days. You and Cianne could use a break." She stood up and took Aidan from the highchair.

Tristan reached for his son. Aidan leaned away, as if he didn't want to go either. His son never refused him. Tristan shook off his son's odd behavior and took Aidan from his mother. "Maybe we can set something up in the future."

Tristan walked to the hearth room where his father was just finishing changing Nadia's clothing. His mother followed close behind. While Tristan strapped Aidan in the car seat/carrier she gathered the children's things.

"Looks like your daddy is ready to go, sweetie," Mr. Bertram said to Nadia. He kissed her before strapping her in her car seat/carrier.

Tristan walked over and checked Nadia's restraints then looked at his mother. He could see she wanted them to stay longer. He felt bad for not allowing them more time together but he worried.

"Excuse me for a moment," he said leaving the room. He walked into the hallway and into the first-floor powder room. Taking his phone from his pocket, he called Cianne. "Mrs. Bertram," he said with a smile.

"Yes, dear husband?" she answered.

He could almost see her smile in his head. "Did I wake you?"

"Not really," Cianne told him.

Tristan didn't contest her claim even though he heard her yawn. For several seconds, he just listened to her breathe. It was so long since he listened to her steady breaths. He remembered when he first discovered that her breathing soothed him. It was a month after their first date when she fell asleep watching television on his sofa. That day he knew he would love her forever.

"How's your parents?" Cianne asked, breaking the silence.

"Good, no… Yeah, good," he said, stumbling over his words. She took his mind away from the reason he was calling. "They really miss the twins, Ci."

"Then why don't you leave them there for a few hours. Isn't there a new possible site Kevin wanted you to see?"

Kevin was his project manager, and the brother-in-law of a man Cianne named Cook. Cook saved her life and that bonded Tristan to his family forever.

"You can check out the site then pick the babies up when you're done."

A drive *would* relax his mind, some. It wasn't as effective as Cianne's presence or her breathing but driving calmed him.

"I love you," he said softly.

"Then let me go back to sleep." She laughed.

"Sweet dreams." Tristan ended the call.

When Tristan entered the room where his family waited, he walked over to Aidan. "Alright big guy, you two are staying with grams and gramps for a few hours," he explained. "You are in charge, be good." Tristan raised his brows high. He looked at Nadia. "You too, little miss."

Mrs. Bertram frowned at his instructions, but Tristan knew the twins understood him. He kissed them both, kissed his parents, then left.

As Tristan drove down his parent's driveway he called Jacobi. He explained that he was leaving the children with his parents for a few hours while he took care of some business elsewhere. Jacobi and Kim were to stay with the children but remain out of sight unless they were needed.

The drive to the site would take a little over an hour according to Tristan's GPS. Avoiding the highway would allow him to enjoy the drive much more but he wanted to quickly get to the site and back. He didn't like leaving the children, especially with his Middling parents.

After driving fifteen miles or so, Tristan began to feel unusually tired. He turned up the radio and rolled his window down. An exit he wasn't too familiar with was coming up but Tristan decided he needed a cup of coffee. He shifted his body a little to the left so the wind coming through the window could hit his face as he took the off ramp that led to a three-way traffic light. He bore off to the right, which was Canyon road.

It appeared to be a long scenic road. There were no gas stations or even another car in sight.

Tristan raised his hand to his forehead. His hand came away wet with perspiration. He was sweating. It was something he didn't do anymore. Confused, he wiped his forehead again and looked at his hand. It *was* sweat.

He leaned forward, keeping the car driving straight as he touched his stomach with his free hand. The onset of pain was tolerable but the sudden itch he felt in the back of his throat and his frantic cough seemed more immediate. Blood sprayed from his mouth, over his dashboard and passenger seat.

Because he never got sick, Tristan knew this was beyond a simple stomach virus. He glanced at his reflection in his rearview mirror. His face was pale and the skin under his eyes looked bruised. On his mouth, he saw specks of blood.

It was then, as Tristan stole glimpses of himself in the rearview mirror, that he noticed the car behind him. Suspicious, he surveyed the red convertible that was close. He couldn't help thinking that his sudden illness and the car's occupants were connected. Ignoring the pain in his stomach and the burning of his eyes, Tristan increased his speed.

The convertible matched his speed.

The two vehicles reached speeds up to a hundred and ten miles per hour as they drove on the empty road. Tristan tried to keep ahead of the convertible but he was finding it increasingly hard to keep focused. His eyes grew heavy and his senses dulled with each passing moment. His speed and control of the car was failing too.

His vehicle toggled from one side of the road, clipping the pursuing convertible, but the driver maintained control. Tristan slowly turned his head and looked out of his side window as the convertible pulled up alongside of him.

Who he saw alarmed him but he had no energy to strike out. Feeling drained, something he was unfamiliar with, Tristan fought hard to stay alert. He called out to Cianne in his mind before his head wobbled and darkness enveloped him.

Caleb cursed. When Tristan began to drive erratically, he decided that keeping a safe distance was no longer an option. He pushed down the gas pedal and sped up alongside Tristan's vehicle. Driving on the oncoming traffic side of the road, he peered into the car. Tristan peered back at him before his head rolled back and his eyes closed.

Caleb veered to the left to avoid being sideswiped again.

He knew that this stretch of road would soon be turning into a curve that overlooked a canyon. So he sped up, passing Tristan's car. Once he was out in front he took his foot from the gas so that his convertible could be rear-ended by Tristan's car. Both vehicles were still traveling at a high rate of speed. Even so, when the car collided with his convertible, Caleb climbed into the back seat of the convertible and jumped onto the hood of Tristan's car.

Caleb used his closed fist to bust through Tristan's windshield. The tempered glass fell in little chunks all over Tristan and the inside of his car. Caleb quickly ripped the seatbelt off and attempted to pull Tristan free of his seat but the car jolted to one side, causing him to lose his grip. Caleb grabbed the steering wheel to straighten the car then looked over his shoulder to gauge the distance of straight road that was left. Road was running out fast but the grill of Tristan's vehicle clung to the convertible's bumper, and the road friction slowed their progression some. He could smell burning rubber.

The convertible was such a nice car. He shrugged.

Caleb turned back to Tristan, who was unconscious. With a good grip this time, he began to lift Tristan out of the driver's seat. The dead weight was not a problem for him and being cautious wasn't his usual thing but he couldn't risk injuring the boy more than what he already was.

As he managed to get Tristan partially free he noticed another car speeding toward them. His inner warnings flared. Caleb narrowed his gaze at the gray car as it slammed into the rear bumper of Tristan's vehicle. He once again lost his grip on Tristan but easily managed to remain steady.

Caleb gathered Tristan's shirt in his fist and raised him again, this time pulling the boy free from the car. Holding Tristan down firmly on the hood, Caleb looked into the gray car, which pulled up beside Tristan's vehicle. The man in the passenger seat sneered at him but the driver kept his eyes forward. Caleb sighed. He had no time for them, yet here he was with his patience wearing thin.

How thin? They would soon find out.

The brooding passenger pointed a gun and began firing at them. Caleb shielded Tristan with his body, not caring what bullets hit him. When the shooting stopped, he raised his hand at their vehicle, lifting the front tires from the road. The car flipped backward in the air a few times before landing hard on its roof.

Perfectly balanced on the hood of Tristan's car, Caleb climbed onto the trunk of his convertible, and tossed Tristan's limp body into the back seat. He jumped into the driver's seat, hit the gas pedal, and twisted the wheel sharply just in time to separate from the bumper of Tristan's car before it went off the cliff. The convertible skidded over dirt and into what was left of the road barrier. He whipped the wheel to the side, causing the convertible to skid again, but Caleb quickly regained control and guided the car back the way they came.

He glanced in his rearview mirror when he heard an explosion, and saw a puff of heavy black smoke and reddish yellow flames that rose into the blue sky behind them. Caleb moved the rearview mirror so he could look in the back seat at Tristan.

"Well, shit," he said, in a matter of fact manner. Beneath the pocket of the khaki pants Tristan wore, a red stain of blood was soaking through the fibers.

Caleb peered at the overturned gray vehicle as he cruised by. One of the men lay still and bloody in the wreckage while the other lay a few feet away on the side of the road. They both looked dead, but…for good measure, Caleb reached his hand out to each unmoving body. He squeezed his hand in a fist then released his fingers into a dramatic flair. He heard every bone in each man's body shatter.

If they weren't dead, they are now.

Bannerman absently rubbed his aching neck. "You know you could have just asked me to come along," he winced. He would have gotten in the vehicle with Caleb with no fuss. He'd been dying to get close enough to the elusive man since hearing that he still lived, because examining Caleb would be like a dream come true for a doctor and scientist.

He relished any opportunity presented to him to catalog what he could about the legend. Even Caleb's aggression and his odd request to bring some of Tristan's stored blood samples didn't get more than a curious look from Bannerman.

He sensed Caleb didn't want to talk during the drive, so against his inquisitive nature he kept his mouth shut. When they pulled in to the parking lot of the less than luxurious motel an hour later, the first thing that caught his eye was the mint green and cream siding. Next, he noted the faded peach doors. The opposing hues and the years of accumulated dirt made him cringe.

Bannerman expected better of the Boogieman. He frowned as he read the sign that towered over the two-story structure. "SHADES MOTEL".

Caleb dressed like a wealthy playboy, so this dirt palace concerned Bannerman. But, who knew what kind of places killers preferred to lay their heads?

Caleb got out of the sedan and walked around the hood to meet him on the other side. "Second floor, third room from the end," Caleb said coldly.

Bannerman's curiosity was peaked. Dirty motel, Caleb the mass murderer, and a couple of bags of blood. *Can you say party?* He should probably be scared but he was too busy taking mental notes every second he spent with Caleb.

When Bannerman reached the room, Caleb reached around him and opened the heavy peach door then stepped aside so he could enter first. Figuring this was unlikely a trap, Bannerman looked into the small dark room before stepping inside.

Someone lay unmoving on the bed. Bannerman hurried inside once realizing who. Never before had he allowed his emotions to override common sense until now. Standing over Tristan, he glanced over his shoulder at Caleb with barely restrained fear for his Soahn.

He lifted each of Tristan's eyelids and noticed his pupils were unresponsive. "You must allow me to take him to the hospital," he said.

"No," Caleb said without hesitation or room to negotiate. "Treat him here."

Bannerman saw that the nightstand was full of medical supplies. He looked to the trash can next to the bed and noted a pile of bloody gauze. *What the hell?* He pulled the floral bedspread down to Tristan's ankles, gasping at the quarter-sized spot of blood that was beginning to soak through the wrapping around his thigh.

◉

Caleb raised his brow at the man's reaction to the bullet wound–he was a doctor, it was a bullet. What's the big deal? "I removed the bullet," Caleb said in a matter of fact way. "He was out before he got shot."

Caleb walked over to the window and peeked out onto the street. He got a room where he could see the entire road clearly. He watched an eighteen-wheeler fly by but movement from Bannerman going into the bathroom pulled his attention back to what was happening in the room.

The sounds of the bathroom faucet turning on and running water reached Caleb but he couldn't see through walls to know exactly what the doctor was doing. Caleb trusted few people, and no, not a single Coesen; but Bannerman had proven to be more scientist than Coesen. Bannerman keeping Tristan's existence secret from his sovereign proved that.

A few seconds later the doctor made his way back to the bed. Caleb watched as Bannerman got to his knees and unwrapped the dressing around Tristan's thigh.

"The wound is nicely stitched."

"I know," Caleb said.

Bannerman smirked at the comment but looked over his shoulder and peered at him with creased brows for several seconds.

Caleb sighed. "Ask your question."

"What was he doing before he was shot?"

"Driving," Caleb said.

Bannerman lifted Tristan's hand and twisted it to look at his fingertips. Caleb noticed they were turning black.

"He's been poisoned," Bannerman gasped as he backed away. He turned to face Caleb, his face drained of color. "He needs to be treated in a hospital."

"Treat him here or he dies. If he dies..." Caleb didn't finish the rest. The ache in his chest returned but he didn't give in to it. Like always, he used the ache to fuel his determination, which reflected on his face.

Bannerman and Caleb stared at each other in silence for a few seconds. Caleb sighed again. "Relax, if I wanted you dead, you'd be the first to know."

The doctor blinked a few times then let out a breath. "Fine then...if you will not let me take him to a sterile equipped facility then I will need some things to treat him here." Bannerman rolled up his sleeves then looked around as if looking for something.

"Just tell me what you need."

The anxious look on Bannerman's face was priceless as he stared at Caleb. Finally, he said, "You're going to want to jot this down."

"Just tell me."

"I have a safe, you need the combination," Bannerman told him.

Caleb tapped his head. The doctor gave him an exhausted look but started to list the combination and the items needed. When Bannerman finished, Caleb walked to the door but looked over his shoulder and said, "Once I'm gone there will be nothing stopping you from leaving this room or calling the Guard. If you care for his safety," Caleb looked at Tristan then back to Bannerman, "then you won't do either. Someone in your organization wants him dead and I need to find out who. Whatever issue you may have with me needs to be set aside for now. Everyone, including my daughter, needs to think Tristan died in that attack today."

Caleb allowed the information he divulged to Bannerman to sink in. The different expressions on the doctor's face told Caleb that he was working through it.

"Tristan's safety has always been my first priority."

Before Caleb opened the door, he said, "It seems we are on the same team."

SHEA SWAIN

Chapter Eight

June

Cianne's dream of happily ever after was fading. She wiped away the irritating tears that rolled over the bridge of her nose and down her cheek to her ear. Forty-eight hours had passed since the Hill Canyon accident and Tristan still hadn't been found.

He'd disappeared. Disappeared…it was such a strange word. To not be found, vanish from sight, or cease to exist.

Over the past couple of days, she'd grown to hate the word. But she hated another word more. A word she heard whispered when they, the Coesens in her home, assumed she wasn't listening. *They*, she thought to herself as she lay on her bed, full of despair.

They, who waited for her to leave the room she hadn't left in the past thirty-six hours. *They*, who waited for her command even though she lacked the desire to give any.

Cianne moved closer to Aidan and Nadia who lay on the bed in between her and Tranae. Her sore eyes focused on her best friend. Tranae opened teary eyes that were staring back. She could see the hurt in Tranae's eyes.

Cianne slowly slid her hand over Aidan and rested it in the empty space between the twins. Tranae reached over Nadia and Cianne soon felt her friend's hand wrapped around hers. Instead of feeling comforted, Cianne's pain of loss pulsed through her stronger than ever. It drove her to bury her head into Tristan's pillow. She silently cried, inhaling what little scent of him that remained on the fabric as her children, Tristan's children, slept.

◉

Louisiana

Perkins drank his beer slowly in the corner of a seedy bar in Louisiana. He chose this place because it wasn't the usual place the Dregan frequented. The Dregan or Dregs, were considered the rogues or the criminal element of the Coesen. Perkins was meeting someone and he needed to do so in a place he knew the person felt safe, or his guest wouldn't come.

His instincts told him that someone else was involved in the killing of Sovereign Harper and he trusted his instincts. Well, he was learning to trust them again.

Now, Tristan was missing, or worse dead, Perkins had to be the man he used to be.

Perkins' gut told him something more was afoot and that Caleb, Cassius' main suspect, was just a patsy. Whoever was behind the murder relied on the Coesen's hate of Caleb to deflect blame, but that was too neatly packaged for Perkins.

Caleb would never be caught on video unless he wanted to be seen. And Perkins was certain that when Caleb killed, no one saw and if they did, they didn't live to tell about it.

Except, one person. Oma.

The identity of the woman who was found dead in the house with Vivian was key. So, in secret, he collected some of her DNA and took her prints. It wasn't easy, but after calling in some favors from an FBI friend of his, Perkins got what he needed.

The dead girl's name was Alicia Reynolds, also known as Lexa. She was a well-trained assassin. Perkins didn't understand why Cassius didn't care about this. Alicia, a Middling by all accounts, was just as lethal as some Protectors.

His FBI friend also told him where to find Alicia's partner in crime, the gentleman who chose what jobs Alicia was offered. With some…coercion, Alicia's boss gave up her address in New York. What puzzled Perkins was that her boss said she hadn't accepted a contract from him in over five months. He'd also stated that Alicia was acting odd; he suspected that she fell for someone on her last job in Louisiana.

A search of Alicia's apartment in New York turned up nothing. It was empty and cleaned out already. But when Perkins left the apartment he noticed a café on the corner. A café Alicia most likely went to regularly.

Being a cop taught Perkins that there are few coincidences, to go where the evidence leads, and to follow your gut. His gut told him to check out the café before leaving New York for Louisiana. It was sunny on that day so he'd opted for an outside table. As soon as he sat down he saw the bright yellow spiraled curls and energetic bounce of a pretty little waitress. And after watching the waitress interacting with a few of the customers, Perkins saw an opportunity.

The waitress was a talker so when she returned with his order he smiled and without much effort, engaged her in conversation. "I'm glad I stopped here. I'm in town for my friend's funeral and was afraid I wouldn't find a nice place to eat. Your shop is right beneath her apartment." Perkins pulled a small photo of Alicia out and presented it to the waitress whose face instantly saddened. "You know my friend?" he asked.

That was all it took. She took the empty seat across from Perkins and told him that Alicia came into the café a lot. The waitress was under the impression that Alicia was an artist who traveled often. After speaking for several minutes, the waitress sprang to her feet, telling him she had something for him. When she returned, she handed him an artist's sketch pad. Alicia left it in the restaurant the last time she was there.

No family had come around and she thought Perkins had a better chance in returning it to them. Flipping through the pad, Perkins discovered that Alicia did indeed have talent.

Almost every page was filled with beautifully detailed sketches.

Now days later, Perkins sat in a bar, hundreds of miles away. He took another slow drink from his glass then placed it softly on the table. He sighed then pulled a twenty from his pocket. His guest wasn't coming. Perkins placed the twenty on the table next to his empty glass. When a woman's hand brushed against his as it reached over and picked up the twenty, Perkins looked up.

At first, he didn't recognize the woman who eased herself into the seat at his table. Her hair was longer, her eyes were dull, and she'd lost a little weight, but she was still breathtakingly beautiful. When she cut her eyes at his ogling her, he swallowed hard then shifted in his seat.

"You have ten minutes of my time, Officer Perkins," she sneered at him.

Perkins relaxed back in the chair. He watched as she raised the twenty-dollar bill in the air. A waitress quickly came over and took her order. "I was hoping you'd come." He knew that just his being in town would catch attention and it would get back to Evelyn Bogdon.

"Well, I suspect you're not here for the crawfish," Evelyn said sarcastically. "I'm here. What do you want?"

Perkins looked at Evie and smiled. Years had passed since they last saw each other. He hoped that some of her anger toward him had ebbed some. The fact that he was still breathing might be an indication that it had. She did tell him that if he ever showed his face in her city again she would kill him.

"I need some information."

"Oh…is that all?" Evelyn asked, continuing her mocking tone.

Perkins leaned forward and placed his forearms on the table. "I wouldn't have come if it wasn't important Evie."

"In that case…" She rolled her eyes, then smiled at the waitress as she approached.

Perkins sat back. Neither of them spoke until the waitress walked away. "Please Evie," he begged.

"Tell me Ryan, you didn't come to Louisiana…risking your life I might add, just so you could ask me to help you for *them*, did you? I'm sorry for your loss but I had no loyalty to your Sovereign when she lived and I definitely have no love for the rest of The Council. You've wasted your time coming here, Ryan," Eve said through tight lips. She lifted her glass and drank.

Perkins eyebrows wrinkled as he watched Evelyn sip her drink. The ankle length black dress she wore had a long split on the side that reached her upper thigh and inched a little further up when she crossed one leg over the other. The dress neckline was high and showed none of her shimmering brown skin other than her shoulder and arms. Evie's hair was long but pulled up, allowing her radiant face to be admired for its devilish beauty. He had never seen her dressed in such a way; he remembered her as a tomboyish type with long cornrowed hair and no makeup under any circumstances.

Their eyes meet briefly before he looked away. She still had an effect on him. "What happened to the Sovereign was tragic Evie, and even if her death wasn't a great loss for you, it was for her family. They deserve answers."

"If you're referring to the three remaining wicked witches who are probably battling over Arkean territory as we sit here, I'm sure their grief will ease once they've agreed on how to split it," Evelyn said then chuckled. She placed her half empty glass on the table.

"No one will be splitting up territories, Evie. And I was speaking of the Sovereign's granddaughter." Perkins looked around before looking back to Evelyn. "She's the true Halo."

She gave him a curious look. "To suggest that some old children's story that has been circulating since forever has finally come to pass is ridiculous," she told him. "I don't believe in fairytales Ryan, and neither should you."

"The Halo is real. Even under your rock, you've must have heard the rumors of a green-eyed beauty. Our news covered the wedding. There are fantastic tales of her Protector and his triumph in the Maatii that are fast becoming legend." Perkins saw a twinkle in Evelyn's eyes but it was quickly replaced by doubt.

She smiled at him as if to say, "You almost had me".

He leaned forward on the table again. "I am telling you the truth, Evie. Her name is Cianne Bertram." He pulled a photo from his jacket and slid it across the table. "She is the daughter of *the* Caleb Scott and Kayla Harper, Vivian Harper's only child. She bares a beautiful full mark encircled by a thin ring."

Evelyn stared at him for a moment, possibly waiting for him to show some sort of sign that he was being deceitful. Then she slowly looked down at the photo and picked it up from the table. After her brief inspection of the photo, Perkins extended his hand. She looked him in the eyes for several seconds before taking his hand.

Ryan Perkins hadn't let Evie read him in over seventeen years. He wasn't particularly fond of her ability to determine if someone was being truthful or not. To him, truth was a biased concept that was based on what someone perceived to be fact. If a person truly believed something was true, then to the reader it was true. Which meant that to really get the truth, the reader would need to ignore the crazies and the psychotic. For her ability to truly work on the person being read the person would have to be reasonably sane and Evie's ability wasn't that strong because it was secondary to her main ability.

Perkins' saw the truth of his words reflected in Evie's eyes. She now knew that he believed what he spoke to be true.

"Kayla died a decade ago. Lilith and I attended her memorial," Evelyn muttered slowly.

Perkins cleared his throat as he felt a stab of pain in his chest. He hadn't heard Lilith's name spoken in years. He fought back the sting and lifted his hand for the waitress. He needed another drink. They were quickly brought refills.

After the waitress left he moved his hand the short distance to Evelyn's, to touch her hand that lay motionless by her glass, but she pulled her hand away before he made contact. "Evie," he said compassionately. He didn't know what he could possibly say to comfort her.

A minute passed in silence between them.

Figuring it was best to avoid the subject of Lilith, Perkins returned to the issue at hand. "Kayla did die then but she had a daughter, Cianne, who was raised as a Middling to keep her safe until she turned eighteen. The Four kept this information from everyone other than the head of the Royal Guard and some high-level Coesen so their male children could be groomed for her Tandot."

"Why would they keep something this important from everyone? So many believe that the Halo is a myth, her being real and alive would have given so many something…someone to believe in again other than those succubae who have been ruining our people throughout the years with their harsh and unreasonable laws." Evelyn shook her head then sucked in a breath. "Wait, the Halo, she's their weapon…a puppet?"

Perkins raised both his brows and let out a low chuckle. "On the contrary, Cianne has refused her throne. She dislikes our laws more than you do. She follows no one and no one controls her." He whispered his next words under his breath, "I doubt anyone could."

Eve smiled at this. "Really?" she said. She looked pensive then said, "What is she like? Is she as powerful as the prophecy foretold?"

"Cianne is gentle and sweet but she is also fair and determined. As for her abilities, from what I've witnessed, she will be very powerful," he said. "But she is grieving, Evie. Cianne has lost her grandmother, her husband is now missing, and she fears for her children's safety. I need your help to find out who is responsible for all her suffering."

Evie reached for her glass and took a drink. She didn't speak even after the glass was empty and she placed it back on the table. Three minutes passed before she said, "Did you say children?"

"Twins, a boy and a girl," he nodded.

Her face beamed with amazement before going expressionless. "Alright. What is Cassius' theory?"

"Cassius' investigation has led him in another direction."

"Still a pompous ass, is he?" Evelyn asked

Evie was never a fan of Cassius, though she was loyal to The Four at one time. That all changed the day Lilith, her younger sister, died. Perkins had never seen a pair closer than Evelyn and Lilith. But Lilith died during a terror attack on the U.S., and Evelyn blamed The Four. She also blamed him.

He was Lilith's Protector. He was supposed to keep her safe above all others, but he was recruited for the Royal Guard and had to do a mandatory Protector Rotation. Often, he told himself that if he hadn't left to serve with the guard, Lilith may not have died such a senseless death. After many years to reflect, Perkins accepted that he may not have been able to save her even if he was there.

Still, Perkins would never forgive himself for not being there for Lilith. He also knew that he could never make Evelyn believe that. Evelyn lost someone dear to her and she needed someone to blame.

Why not him? He already blamed himself.

Despite her wavering devotion to The Four prior to Lilith's death, Evelyn was now convinced that The Four were cruel dictators who put themselves above the people. Evelyn became anti-Four and was very vocal about her views. She was so vocal she was stripped of her title and labeled a Dregan. Evelyn's name resides on The Royal Guard's wanted list.

Perkins grimaced. "Yeah, he is. Even with his abilities fading he still goes out of his way to make everyone around him feel inferior."

Evelyn nodded, as if she understood.

Perkins sighed. "Evie, I just need you to point me in the right direction. That's all."

"So being an ex-Royal Guardsmen hasn't won you any fans, and now that you don't carry the Brand of The Four Tribes anymore you need the assistance of a Dregan."

"That about sums it up," Perkins admitted.

Evelyn stopped a waitress who was walking by their table. She asked for two more drinks. They remained quiet until the waitress returned, sat the drinks in front of them, then left. Evelyn lifted her drink and motioned for Perkins to do the same. He did.

"To the new Sovereign and Halo. If she takes the crown, may she rule with the fairness and compassion her forbearers wouldn't."

Missing four weeks

Cianne heard voices coming from the library as she descended the stairs. It was Father's Day and she decided earlier that morning to avoid everyone today if possible. That was until she heard Dr. Bannerman's voice and curiosity got the better of her. Soon, she stood off to the side of her library's entryway, unnoticed but with full view of everyone in the room.

Whodai sighed, "She hasn't actually come forward to take responsibility but…"

Cianne felt a chill run up her spine.

"It's a direct challenge," Langley chimed in, "She's recruiting loyalists and Dregan alike. Anyone who believes in her cause is rebranding themselves with the image of a flame on their wrist. She threatened Tristan in front of all of us and she could have easily acquired Death's Door. What little evidence we have points to Chandra, there's no denying it."

Cassius rubbed his brow.

"No one will judge you Cassius, if you decide to sit this one out." Whodai laid his hand on Cassius' shoulder.

Cianne winced. Cassius was a Quende. Would he choose to support Chandra, leader of the Quende? His tribe? She saw the how conflicted he was. His eyes reflected his turmoil ever since Whodai came to them a week after Tristan's disappearance with information that Chandra may have been involved.

"I'm fine," Cassius jaw tightened. "We will handle it like any other threat. Whodai, you will take the lead in the investigation."

"And the search for Tristan?" Zeta's eyes moved from Cassius to Whodai.

"It's been over three weeks and nothing," Cassius said. "Just a burned-out wreck and skid marks from a possible second vehicle is all we've got."

"We should continue," Whodai said.

Cianne sighed. Whodai wanted to find Tristan. She knew he was the best choice when Cassius told her that he was appointing Whodai to help with the investigation of Tristan's disappearance and to aid in protecting her and the twins.

"Continue with what?" Cianne stood in the entryway, visible to all.

Everyone turned their heads to see her. Each of them stood immediately but Cianne waved her hand, dismissing the formalities as she walked into the room.

"Continue what?" she asked again.

"We were discussing if continuing the search for Tristan is logical. I feel we need to focus on who's responsible," Cassius said.

Cianne shook her head furiously. *What are they saying? No!* "I don't care who's responsible. I just want Tristan found." Cianne looked to Zeta who sat down first. Zeta put her finger in her mouth and began nibbling on her nail.

Everyone else slowly sat after Cianne took a seat.

"Nothing has been decided," Langley said quickly. He sat next to Cianne and took her hands in his.

"Tell her," Cassius demanded as he looked to Bannerman.

Cianne hadn't heard from him since he arrived at the mansion a few days ago. Her eyes fell on Dr. Bannerman.

The doctor looked at her for several heart beats, then he sighed, "The substance that was found on the steering wheel of Tristan's vehicle that day is called Death's Door. It is absorbed through the pores. The tips of one's extremities turn black after exposure. It kind of resembles frost bite. Death's Door is usually fatal. People who've been exposed will normally die within a few hours."

"Damn it Bannerman! Don't give her false hope!" Cassius yelled out. He looked at Cianne, "Death's Door has a 100% fatality rate, Soahn. It is extremely rare and very precise."

Cianne felt all eyes on her. But all she could do was stare at Dr. Bannerman, who lowered his head. When she realized Bannerman wasn't going to confirm or deny Cassius' claims, she looked around the room, briefly meeting everyone's eyes.

Well, everyone except Langley, who was looking intensely at Dr. Bannerman. When Bannerman looked up and saw Langley watching him, Cianne saw his eyes widen for only a split second.

What was that? she asked herself. Then she realized she had to address the room.

"You all want to give up looking for him?" Cianne asked in disbelief. She looked around the room to faltering gazes. Everyone other than Cassius and Whodai lowered their eyes. Those two were warriors; they stood firm in whatever they believed should be done. From the conversation, they were having before she entered the room, Cianne knew they weren't in agreement. But Cassius was responsible for making the decisions.

Why is Cassius doing this? Why doesn't he believe?

Her body stiffened. "Tristan is alive!" she screamed.

"He was poisoned, and a large amount of his blood was found, Soahn. I know it's hard but you have to accept the facts," Cassius said, with disturbing reason.

"I know he's alive," Cianne said as she jumped to her feet. "When a person I love dies," her eyes burned with tears, "…I feel him. I love Tristan with all my heart and I don't feel that he is gone. I know he is still alive." Cianne couldn't hold in her emotions. Tears streamed down her face.

"We don't mean to upset you," Langley said as he stood.

"You can't know what I mean because you don't love him like I do," she said helplessly. She backed away from Langley, suddenly feeling claustrophobic. Breathless, out of the corner of her eyes she saw Cassius look at Bannerman. Dr. Bannerman held his hands out toward her but she shook her head. "Listen!" she cried, backing away. "You don't understand."

"Let's just try to relax," Dr. Bannerman said to her.

"Don't tell me to relax!" she shouted. The tears were running down her face now.

As Bannerman and Cassius stalked toward her, a ripple of hot air left her body. The heat came out as an invisible wave, passing through them. Surprise and pain appeared on their faces as they slid back several feet from her. Langley, unaffected because he stood behind Cianne, watched in horror as the men hit the far wall hard.

Whodai stood up but didn't move. He just watched her with hooded eyes. Zeta muffled a shriek but stayed seated.

Cianne's chest moved up and down as if she'd just run a mile. Her eyes were puffy, red, and flowing with tears, but she still focused on Zeta. "Tell them Zeta," Cianne demanded. "Listen to your heart. They don't understand." She motioned to the men in the room. "They don't know what loving him is like…but you do." Cianne looked into Zeta's eyes and begged, "Tell them you feel him. Tell them he's alive."

◉

Zeta looked at Cianne as if she had been slapped across the face. Sadness, fear, and guilt swelled inside her but she didn't have the strength to deny Cianne's claim. It was true, she was in love with Tristan, but she had no idea that Cianne knew.

She thought she was careful not to show her true feelings. Still, Cianne, the woman she loved as a sister and respected as her queen, knew.

Zeta's face reddened as she looked around the room. Whodai watched her with apathy mixed with something she didn't recognize. *Oh,* she thought, *maybe it's sadness.* More than anyone, he must know how it felt.

Cassius, who had recovered from slamming into the wall, watched her with anger and disappointment. Bannerman, still righting himself, just blushed as if the news was too personal for him to know. And Langley…he just looked at her with a sorrowful expression, as if he knew all along but respectfully kept the information to himself.

Zeta felt as if her skin was tightening around her bones. She wanted to escape. To run from this place until her legs gave out. She looked to the entryway as her inner voice cried for shelter. But instead of running, instead of hiding, she walked over to Cianne, who was a distraught mess at this point.

She wrapped her arms around Cianne and held her tight. "I never meant to love him, but I know that nothing but death would keep him from you," Zeta said softly into Cianne's ear.

Cianne, overwhelmed with grief, pulled away from Zeta. *How can they doubt me, especially Zeta?* She moved her gaze over each of them. She felt Langley move behind her. *No…*she didn't want to be touched.

Langley was pushed back down into the seat he occupied before he stood.

Cianne heard his breath leave him but he didn't move to stand again. Frustrated with them, Cianne covered her mouth and ran from the library and straight to her bedroom. The bedroom door slammed shut with only a thought from her. She threw herself onto her bed and screamed Tristan's name.

Chapter Nine

Tristan popped his eyes open and clutched his temples. It only lasted a second, but the sound of Cianne's voice exploded in his head, ricocheting through it like a weapon instead of a gentle caress. When the pounding subsided, he let his hands slide down over his eyes.

Aware, but a bit cloudy, he felt his face under his fingertips. It was as if he hadn't felt his fingers moving or his face in years. Tristan pulled his hands from his face and looked at them. He wiggled his fingers in front of his eyes. Confused, he moved both his legs but soon realized they were covered with a sheet.

He was in bed but it felt…odd. The scent of it, the room, wasn't familiar.

Grimacing, Tristan eased himself up in the bed then pulled the sheet back. He touched the sensitive area of his thigh that was wrapped with a bandage. More confused than ever, he got out the bed and stood. It took time for him to find his balance; he dismissed it but moved slowly.

This wasn't his bed. Not his bedroom.

Get home. Cianne and the kids are waiting for me.

Tristan looked around the room for an exit but noted his surroundings. The room contained a bed, a dresser, and a chair. All the furniture was mahogany and looked well-made and heavy. There were no decorations in the room at all, other than a pair of long black curtains that covered a large window.

Aware that he only wore a pair of long basketball shorts, Tristan walked over to the drawer for a shirt but all the drawers were empty. He looked to the closet.

When Tristan moved his right foot toward the closet, he stopped. Feeling lightheaded he braced himself on the dresser for a moment before pushing off and making his way to the closet. Inside he found some sweat pants and a sweat jacket hanging up.

Running shoes were on the floor under a number of empty hangers. Tristan quickly pulled the sweat pants up his legs, using the wall to brace himself. He moved his arms into the sweat jacket sleeves and zippered it up. Dressed, he put on the sneakers, shrugging at the realization that they fit. Actually, all the clothing fit even though he didn't recognize any of it.

Pushing that disturbing revelation out of his head, he went to the one door that was shut. The other door was open and it led to a bathroom.

Tristan placed his ear to the door and listened. When he was sure no one was on the other side of the door he opened it. "A cabin," he said aloud. He couldn't tell from the bedroom but now, looking around the open space, he could tell it was a mid-sized moderately furnished cabin. Only everything looked as if it had never been used.

Tristan wobbled out of the doorway and into the open space of the cabin. He stabilized himself by leaning on the wall then made his way across the living area to the front door. Slowly he turned the knob and was surprised to find that the door wasn't locked. Opening the door with his left hand and bracing the frame and the door with his free hand; he quietly eased the door open.

Tristan peeked out of the door. As far as he could tell the coast was clear. He stepped outside and looked around.

Nothing but trees.

He walked down a few steps and looked down at the ground in front of him. *No car tracks*, he thought. *How did I get here?*

It didn't matter. All that mattered was getting home.

Tristan took a step, but before his foot fully touched the ground he angled forward, dug his back foot into the ground, then took off in a sprint into the forest. He couldn't manage his full speed because his body ached and he felt weak. He didn't know how long he was out of it or how long he'd been in the cabin. But, his body wasn't thinner and he didn't feel dehydrated so he figured that he couldn't have been out for long.

He *was* starving, though.

He wasn't certain why his leg was bandaged but he was still mobile and able to cover about five miles in less than ten minutes. His only thought was to make it home to his family. But soon he realized he had no idea the direction he was headed or how long it would take for him to get out of the woods.

Tristan stopped in a clearing to check his aching leg and to maybe climb a tree to see if a road was nearby. Not to mention he needed to catch his breath, surprisingly.

Why am I winded?

He could normally run for thirty miles without getting winded. Yet, here he was, leaning on a tree, trying to catch his breath. As he breathed, he pulled the waist of the sweatpants down below the bandage. He was bleeding. He shook his head but it was something he couldn't avoid right now.

Just as he was pulling the sweat pants up he felt something hit his upper right arm and shoulder. Tristan hit the ground hard. He rolled a few times over some crunchy leaves, hard rocks, and branches beneath him. He grabbed at his arm and shoulder with his left hand as he looked up and saw the bear that was already bearing down on him.

Shit!

Tristan tried scrambling to his feet but the bear swung at him again and he fell to his butt. He grunted. Feeling tired for the first time since he became a Protector, Tristan pushed with his feet, sliding away from the bear on his butt. His energy was spent. He drained himself running and had no energy left to fight with.

The enormous black bear stood over him, growling. Tristan had no other choice but to cover his head, ball up in the fetal position, and hope that the bear would think he was dead. Bracing himself for the bear's anger, Tristan thought of Cianne and his children.

When Tristan didn't feel sharp claws slicing through his flesh, he slowly lifted his head from under his arms. Lying a few inches from him on the ground was the massive bear, and standing directly over it was Caleb.

Tristan sat up slowly. He placed his elbows on his knees and let his hands dangle between his legs. He looked to the bear that lay lifeless next to him then to Caleb who was watching him impassively.

With his head held high, Tristan said, "I'm not the begging for my life type."

"Good, because begging doesn't work with me."

Tristan blinked his eyes as Caleb raised his hand. His head suddenly became foggy. He knew what this was and was only able to say one word before passing out. "Don't…"

When Tristan woke, he found himself back inside the cabin and in the same room. Again, he lay in the bed, only this time he wasn't able to move freely. With great effort, he raised his heavy arm and touched his bandaged shoulder.

He chuckled. That damn bear had sliced through his flesh as if he was made of margarine. He pushed the pain out of his mind and tried to sit himself up but all he could do was move his legs a little. Angry, he was about to call out but the bedroom door opened and Caleb strode casually to his side.

Unable to fight, Tristan watched as Caleb tapped his arm then stuck a syringe in his vein and injected a dark fluid into him. Caleb then pulled down the sheet covering Tristan, exposing the shorts and his bare legs. Tristan immediately noticed there was some type of device attached to his leg.

"It's similar to the monitoring devices that criminals on house arrest wear but you shouldn't confuse the two. Your device will not alert me if you go outside your designated area. What it will do is send a charge through your body that will cause you immense pain until you return to your designated area…or you'll eventually drop where you stand."

Caleb left the room but immediately returned. He placed a plate that contained a sandwich and fresh fruit on the dresser. *"You have the run of this room and the bathroom."* Caleb pointed to the door in the back of the room then turned to leave but stopped. He didn't turn around but continued to speak telepathically. *"You're experiencing hearing loss. It's temporary."*

My hearing is gone?

Earlier, his need to get away was so vital he didn't realize he couldn't hear a thing.

"Why haven't you killed me yet?"

"I considered letting the bear have you but, I need you alive," Caleb transferred. *"Eat…you've been unconscious for almost a month. Any longer and I may have had to insert a feeding tube. Oh, and Happy Father's Day."*

A week later, Tristan still was still looking for a means to escape. His gracious host left him alone for hours on end, and sometimes for days. With no television or books, he felt as if he was going crazy but he didn't want to give Caleb the satisfaction.

Most days he just slept. It was the only way he could get a clear image of Cianne and the twins. The rest of the time he spent working out in his room. It was his attempt to remedy the weakness he was experiencing in his limbs.

During the long week, Tristan also tested the ankle monitor. It did exactly what Caleb said it did. Each time he ventured beyond the invisible barrier a few feet past the kitchen, he ended up screaming on the floor in unimaginable pain so terrible that he did indeed pass out after pissing himself.

He always woke sometime later, wiped clean and in the bed. Just thinking about it made him seethe with anger.

When he heard the front door open, Tristan sat up on his elbows and looked through the crack in his bedroom door. Caleb was gone for two days and though Tristan wouldn't admit it, he was lonely. Plus, he was tired of eating cereal.

Tristan's hearing was almost normal, at Middling range, but not where it was before. So, he didn't hear the light footsteps Caleb made as he walked through the cabin and up to the bedroom door. But the smell of the hot food Caleb carried filled the air; it was pulling at him through the door, but he didn't move.

He defiantly placed his hand behind his head and looked up at the ceiling. Tristan didn't acknowledge Caleb when he tapped on the bedroom door but Caleb entered anyway.

Caleb walked over to the bed and placed one of the bags he carried, beside him.

Tristan glanced at the bag then watched as Caleb sat on the floor against the far wall a few feet away. He barely had time to catch the canned soda that was flying at him. If he hadn't caught the can, it would have hit him in the face.

Still shocked, he stared at a silent Caleb who was pulling food from the other brown bag and started to eat. When Caleb didn't acknowledge him, Tristan said, "So…we're supposed to fucking sit here and eat like friends?"

"No, we don't have to." Caleb started packing up his food. "But I expect you to be civil."

"Did you see them?"

Caleb looked at Tristan blankly before he relaxed back on the floor. "No, but I have someone watching them for me. She misses you."

Tristan felt the familiar pain that always surged through him whenever he saw Cianne's tears. He looked up at the ceiling to compose himself then back to Caleb who was eating as if he had not a care in the world. Anger raged in Tristan in that moment. He hurled the soda can at Caleb's face as hard as he could.

Caleb caught the can without looking then sat it down next to his leg on the floor. "That wasn't exactly civil."

"Why am I here?" Tristan hissed.

"Keep you alive; keep Cianne sane. Keep Cianne sane; save the world."

Tristan frowned, "What?"

"I've been given the task of keeping you alive. Doing so is difficult when you surround yourself with people who want my head on a platter." Caleb looked up at him. "The recent attempt on your life has given me the opportunity to keep you alive *and* allow me to find out who's behind Vivian's murder *and* your attempted murder. Until then, you stay here, you stay safe."

"Because you're not behind all of this," Tristan said with irritation.

"No, I'm not," Caleb said plainly.

Tristan's face paled. "If that were true then shouldn't you be keeping Cianne and the children safe and not just me?"

Caleb raised a brow. "My daughter will be fine. I also pity the person who is ignorant enough to mess with the twins. You, on the other hand...." Caleb shrugged.

This is madness. Think Tristan...think...think.

"Cianne will think I'm dead. Your plan is fucked."

"She knows in her heart you live," he said in a low tone. "As long as she has hope she won't slip into the darkness." Caleb looked down at his food then began to eat.

The smug bastard is actually eating.

Tristan watched with hooded eyes as Caleb ate. It didn't take long for his hunger to grow unbearable so he opened the bag, took out the sandwich, and ate in silence. As Tristan ate, he tried hard to remember how he got into this situation.

He remembered dinner with his parents, then feeling sick. *Caleb said he saved me. Did Caleb save me?*

His memory was fragmented. He remembered that Caleb was there but not much else. But even though his memory of the event was incomplete, he had no doubt that if Caleb wanted him dead, he would be. So, for now, he would bide his time and wait for an opportunity to get away and back to his family.

Cianne found her mind wandering so she tried to focus back on the phone call. She waited for a pause in the conversation before she said, "No. Really Brian, we are fine." She and the children were fine, financially. In fact, Langley informed her that the Arkean royal family gathered quite a fortune over the years and she and the children were the only heirs.

"Mr. Bertram will handle all of Tristan's finances until he returns," Cianne said. "It's the way I want it." She listened to Brian speak as she looked over her shoulder at Tranae who played with Nadia and Aidan on the grass a few feet away.

Does he think Tristan is dead, she wondered? The others did but it didn't matter. When Tristan returned, he would prove them all wrong.

Her spirits lifted a little when Brian asked about Tranae.

"Tranae is here. If you want to speak to her-"

"No," Brian said, cutting her off. "No, I don't think so but, how is she?" he finally asked.

"She misses you." Cianne sighed, "She misses you a lot."

"Yeah…I know," he murmured. "I just can't be what she needs right now. Look, tell her congratulations on getting that internship at the pharmacy. I know she'll do great. Look Cianne, I'll talk to you soon. Thanks for the pictures of the kids." Brian took in a deep breath. "…and Cianne, what doesn't kill us just makes us stronger."

"That's what you keep telling me. I'll talk to you soon, Brian. Goodbye," Cianne said.

With her back still to the children and Tranae, Cianne rubbed the bridge of her nose. She was exhausted. She was eating less and the headaches were back. It took all she had to keep going without him but she needed to. Tristan would expect her to keep things in line for when he returned. She planned to make him proud.

"Come home, Tristan," she whispered.

"Excuse me, Soahn?"

Cianne rolled her eyes but turned her head slightly to her right to acknowledge her guest. "Please Whodai, call me Cianne." His smile was apologetic when she turned to face him. "I apologize for taking so long. I'm ready now."

"It is my honor and duty to wait for you, however long it takes," Whodai said as he gazed into her eyes.

Cianne looked away before he saw her flushed cheeks. Whodai had a way of making her feel as if she was being inspected.

"They are ready for you," Whodai informed her. He moved his hand under her elbow and escorted her across the lawn and into the house. "How do you feel?"

A breeze moved around Cianne, blowing her long tresses over her face as he pulled the double patio doors open. She brushed her hair away from her face. "I'm alright."

…and she was, mostly.

They made their way through the house, heading for the underground room Tristan constructed when the house was built. To her, it resembled some kind of panic room so she named it The Tomb.

Whodai stopped abruptly, took hold of her shoulder, and turned Cianne until they were face to face. His stare was intense. "If you would prefer to postpone this, for a week or so…"

Cianne smiled. Whodai, always the gentleman, was trying to protect her. She placed her hand on his arm, feeling his muscles flex as he tensed under her touch. Feeling as if she'd overstepped some boundary, Cianne quickly removed her hand.

"It's fine Whodai," she said, beginning her stride again.

Whodai walked beside her. "Do you know how everything works?"

She did. Vivian insisted that she learn to execute the Veris because only their bloodline held the ability to open the plane. The Veris was the only way the Council of Four was able to meet without the fear of the entire Council being exterminated in one swift move.

"I know the gist of it," Cianne said.

Similar to the Maatii, the members of The Four appeared in a common room on an astral plane. While in this celestial state their physical bodies are vulnerable and are watched over by their Protectors in a secured room.

"Good. Zeta will be inside the room with you. Jacobi will be outside the door and Felix will be here." Whodai motioned to Felix who stood outside of a small sitting room located between the formal dining room and Tristan's home office.

The room was shaped like a half circle with white walls except for one which was a pale gray with two very thick floor-to-ceiling glass mirrors on it. Two white half circle seats faced each other in the center of the room. In between the seats was a round smoked glass coffee table. A very large soft grayish-blue rug lay beneath the seating and table.

Cianne glanced around the pristine room then turned to Whodai who stood just inside of the doorway, watching her. "Where will you be?" she asked

"I'm going back to the Canyon to take another look. See if there is anything we may have missed," he said.

She sighed, "Cassius has been there a half dozen times. He said there's nothing there."

"I just want to be sure." Whodai grimaced, then said, "There are wild animals in that area. They could have taken something."

Cianne looked to her hands. Her once long natural nails were gone. She bit them down, some even to the skin.

"If I've upset you, please forgive me," Whodai said politely.

"No," she said as she shook her head. Her hair fell over her shoulder with the movement.

Whodai's eyes appeared to gloss over as he moved forward a step, but he didn't take another. Instead, he shut his eyes tight for half a second then shook his head.

"Whodai, are you alright?" She reached out but held off touching his shoulder.

He nodded.

Cianne tilted her head as she rubbed her hands together. "You haven't upset me. It's just that you are going far beyond what Cassius asked of you. I want you to know that I appreciate it."

Whodai and Jacobi were the only ones still searching for Tristan. Jacobi was on Guard duty most days so he could only search in his free time but Whodai followed no set schedule. Both of their efforts were purely voluntary. Cassius was vocal in his opinion that their efforts were useless, bluntly stating that "finding the responsible party is more realistic than looking for a body."

"Soahn, there is nothing——," Whodai said.

"Please...call me Cianne," she interrupted.

Whodai stared at her for a long moment then smiled. "I will do my best to remember." He lowered his head in a bow.

Cianne almost smiled as she watched Whodai exit the room, then she remembered why she stood in the room. The Tomb was programmed to not open unless the outer door was closed. Once the door was shut, Cianne walked over to the mirror and gently placed her fingertips on a scanner located on the back of one of the mirrors. A red beam of light scanned over her eyes then there was a hiss whispered through the room as if air was being released. The mirrors parted to reveal a lit staircase to the underground room.

Chapter Ten

The Veris
June 27th

Cianne, whose projected image was solid, sat on a white bench above a floor of bright light. She took in a deep breath as she studied the magical room. Cianne's gaze followed the long sheer sheets of fabric that hung from above until they vanished, or more like blended into the invisible ceiling. The floor was basically air or mist.

Over to her right, sitting on a similar half circle bench was the misty image of Eldra. On a third bench sat Brenna. Cianne brought them to this room by some type of astral projection ability but the room and all its details seemed to be of its own design.

To Cianne's left, the fourth bench sat empty.

"Good day," Brenna said with a smile. She looked to Eldra, raised a brow, then back to Cianne. Her smile seemed to widen as she admired Cianne's solid form.

"Good day," Cianne said, hesitantly.

"Good day," Eldra said. Her face was pleasant but lacked a smile.

"I welcome you, Cianne and I thank you for bringing us together, under the circumstances. Eldra and I realize this is a difficult time for you but there are some things you need to be made aware of," Brenna said. The urgency in her tone was apparent. Her smile had vanished, replaced by a more serious, penetrating stare.

"The reason we requested this meeting is to inform you of what is happening." Eldra said, a little more subdued.

Cianne sat still and listened.

"Within the next few weeks every Coesen will know of your existence," Brenna told Cianne.

"I thought that everyone knew already." Cianne said slowly.

"Only VIP's and Vivian's region, who watched the broadcast from Coesen News Today, were told. We planned to unveil you at a proper time but things have changed," Eldra sighed.

Brenna began again. "Once this happens, once everyone knows that you are among us," she paused, "well…we aren't in the position—"

"Our position is fine," Eldra interrupted.

Cianne didn't look to Eldra, her attention stayed on Brenna.

"There are Coesen who will see your birth as an end of days. It is said that with your birth the heavens opened, and the two sleeping messengers will awaken to be released upon the earth. The messengers, Death and Life, will await your command. A struggle will commence and in the end, messengers will bring about the destruction or rebirth of all.

"These are the very words Oma spoke over a hundred years ago. Most see Oma's words as a revelation or opportunity, the classic struggle between good and evil in which life prevails. Others seem to take the words more literal and fear the power you wield. These are the Coesen your mother feared and whom the Council of Four protected you from all these years." Brenna stopped and looked over to Eldra before continuing. "We have reports that Chandra may have had counsel with these Coesen."

Cianne looked from Brenna to Eldra, then back to Brenna. "Chandra has never been a fan of mine."

"You must understand, Cianne. We all wanted to punish your mother for her crimes—"

"Brenna please," Eldra interrupted again, "telling Cianne all this is not necessary."

Brenna looked to Eldra. "Everything is necessary, Eldra. We need to tell her everything." She looked back to Cianne. "When we found out who fathered you, it infuriated us all, but no one more than Chandra. We suspect that is when she convinced herself that the prophecy was a warning instead of a gift. We need to prepare."

"For what exactly?" Cianne asked.

"For war, of course," Brenna said, then frowned.

"Brenna please. There hasn't been a war since the Originals." Eldra looked to Cianne. "Cianne, we want to be careful and protect you and the children from any threat. But we cannot protect you fully unless you accept your birthright. Once you do, we will present you and your children to our people properly and declare that you *are* the Halo. Then this issue with Chandra will lose steam," Eldra said.

"You think that the Coesen will bow to me then?" Cianne laughed bitterly. "My husband is my Protector. I've broken your sacred law."

"You are the Halo, Cianne. Change the laws," Eldra said with conviction.

"Listen," Brenna said, "Chandra may be able to gather a few radicals, but the majority of the Coesen remain loyal. They've waited for your arrival." Brenna smiled wickedly then continued, "Yes, Chandra or some other faction may test our strength, but they will fail."

"I don't want a war. I didn't want any of this," Cianne said, pleadingly.

Without a sound or sign of warning, Caleb appeared.

Cianne stood and her first observation was that his form was just as solid as hers as he floated in the center of nothing.

He grinned then said, "Good day ladies."

Neither Eldra nor Brenna had a chance to speak before Cianne sent them back to their physical bodies. Her anger rolled off her in waves that seemed to affect the mist around them.

"I just want to talk," Caleb said. When she didn't respond, Caleb moved a few solid steps toward her.

He stopped when she tilted her head and narrowed her eyes. "There's nothing we need to talk about, unless you're telling me where you are so that I can come and end your long-suffering existence."

"Please Cianne," Caleb begged, "just listen."

"I wanted to believe that you had nothing to do with my grandmother's death but you never even tried to deny it." Tears rolled from her eyes as her body shook. "I blame myself you know. If I hadn't wanted you around so badly, to have my father in my life, maybe this wouldn't have happened. I convinced everyone to lower their guard. I lowered mine." She looked away for a moment. "Now Vivian is dead, and as a result, Tristan has been targeted by Chandra who incidentally wants you dead." She sniffed. "I will not trust you again…father."

Her form dissolved. When Cianne opened her eyes, she was sitting in a chair in the Tomb. She wasn't sure what she looked like but her body still shook with rage.

"What happened?" Zeta scurried over to her. Kneeling, she took Cianne's hand in hers.

Cianne blinked several times. Her heart was racing and the green of her eyes was fighting the red specks that threatened to show through. After several seconds of fighting for control, she said, "Caleb, is what happened."

Whodai walked around to the end of the bed and sat on a bench. He would prefer to be in his own place, in his own bed, but he had to stay close to West Hills in case he was needed.

So, the Eglin Ker, a high-end hotel with all the amenities to which he was accustomed, was his temporary address for now.

After drying his hands, he placed the towel next to him on the seat then answered his cell phone.

"We may have a problem, Soahn," the caller said. "Perkins has been poking around in Louisiana for almost a month now. He has help."

"I will handle it," Whodai said. "Where are you?"

"I'm a few miles away from the main property. I'm supposed to be checking the perimeter." The caller paused then continued, "Look, I just don't think it makes sense, me being here anymore. My skills are being wasted. I can go to Louisiana and take care of Perkins myself."

"Everything is going along as planned. I need someone I trust at the house with Cianne and as long as you stay put, the plan will work. Those assholes almost screwed up everything with that Tristan fiasco but you cleaned the accident site up nicely. No one knows who was chasing Tristan the day he went over that cliff." Whodai was still a little upset that Tristan was able to somehow kill his men before dying but it didn't matter. They were expendable. "I need you there."

"Yes, Soahn. When do I kill the children?" the caller asked.

A groan behind Whodai made him turn his head and glance over his shoulder. Behind him, gagged and tied to the bed with only a thin sheet to cover her nakedness, was a young woman. She was chosen for her appearance and age. With long dark hair that flowed over her breasts, smooth sun-kissed light brown skin, and a delicately beautiful face, she bore a striking resemblance to Cianne.

A beauty yes, but to Whodai she did not compare. She was just an appetizer and he longed for the main course.

"I will do it myself when the time is right." He lifted the champagne bottle that fell over when his toy tried to run from him. He refilled one of the two crystal flutes that sat next to him. Whodai put the glass to his lips as he stood, turned around, and drank slowly while he admired the young woman.

"That wasn't the plan," the caller said with irritation.

Whodai didn't reply right away. Instead he savored the taste of the French champagne he ordered for him and his guest. He believed that everyone should have an excellent meal and taste superb champagne before dying.

"I will explain my reason once. If Cianne was to lose the children now, she may not recover so easily. I want her broken," he admitted, 'but if we drive her insane she'll be of no use to me."

"What are we going to do about Caleb?" the caller asked nervously.

"With him being blamed for Vivian's death and that little stunt he pulled last week during the meeting of the Council, Cianne wants him dead. I figure he will keep his distance and my plan will play out smoothly," Whodai said confidently.

"How long do you think you'll be able to keep all this from Soahn Eldra?"

With the mention of his mother's name, Whodai felt his calm diminish. His toy must have seen it in his eyes because her eyes grew wide and a low squeal escaped her lovely mouth. But Whodai reeled in his emotions.

"Let me worry about my mother. All you need to do is play your role. You've earned Cianne's trust, which was the hardest thing you had to do. She has even offered you a room in her home. Your job is to be my eyes and ears and to induce a few nightmares. I'll send someone to handle Perkins." He turned, stood, then walked a few steps away from the bench." Don't make me regret choosing you."

Whodai glanced over his shoulder. The woman shivered when she met his gaze. He smiled. She was indeed beautiful; he only chose the most attractive women for his bed. Her name, her story, none of that mattered. For just one night, the women were all Cianne. This one though, he might keep a while longer. Her hazel eyes were a problem, but if he plucked them out…

"Don't bother me again unless there's an emergency. I'd like to get back to my guest."

He ended the call then placed the phone on the bedside table. Shirtless, with only a pair of jeans that hung low off his waist, Whodai flexed his lean muscled frame as he gave the young woman a wicked grin. Poor thing didn't look like she would survive more than a day.

I will just have to make the best of it.

Chapter Eleven

Tristan got up from the bed and limped to the bedroom door where the mouthwatering aroma from the kitchen was stronger. The pain from the bear attack and the bullet wound in his thigh ached, causing his body to scream in protest but he was too hungry to care.

He steadied himself in the doorway and looked out into the kitchen where Caleb stood over the stove with a fork. The food in the pan sizzled as Caleb moved it around.

"Hungry?" Caleb asked.

Tristan didn't answer. The hate he felt for Caleb was so thick he could feel it in his throat but he wasn't capable of doing anything about it now. Caleb did something to his ears while he was unconscious, making it difficult to hear. And Caleb injected him with some drug. What the injection was, he didn't know. He just knew that after the injection, he felt invigorated, almost brand new, yet still sore.

Caleb looked over his shoulder at Tristan briefly before turning back to the stove. He pulled two plates from the cabinet and filled them with food then placed them on the table.

Tristan took a step out of his room but hesitated then quickly stepped back. After his last escape attempt, Caleb jailed him in his room.

"I extended your perimeter."

Tristan was starving but he took his time as he made his way to the table. He didn't want Caleb seeing him limp and he definitely didn't want to fall like he had minutes ago in the bathroom. For some reason, he was getting weaker and he really didn't want Caleb to know.

Tristan sat with a stifled grunt, picked up the fork, then started eating. His plate was clean when he raised his head and noticed Caleb watching him with that impassive creepy stare of his.

God, I hate that fucking stare.

He knew now how Cianne felt about his own stoic looks. Only, he had nothing on Caleb. The man's lack of emotion coupled with his deadly skills were a lethal combo.

After a few moments of that uncomfortable death stare, Tristan grunted, "What?"

Caleb said nothing. He just slid his untouched plate across the table.

Tristan hesitated but in the end his hunger won over. "Thanks." He ate slower this time. When he was done, he glanced up at Caleb before sitting up straight and taking a drink from his glass. "Did you check on my family?"

Tristan placed the glass on the table. He hated to ask his captor for this but he had no other way of knowing. Plus, he needed to talk. Being cooped up in that small room for over month with no conversation was taking its toll.

"No," Caleb said. He held up an odd-looking bullet. "I've been looking for the person who made this."

Somehow, Tristan knew that it was the bullet that hit him, but before he could say anything a wave of dizziness hit him.

Caleb inspected Tristan's face. "Are you experiencing any weakness?"

He saw the answer in Tristan's eyes briefly before the kid was able to shake it off. Tristan needed to learn how to hide his weaknesses better, Caleb decided.

Something else I must teach him, he thought.

Tristan's expression suddenly grew angry. "You need to go check on them."

"I can't. Cianne will attack and I may inadvertently harm her." Caleb stood up, grabbed the empty plates, and walked over to the sink.

"Can you blame her?" Tristan asked him. "It's not like you're making all the right moves."

Caleb glared over his shoulder at Tristan. The little bastard had no idea what moves he made for his daughter. "Everything I do is for Cianne."

Tristan frowned at that, or he grimaced. Caleb wasn't certain if the look was due to pain or because he didn't agree.

"Like letting her think I'm dead? That's going to get you the father of the year award. Do you even know what love is? I bet you don't—"

Before Tristan was able to complete his comment, Caleb leaped across the room and grabbed him by the throat. He watched Tristan gasp for breath as he held him high in the air. Tristan's flailing feet kicked over the chair he was seated on seconds earlier. He dug at Caleb's hand for relief.

"I don't know what you've read about me in those books they gave you and I don't care. So, we're going to start off with a clean slate, you and I. Get to know each other." Caleb tilted his head as he watched Tristan's eyes roll. He loosened his grip so Tristan didn't pass out. He wanted to make sure everything he said was heard loud and clear. "A few things about me…I don't answer to anyone. I don't play with my kills and I don't like it when people think they know what or how I feel." Caleb was impressed that there was no hint of fear in Tristan's blue eyes that angrily stared back at him. "Please try to stay on my good side, son. My intent is to keep you alive and return you to your family. The state you're in when I return you will depend solely on you." Tristan tried to speak but only managed to squeeze out a few muffled words so Caleb dropped him to his feet.

Tristan clutched the edge of the dining table, bent over and coughed several times, before righting the chair and dropping into to it. Caleb sat down and watched as Tristan rubbed his throat.

"Actually," Tristan said calmly, "there isn't much written about you in the Annals."

Caleb shrugged.

"So, what's your story then?" Tristan asked then took a sip of water, but he grimaced when he swallowed.

"Why would I tell you my story?" Caleb asked.

"You just said we need to get to know one another. Besides, you have no books, no television, and no games here. You claim you want to keep me alive but I'll be dead of boredom in another day or so." Tristan leaned forward. "Haven't you ever wanted to tell your version of things?"

Caleb thought over it. To tell his story to anyone would be a first. To tell it to Tristan…well, it might allow the boy to understand his actions better. Caleb didn't really care how Tristan felt about him but if the kid knew his path, it might prove that they aren't so different.

Caleb sensed it the first time he saw Tristan. He and the boy had the same unruly spirit. It was that same spirit that most likely attracted the Source and what made Caleb what he is today.

Yeah, he thought, *Tristan needs to know how close to the edge he actually is.*

"Alright," Caleb said, "but for my life story, you will act civil, take your injections without question and…allow me to train you."

Tristan frowned. "What's in the needle?"

"It's keeping you alive," Caleb said with no inflection of tone or emotion. "That's all you need to know for now."

It contained a special mix Bannerman made specifically to keep the poison, Death's Door, closed. The injection was effective for at least three weeks, then the poison would start wreaking havoc again. Without it, Tristan would experience weakness, pain, bleeding, and then death within days.

"I'll take the injections for now," Tristan said. He got up, went to the fridge and pushed the lever for shaved ice to fall into his glass. When he returned to his seat he rolled the cold glass over the red hand print on his throat. "You can train me too. I'll prove to you that I'm not as weak as you think I am. The sooner you're convinced I can handle whatever comes at my family, the sooner I'll be home."

"The terms are agreeable," Caleb said.

"Alright," Tristan said. He placed the glass on the table then leaned forward. "My schedule is clear, so..."

Caleb shook his head at Tristan's impatience but said, "I should start when my life really began. My mother was sixteen when she married my father, Fredrick Scott. He was twenty-seven and the son of a wealthy southern landowner who died and left everything he owned to his only child. I'm not sure if my parents were in love but I do know that they respected one another. Love, to most in that time, wasn't a condition to marry, security was.

"My mother, a gentle and beautiful woman, wanted her children to have what she referred to as a civilized gentleman's education so she sent my brother and me abroad to stay with her relatives. We were never told why she wanted us to return to the Americas and we never asked. Though it felt as if I was leaving the family I had grown to love behind. But my brother and I left London with our father without a word of defiance.

"When my brother and I left Maiden Hall as boys, construction was underway. It was the largest of my father's three plantations and he wanted the house to be grand. A place my mother could be proud of and to show off his wealth. My brother Fredrick, named after my father, was eleven. I was nine when I last set eyes on my home. We returned as men.

"Maiden Hall was an enormous and magnificent plantation with slave cabins to house a large sum of slaves, houses for the overseers' and their families, a smokehouse, barns, stables, silos and gardens. There was also a small school house and a chapel on the property. In the center, surrounded by flowers, trees, and a beautiful green lawn was Maiden Mansion. For Fredrick, it didn't compare to the elegance of London but to me, a young man full of dreams, Maiden Hall was amazing.

"I suppose my tale really begins on the night of our return. It was late and we were tired from the journey so our father decided that we would stay at the neighboring plantation for the night. I could not sleep. Restless, I suppose, or maybe I was excited to see the places from my childhood I scarcely remembered. Whatever the reason, I crept out of my offered room and saddled my horse. It didn't take long for me to reach the lake that split the two properties. It was one of the few things I remembered enjoying before leaving home.

I found my favorite tree, a large live oak with branches that were low and spread wide. I climbed it and easily fell asleep in the comfort of the southern night air. I slept peacefully until I heard some splashing in the lake beneath me. It was a colored girl and she was the loveliest creature my eyes had ever seen. Her smooth skin, which instantly reminded me of the color of toasted wheat, shimmered as the moon's bright light illuminated the water that moved over her.

"Her eyes were round, with the darkest lashes and brows that made their brown color seem lighter, richer. Her long nose, full lips, and high cheek bones were perfectly proportioned for one so delicate. In my day, people referred to mixed race people as mulatto and I'd seen a few by that time. All her features and that midnight black hair put me in the mind of a mixture of Mediterranean and African descent. Whatever she was didn't faze me. All I knew was that she was breathtaking.

"I wasn't sure why I didn't say anything to her, to let her know that I was there. Instead I sat in that tree, my tree, frozen. I watched her gracefully swim in my lake like it was where she belonged. It didn't take long for me to imagine myself in the water with her. That I could feel her coal black hair cascade over my fingers as the small glistening streams of water drained from it and down my arm. That she would look at me with the same wonder and curiosity I looked at her with. At fifteen I was not innocent and hadn't been for some time. But this girl, she made me regret all my indiscretions.

"Time stopped for me as I sat in that tree fully content with just watching her. But I knew that light of day would be coming soon. I also knew that she wasn't supposed to be in the lake, and that if she were discovered she would be punished. I, like my mother, disliked violence, especially the kind that was inflicted on slaves. I didn't want my homecoming scarred with this beautiful creature's blood so…I threw an acorn into the water to alert her of the time."

Maiden Hall Plantation
Mid-Summer of 1821

The water was warm and soothing, giving Marda a false sense of security. It made her feel like she once had, before she was brought across the ocean to this place she could never embrace as her home.

For five years, she remained a captive.

The lake was the only thing she could enjoy, secretly of course. Time spent in the lake behind the great house allowed her to imagine she was home. If only for a moment.

The quiet calm that swept over Marda when she was completely submerged under the cool water felt amazing on her aching muscles. The way the ripples on the surface caressed her skin, it was as if her mother was touching her. Easing her fears over the vast distance in which they were separated.

The lake was what kept her sane.

Marda knew there would be consequences for breaking the Mistress' rules. It was the one rule the Mistress wanted them to abide above all others.

"Don't leave the house unless you are accompanied by another." The Mistress' gentle words replayed in Marda's head.

If she was caught, the punishment would not fit the offense. No, it would be severe and painful.

"I cannot keep you safe if you disobey the rules."

Marda cleared her mind and relaxed her muscles, allowing the water to swallow her. Soon she wouldn't be able to sneak out in the late of night to take a dip in the lake. Mr. Scott, her Mistress' husband, was returning in a few weeks.

She'd heard hushed talk of him from the others. They said Mr. Scott isn't as kind as Miss Catherine. They said he was the one responsible for hiring Shaw, the hateful overseer who mistreated the slaves who work in the fields.

If he likes Shaw, then Mr. Scott can't be nice.

Marda didn't care for Shaw or the way he watched her the few times their paths crossed. She was told by Tempie, the head house slave, to stay clear of Shaw. Marda did her best to avoid him at all cost. She also followed all the rules.

Except...

Swimming was the only thing she had ever done that the Mistress would be angry about. If she was caught disobeying the rules she had no doubt that Shaw would be the one tying her to the large whipping oak to deal her fifty lashes. The devious smile he kept on his face flashed in her mind. The thought, a frightening one, almost caused her to breathe underwater. She rose to the surface, gasping until she was able to catch her breath.

Relax, Marda told herself. She enjoyed the pond over a hundred times and hadn't been caught yet. Plus, tonight was special. Today was the anniversary of her thirteenth dry season or year and swimming was her way of celebrating. Being whipped if she was caught would be worth it. Besides, she wouldn't stay out too long.

At least that's what she told herself two hours ago when she stripped down and got into the water.

Marda lowered her head under the water again and rose up slowly. Her loosely braided hair unraveled and was cascading over her face. She raised her hands up out of the water and smoothed her tresses away from her eyes so that she could see the night sky. The moon's position told her that time had gotten away from her.

Marda decided it was time to swim in so she looked around the shore line to make sure she was still alone. She moved to swim to shore but stopped when she heard something hit the water a few inches in front of her. Marda didn't see what hit the water, but she saw the ripples the impact caused.

Frightened, Marda turned and waded in a complete circle to find the source. *Maybe it was some animal*, she told herself, not finding the source. *It's nothing*. With wide eyes, Marda strained to see in the dark lit by moonlight. *It's nothing*, she convinced herself.

Something hit the water again; this time it landed right beside her. Only, Marda saw the direction it came from before the spray of water from the impact splashed over her. She followed the arc the object took.

To her shock, she saw a dark form of something…no…someone in one of the towering trees. The person was stretched out on a thick branch several feet away, watching her.

"The sun will rise soon and I'm certain you don't want to be discovered out here."

The unfamiliar voice sounded different from the people on the plantation. His pronunciation was sharper, and his tone was kind, but it left no allowance to question. Only, he sounded young. But there was no way to tell his age from his outlined form in the darkness.

Marda didn't say a word as she swam for the shore. Climbing out of the water, she pulled her clothing over her nakedness in a frantic rush. Not once did she look back as she ran toward the main house. Her heart raced as she opened and closed the cellar door as quietly as she could and went to her pallet in the corner.

She waited for the sound of footsteps above her as she lay in a protective ball. Marda cringed at the thought of the leather whip that would slash into her back like it had for so many other slaves before her. Her hands will be shackled to the big oak near the cabins for everyone to see. That was the rule, everyone had to see.

Marda waited.

The next morning
Marda glanced at Jai before putting the scrub brush in the bucket and pushing off her knees to stand. The Mistress called for them. Marda didn't tell Jai about her late-night swimming or that she'd been caught.

Her head ached as they walked side by side through the house to the dining room. But unlike Jai, Marda was sick with fear, and she kept her eyes on her feet. When Jai and Marda entered the room where the Mistress waited, Marda glanced up then looked back at her feet.

"I so hoped we had more time to prepare for your homecoming, Fredrick," Catherine said to a tall man. Catherine turned to regard them, then said, "Ready the boys' rooms right away."

"Father wanted to travel before the heat set in."

Marda heard the man's name when she entered. She knew that Fredrick, at seventeen years, was the eldest of two sons and the spitting image of a man she saw earlier that morning walking through the halls. That man must have been Master Fredrick, the Mistress' husband.

"Yes'm," Jai said as she took Marda's hand and hurried out of the dining room. "You take the Young Master's room; I'll do Master Fredrick's."

Marda slowly walked to the room of her Mistress' youngest son as she wondered when her world would be turned upside down. When would the stranger tattle? The not knowing was stressful.

She pushed open the bedroom door and straight away started picking up scattered clothing off the floor. When Marda heard someone clear their throat, she scrambled back into the door, unwittingly closing it and shutting herself inside with the newcomer. With her gaze to the floor she spun around to open the door.

Open, she thought as she fumbled with the knob.

"Wait."

Marda knew that smooth deep voice. It was the same voice from last night. She stopped trying to open the door but was too afraid to turn and look at the face of the person who'd caught her naked in the lake the night before. When she heard movement behind her, Marda's heart almost stopped. Footsteps told her he was closing the distance between them. Marda pivoted and soon saw his booted feet beside her.

"Do you speak?" he asked her.

Marda didn't answer.

"You needn't be afraid of me. I just want to give you this."

Marda closed her eyes tight as she felt his warm hand touch hers. She tried pulling her hand away but he caught her by the wrist then he placed a piece of cloth in her hand. Marda opened her eyes and looked at her hand. She saw her head wrap.

"You left this," he said softly.

Marda looked up slowly, focusing on the crisp white shirt he wore. She continued to raise her head until she was staring at the young man who was holding her hand so gently. His hair resembled the warm golden sand that she once felt between her toes when she was a young girl. It was unruly but perfectly so, flipping up at the ends to almost cover his ears while the front brushed the top of his brows. His face looked young and innocent but he had a strong chin and cheek bones. His skin was sun kissed and his lips, the top thinner than the fuller bottom, looked swollen.

Maybe he bit his lips like I often do.

He was the most beautiful thing she ever saw. He looked nothing like his brother, who was also quite handsome. No, this boy resembled Mistress Catherine and he had her most mesmerizing feature.

"Caleb," a husky, authoritative voice echoed up from the first floor.

"I'll be right there, sir," the boy called out, but he continued to hold onto Marda's hand.

They held each other's gaze for a few seconds more. Then he lifted her hand to his lips, and before she could muster the strength to pull away, he kissed her hand then allowed it to slide from his. He smiled then stepped around her, opened his bedroom door, and left the room.

Sighing from relief that the encounter didn't go the way she thought it would, and that she had her favorite head wrap back, Marda relaxed her tense stance. She went to work on cleaning the bedroom but couldn't get the image of his smile or his eyes out of her head. In fact, her day was filled with thoughts of Caleb, and that made her heart race with anxious thumps.

Marda kept herself busy and out of sight so she wouldn't be caught staring at him if their paths crossed again. But to her displeasure, he also kept out of sight. Caleb affected her in a way she couldn't explain. Even as she fell asleep that night, a vision of his eyes calmed her homesick heart.

Caleb is 17 Marda is 15
Fall of 1823

Marda walked slowly down the dirt road toward the main house. The cool evening air moved around her body, chilling her to the bone. She straightened her covering over her shoulders and bunched it to her chest. The sun was low in the sky when she was sent from the main house by Tempie, with goods for Mistress Shaw.

It was dark out so her steps were quick. Rarely did she leave the house without someone accompanying her but everyone else was busy getting ready for some big dinner party her Mistress was hosting in a few days.

I should have parted ways sooner, Marda thought. When she arrived at Mistress Shaw's home, the sweet mother of four younglings was overwhelmed even with her young colored girl's help. So Marda stayed to help with things and now found herself in the dark with only a small candle to light her way.

She hummed a hymn in her head as she strolled along her way. Everyone on the plantation worked real hard, waking before dawn and retiring when it was too dark to see, so the path to the house was bare. Though alone, she was not afraid. She knew everyone.

As Marda moved closer to the stables, she heard a faint noise. Knowing that the animals were in the stable, she didn't make much of the noise and kept on her way. It wasn't until she was almost beyond the structure that she heard someone speak.

"Hey there, little colored girl."

Marda stopped as Shaw stepped out of the shadows and in front of her. She took two steps back and immediately lowered her head. She tried to not to panic and kept calm by rubbing her apron hem. All the house slaves were warned to stay away from this overseer. She heard he was a hateful man who took pleasure in causing folk pain.

When Shaw grabbed for her, Marda attempted to retreat but he took hold of her forearm and pulled her into the dimly lit stable. The dirt and hay gathered at the front of her shoes as she tried to burrow her feet into the ground for leverage, but it was no use. He was stronger.

"Don't fight me, you hear," Shaw ordered, his mouth close to her ear. "Been waiting for my chance at you girl."

Marda winced from the pain of his grip. She gagged at the smell of the day's work all over him and the scent of drink on his breath.

"Had my eye on you for some time girl, but your misses keep you close."

Shaw took Marda's other wrist, ignoring her futile struggles, and slammed her body against the side wall of the building. He hiked her arms above her head, making it hard for her to look away.

She hadn't looked directly in the face of the infamous Shaw since he purchased her on the block. He was unnervingly handsome with defined angles that gave him a high-born polished look. Wet and oily blonde hair fell down the sides of his face and to his shoulders. The gray eyes that stared hungrily at her were soulless and dead.

"Now hold still. I got something special for you. Something you gone like."

Shaw kissed down her neck, leaving warm saliva behind. He coupled her wrists in one hand and pulled up her dress and caressed her thigh with the other. Marda whimpered as she fought to turn her head away, just managing to squeeze her head to the side giving him access to her jaw.

He licked her skin just below her ear.

Scared and still reeling from the shock of being dragged into the stable by Shaw, Marda found it difficult to think clearly. For a moment, her mind shut down, but the ache from her arms being held over her head brought her mind racing back to the hell she was experiencing.

Shaw had her balancing barely on the tips of her toes, unable to gain any footing. His hand searched desperately for the edges of her undergarments.

Tears rolled down Marda's face as she struggled in vain, understanding that this was to be her fate. She closed her eyes and hoped that after he took her innocence that he'd take her life.

"Sir please, the misses sent me to fetch her. We are expected."

Marda's eyes sprang open as hope filled her. *Jai*!

Shaw whipped his head around, but didn't let go of her. He looked Jai over as she stood behind him. Marda also noticed a small stable boy hiding behind Jai.

Did the boy go after Jai?

Shaw smiled a wicked smile and let out a chuckle that spoke volumes. Marda knew he would make the stable boy pay for fetching Jai. She cringed knowing what the boy would endure, but by the way Shaw looked, she worried more for what he planned to do to her and Jai.

"Have not seen you both together since I bought you from the block. Come here, girl."

Caleb walked into the stables with Winter, his beloved stallion, not expecting the gathering of people. It didn't take him long to figure out that he interrupted something. Jai, his mother's slave, looked frightened but determined. He followed her gaze over to Shaw, who was grinning, then to Marda whose face was strained with pain. There was also a stable boy present, who cowered behind Jai's skirt.

"What's going on here?" Caleb asked Shaw, but his gaze fell on Marda.

For the first time, her tear-filled gaze fell directly on him, her eyes pleading for his help. He blinked as his gaze moved from Marda's eyes down to her exposed thigh. A storm of anger brewed inside him when he saw Shaw's hand caressing her there.

"What is going on here, Shaw?" Caleb demanded. This time his voice was filled with anger and his eyes narrowed. He grew angrier when he realized that it was under these circumstances that Marda finally looked him in the eyes, again. Not because she wanted to see him but only because she was scared of Shaw and what he wanted to do to her.

This wasn't the way he wanted it to be. Since returning to Maiden Hall, Caleb felt an unfamiliar pull to the beautiful girl he found swimming in the lake behind his house. But she never met his gaze or spoke, even when given permission. A frown seemed all she was capable.

"Nothing going on, yet." Shaw then raked his gaze over Marda in a way that made Caleb's stomach churn. "Get the young master's horse, boy," Shaw told the stable boy without taking his eyes off Marda, "so he can retire."

Caleb fisted his hand around the reigns he forgot he held.

Shaw was important to his father, but in Caleb's mind there was no solid reasoning for slavery. That made it difficult for Caleb to acclimate to life on the plantation he was so excited to see. Unlike his brother Fredrick, who had an enthusiastic interest in the family business now, Caleb had no desire to be a planter and cared less for plantation life. He believed that everyone should be paid a fair wage, but people like Shaw loved the power slavery afforded them.

That disgusted Caleb.

Caleb looked down as the stable boy finally grabbed for Winter. He glanced at the frightened boy as he gave over his horse, knowing it was up to him to do something. With his mind made up, Caleb looked back at Jai, and in the most authoritative voice he could muster, he moved forward and said, "Jai, Marda get back to the house now!"

Shaw didn't let go of Marda right away. Instead, he and Caleb stared at each other, one waiting for the other to fold. But Caleb stood his ground and refused to shy away. He barely held in his relief when Shaw slowly lowered Marda's arms, allowing her feet to touch the ground. Once her feet were on the floor she hurried past Caleb and into Jai's arms.

"Be seeing you now, girl." Shaw's smile was a warning.

Marda hid her face in Jai's chest, but Caleb saw the way her body shuddered at Shaw's threat. Caleb buried the need to comfort her and motioned for them to get. He watched as the two hurried out of the stable and up the dirt path, holding tightly to each other, never looking back.

Once their silhouettes faded into the darkness of night, Caleb turned to face Shaw. He could hear the stable boy settling Winter, but he kept his attention on the overseer.

Shaw rolled his shoulders then chuckled as he lazily walked by Caleb, toward the entrance of the stable. "You think no one see the way you look at that colored mute."

Caleb's eyes grew big.

Shaw's smile widened as he raised his hands in defense. "It's alright. I get it, you want her for yourself. A man got his needs. She young and ripe made for hard work and pleasure, you know."

Caleb felt disgust and panic wash over him as he stared at Shaw. The man had a reputation as an effective overseer, and was sought after by many planters before coming to Maiden Hall. But Shaw was also known for his cruelty and lust. It was rumored that Shaw had over a dozen children on different plantations, but his wife, Mary, had only birthed four. The other children are said to be born of slaves.

"She's different, that one is. The other coloreds see it too, and it ain't just cause she easy to look at." Shaw cleared his throat then spit on the ground, close to Caleb's foot. His wicked eyes focused only on Caleb. "She walks around like she's some kind of royalty, ya know."

Caleb didn't look away, wanting to show he wasn't afraid.

"Ever wonder what it sounds like when a mute scream?" Shaw kicked up hay with his foot before turning around and walking slowly out of the stable.

Caleb only relaxed when Shaw was gone. He unclenched his fists, feeling the half-moon impression on his palms. He wasn't certain how he felt about Marda. She intrigued him in ways he was unable to express, but he was sure of one thing. Shaw wasn't getting his hands on her. Ever.

For weeks, Caleb pondered over what Shaw said to him in the stables that night. If what he felt for Marda was written all over his face, then he needed to be careful. From then on, every interaction was short, if he interacted with her at all.

In an attempt to free his mind of Marda, Caleb avoided her. He spent his free time away from Maiden Hall visiting John Scott, kin of his father, who owned a shop in town. He told himself that after the incident in the stables, Marda wouldn't venture far from the safety of the main house again.

Three months later.

Marda worked as fast as she could to hang the clothing she and Jai twisted free of water on the drying racks. It was early eve and light was still left in the day, and the wash house wasn't far from the main house, but ever since that night in the stables…

Well, Marda didn't like being outside the house when it was dark out. Or any other time, for that matter.

With chilled fingers, she pinned a garment then plucked another from the pile.

When done with her task, Marda gathered the dry clothes in her basket then hurried out of the small structure only to stop in her tracks. Shaw was propped against the fence post. Jai stood in front of him, but Shaw still saw Marda. When her wide eyes met his slanted gaze, he smiled then winked.

Marda hesitated. His awareness of her fear of him was apparent by the slow smile that spread across his face but she squared her shoulders, hiked the basket higher on her hip, then walked along the path that would lead her past him. When she was a few feet from him, Shaw pushed off the post and stood directly in her path. Marda slowed. She glanced at Jai who looked just as scared.

Shaw reached for her apron, but Jai grabbed his hand.

No…

But there was no stopping him. Marda cringed as Shaw's hand rose then came down hard across Jai's delicate face. The blow made Jai stumble sideways. Marda dropped the basket and grabbed Jai by the arm. Dazed, Jai supported herself on

Marda for a split second before straightening herself and pushing Marda away.

"Go back to the manor," Jai ordered. Her tone was never harsh, until today.

Marda didn't move. She just stared at Jai, confused. There was no one around. Why didn't Jai use her ability to hurt him? She could, so, why didn't she?

Instead of punishing *him*, Jai pushed Marda, causing her to lose her footing. She fell to the ground. Shocked, Marda looked up at her. Jai's lip bled and swelled where Shaw hit her but her face didn't reflect pain. It was determination Marda saw.

"Go now," Jai said again.

Marda pushed to her feet. Shaw didn't try to stop her when she stumbled away. She looked back as she hastened up the path. On Jai's face she could see fear and anger but when their eyes met, Marda also saw a hint of relief.

Chapter Twelve

Perkins was surprised when he heard a knock at his hotel door. "Just a minute," he yelled.

For two months, he did everything possible to cover his tracks. He didn't tell anyone other than Tristan that he was going to investigate on his own. He had no contact with the Coesen Guard and he left them no way to locate him. Yet, when he looked through the peep hole he knew it was Cassius who stood on the other side of the door.

Perkins pivoted around and did a few hand signals, telling Evie who it was on the other side of the door. "I'm putting something on," he told Cassius through the closed door.

When Perkins glanced back at the sofa, Evie was no longer there. He quickly made his way to one of the back rooms. She stood next to one of the large windows.

"You can't jump," he joked.

"We can't let him find me here either," Evie said with a shrug. She opened the window as quietly as she could to put her bag strap over her head and shoulder before stepping onto the fire escape. "Ask yourself this, Ryan, why is he here?"

"Cassius would have never betrayed Sovereign Harper." Perkins whispered as he walked over to the window and crouched down.

Evie looked down onto the street below, he assumed to make sure it was clear, then she squatted so they were eye to eye. "All I know is that the informant who told me that your mystery girl Alicia Reynolds was involved with Zuri, also gave me the heads up that someone has taken notice of our snooping. Now, my informant is dead and Cassius is here. It's all a little too convenient for me." She frowned when he didn't respond. "Fine," Evie said, "it's your ass. If you survive the next hour, call me." Evie quickly descended the metal steps.

Perkins had no time to think it over. He hurried to the bathroom and took off his shirt. He put a dab of shampoo on a washcloth and rubbed until it was full of suds. Then he rinsed the cloth until the suds were almost gone and rubbed the dripping cloth over his face and hair. He wiped it over his upper body then put the shirt back on and buttoned it up making sure to skip a button so that his shirt was buttoned up wrong. He pulled off his shoes and socks and wet his feet. Perkins then grabbed a towel, placed it around his neck then went to the hotel door.

When Perkins opened the door, Cassius was leaning against the far wall. Perkins stepped back and extended his hand, motioning for Cassius to come inside.

"I apologize for not calling first," Cassius said as he walked into the hotel room. He looked around the mid-sized accommodations then turned back to Perkins with a look that suggested the room wasn't fit for an animal, let alone a Coesen. "How about we take a walk."

Perkins rubbed the towel over his damp head for effect. "Alright," Perkins agreed. "Let me finish getting dressed. You can have a seat." Perkins didn't look back to see if Cassius would sit. Instead he started toward the bathroom, leaving his wet footprints to mark his path.

"So, what can I do for you Cassius?" Perkins asked as he and Cassius walked down the busy street ten minutes later. He kept watch of all the people around him as they strolled. Evelyn's words of warning still rang in his head.

"I wanted to see if you found what you were looking for," Cassius said. "You've been at this for a while now."

The two men held each other's gaze for a moment as they continued to walk.

"No," Perkins said with a smirk, "nothing yet."

Cassius stopped and faced Perkins who casually reached into his pocket and pulled out a pack of gum. He watched Perkins inspect the pack then turn in place. When Perkin's saw a convenience store to the side of him, he crumbled the pack in his hand and threw it at a trash can that sat on the sidewalk near the street.

"Can I get you something?" Perkins asked as he motioned to the store.

"I'm good," Cassius said. He tried to hide his contempt for the area and all it encompassed as he responded. He didn't follow Perkins inside the little convenience store. As an alternative, he turned around and watched traffic move on the street. After a few minutes, he cursed. He didn't want to be here, in this place a minute more. "How long does it take to buy gum?" he said under his breath.

Cassius sighed as his gaze found the pack Perkins tossed at the garbage can. The gum pack lay amongst the litter on the sidewalk. He leaned forward, taking a closer look at the pack. There were still a few pieces left inside.

"Shit," he cursed then immediately ran into the small liquor store. He looked up and down the two aisles. "Is there a back door in this establishment?"

The clerk looked up from his magazine as if annoyed and pointed to the rear of the store. "Yeah, but it's locked. I got the only key." The young man said holding up a chain that was around his neck with a single key on it.

"Sure," Cassius said sarcastically. He swiftly walked to the rear of the store where he found the door ajar. The store clerk came up beside Cassius with a surprised look on his face.

◉

Perkins went to the other hotel room he procured for a situation just like this. Inside, he gathered some clothing, money, and his spare guns before calling Evie. The instructions in the message he left were clear. Don't go home, just go somewhere and lay low until ten pm then meet him at the park.

They met in the same spot a few days before and he knew she would know the location.

Perkins looked at his watch again. It was ten after ten. "Shit," he said, then stood up. He paced and grabbed his head. "Shit," he said again.

Twenty minutes later, Perkins anxiously stood in front of Evelyn's house. He didn't need his Protector abilities to sense that something was seriously wrong. A large shadowed form that wasn't Evie moved behind the window, causing him to drop behind a car parked near the curb.

Is she seeing someone or…

After watching the front of the house for a minute or so, Perkins decided he needed to enter through the back. Perkins took a deep breath as he slowly pushed Evie's back door open and slid inside. There was nothing immediately screaming out at him but he trusted his instincts. If all was fine, Evie will just be upset about him stalking around her house. So, he crept through the rancher style home, quietly making his way to Evie's bedroom where the door sat open.

Perkins' heart sank when he peeked inside and saw Evie on the floor, face down beside her bed. Her hair was knotted and disheveled. Her shirt was raised, leaving her lower back uncovered. The stretch jeans she wore were ripped but thankfully still on. One of her shoes was on her foot, the other was gone.

She fought her assailant.

Kneeling beside her, Perkins rolled Evie over. Her face was swollen and bruised, and blood ran from her nose. He placed his hand behind her neck to lift her head but his hands grazed over something hard. She moaned.

"Damn it Evie," Perkins whispered in her ear. He raised her head up more and placed his forehead to hers. He closed his eyes, willing her to wake up, to heal, to come back to him. He wanted to tell her so many things. Tell her he was sorry that he let her and Lilith down. To tell her that he wanted to be more to her and always had.

"Why did you come back here? I told you not to come back here."

Evelyn raised her clenched hand slowly and brushed his cheek. Her eyes were still closed but hope washed over him. She was alive. He felt her fist press against his cheek so he took hold of her wrist. When she opened her hand, Perkins took the paper she revealed.

Evelyn slowly opened her eyes. "Find Zuri," she breathed.

"That's going to be a bit difficult if he's dead."

Perkins turned his head and stared at the average sized man standing in Evie's doorway. He only had time to log the man's mature face to memory before he felt a devastating blow to his chest that knocked Evie out of his arms and pushed him back into a shoe stand across the room.

The assailant's eyes burned with wickedness as he stood by the bedroom door again with a menacing smile on his face.

Perkins grunted in pain as he spat out a mouthful of blood. He slowly got to his feet. "Get out Evie!" he shouted, as he pulled his gun out and aimed. But she didn't move. She lay on the floor, staring at him with hollowed eyes.

"Let me introduce myself, Guardian Perkins," the man said. "My name is Bernard but you may know me by my last name, Givens." He walked slowly now, as opposed to the lightning speed at which he moved when he hit Perkins.

Seemingly amused, Givens moved toward Perkins with no fear of the gun pointed at his head. "Assuming you've forgotten who I am or what a Protector can do," he continued toward Perkins, "that piece of shit gun isn't going to save you."

Closer, Perkins said to himself. *Come a little closer.*

Perkins remembered Givens and all the victims he'd killed to gain an order of death from the Royal Guardians.

Closer. Closer.

Perkins fired but Givens moved at the last minute, avoiding the bullet with speed and grace that only a skilled Protector could. "No, this piece of shit gun won't save me," Perkins said with a satisfied grin, "but she can." He held out a small oval silicone device with two little wires coming out of each end. Perkins rotated his hand and the device dropped to the floor.

Givens' carefree expression turned to panic as he watched the Inhibitor he must have placed over Evelyn's spine fall to the floor. His gaze trailed from the Inhibitor to his feet where one of Evelyn hands was wrapped around his right ankle. Givens' eyes widened when they met Evelyn's.

Perkins saw Evie's eyes narrow with hate a second before Givens' entire body burst into flames. He hurried to Evie's side and dragged her from Givens' flaming body that bumped around the room setting everything it touched a flame.

Once they were clear of the flames, Perkins lifted her to his chest and carried her out of room, down the hall and through the front door. When he reached the curb, Perkins sat with her cradled in his arms. He inspected her scorched arm and hand. It was charred, with red lines glowing under the burns.

"Evie…Evelyn," he whispered. Perkins peered into her unresponsive but still beautiful face. After a few seconds passed, he reluctantly felt for a pulse. A debilitating pressure built in his chest, almost knocking him back. His body swayed but he remained seated upright with her still cradled to him.

Perkins let a faint gasp slip out as he sucked in a breath. He clumsily climbed to his feet with Evie still in his arms. Perkins walked the three blocks to his car with a new resolve.

He opened the rear door and gently placed Evie's body in the back seat, tearing his eyes from hers only when the locket around her neck reflected the light of the moon. Perkins' hands slipped around her neck and unfastened it. He knew at once that it was Lilith's necklace, he saw it around his ward's neck every day when they were younger.

Opening the locket, his heart sank. On one side, a picture showed Evelyn, Lilith and him hugging each other and smiling. He remembered that day because it was the day he told Evelyn he loved her. The day after, Evelyn gave herself to him completely. It was that day he treasured above all.

On the other side of the locket was a picture of him, the day he completed the Maatii and became a Royal Guardian. He waited until they graduated college and for Lilith to move in with her boyfriend before he told her and Evie he was planning to complete the Maatii so he could serve his four-year rotation protecting the Royals.

Lilith was excited and supported him. Evelyn, who gave him the brush off after his declaration of love and after making love to him a year earlier, told him he was a fool and she couldn't believe he would leave Lilith unprotected when he could just join the local Guard to serve his rotation.

Perkins' heart broke as he held the locket tightly before placing it around his neck. He chose the Royal Guard versus the Coesen Guard to get away from her. To heal the broken heart Evelyn had so easily dismissed. But he never stopped loving her. Evelyn still owned his heart all these years.

Perkins kissed Evelyn's cold lips. All the heat had left her body now. Pyros like Evie usually held onto their core heat and some curious electricity, allowing them to hold on to life longer than other Coesens when their bodies experienced trauma. But Evelyn was beaten so badly that she didn't have enough heat to sustain her life and kill Givens too.

She sacrificed herself, choosing to kill Givens to save him.

"Why?" he whispered, "why save me?"

Realization hit him so hard he fell back through the open car door on his ass. He rested his elbows on his knees and covered his face with his hands.

Evelyn befriended him instantly when the Source chose him as Lilith's Protector. The three were inseparable but he always thought she hung around to keep an eye on her sister. Evelyn took his first kiss and he took hers but it had been on a dare at a party so he thought she didn't treasure it the way he had.

He remembered she dated some throughout high school and college but never really latched on to one person. Lilith often joked that Evie always kept men at a distance, except for him. Only, she never gave him a hint of interest, never said she wanted more even though he did. She led him to believe she only wanted to remain best friends. They were the three musketeers until she came to his dorm room one night, giving him her virginity that he'd been so certain she gave away years ago.

All those years…

"Damn it Evie, why didn't you tell me that you loved me too?"

Chapter Thirteen

Cianne smoothed her hand over her dress before she opened her bathroom door. She paused then tightened her grip on the door knob as she stared at her friend in the sitting area of her bedroom.

Tranae stared back but said nothing.

Cianne broke the staring contest first by looking to the small table where her favorite morning drink sat waiting. Sighing, she noted that it was nine in the morning as she walked over to her bed and laid the robe she carried on top.

"Good morning," Cianne said eventually. Her voice was a little shaky.

"Really, Cianne?" Tranae said.

Cianne turned to look at her closest friend in the entire world. She missed Tranae. Missed the happier times. "I'm dealing the only way I know how."

"Is that what you call what you're doing? You're dealing?"

Cianne looked away from Tranae's accusing glare. She was the one who had to deal with all the loss. She had to cope the best way she knew how. Cianne thought that Tranae would understand. Only, no one understood. How could they?

Cianne walked over to the chair next to Tranae and sat.

It was Tristan's idea to have the seating positioned here in their room. He said it was so they could watch the sun set and rise together. He said that watching such a beautiful event still took his breath away.

"And who better to sit and watch it with?" he'd asked her. "With you, the only woman who has ever taken my breath away."

Cianne wasn't too fond of the daily event then, or the way Tristan set up the two chairs and small table between them. Now, she was grateful to him for arranging the furniture this way.

Tranae lifted her hand with her fingers splayed out. "Dealing involves," she said as she lowered a finger for every number she counted down, "not taking my calls." She lowered another finger. "Or Brian's. You locked down in this house." Finger three went down. "And avoiding the world as it goes on without you," she said, lowering finger four. "Is that you dealing?" Tranae slid to the edge of the chair and turned her body toward Cianne. "We've been friends for a long time, Cianne. I know you're hurting but you have to allow me to be here for you."

"I love you, Tranae," Cianne said. This time when she spoke she looked into Tranae's eyes. "But you can't help me with this."

"Because I'm not like your new friends," Tranae said with agitation. She sat back, narrowed her eyes, and twisted the corner of her mouth.

"Partly," she admitted. Cianne wouldn't allow another person she loved get hurt.

Locking herself away, with only her children for company, Cianne had time to go over everything that happened in the past two years. The common factor in all the tragedies was her. From the very beginning, if she told her mother about her headaches instead of lying so she could go on that stupid field trip... If she listened that day, none of this would have ever happened. Her life may not have been better, but Tristan would not have suffered because of her.

God, he may still be suffering...because of me.

Things were clearer to her now. With the Coesen was where she should have been from the start. They knew death followed her. They are better equipped to handle someone like her. She now understood why the Coesen kept their dealings at a minimum with Middlings. She couldn't allow any more casualties by association.

Bianca, Cook, Nick and his friends, and God knows how many others died because of her. No one else would suffer because of her, and the only way to make sure of that she needed to cut all ties with everyone she loved in the Middling world.

"But mostly because I don't want any help from you. I'm not the weak girl I was two years ago, Tranae. I don't need you to take care of me anymore." Cianne turned away from Tranae and looked to her bedroom door. She imagined the door opening, and it opened with ease.

I'm doing the right thing protecting them from me, from this new world that has consumed me.

With her mind set but her heart breaking, Cianne turned to face Tranae who looked concerned to the point of tears. "I don't need or want your sympathy." Cianne spoke with a calmness that chilled her own soul as she dug her nails into the arms of her chair. "What I do want is for you to leave. I would ask that you call first before dropping by again."

With an open mouth gape, Tranae tilted her head and stared at Cianne for a moment. When Cianne's facial expression didn't change, Tranae stood up. "Wow." She laughed cynically as she made for the bedroom door. Tranae stopped just before exiting.

Cianne felt Tranae's eyes on her back, and again she was pleased with the way the seating was positioned. If she looked into Tranae's face now, it would definitely stir up emotions she was trying so hard to suppress.

"I know that you are going through hell right now but that is no excuse to treat the people who love you like shit." Tranae paused, and Cianne knew that she was trying to shake off the anger before speaking again. Tranae exhaled. "I'm here, so I am going to spend some time with my god children. I can see myself out when I'm done."

When the door shut, Cianne let out a gasp. She felt sick to her stomach and wanted badly to go to the nursery and apologize to Tranae. Instead, she took a deep breath and solidified her resolve. This was how things had to be. Cianne took another deep breath then mentally swatted at her emotions.

After today, she told herself, *handling my emotions will come easier.*

She pulled her knees up to her chest and placed her feet on the edge of the seat cushion. She sat that way for what felt like an eternity before she again noticed her morning drink on the side table. It was a special mixture of fruits and natural ingredients that Vivian started making for her when she was pregnant.

Cianne loved the drink so much that she had one prepared for her every morning. It was said to relax a tense spirit. During her pregnancy, Cianne felt no benefit from the concoction. But now, after her morning glass she felt much more relaxed, almost serene even. She lifted the glass to her lips and drank.

When Cianne left her room later that morning, she looked down the hall to the nursery. Kim, one of three Protectors that currently resided on the property, stood outside the nursery door. Kim was tall, lean, and deadly, but with all her training and experience the mature Guard had a way with the children that Cianne couldn't deny.

If Kim was outside of the twins' room it meant that Tranae was still inside.

Kim gave Cianne a concerned look but didn't speak. Cianne lifted her hand slightly, signaling that everything was fine. She turned away from the direction of the nursery and descended the stairs. The plan: get something quick to eat then return to her room before anyone noticed her.

Inside the kitchen, Cianne went right to the refrigerator and scanned the shelves.

"Good Afternoon."

The voice sounded foreign, British maybe. Cianne went rigid and her grip tightened around the handle of the refrigerator.

Who is in my house?

Cianne looked over her shoulder to see the visitor. Whodai sat at her kitchen table looking so polished in his tailored gray suit and pale blue dress shirt that he looked out of place. Her mind immediately flashed with images of Tristan and how he too looked like a GQ model on a photo shoot no matter what he wore. She shook the thought of her husband out of her head before she blushed.

"Hello Whodai." Cianne grabbed a bottle of juice before closing the refrigerator door. Turning, she walked over to the table and took a seat across from him. "I'm having a not-so-good afternoon," she admitted.

"Anything I can do to help?" Whodai asked politely.

"I didn't know you were going to be here today." Cianne moved on to another subject. There was only one thing she needed. But no one seemed to be able to find Tristan as of yet.

"Cassius had some business to take care of so you get me for a few," Whodai smiled. The edges of Cianne's lips turned up slightly. "Afternoon getting better?" he asked.

"I guess it is."

Whodai had only been in her company a handful of times yet each time he made her smile.

"I've made you smile. I figure that's more than the cantankerous Cassius has ever gotten from you."

"Well," Cianne said coyly, then chuckled.

Whodai raised one of his brows causing his youthful skin to wrinkle on his forehead. "Foul mood minutes ago, now you're laughing."

"Well," Cianne said, drawing the word out, "it's your accent. Your British accent sounds kind of funny."

"Would you prefer I speak to you like this?" Whodai's British accent was gone. He now sounded as if he were born and raised in New York.

"Wow." She laughed. "I thought only actors could do that."

"It's a gift," Whodai boasted.

Cianne took in a breath and slowly exhaled, an attempt to get all the residual laughter out. "I prefer you to be yourself. Talk in your natural voice." Cianne opened her orange juice and took a sip. "Is that your ability, mimicking sounds?"

Whodai gave her a confused frown. "Tristan didn't tell you what my ability is?"

"No." She shrugged.

Whodai looked pensive then he lifted his glass. He realized it was empty so he sat it down in front of him. "My abilities are much like a Protector's. I have speed and strength."

"Imitating accents is just something you do for fun, then."

"Basically, though I like it when you smile so I'll be using my native brogue more. I enjoy when you give me a proper smile." Whodai held her eyes for moment before she looked down to the papers in front of him. He casually but quickly flipped the papers over.

He doesn't want me to see what he's doing. "What are you working on?" she asked.

Whodai sat up in the chair as if it were possible to sit any straighter. "I am reading over the investigation report I've prepared for Cassius."

"Tristan's case?" Cianne stared at him, watching his reaction. He didn't flinch or look away so she looked back to the papers.

"Yes."

She bit down on her lip then asked, "What does it say?"

"I could lie to save you from any more heartache but that would risk the friendship I feel is building between us, especially if you can Truth-see. So…" Whodai slid the report across the table to her.

Cianne read the report carefully before placing it back on the table and sliding it back to him. The report confirmed what she already knew. That Tristan's steering wheel was poisoned. That the poison undoubtedly entered his body and that a large amount of his blood was found ten weeks ago. It also stated that Whodai dedicated a large number of man hours searching the crash site and the surrounding desert for any clues as to where Tristan could be.

It concluded with Whodai's recommendations. He wrote that all evidence suggested that Tristan Patrick Bertram was indeed deceased, but he felt that the case should remain open and active at this time.

Whodai's gaze bore into hers. Without turning away, he said, "I'm sorry."

"For what?" she asked. She looked around him and out of the kitchen window. When he didn't reply, she asked, "Have you ever been in love, Whodai?"

Whodai's fingers flipped the corners of the paper up as he continued to stare at her, but she kept her focus on the birds that flew outside the window.

"There was someone," he said finally.

"What happened to her?"

"Well, for years I worked really hard to be the perfect man I felt she deserved. I trained and studied until I was unrivaled, just to prove to her I was worthy. But when I finally got the opportunity to tell her how I felt about her, it was too late. She found someone else."

Cianne thought about what Whodai told her. He devoted his life just to prove himself worthy of the woman he loved. *He might understand me.* "Does her being with someone else change how you feel about her?"

Whodai drew his brows in. He stared at her with such intensity that she almost looked away. *Was my question too personal? Did I cross a line?* Just when it occurred to her that he wasn't going to answer her, she heard him suck in a breath.

"No," Whodai admitted.

"So, you know that when you truly love someone that nothing or no one will ever change how you feel." She felt her eyes fill with tears but she held them at bay. Whodai nodded. "Until I have undeniable proof that he is dead, there is still hope."

"If you believe that," Whodai said, "then why have you barricaded the children and yourself in this tomb of a house? Why do you avoid your friends?"

"You're right," she admitted. "I shouldn't be barricading us in here and I have to work on that. But my friends are another matter completely. I don't want to endanger their lives more than I may already have. Chandra may have had something to do with Tristan's accident and if she did, no one I love is safe. Not to mention, Caleb is still out there somewhere plotting as we speak. I don't want anyone else I love hurt because of me."

"You've cut them off?" Whodai asked.

It sounded so harsh the way he said it. "That's the only way."

Whodai looked away, as if he was thinking. "Being a Coesen does present an issue when your friends are delicate Middlings. I agree with you, but speaking as someone who would like to be your friend, I have to say that you need to maintain a relationship with them, especially with Tristan's parents. They are your family and your children's grandparents."

He was right. She did have to have a relationship with Tristan's parents. When he returned, Tristan may not forgive her for shutting them out. But as for Tranae and Brian, she couldn't risk destroying them. "Maybe," she said.

Whodai smiled. "In the spirit of friendship and the fact that you have been a shut-in for weeks now, what do you say we take the children out for lunch, maybe to a park as well?"

"You've been working toward that offer this entire time, haven't you?" She smiled.

"My intentions were to get you out of the house for some fresh air but you supplied the ammunition. I believe the children have never been to the zoo. So, what do you say? We go to lunch, the zoo, and maybe you can call the Bertrams to see if I can drive you and the children by later. I'll guard the perimeter myself."

"You've got it all planned huh?"

"All I need is for you to say yes." Whodai smiled wide. As his full lips parted, his perfect white teeth glistened.

"Alright," Cianne said, giving in. "By the way," she said, "that Truth-see ability you mentioned earlier, it hasn't kicked in yet. But when it does…I'm going to find out who your mystery woman is."

Whodai shrugged then smiled. "I'll go prepare the vehicle."

Chapter Fourteen

Caleb realized that sounding threatening when speaking in a hushed tone over the phone wasn't coming off so well. He paced the floor of his bedroom with the edge of his cellular phone resting on his brow. Obviously, the urgency he was trying to convey wasn't being understood, or perhaps his not killing the good doctor after he treated Tristan in that hellhole of a motel almost three months ago was a mistake.

Things were much simpler when he only relied on himself and killed anyone in his way.

Damn it, he thought as he squeezed his eyes shut in frustration. One time. That is all it should take to get what he wanted. One chance for them to do it or die. The doctor needed to be reminded of who the hell he was dealing with.

Caleb took a deep breath then put the cellular device back to his ear. "Let me be clear here just in case you don't understand. There are only five people whose life I value above my own. One of them is in the other room. If you have any concern for your life or the Protector assigned to you, then you will tell the girl to get on U.S. 95 heading north. If I have to leave here to procure the new treatment Tristan needs, you can kiss both your ass' goodbye."

There was silence from the other end then Bannerman spoke. "What do I tell her?"

"She's a fucking soldier. Tell her nothing. Just give her the new injections and tell her to drive. I will find her." Bannerman was about to speak but Caleb cut him off. "You have two days for her to get to my checkpoint before I pay your old Protector a visit doctor." Caleb disconnected the call.

He placed the cellular in his pocket, opened his bedroom door, then walked out into the common area. He looked across the room and through a large picture window where Tristan sat on a lounger on the porch.

Caleb walked slowly toward the front door as he kept his eyes on the figure on the other side of the window. He stepped onto the porch and sat down on the chair next to the lounger. Caleb's eyes dropped to his feet. He moved his foot off of the blanket that was gathered on the porch. His gaze traveled from the blanket beside his foot to the top of the blanket that was secured just under Tristan's chin.

Caleb focused on Tristan's face. The kid looked bad. If it weren't for Caleb's exceptional hearing, he would think Tristan was a sitting corpse.

"I'm awake," Tristan said. He slowly opened his eyes and rubbed his head. His voice was barely audible.

Caleb turned his gaze to the tall trees that surrounded the cabin. The strong, healthy man Caleb knew Tristan to be was now a lethargic shell of himself. Just a few days ago, Tristan sat at the kitchenette and made a deal with him for his life story. Now, Death's Door was working fast to put him six feet under.

Thing was, whoever was behind the poisoning didn't consider that Tristan wasn't like other Coesens. Hell, he wasn't a Coesen at all but he was powered by the Halo, and because of that he was still alive.

Keeping him alive was the problem now. But Caleb had faith in the hybrid treatments Bannerman created, to do just that. It had to work or all of what he did would be for nothing.

"I didn't take you for the worrying type," Tristan said then grimaced. He tried to hold in the cough that followed but was unsuccessful.

It sounded as if he was hacking up a lung.

Caleb continued to watch the trees and the leaves as they gently swayed. When he turned to face Tristan, he made his face the way it always appeared, unreadable.

Tristan chuckled as their eyes met. As suddenly as his laughter began it stopped. Tristan's expression became serious and his mind seemed to wander. "I know you think you have to keep me here. But promise me if you can't stop the poison, that you won't let me die here. Promise me you'll take me home while I still remember who she is. I want to be with my wife and children when I take my last breath."

They both knew the injections were a temporary fix, and the length of his healthy time between them was growing shorter and shorter.

Caleb didn't respond. He just stared coldly back at Tristan then looked back at the trees. "Are you ready to go back inside?"

Tristan shook his head. "You're kidding, right? This is the first time you've let me sit out here to just relax, instead of drilling me with your fist." Tristan closed his eyes and let the breeze brush over his face.

He glanced at the entrance to the Cabin and shuddered. That's what he named the place because it was simply what it was–a three-room cabin with all the amenities of a modern home, only it was deep in a forest and Tristan had no idea where.

He had no way of escape and the poison was killing him. Tristan heard Caleb talking to someone the past few days. Apparently, the original formula of the injections wasn't working anymore. They lasted two weeks at first, now they didn't last two days. Soon they wouldn't work at all.

From what Tristan gathered, Caleb and whoever he was working with had come up with a new formula but the guy didn't want to use it yet. It was too raw, never been tested. From Caleb's responses, he didn't see a need to test it. He seemed confident it would work and he wanted the new formula injections as soon as possible.

One didn't have to be a genius to know why. Tristan was fighting for every breath he took; he could hardly keep his eyes open and was so sluggish he didn't want to move.

Depending on someone, especially Caleb—the man he hated—was against everything he was. He didn't hate the guy so much, now. Caleb was turning out to be quite interesting.

"How about you continue telling me your story?" Caleb started to protest but Tristan cut him off. "Your story and in return I let you train me…that was the deal. That is, unless you see no reason to keep such a deal; maybe you believe I won't be alive to train."

Caleb glared at him for a moment. "Remind me where I stopped," he gritted out.

"Your family just discovered that Jai was pregnant."

"Right," Caleb said. He extended his legs out in front of him. "My mother was very upset. You see, she didn't want Jai or Marda to know of men until they were more mature. Everyone knew my mother was partial to the girls. They were not to be touched.

"Jai refused to tell who she'd been with. Her silence outraged my father. He threatened to sell her if she didn't tell him. Although frightened, she still refused. In the end, my mother convinced my father that Jai was irreplaceable to her so he relented and allowed her to stay."

"That was human of him," Tristan said under his breath.

"It was a different time. I don't expect you to understand. Hell, I didn't and still don't, but it's the story you wanted to hear. So, listen and try not to judge." Caleb lifted one of his legs over the other and relaxed back. "That was also the year my brother was married. He courted Abigail Madison from

Holly Oak plantation since the day we returned home and stayed at that neighboring plantation.

"By this time, I lost my fascination with Maiden Hall. It was a beautiful and majestic place but it held no place in my heart. During my time there, my view of the place had been marred." He sighed. "My feelings for Marda had grown over the years even though I tried desperately to push them away. I needed to stay as far away from her and Maiden Hall.

"To do this, I frequented the city of Dominion. I called it the 'Hole' because I never really cared enough to refer to it by its proper name. It's known today as New Dominion, South Carolina. My father's uncle, Henry Scott, had a very lucrative shop in the bustling city. Uncle Henry had a daughter that married well. So, with no sons to take over the business for him, he expressed an interest in me learning the trade so that I could someday take ownership.

"My father had different plans for me, but after seeing how unhappy I'd been since coming home he agreed that I should be my uncle's apprentice. It was either allow me to apprentice or send me back to my mother's relatives in Europe. Mother didn't want me leaving the States again, thus agreeing to let me apprentice for my uncle.

"Life in Dominion was much more exciting than the plantation life. The ports allowed newcomers almost every week. The shops and different people kept me much busier than my carefree days at Maiden Hall. I learned quickly and liked the retail business. There was much more to do for my leisure in town which kept me from consuming myself with thoughts of Marda.

"Uncle Henry was into boxing. Watching two men fight in the center of a room for the first time was the most spectacular thing I had ever witnessed. From that day on, I was captivated with fist to cuffs. I went to the matches whenever I could and eventually I learned to pick the winners and place bets of my own.

"For months, I kept myself occupied with work and boxing. Marda entered my mind from time to time but I did my best to not dwell on her or her life at Maiden Hall, for there was no future for me there. I tried to convince myself that feeling anything for her was juvenile and I was a man now. I thought that as long as I stayed away, my feelings would dissolve.

"I managed to stay away from Maiden Hall for months before I was taken back against my will."

Maiden Hall Plantation
Caleb 18-Marda 16
Mid-July 1824

The door burst open with such force that the knob hit the wall hard enough to leave an impression. The door sprung back and hit Henry Scott in the elbow as he and young Fredrick carried Caleb's limp body into the room.

"What ails him?" Catherine asked. She hurried to the bedside.

"Do not get too close," Henry panted in his thick southern drawl. He was still catching his breath from carrying Caleb, but managed to pull Catherine away from her son.

Catherine pulled free of her brother-in-law and moved to her son's side. She struggled but managed to unbutton and push Caleb's top shirt off his chest. It was wet all the way through from water or perspiration.

"We know not what put Caleb under," Henry grunted. "Three days passed, the young sir was in good spirits before he was stricken down with fever." Henry backed away from the bed as he spoke. "The physician knows not what to make of it." He moved out of the room just beyond the doorway.

Fredrick moved aside when his father pushed by him and entered the room. Senior focused on his youngest son who was sprawled out on the bed then to his wife who looked up at him with glistening green eyes, pleading for him to do something.

"I encouraged his cause, Senior," Catherine sobbed to her husband, "It was I who rallied for him to reside in Dominion in an attempt to keep him satisfied."

"I warned you that no good would come of it, Catherine," Fredrick Sr. said as he shook his head. Senior looked over his shoulder. His eyes found his eldest son first. Young Fredrick's expression was full of worry as he peered at Caleb. Next, Senior pinned his brother, who stood outside of the room, with a hard gaze. Fredrick Sr. went to his brother.

Young Fredrick followed his father. The three men talked in hushed urgent voices as they passed Tempie on the stairs, neither of them noticing that they had narrowly missed knocking the pitcher of warm water from her hands as she rushed to Caleb's room.

When Tempie entered the room, Catherine was fighting to remove the rest of Caleb's clothes. "Let me do that, Missus," Tempie said. The plump old slave took his clothes off in a matter of minutes once his mother moved aside. Tempie pulled the thin sheeting she placed over him for privacy down as she wiped him down with lukewarm water.

When Fredrick Sr. returned, Catherine was pacing the floor. She looked to him, anxiously waiting for him to fill her in.

"The physician will arrive in the morn." Fredrick Sr. said as he walked toward his young wife. Catherine looked aghast then spun away from him. "I…," Fredrick Sr. started to say but stopped. He stalked over to one of the far walls and leaned on it.

Catherine walked over to the other side of the bed, sat down in the chair Tempie retrieved from under Caleb's writing desk, and took Caleb's hand in hers. They waited.

"Missus Catherine," Tempie said in a hushed voice. "Missus Catherine." Tempie touched Catherine gently on the shoulder.

Catherine shifted in the chair before slowly opening her eyes. Her body was stiff but she managed to sit up in the chair without groaning. Her face scrunched up as she looked around the room before getting to her feet. "Have I slept long?"

"Not long, Missus," Tempie answered. "Doc's already done. He say ain't nothin' more he can do. He say it's up to the young master." Tempie's head hung as she walked over to the table and sat down the tray she carried.

"Who sits with him?" Catherine asked. She smoothed her hand over her stomach as she looked out of the library window to the cottage that sat a good distance behind it.

"Young master Fredrick, Missus" The tea pot made a low chime as Tempie touched the pot to the tea cup when she poured. "I'll prepare you some meat, Missus."

"No Tempie." Catherine pushed to her feet and exited the library doors. She walked across the back lawn toward the cottage where Caleb was moved two days earlier, before Tempie could say another word. She didn't like the idea of moving her son to the tiny bare dwelling she and Senior occupied during the construction of the main house. But Caleb's illness had gotten much worse and the town physician abandoned him, fearing Caleb was contagious.

Senior rode out, searching for another physician the day before.

The high fever was now paired with his loud screams and cries of agony. Cries that suggested a man was being tortured. When Caleb wasn't screaming, at those moments when he was aware, he mumbled unintelligible words. The past few days were hell at Maiden Hall and it seemed the upcoming days weren't going to be any better.

No one believed that Caleb would survive whatever ailed him. Her son had only seen eighteen winters. He was a man to society, but to her he was just a boy.

Catherine stopped in her tracks to take a needed breath. She rubbed her forehead with a shaky hand as she continued across the green. Fatigue and grief were taking a toll on the young and beautiful Lady Scott. After just a few hours of her fumbling with limited knowledge of caring for the ill, she surely thought she would go insane. Most of all, Catherine feared what she would become if she lost the son she loved so dearly.

She took her son's illness the hardest and now with hope scarce she couldn't bring herself to look upon him in the state he was in. She refused to see him suffer. Unable to listen to his tortured cries, she kept her distance and relied on reports to know of his well-being.

Stopping again, Catherine placed her a hand over her mouth and the other over her stomach. She couldn't bear to see him in his worsened state. She cried as she turned, and slowly walked back to the main house. She wasn't strong enough.

"Fetch Jai for me, Tempie," Catherine ordered as she entered the library. When Tempie scampered off, she sat down by the window once again. Her eyes blurred as tears ran from her eyes. Catherine needed help with Caleb's care and only one person was brave enough to volunteer.

"Missus, she here," Tempie announced as she stood in the doorway a few minutes later.

Catherine turned her head around slowly to see Jai beside Tempie, her head low. Catherine avoided looking directly at Jai's stomach. She made an effort to avoid looking at the beautiful young woman's stomach since discovering she was with child.

"Jai…" Catherine started but faltered.

"I'll care for him, Missus. Like my own," Jai assured her.

"I know you will, Jai," Catherine sighed. She couldn't help looking to Jai's distended stomach.

Catherine absorbed the little hump where there previously was none. Tears rolled down her eyes and fell to her pale purple laced dress. The usual questions barged their way into her mind.

Is it possible that Senior's babe grows inside Jai's belly?

Is it my husband's shame or that of one of one of my son's?

It was common for white men to use slaves for their pleasure, especially one as comely as Jai. Only, no woman of class would openly speak of it.

Was she doing the right thing by allowing Jai to take care of Caleb in her state? If she lost her youngest…

Catherine shook her head but struggled to get the words she wanted to say out. She sobbed as she lowered her eyes. "I cannot allow you to do it," she said.

What if the babe is Caleb's?

If she allowed Jai to care for Caleb, surely, she could be sending the woman and her unborn babe to their deaths, and she would not risk his only offspring if the three of them should succumb to this illness.

Jai walked to Catherine's side and kneeled on the floor beside her leg. "I will care for him Missus, just as you have with me and Marda. I will be fine."

Catherine sighed. There was no one else she trusted more, and all the other slaves were scared to go near Caleb. She heard whispered talk of devils and demons. Some of the slaves spoke that Caleb was paying for the sins of the Scott family. Some, like her, wondered if one of the Scott men was responsible for Jai's abuse and condition. Others whispered talk that God struck the treasured youngest son down for his father's lust of coin and for turning a blind eye to an abusive overseer.

Catherine didn't know why she was being punished. All she could do was pray.

"Thank you," Catherine said as she closed her eyes and let out a deep sigh.

Jai quickly gathered some needed items then hurried to the cottage. She tapped on the door twice before Fredrick opened it. He immediately replaced his surprise with a look of resolve as he stepped aside to allow her entry.

"Mother has decided, then?" Fredrick asked as he pinned her with his stern gaze.

Jai looked at him and nodded, then nervously blinked a few times but didn't look away. Fredrick nodded with a resolved grunt. He looked to her stomach, and for a moment Jai noticed how uncomfortable he was.

He cleared his throat then said, "You are not to leave him alone."

She nodded.

"Be comforted that no one will bother you here." Fredrick eyed her belly again but turned away and walked over to the single bed in the cottage. He stood over his brother for a short while then Fredrick walked to the door and left without another word.

Jai placed her things near the far wall of the cottage where someone made a pallet of bedding on the floor. She then went to Caleb, knowing the cause of his condition when she first overheard the women in the kitchen talking about it. That night she tried to see him but the Scotts never left his side. It wasn't until the slaves got to spreading fear around the plantation that she figured she'd get the opportunity to see him.

Jai got to her knees so that she was able to speak into Caleb's ear. "Caleb, focus on my voice," Jai whispered. There would be no calling him master anymore. Not when they were alone, that is.

Caleb didn't move or let her know that he heard her.

"I know you can hear me, Caleb. I have come to help you manage the pain. All you need to do is think of something that makes you happy. I will do the rest."

Pain is unavoidable and necessary to exist. It reminds us that we're still alive. Depending on the recipient, the cause, and degree of pain one can bear, varies greatly. A person will do anything to stop it when they are subjected to pain but after it's over; do you really remember how dreadful it felt? Can

*you accurately describe what you were feeling? Or does the mind protect us from ever really remembering? – **Lost Journals of Caleb Scott***

Marda listened. The main house was quiet. It was dark out and everyone was usually asleep at this time of night. Master Scott was still reading an hour ago but he was surely asleep now. Marda knew he was exhausted.

Mistress Catherine was who she worried about. The Mistress was unable to sleep the past couple of weeks, but since Caleb made a turn for the better, Mistress Catherine slept the entire night last eve.

Marda suspected the Mistress would do the same tonight.

She took small careful steps. The kitchen wasn't as easy to sneak out of, but since the Mistress discovered Jai was with young, she demanded they sleep in the kitchen instead of the cellar. The Mistress didn't understand. If a white man wanted them…he'd find a way.

Marda stilled when the wood floor creaked under her bare foot. She spared a glance at Tempie, then looked at Jai. Tempie, who slept beside the door that led outside, was still sound asleep. Jai wasn't a concern either, being as she wore herself out helping young Master Caleb. The only reason Jai was even inside the main house was because the Mistress ordered her to retire from his side for a spell.

Jai wasn't going to wake.

Marda forced herself to slow, but her excitement was overwhelming. For the second eve, she was going for a swim in the lake that separated the Holly Oaks Plantation from Maiden Hall Plantation. She hadn't been able to sneak out for so long that anticipation rippled through her.

Walking barefoot through the grass, Marda followed her usual path. A swim was what she needed. Her body and mind were pushed to their limits with not only chores, but because she had Manifested. According to Jai, when some Coesen came of age a gift was bestowed to them. These select Coesen acquired the ability to do magnificent things. Some beautiful, some dangerous.

Marda's ability was more one of beauty than of harm but she prized it all the same. Even if she had the skill, she didn't think herself capable of wielding harm to her captors for their wrongdoings toward her and her countrymen. To loathe but not desire to harm, it was that odd sentiment that muddled Marda's mind. Nevertheless, Jai was dedicated to helping Marda master her new ability.

Gaining understanding of her ability was cumbersome in a place like this. Where they were from, Jai said people used their unique gifts openly. But she couldn't allow anyone to discover her ability or she'd surely be hanged.

A hint of fear slithered up Marda's spine as she continued along the moonlit path, her footfalls sure. She pushed aside her fears and tried to conjure happy thoughts, but when her fears weren't plaguing her, images of Caleb crept into her mind. Marda felt indifferent to the pale people who called themselves whites, except for Mistress Catherine whom she cared for dearly. So, it confused her why Caleb was often on her mind.

When he left for Dominion, she felt offended as if it was an affront to her. Why feel this way for a man who mattered not? But for whatever reason, the thought of him had her so twisted up inside it made her days fitful. That was more than enough reason to go for a swim. Besides, it was her sixteenth year and swimming in the lake was the annual gift she awarded herself. No matter that she swam last eve as well.

Marda smiled as she undressed under the cover of night then took care to step over the pebbled beach. She never considered that she might have an audience.

Shaw waited with an anxious smile as the nigger unclothed and walked into the water. She was beautiful and untouched, a perfect morsel for his appetite. His body went rigid with anticipation, his penis already stiff.

Earlier this afternoon, Shaw overheard a slave speaking to another. He often hid when encountering the animals, to foil plans of rebellion, but neither spoke of such. What they spoke of was much better than running down a nigger to whip. They spoke of the beautiful mute house girl who never left the manor long enough to court. One of them saw her last eve, walking alone near the lake.

They spoke of going this eve to encounter the girl, but Shaw came out of hiding. He beat both of them good, so that the two would never think of nearing the house, the lake, or his mute little whore again. He waited too damn long to get his hands on the one they called Marda. Since he chose her and Jai to purchase, he'd been biding his time.

Now was his chance.

He stayed himself, waiting quiet-like, as she swam. Shaw watched her limbs move naturally in the water like she swam on the regular. When she rose above the water and her round breasts glistened in the moonlight, he licked his lips. The urgency inside him burned to the surface. Shaw could wait no longer.

"Hey gal," he said, stepping out from behind a great oak.

Fredrick raised his heavy head and tried to focus on his mother's words. She spoke again but he only frowned as his shoulder rocked to and fro.

"Where's Caleb?" Catherine asked a fourth time as she shook her son awake.

Caleb?

Fredrick wasn't fully able to process everything in his drowsy state but he heard her say "Caleb" loud and clear. He looked around her and gazed at the empty bed and the sheets that were in a pile on the floor.

"He was here asleep," he said. He couldn't hide the lift in his tone that signaled his surprise. Fredrick hurried over to the door and looked out into the night. When he looked down he noticed the grass was flattened with footfalls.

"We must find him," Catherine urged.

Fredrick knew his mother was frantic with worry. She waited for the physician to announce that Caleb was out of danger before she even ventured out to the cottage for a brief stay. It was obvious she feared he would regress, but she remained in high spirits. She limited her visits to nights, when Caleb rested.

"He is not sturdy enough to be out of bed. He will harm himself."

"I will find him, Mother," Fredrick said, looking over his shoulder at his mother. She was visibly beside herself, her wide expressive eyes filled with worry.

Fredrick grabbed a bronze candlestick then stepped out of the cottage onto a crushed area of grass. His mother followed close behind. He lowered the light and followed the impressions Caleb left behind. Some of the grass just had foot impressions but there were also sections that looked as if Caleb lost his balance and fell, then possibly dragged himself further.

A loud grunt and the curse that followed startled them.

"Stay close," Fredrick ordered as he took his mother's arm. He cursed himself for not bringing a weapon, but he found comfort in the weight of the candlestick.

The two moved quicker in the direction of the noise which happened to be the same direction Caleb's path led. As they moved closer, Fredrick made out figures on the ground in the distance. He handed his mother the candlestick and sprinted the rest of the distance. His fear rose when he saw that one of the still figures was his younger brother.

"Caleb!" Fredrick yelled. He ran faster, choking on the air he inhaled.

His urgency wasn't for Caleb now as he came to a stop a short distance from the scene but close enough that he could make out details. Beside the dirt and rocks of the water's edge, lying still was the naked figure of a colored girl he would later know to be Marda. Beside her, on his knees and partially unclothed was Shaw, a severe individual who was more beast than man in Fredrick's estimation. Standing behind a wide-eyed and visibly frightened Shaw, was Caleb with a fist full of the overseer's stringy blond hair.

"Caleb?" Fredrick called out to his brother again.

"Please…" Shaw's voice shook but he said no more when Caleb tightened his grip.

What ensued next was unbelievable, and Fredrick wouldn't have believed it if he didn't see it with his own eyes. Caleb regarded him and their mother, who just then reached Fredrick's side, with glassy vacant blue-green eyes. Fredrick saw no recognition in his brother's eyes. Caleb turned his attention back to a wriggling Shaw. Fredrick heard his mother gasp but he didn't take his eyes off his brother.

"CALEB!" Fredrick tried once more to get through to him.

With Frederick and their mother as the only witnesses, Caleb let go of Shaw's hair and pushed him hard to the ground, face down. He then straddled Shaw, dropping to his knees. Caleb placed his right knee in the middle of Shaw's back then pulled the man's head back with a sudden jerk. The sound of bone snapping split the air. Catherine screamed but it was too late. Shaw's body fell to the dirt.

Caleb stood, his handsome face blank. He took five steps toward the naked figure a few feet away then dropped to the ground like a sack of potatoes.

Catherine listened just outside the doorway to her husband's study. One hand covered her mouth to keep herself as silent as possible. She inched closer as the conversation changed to Shaw's whereabouts.

"Have you located him?" Mr. Scott's voice was powerful and abrupt.

"No sir, Mr. Scott." David Abernathy winced.

Catherine imagined David shifting from one foot to the other the way he often did when talking to her husband.

David sighed then said, "He most likely liquored out and resting beneath some oak…sir."

"Some of the men think he gone after his Missus, sir. Seems she gathered up her young and their belongings and took passage to the north. Here tell it, she has family in those parts."

Catherine wasn't certain, but the man who now spoke could be Walter Hutchings. He was a fresh hire. He wasn't predisposed to keeping his thoughts hidden like the other men her husband hired on. She liked that.

"Shaw left for a visit with his relatives? He made no such plans with me," her husband said.

Walter cleared his throat. "My Missus says Shaw's wife left him. Seems she had a notion he was finding pleasure with some of the colored girls on the property. Even may have spawned a few young."

Catherine winced. She knew what Walter said was true from the scene of last eve. Her anger rose but she bit her lip not to burst inside her husband's office and confess what she knew. Not because she wanted Shaw found, but because her husband should know the scoundrel he hired on. What Catherine did instead was calm her anger. She didn't care what her husband thought now, as long as he didn't discover the truth of what really happened to the overseer.

She was the one who kept her head last night. She ordered Frederick to fetch Tempie and Jai while she stayed with her unconscious son. When the three returned, Catherine told

Fredrick to take Caleb back to the cottage before returning with a horse drawn wagon and a couple of shovels.

Catherine covered Marda with the blanket Fredrick asked Tempie to bring, then Jai and Tempie carried the unconscious girl back to the house. The two women were sworn to secrecy, and for the first time in her life Catherine threatened her slaves with violence if either of them ever spoke a word of what they did and what she planned to do.

Catherine assisted Fredrick as much as she could with loading Shaw's body into the wagon. She silently prayed to her Lord as she sat soundless beside her son as they rode deep into the forest. They buried that horrid man, leaving no markers for the grave.

"Where did Abigail get off to?" Catherine asked as she entered the cottage. She snuck off before the men finished inside the study but had not run into her daughter by marriage the entire morn.

Fredrick looked up at her. His face was two shades whiter and lined with worry. "I told her to spend a few days with her mother."

"Fredrick," Catherine said, touching her son's face and looking into his eyes, "we can't act any different." He blinked. She saw the worry in his eyes. "Everything is going to be just fine as long as we keep quiet."

"Our telling isn't what worries me mother."

"Jai nor Tempie will speak a word to anyone, I can assure you," she said quickly.

Fredrick shook his head. "I know they are loyal, mother. I need no persuasion to that fact," he said, then looked at Caleb. "You didn't see how empty his eyes were, nothing was there. What if Shaw wasn't the first?"

"Don't be daft, Fredrick. Your brother is not the wicked sort. He seems on the mend, but he is still unwell. Once on his feet, he will be his old self," she said confidently.

"He broke a man's neck with such ease, mother." Fredrick stood. "As if it were as easy as taking a breath. I know of none strong enough for that task, do you?" He grabbed his mother by the arms and looked at Caleb then to her. "I fear for your safety if he were to wake."

Catherine's lips stretched thin. "The fever caused him to have a touch of madness. Sometimes the madness can give people strength or cause them to act out of their heads, but it is over. Caleb will be himself again." Her English drawl was stronger with anger behind it. "Shaw wasn't a man of quality and I will not have my son punished for one such as him."

Fredrick let her arms free. "Shaw was not a kind man," he whispered, more to himself than to her. "One would only need to witness how the man handled the slaves."

"You have no need to fear your brother. He will be fine once the fever passes."

Fredrick nodded in agreement. He slumped back down on the chair at the end of Caleb's bed. "How is the girl?"

"She is bruised but it seems Shaw didn't have time to ruin her."

"You mean like he did with Jai." Fredrick winced; regret masked his face.

He avoided Catherine's astonished gaze. "He was the one who sired the babe she carries?"

"Abigail says that is why Mrs. Shaw went north. She discovered the truth of the matter. I should have advised you of this sooner but..." He lowered his head, letting his explanation fade out.

Eventually she looked away, realizing his discomfort. She walked over to Caleb and laid her hand on his forehead.

Fredrick sighed. "Does the girl recall what happened?"

"She remembers biting Shaw but remembers nothing after he hit her across the face." She sat on the bed next to Caleb. "I see no need to tell Caleb what happened." He slept peacefully as she rubbed his wet hair from his face. "Everything will be fine, Fredrick. All we have to do is take care of Caleb," she whispered lovingly.

"Yes mother," Fredrick said quietly.

Catherine looked at Fredrick who looked deep in thought. He opened his mouth but closed it. Soon after, Fredrick's worried gaze turned to what she knew was pride, as he looked upon his sleeping brother.

Chapter Fifteen

Caleb sighed. "My mother and brother kept my murderous act a secret for a long time, even from me." For two days Caleb told his story in full detail to a weak but alert Tristan in intervals. But the kid needed to rest now so Caleb got up from the chair and helped Tristan to his feet. He wrapped Tristan's arm around his neck, supporting most of Tristan's weight, then walked toward the bedroom. He helped Tristan to the bed then went to stand by the door.

Tristan took a deep breath before speaking. "You were Marda's Protector," he said.

Caleb agreed with a nod of his head.

With awe written plain on his face, Tristan asked, "How did you do it? How did you move in the last cycle? From what I've read, it is virtually impossible to stand let alone do what you did."

"All I know is that when you hear the cries of someone you love, who also happens to be under your protection...but I suppose you know how that feels." Caleb winked. "Fredrick eventually told me that I most likely crawled the last few feet to Marda and Shaw." Caleb turned toward the door. "I have to make a run. I'll be back before morning."

"Wait," Tristan said, "you never told me what Jai's ability was."

Caleb tilted his head, "You're really interested, aren't you?"

"Your life's story is my only entertainment," Tristan said as he caught his breath. He took in a deep breath then an onslaught of coughing commenced.

Caleb moved to his side with tissue in a flash, covering Tristan's mouth. He moved so fast from the doorway, to the bathroom, then to Tristan's side that he knew Tristan's eyes didn't even track the movements. When Caleb removed the tissue, dark red blood was soaked through it.

Tristan looked at the speckles of blood that hit his robe and sheets. He sighed.

Caleb wiped Tristan's face clean with a gentleness he didn't think himself capable, then helped him to lie back on the bed.

You are cold, heartless, removed. This is only a job. Keep the boy alive, make your daughter's life a happy one. That was all. He couldn't afford to get attached.

Already, Caleb lost his patience with Dr. Bannerman and that wasn't like him. He would do his best to keep the boy alive. That's all he could do. Caring for him was not a job requirement.

With his new resolve, Caleb made sure Tristan was comfortable before he spoke, "Jai was what The Coesen calls a Fantom. She, and others like her, can create illusions, dreams or mirages in a person's mind. Some Fantoms are so strong that they can blur the lines between reality and illusion. Once, I watched Shaw whip a field slave on the block for attempting to run away. That slave didn't so much as flinch during the harsh punishment. He didn't make a sound, but ended up dying tied to the post that day. That man died with a smile on his face.

"Like all the slaves on the plantation, Jai was ordered to watch. She later told me that she asked the slave's permission to help. With the slave's acceptance, she made it so his mind was somewhere else. He died happier than he had ever been in his life."

Tristan frowned. "But he died."

"I asked Jai once if she thought that taking his mind wherever she took it attributed to his death. She told me that death was his freedom and that's what he wanted, his freedom." Caleb walked toward the door. Without turning back, he said, "I don't think dying would be so bad."

A few hours later, Caleb pulled his truck behind an SUV on the highway. He reached over to his passenger seat, picked up the portable flashing police light he owned, and placed it on the roof of his truck. Half a minute later, the SUV pulled off the road.

Caleb got out of his vehicle with a flashlight in hand. He turned the flashlight on and pointed it at the driver's side mirror as he walked up, causing a bright glare to make it hard for the driver to see his face reflected in it.

"Do you know how fast you were going?" he asked.

"I wasn't speeding." Zeta said with confidence.

She squinted as he shined the light in her face. After a second or so, he moved the light and she saw it was him. But Caleb gave her no time to react. He raised his hand. Her eyelids instantly lowered and she slumped down in the driver's seat of her vehicle.

Zeta came to, slumped over on a sofa in a place she didn't recognize.

Caleb!

Inside she panicked but her face only reflected a perfected calm.

Never show fear, never show pain. Those were the first lessons of the Royal Guard training.

She sat up and looked around the room slowly until her gaze landed on her abductor. As soon as their eyes met, Caleb raised his hand. Against her will, Zeta felt her body rise from the sofa. Her breathing quickened and fear beat at her head as her stiff body levitated a few inches from the floor and moved toward him. Unable to speak no matter how hard she tried, Zeta realized she could do nothing to protect herself.

When she was close enough to him, about arm's length, Caleb led the way to a closed door. With care, Caleb quietly opened the door then backed away so Zeta was able to see inside. The only reaction her body would allow was the sudden widening of her eyes. Then, all too fast, Caleb eased the door shut, ignoring her mental cries she knew he heard to let her free. Her body floated away from the door and she was placed on the sofa again.

Zeta sat on that sofa, frozen and unable to speak. She felt alone in the silent prison of her mind, knowing what no one else but her and the psychopath who abducted her knew.

"Your reaction in the next thirty seconds will determine if you live. Do you understand?" Caleb asked Zeta, breaking an hour-long silence.

Zeta felt a mysterious pressure lift from her head. When Caleb looked at her expectantly, she realized she could move, but only her head. Zeta nodded yes, indicating that she understood.

Caleb nodded.

With that simple action, Zeta had full control of her body again. But she didn't move. She just sat there with her eyes locked on her abductor.

After a minute of him staring at her as if he was reading a set of instructions, he spoke. "On the table in front of you is the case Bannerman gave you. Have you let the case leave your sight at any time before I stopped you?"

Zeta shook her head from side to side.

"Good," Caleb said as he stood. "Would you lead the way please?" Caleb motioned toward the room Tristan was in. He picked up the case from the coffee table and followed her.

Inside the room, Zeta stood against the wall while Caleb injected Tristan with one of the syringes that was inside the case. When the needle punctured his arm, Tristan opened his eyes and stared at Caleb.

"What day is it?" Tristan asked. He seemed to have some difficulty keeping his eyes open.

"It's the ninth, middle of the night."

Why did Caleb lie to him, she asked herself? It was the middle of the night but it was August 10th. Tristan must have slept two full days but Caleb obviously didn't want him to know that.

"These new injections are going to make you feel much better but you need to rest."

Caleb's voice sounded unusually soft and caring. Every time Zeta heard him speak before, it was always imposing and rough. She frowned but said nothing as she watched Tristan's eyes close and his head fall to the side.

"What's wrong with him?" Zeta asked. She wasn't able to keep her native French accent from infusing itself into her speech due to her confusion and worry. She spun the glass in front of her in slow circles as she tried to avoid making eye contact with Caleb.

"He was poisoned by someone in your camp, remember," Caleb told her as he leaned back on the countertop with his arms crossed over his chest.

She looked up and met his gaze. "My camp? How is he still alive?"

"I've been keeping him alive," Caleb said. "I killed the two who carried out the orders but I am still looking for the one who gave them."

"Impossible. Besides, there were no deaths reported in this region at that time, let alone two." Zeta rolled her eyes. "I am a member of the Royal Guard. I would have been informed of any deaths that close to the Royal family."

"None of this is sinking in for you, is it? People in your organization already killed your sovereign, and now they want Tristan dead. Now, one person may be responsible or it may be two or more separate factions that want the same results. I don't know yet. What I do know is the Coesen are virtually leaderless. Now would be the time for someone to step up and claim the crown. There are bound to be a few Coesen who aren't as…loyal as you are."

"We all presumed Tristan was dead for the past three months but you saved him and have kept him alive," Zeta said, but she was basically thinking out loud. *Why? Maybe Caleb is right.* "If we don't know who it is giving the orders then he will never be safe."

"I brought him here to keep him alive and to find the person responsible. For Vivian's death and the failed attempt on Tristan's life."

"But you're keeping him from his children, from Cianne." Zeta stared at him with fresh anger.

I gave up. I told her he was dead.

"Cianne never stopped believing." Zeta looked away. She was angrier with herself than she was with Caleb. After a few moments of silence, she said, "You know I have to report this to my superiors." She frowned, then added, "You knew I would…you planned to kill me to keep your secret this whole time, didn't you?"

"I was hoping I wouldn't have to," Caleb said as he pulled a small object from his pocket and held it out in front of her.

Zeta stood, pushing her chair back. "How did you get that?" She gasped as she reached for the necklace. Before she touched it, she stepped back and covered her mouth.

"You know it cannot be taken. It has to be freely given, and not under duress or persuasion," he said, reminding her.

Chapter Sixteen

Missing 3.5 months.

It was a peaceful brightly lit summer day. A large yellow and red checkered blanket lay over the lawn with a brown open rattan basket on top, displaying some of its contents. A few plastic containers, silverware, some bread, and two of four wine glasses were still inside the picnic basket. A bottle of wine sat on a cutting board next to the basket with two full glasses, and a spread of various cheeses and grapes lay untouched.

Cianne sat on the blanket with her legs out to the side, leaning most of her weight on one arm. She focused on the basket as she wondered how she got to this place—outside and on a picnic.

"Wine?"

Cianne, somewhat startled, closed her eyes and placed a hand over her chest. She attempted to calm herself as she processed the familiarity of his voice. She knew it intimately and his tone always pulled at her heart, but there was something different about it, something foreign.

She opened her eyes, and when her eyes met Tristan's she instantly squeezed them closed again.

"If you'd rather have water," he said with a smile. Positioned on his knees, Tristan rummaged through the basket, pulled out a bottle of water, and placed it within her reach. He reached inside the basket again and took out a

container filled with salad. "You alright?" he asked. His concerned tone made her chest ache with every beat.

It is him. It is Tristan.

Cianne pried her eyes open and allowed herself to study him. As he placed the container on the blanket he frowned at her. It was more than three months since she last saw his face, his smile, the body she longed to feel against hers.

"Cianne?" he asked, brows still wrinkled.

Her gaze jolted back to his, "I'm fine," she rushed out.

He smiled then went about placing food on their plates. Only it wasn't "her smile". It was different...odd, but did it matter?

"You're here," Cianne breathed.

Tristan's brows wrinkled. "Uh," he said as he stopped what he was doing, "where else would I be sweetheart?"

Sweetheart? Had he ever called her sweetheart? Oh stop, she scolded herself. "You haven't been here for so long," she whimpered.

Clearly softened by Cianne's tears, Tristan went to her. He pulled her with minimal resistance into a tight embrace. "I've never really left you, not really. Now is the time to be strong Cianne," he said in her ear. "Please, be strong."

Closely, they held each other until Cianne moved her head up to look at him. She pulled back abruptly, falling back onto the blanket. She kicked away from him as she screamed hysterically.

Tristan's hair changed in front of her eyes, along with the rest of his features as he reached out to her. His eyes, a calm blue, transformed to her own blue-green. His nose became more aristocratic, long. She watched in horror as Tristan transformed into Caleb.

Cianne pushed her feet out to gain some distance, but Caleb was fast and had her pinned to the ground in no time. He raised one of his hands high. The sun's light reflected off the double edge hunting knife he held in it.

As Cianne screamed, Caleb brought down his hand, forcing the sharp blade into her chest.
"Be strong." ...was all she heard.

Whodai took each step with restrained yet cautious excitement as he climbed to the second floor. When he reached the top of the stairs, he moved to Cianne's bedroom with caution. He knew that she wasn't sleeping well and he didn't want her to catch him if she was awake. But the sound of a male voice coming from her bedroom urged him to move faster.

Concerned, jealous, and a bit anger…Whodai was at her door in a flash, peeking through the small opening, unseen with a clear view.

"Soahn, wake up." Felix placed his hand on Cianne's shoulder and gave her a gentle shake.

Whodai bristled at Felix's audacity to touch her but said nothing to announce his presence. He even managed to stay quiet as he witnessed Felix face paled as he stumbled away from Cianne, who popped her eyes open. Whodai almost retreated himself. Not due to fear, but shock.

Her eyes were completely blood red.

Felix, a seasoned Protector, tried to dart away. His eyes even met Whodai's but before he could say anything, Cianne sat up on the bed and Felix was yanked back by some invisible force. Felix thrashed and kicked, knocking over a vase that sat on a high table with his foot as he clawed desperately at his neck.

He can't breathe, Whodai thought as he watched as Cianne seemed to regard Felix for a few seconds. Her vacant eyes stared at the Guard without compassion. When she tilted her head, Whodai sheard the snap of Felix's neck then a thud as his body fell limp to the floor.

The sight prompted Whodai forward and into the room. He only managed four steps before being forced to his knees.

"Cianne," Whodai strained her name out. He tried to stand but realized his body was no longer under his control. "Release me now."

Cianne turned to face him. Her eyes were still red, her expression blank yet devastatingly beautiful.

Whodai stifled his desires and focused on surviving. "**Release me**," he commanded. What he didn't expect was how easily Cianne ignored his demand. Not only did she ignore his demand, it must have agitated her because her response was instant and excruciating. Whodai gritted his teeth because he was unable to scream. It felt as if he was being squeezed, or his skin was shrinking, crushing him in the process.

He fixed his eyes on hers, silently pleading with Cianne but she looked at him like he was of no importance, a lower being, something she wanted to see die slowly.

Dying was exactly what he was doing. In the haze of near unconsciousness, Whodai heard a faint, fading sound. His eyes fluttered to the baby monitor that sat on her nightstand.

One of the children was stirring, possibly waking. Whatever the case, Cianne's attention turned to the monitor. With his vision waning and death clawing at his soul, he was shocked to find himself suddenly flat on his back sucking in oxygen.

Cianne's attention strayed from him entirely as she slowly walked by his sprawled-out body, seeming to forget or care that he was even there.

Minutes passed as Whodai lay on the floor, choking and gasping. No one dropped him on his ass in a very long time. His body never felt the pain he just endured. But aside from that, he was intrigued by the show of power that Cianne just displayed without lifting a finger or saying a single word.

When he was able to move, Whodai struggled to his hands and knees. He stayed like that for a moment before getting to his feet. He stumbled through the empty hallway, comforted by the fact that it was still night and everyone other than the Royal Guards who watched the perimeter was asleep.

The nursery door was closed so Whodai pushed it open as he leaned on the door frame for support. Cianne was sitting in a glider with Aidan snuggled in her arms, rocking steadily. Her eyes were once again their glorious green-blue hue and her lips curved up into a worrisome smile when she saw him.

"Is everything alright?"

Cianne wiped the tears from her eyes and turned her head a bit so that her profile could be seen. "Yes, Eleanor?" She hoped she didn't sound as impatient to her children's caretaker as she sounded to herself.

"Mrs. Bertram to see you, Soahn," Eleanor said, sounding nervous.

Anyone would be nervous under the circumstances. Eleanor was a Coesen, though she was one with a latent gene who had no abilities, seeing the lifeless body of a person she worked with was still jarring. But, Cianne assumed that when Langley offered the woman the position he explained that working for a Soahn would be more complicated than working for some of her usual employers.

Eleanor gave Cianne a sympathetic nod, then lowered her head. She didn't move right away. She just raised her head and stood still for a moment, looking at Cianne.

"Yes."

"Thank you for allowing me to stay on, Ma'am."

After she was told of the murder, Cianne dismissed most of the staff aside from a small group of Royal Guards. Eleanor was quite attached to the children and Cianne knew she would miss them dearly, having none of her own as it were.

Cianne nodded.

Eleanor seemed to want to say something else but bit back her words and blushed. She turned on her heels and headed toward the entry but Nadia caught her attention.

Using a push toy, Nadia pulled herself up to a standing position. The ten-month-old pivoted her body to face Eleanor while letting go of the chair. Holding both arms out wide, Nadia took one step toward her before falling on her bottom.

Cianne could see that Eleanor wanted to pick Nadia up before the tears started. But instead of crying, Nadia's painful frown turned to a look of confusion. Nadia turned her head toward Aidan, and instead of crying like she often did, she crawled over to where her twin was playing and picked up a large plastic block and began to play with it.

"Is there something else, Eleanor?"

"Uh, no…no," Eleanor said quickly. "I'll show Mrs. Bertram in now." As Eleanor left the room she looked back at the twins who played together on the floor at Cianne's feet.

Cianne was sure Eleanor knew that something transpired between the twins. No doubt, the caretaker witnessed their silent communication before. It was also clear that Aidan had the ability to soothe Nadia. More than Cianne could at times.

If Eleanor knew, it seemed she kept it to herself. Her discrete nature was one of the reasons Cianne let her stay on. She hoped nothing happened to the nice woman to make her regret the decision.

Cianne smoothed back the strands of hair that fell from her single braid then adjusted herself in the chair so that she sat straight up. She cleared her throat then tried to relax. Both of the children looked over to her at the same time. Aware as always.

For three and a half months she hadn't heard, seen, touched, or tasted her husband. He missed weeks of their children's growth and bonding with them. He wasn't around to drive away the nightmares. But nightmares were the least of Cianne's worries.

Whodai reported to her that an assassin entered her home last night while she was in the children's room, and killed Felix. Felix was one of her Royal Guards, and if he was taken down so easily… It wasn't safe for her and the children in her home anymore, without him. Tristan built them a house, not a fortress.

Sighing, Cianne noticed that her son was watching her, his tiny cherub face pinched with concern. "I'm fine, Aidan," she told him. Her son turned his head and returned to playing. Nadia didn't seem to notice her mother's mild panic attack and played as if nothing was wrong.

"Are you…fine?" Mrs. Bertram asked as she entered the room.

Cianne offered her mother-in-law a forced smile. Her eyes were already watery and she didn't trust her voice to not quiver.

Mrs. Bertram walked around the chair and sat down on an ottoman next to Cianne's feet. "I came as soon as I got your message. Are you alright, dear?" She placed her hand on Cianne's leg. "Are the kids alright?" Mrs. Bertram turned her gaze on the children.

Cianne took a deep breath. Guilt was taking hold of her. Her eyes were already sore from crying, and they began to ache as she fought back tears. It was always a struggle to be around Tristan's parents, knowing she was the reason for their pain. She knew loving her would end badly for Tristan.

"We're fine… But, I needed to see you because," Cianne said then paused, "I wanted to tell you that we are going away for a while."

"When are you leaving?" Mrs. Bertram's next question came immediately after the first, giving Cianne no time to answer. "For how long?"

"We leave today. I haven't exactly thought about the length of time. I'm sorry I have no answer for you." Cianne knew she wouldn't return until she was sure that the Bertrams, Tranae, and the other people she cared about were safe. She was the cause of the danger, the target. That meant her leaving was the only solution.

"Where will you go?"

"My grandmother willed me her estate in Canada. I've been anxious to return to settle some matters for her but I just…" Cianne stopped. It wasn't her nature to lie. She didn't want to leave her home. The bed *they* shared. The one place she felt connected to *him*.

Mrs. Bertram looked sad but there was also sympathy reflected on her face. "Losing Tristan has been hell for all of us, Cianne. But you have to stop torturing yourself. It was no one's fault. It was a car accident sweetheart, a mishap that was out of our control." She took Cianne's hand in hers and smiled. "A change will do you good, Cianne. We can talk about us visiting once you're settled."

Cianne stood. She waited for her mother-in-law to stand before embracing her. "Thank you for being so understanding."

"I love you sweetie." Mrs. Bertram squeezed Cianne before letting her go. "Now," she said turning to the children, "I want to spend some time with my little darlings."

Cianne watched as Mrs. Bertram played with the twins. She wondered, if her mother-in-law knew everything, all of what Tristan endured because of her, and that she was responsible for his disappearance…would she be so understanding?

Chapter Seventeen

Maiden Hall Plantation
Caleb 18 Marda 16
Late summer of 1824

Caleb felt something wet and soft graze over his forehead, then his cheek. Unsure what it was, he opened his eyes and at the same time reached out and grabbed the delicate wrist that hovered above his face. He heard the soft exhale from the woman he restrained, but he didn't look at her.

He didn't much care for looking into the faces of the widows or whores he took to his bed the morning after. He preferred to be long gone before the rooster's crow.

"Where am I?" Caleb asked but still didn't look at the woman. Instead he studied the small but vaguely familiar surroundings.

When the woman didn't respond, Caleb tightened his grip. He heard a yelp of distress, then a bevy of odd sensations assaulted him. Nausea, anger, and intense apprehension seared through him all at the same time. Confused, Caleb released the woman's wrist before turning his attention on her.

Seeing who it was, Caleb released her arm. At once, the nausea and anger faded but he still felt uneasy coupled with shame. He watched Marda cower away to the far wall where she regarded him with hooded eyes as he lifted the sheet up and stood. Caleb extended his hand toward her but retracted it when she moved back more, as if she were trying to disappear into the wall.

She fears me now.

Caleb stroked his hand over his head nervously, as he looked around the cottage. He then sat on the side of the bed and closed his eyes. He remembered the dreams, a voice telling him *strange and wondrous things.*

He angled his head as sounds bombarded him. A rodent scurried to his left but he heard the motions as if they were amplified. He moved his head upward, focusing on the sound of what he somehow knew was a bird landing on the chimney brick on the roof. But it was the strong sound of rhythmic thumping that took precedence over the other sounds.

Caleb opened his eyes and focused on Marda again. He blinked slowly in an attempt to clear his head. Yet, he knew the sound was her heart beating because he could actually see the subtle motion of her chest. The longer he watched her…the slower her heart beat. She was calming.

"How is it that your life force calls to me above all others?"

Marda didn't answer him but she did move a few steps away from the wall.

"Have I damaged you?" he asked.

Marda shook her head as she quickly walked over and picked up the cloth she dropped on the floor. She rinsed it in the basin then motioned to his face.

Caleb nodded.

He admired her while she gently moved the moistened cloth over his face again. Marda was beautiful, devastatingly so. Her symmetrical features were delicate, her skin reminded him of ginger biscuits, her dark eyes were enchanting, and her long hair was dark as coal but looked soft as silk.

When he raised his hand and covered hers, Marda stilled but she didn't pull away. Instead, she allowed him to slowly guide her strokes along his jaw.

Caleb pulled the cloth from her hand so that her fingers pressed upon his bristled face. He sighed, closed his eyes, then tilted his head into her callused palm. For a short while, he just settled into her touch.

"Jai explained what is happening to me. She came to me in my dreams. Spoke of where you come from and the wondrous things your people can do. I know what is expected of me, though I fear I may not be the worthy choice. I don't mind admitting I am coarse in..." He opened his eyes and looked into hers. "Marda, if you could feel only a tenth of what I feel for you..." he began.

She stared blankly back at him.

Caleb boldly touched her cheek. "Please Marda, say something."

"Sir, I am not permitted to feel."

He stared at her in amazement but, somehow, he knew she could speak. Something inside him always knew it to be true, but when she did he stopped breathing. Her voice was low and her accent heavy, making him want to savor every word. Only what she said tore at his heart.

Marda sighed. "But I do feel. If you are asking me what I feel..."

Against his instincts, Caleb nodded, sensing he would regret her answer.

Before he could change his mind, Marda yanked her hand from his face.

"I feel nothing, sir. I was taken from my home, my people, and brought here to serve the needs of your relations before I attend to my most basic needs. I am an animal, livestock, unworthy to pale folk and believed incapable of sentiment unless you lift my skirts to force yourself upon me. I should be happy then."

The cottage door suddenly swung open and Marda immediately took two steps away from him and lowered her head. Caleb stared at her beautifully sculpted form as she stood perfectly still. Her long satiny hair was pulled away from her face, parted in two halves, and braided into long plaits that fell down over her back. Her skin shimmered from the light that came into the cottage from the doorway.

Caleb knew that as long as his brother was in her presence that he wouldn't see Marda's coal black lashes flutter open to reveal her dark brown eyes. If there was any benefit from her submissive stance, it was that her head was lowered and she would not be able to see the pain reflected in his eyes from the truth of her words.

"Little brother!" Fredrick sang out. He crossed the gap between them in just a few strides. "By God's good grace," he said before he pulled Caleb up and into a tight embrace. Fredrick patted him on the back then released him. "Father and Mother will be comforted to see you about."

Caleb secured the sheet around his waist. "I must be properly attired."

"Marda, assist our young master," Fredrick said boisterously. He spun on his heels and strode toward the door.

"No," Caleb said. His voice cracked as he called "no" a second time, stopping his brother in his tracks. "I can manage on my own." Caleb looked over at Marda who stood awaiting his command. "Leave me," he ordered.

Marda glanced at him but lowered her eyes and hurried around Fredrick to take her leave.

"Caleb?" Fredrick questioned.

Caleb looked to his brother. He saw a hint of fear but couldn't be bothered why just yet. Never before had he given Marda a command or spoken to her with such venom but he had been rejected. It hurt like hell.

It was Sunday eve and the usual custom was to enjoy large meals with several guests in attendance at Maiden Hall. Caleb didn't object when his mother used the opportunity to honor his recovery but he was in no mood to entertain.

Caleb sipped his beverage as he looked upon Marda, who stood in attendance. She was dressed finer than he'd ever seen, in a canary yellow print and lace gown with an ivory apron. It was customary for Jai, who was very skilled, to stand quietly in a corner to wait for instruction and serve. With Jai round with child and close to her time, Marda was expected to serve in her place.

"Caleb, you remember Elizabeth Kent?" Fredrick asked.

Lowering his glass, Caleb regarded Fredrick. Had Fredrick seen him watching Marda? If he did, his brother gave no indication he had. Caleb gave his brother his full attention.

Fredrick added, "If I recall, you used to call her Lizzie,"

Caleb turned his attention to the pale delicate beauty who sat directly across from him. He didn't notice her until now. Elizabeth had golden-brown silky hair that was tied up with white ribbon and pearls. Her soft pink lips parted when their eyes met and her cheeks soon flushed a faint red.

So…this dinner is a ruse for a matching.

"The Lizzie I remember would prefer pantaloons to a gown," Caleb said, then smiled.

"I have retired my old frocks for silk and bows, I'm afraid. Climbing trees and torturing toads is far removed, sir. Just as I hope pulling little girl's pigtails and frightening them with garden snakes is behind you." Elizabeth smiled.

"I'm afraid I've lost my ardor for pulling pigtails. Though, if I should stumble across a garden snake and the urge to throw it at an unsuspecting lass presents itself, sentimentality may overwhelm my good sense." Caleb didn't smile until he noticed he had everyone's attention.

The room erupted in laughter, though he suspected it was led by his mother.

Elizabeth smiled again as she anchored her attention on Caleb.

Being well-practiced in the wants of women, Caleb felt her desire. Whores and widows were the lot he usually entertained. A wife was not an option now and may never be if he were being frank with himself.

Caleb resisted the pull to glance at Marda, so he looked down at his plate. After several minutes of side conversations around the table, he heard Elizabeth's smooth voice again.

"Do you not fancy my new gown?" she asked.

Caleb looked up to see that everyone around them was engaged in private conversation, and Elizabeth was looking directly at him. He swallowed his wine then spoke as politely as he could manage, "I am not a man of fashion, Miss Kent."

"I think you are quite fashionable," Elizabeth argued.

Caleb didn't know how to respond to that. He didn't feel charming at the moment, let alone care how he dressed.

"Take a bow mother," Fredrick teased as he winked at her. "You see, Miss Kent, mother still dresses him."

The guests found humor in this too and laughed.

Caleb smiled again, but for the rest of the meal he sat in silence. He honestly had no desire to talk politics, clothing, farming, or life in general.

After dinner, Caleb strolled the shore by the lake. He eventually rolled the sleeves of his shirt, having discarded his waistcoat on the path, and climbed his favorite tree. He moved quicker and with more confidence than he ever had before. He would learn all the things he was capable, but right now he just wanted to forget what he'd become and how it included Marda.

He sat on his favorite branch and admired the fading light of the sky but his mind wouldn't settle. He had so many questions to ask Jai. He also wondered if Marda was going to resume speaking to him, or did she plan on shutting down again.

Does she hate me?

Caleb's mind was everywhere, which would explain why he didn't hear someone approaching.

"Looking for snakes?" Elizabeth asked as she looked up at him from below.

"No," he said. Caleb sighed, then jumped down, landing in front of her. "If I was rude before, I apologize."

"Wow…" she said as she blinked in amazement.

Caleb realized that he jumped from a high branch in a manner that could injure an acrobat. He bent and rubbed his ankle as if he hurt himself.

"Show your abilities to no one unless you or your ward is in danger," Jai's warning sounded in his mind.

"Are you injured?" Elizabeth asked, bending.

Caleb stepped away from her then shook his head.

Elizabeth smiled. "Alright." She stood as well. "You weren't rude. I'm glad you remember me enough to be yourself." She subtly moved forward, showing off her cleavage. "Do you remember our favorite game?"

"We should return to the manor." Caleb moved past her and made for the manor.

Elizabeth ran to catch up. "The one we played when no one else was around?" She stepped in his path, wrapped her arms around his neck, lifted on her toes, and kissed him.

For a moment, Caleb was too stunned to move. But when her tongue pried for entry, he took Elizabeth by the arms and moved her back, breaking the kiss. "Miss Kent, you should not be out here alone," he said.

She struggled to kiss him again but sighed because he gave her no purchase. "I'd rather you call me, Elizabeth. I know I will fancy the way you say my name."

Because he wasn't sure how much pressure to use without hurting her, Elizabeth managed to pull her hand free, and she used it to rub the back of his neck.

Her hands felt nice but…

"What will your family say when they've caught you with me, alone?"

"They will say that I've made an excellent choice. It is what both our families want, Caleb. That's why my family was invited here tonight. They intend to match us."

Curious, he grinned. "And you approve?" There was a sparkle in her eyes he'd seen before. One he needed to dim.

"Very much so," Elizabeth said as she leaned inward again.

Caleb leaned back to avoid her kiss then pulled her hand from around his neck. "You really shouldn't be out here without your girl. There will be rumors and your reputation may be ruined." He could not deny her beauty but he had no interest in her. Well, none that was honorable.

"Don't worry," Elizabeth said, smiling. "We're not alone, not really. Your mother sent her girl with me."

Elizabeth tried to lean into him again but he held her away.

Caleb's eyes widened and his pulse pounded as he scanned the area while avoiding Elizabeth's advances. His eyes were altered just like his hearing but he was still learning to filter the sudden contrasts. Yet, it was easy to find Marda sitting alone on a bed of grass a hundred feet away, with his waistcoat in her care.

"I'll walk you back to the Manor, Elizabeth." He took Elizabeth by the hand and gently pulled her along. Reluctantly, she allowed it but pouted the entire way. It was clear that she was little Lizzy no longer.

Marda followed the two at a distance. By the time she reached the manor, Caleb was headed for the cottage as Ms. Elizabeth watched him from the grand porch. Marda's mouth spread into a slight smile as she made her way to the kitchen entrance.

For reasons unknown to her, Marda took comfort in the fact that Caleb didn't fall into Elizabeth's arms like the woman intended. The thought of that woman placing her lips on him angered her.

But why?

Later, after all her work was done and she lay on her bedding, she touched her lips with her finger tips. She imagined Caleb kissing her earlier, instead of just reaching for his waistcoat.

What would it be like, kissing Caleb Scott?

Marda continued to wonder as she drifted off to sleep.

Chapter Eighteen

Missing four months
September 8th

Cianne opened her bedroom door and ran down the hall to the room she chose for her children as the alarm boomed throughout the mansion. She originally thought the room was too far from hers.

It was.

By the time she reached the door and turned the knob, her chest was heaving from her full-out sprint and panic. She knew they were safe. If she concentrated enough, and depending on proximity, Cianne could reach out to them and know. But only when she burst through the door did she allow herself to calm.

Cianne stepped inside the room then locked the door behind her. She was grateful for soundproof walls and doors so the alarm couldn't be heard inside the room. The only reason she knew it was still blaring was the red flashing light located on a wall panel beside the door.

She walked through the extravagantly decorated room she had no input on, to where the two cribs were located. One crib sat empty so her focus moved to the one both children slept in. Cianne found them in their usual position, back to back and sound asleep. She smiled.

When she heard footsteps rushing toward the bedroom, she steeled herself as she faced the door and the possible intruder. The knob on the door rattled and her heart sped up.

"Cianne, open the door."

It was Cassius. Cianne rushed to the door and opened it. Cassius looked around her to see into the room then looked at her.

"They're fine," she whispered. Cianne noticed the alarm was silenced so she stepped into the hallway but left the door slightly ajar. "Is-"

Cassius raised a finger to quiet her, turned his head, then pressed some ear piece and spoke. "Top floor secured. Lioness and cubs are safe." He focused on Cianne. "Someone tried to breach the outside perimeter but failed to get on the grounds. I have two teams out searching for the perpetrator. I don't think he's gotten far." Cassius looked into the dimly lit room at the cribs. "Are the children alright?"

"They're fine," Cianne told him as she closed the door behind her. "I can't live like this. My children can't live like this," she told him. "I moved here because I was told we would be safer but this is never going to end, is it? This is the fifth incident in three weeks."

"Not safe, Soahn," Cassius said then sighed, "Safer, better protected. Ark Mansion is the best place for you and the children." His eyes grew distant as he touched his ear piece. Then his brows softened as he gave Cianne his full attention. "Try to relax if you can, maybe try and get some sleep."

"As if I could possibly sleep," Cianne sighed. She left Cassius where he stood and went back into the children's room. She sat in the glider, put her feet up on the stool, and pulled the afghan over her legs. To sleep would mean dreaming, which meant nightmares.

The nightmares were brutal and always left her gutted. They were making her jumpy and suspicious of everyone and everything. It was best to just stay awake.

Cianne relaxed into the chair and thought of the life she always wanted. The life she once had. A life that was simple and perfect with her children and Tristan.

The sound of thunder shook Cianne awake. She was still seated on a comfy glider in the nursery. She must have fallen asleep. Cianne took a deep breath as she lowered her feet to the floor and swept her hair away from her face. Leaning forward, she peered at the cribs.

Cianne jumped to her feet. She darted across the room to the two empty cribs. Her mind went blank with fear as she lifted the sheets in her hands. She gently reached out with her abilities to feel for them, their presence. But with herself in such an emotional state, her abilities were unpredictable and she didn't feel them.

She hurried to the nursery bathroom. No children.

Cianne stormed out into the hallway to her bedroom, then to one of the unoccupied rooms beside hers. No twins. She could reach out to them mentally, try to touch their minds. But she feared she might damage their fragile minds if she pushed too hard. Cianne hated her abilities and stopped practicing using them once Tristan…since he wasn't there to help her. Plus, the only way she can keep the people around her safe was to avoid using her abilities.

"Good afternoon, Soahn."

Cianne whirled around to see one of the many maids who worked at the mansion. Her name was Stella.

"I… I can come back later, if you like," the woman stuttered.

"The children," Cianne said, trembling with worry, "where are the children?"

"In the kitchen, Soahn, having lunch," Stella said. Her face paled.

Stella feared her. Cianne knew some of the staff might find it hard to warm to her but she never thought they'd fear her.

Sighing, she moved forward. Stella had little time to move as Cianne hurried from the room and down the stairs, not even considering how she was dressed.

As Cianne neared the kitchen, she slowed when she heard laughter. Curiosity replaced her fear.

"Hey mommy," Whodai smiled. He looked up at her as she entered the kitchen.

Nadia sat on the kitchen counter as Whodai wiped her face clean with a towel. Her dark curly ringlets created an obstacle for him as she laughed and wriggled to get free of his grasp and move into her mother's arms.

"Would you like an apple butter sandwich?" Whodai asked, as he walked Nadia over to her.

Cianne opened her arms and pulled the playful toddler into a snug embrace. Only when her lips touched her daughter's cheek did her rigid posture relax.

"I heard you upstairs," Whodai said. He palmed the back of his neck as he looked at his feet. Then he turned and walked to where Aidan sat quietly. He looked over his shoulder at her. "I'm sorry if I worried you."

Cianne smiled at her son then registered what Whodai said. She asked, "You heard me…upstairs?"

"Remember when I told you that my ability was sort of like Tristan's? Well, I can hear really well. The second floor, if I try hard."

"Oh." Cianne let the word fade as she tried to remember if she ever said anything embarrassing while he was in the house.

"I thought you knew…about the hearing. I apologize if I-"

Always the perfect gentleman.

Cianne cut off his apology. "It's fine," she smiled with relief. Following him over to the table, she sat down next to Aidan who was getting his face and hands wiped. Unlike Nadia, Aidan sat still while he was being cleaned.

Cianne's heart pulsed when her son smiled at her. He didn't smile often. She suspected he knew he had his father's smile and wanted to protect her. That was her theory, anyway.

She watched Aidan lift a small cup to his mouth then frown. Cianne reached for the cup but Whodai got to it first.

"I'll get it," he said. He refilled the cup, gave it to Aidan then made Cianne an apple butter sandwich. "Cassius told me you had a rough night when I arrived to relieve him. I came to the nursery to check on you but you didn't hear me knocking. On the other side of the door, I heard you breathing; it suggested that you were still sleeping. But the kids were awake." He sat down on the other side of Aidan. "We figured we'd let you sleep."

"You've been with them all morning?" Cianne glanced at the clock and grimaced. It was after one in the afternoon.

Whodai laughed. "Don't look so horror-struck. Eleanor had some errands to run. We didn't burn the house down and the kids are really sweet. I enjoyed spending time with them." He reached to the center of the table and used tongs to place four more apple slices on Aidan's plate.

Aidan picked up an apple slice and began to eat it.

"So, I was thinking that I could hang out with you guys today." Whodai smiled.

Cianne smiled, suspiciously. "Hang out?" She picked up an apple slices and bit into it.

"Ok," Whodai said as he adjusted in his seat, "I was told to shadow you and the children."

Cianne reached for another apple slice and handed it to Nadia.

"I honestly do enjoy spending time with you guys. I hope to be good friends with the twins, and you. Someday."

"Well," Cianne dragged out the word, "since you've put it that way. Do you think you could watch them while I take a shower?"

Whodai stood and took Nadia as Cianne handed her over. "Take your time," he said. He sat Nadia back in her high chair and placed her juice cup in front of her. He tried not to watch Cianne as she poured some juice in a glass then drank it.

Hell, he was having a hard time trying to push the images of her in the shower, with hot soapy water running down her smooth skin, out of his mind. The only comfort he had was that he planned to be showering with her very soon. *Cianne will be mine.*

Chapter Nineteen

Tristan felt the devastating force of Caleb's elbow as it collided with the left side of his jaw. That blow alone would have been enough to put him down for a minute or so, but Caleb followed it with a palm to the chest that would stop the heart of a Middling.

Tristan slid several feet back, stopping only because the tree he hit was rooted deep inside the ground and was too strong to fall over. He dropped to his knees and fought to breathe.

"We're done for the day," Caleb said. He walked over to Tristan and extended his hand.

Tristan smacked the offered hand away. "No," he hissed, looking up. "Again."

The pain in his chest was nothing compared to what he felt each day he was away from his family. He grunted as he got to his feet, ignoring the disapproving look, or maybe it was compassion, on Caleb's face. Either expression angered Tristan so much that he turned around and yelled out as loud as he could, causing the sleeping forest to wake.

"Damn it, Caleb," Tristan yelled, turning back. "I'm fine. The new medicine you're pumping into me is doing its job. It's working, what else do you want from me? You hold me here against my will, fine. You perform some kind of operation on my ears without my permission, that screws up my hearing, whatever. You inject me with a mystery cocktail I haven't even questioned you about, that keeps me alive. No problem.

"Then, you tell me you want to train me before I can go home. So, I train. I've done everything you've asked of me. I just want to go home but you won't let me until I somehow show you I am no longer the weak link in the family. For fuck's sake, pocket your sympathy and just train me."

Nothing else mattered. Not the pain, the bruises, the demoralization. Nothing mattered to Tristan other than getting home. That meant training hard and…learning all he could about Caleb Scott.

"Tomorrow," Caleb said, sounding resolute. "You have less than ten seconds to get to the cabin or the ankle bracelet activates." He strolled away, leaving Tristan standing in the clearing.

When Caleb reached the house, Tristan was on the sofa wiping his head with a towel. The boy was much faster and stronger since the start of the new injections three weeks ago. He would not have survived that hit then.

He and Bannerman hoped the new injection will keep Death's Door at bay for longer periods of time. It was a few days past the last serum's longest effective time, and Tristan was still going strong.

Caleb got a bottle of water and started toward his room.

"So," Tristan said, "how did you deal with Marda's rejection?" He stretched his feet out so that they rested under the coffee table and leaned his head back over the back of the couch to look at Caleb.

Caleb stopped just outside his bedroom door. He'd been anxious to get back to his room the entire day. When he checked his P.O. Box that morning, he found the information he requested from Richard.

Richard Scott was a Middling he trusted with his life and all his secrets including the secret of his true identity and what he was. Twenty odd years ago, when he returned to United States to locate a specific Coesen, Caleb took the opportunity to befriend his brother's only living male descendant. At the time, Richard was newly enlisted in the U.S. military. Upon meeting Richard and talking to him, Caleb sensed that he could trust his secrets with the open-minded young man.

Richard, a big deal in the army, was the only man Caleb trusted with something as important as investigating the strange bullet he dug out of Tristan's thigh. He accepted the fact that Richard could find out some things faster and easier than even he could.

When Caleb opened his lock box at the post office two counties away and saw the package, he knew that Richard had come through again.

"You want to know why I have no television or radio? You're smart, so I'm sure you already know the answer but just in case you haven't figured it out yet, I'll tell you. I enjoy the serenity of being alone." Caleb opened his bedroom door.

"Really, I would have never guessed," Tristan said, then smirked.

Caleb could sense that the boy was still annoyed that his training was cut short. Then the dark energy radiating from Tristan changed. The sudden difference had Caleb turning around. Tristan turned his entire body around so that they had a clear view of one another. The boy also had a huge smile on his face. It was the kind of smile that brought out a smile from anyone privileged enough to witness it.

"Tell you what," Tristan said, crossing his arms over his chest, "you tell me some more of your story and I won't bother you when you look through that mail you've been stressing over all day."

What is this, a battle of wills?

The boy should know that he shouldn't negotiate with terrorists or infants. Tristan could be classified as both. Maybe a broken collar bone will encourage him to mind his own business. Though, Caleb couldn't help but admire Tristan's skill. The boy was dangerously fearless and clever. They were qualities he admired, but not in a son-in-law.

Why couldn't the man Cianne fell for be a bookkeeper or a dentist? But then again, if Tristan was a mild-mannered Middling, Cianne and his grandchildren would be unprotected. Caleb needed them protected because, aside from this little revolution amongst the Coesen, he felt the worst was yet to come. Which meant that dangerously fearless and clever was a plus.

Caleb was seated in the chair before Tristan even noticed he moved. "I left Maiden Hall. Went back to my uncle's home in Dominion. Marda wasn't in any danger at Maiden Hall since I was told at the time that Shaw had disappeared. My mother didn't allow her slaves to be mistreated so my being near her wasn't necessary. At least that's what I told myself."

Caleb pulled his vibrating flip phone out of his pocket and looked at the number that popped in the display window. He then placed the phone on the coffee table in front of him, confident that Tristan wouldn't reach it before he did.

"I kept up appearances and visited from time to time. Jai, of course, insisted that I stay at Maiden Hall. She wanted to teach me the ways of her people and my responsibility as a Protector, but I was arrogant enough that Coesen law meant nothing to me. I was the captain of my ship and no one would make me a slave. It was ironic how things worked out.

"Returning home to see Jai when she gave birth to her child was the last time I spoke to Marda for some time. I made every effort to avoid interacting with her when I came home after that, which was not often. During my time home, I kept busy with work and frequent dinner parties. Being an educated young man with two wealthy parents and with women considering me handsome, I was somewhat of a catch.

"I attended those parties and behaved like the wealthy gentleman I was raised to be. Polite and educated with a hint of arrogance. It was only a show. I despised everything about the antebellum South but I had no intention of publicly spiting the source of my family's wealth nor would I embarrass them at these gatherings. As for my many admirers, I had very little interest in them as well. My heart belonged to someone who wanted nothing to do with me."

"I don't know what I would have done if Cianne didn't finally give me a chance," Tristan sighed. He placed a hand over his heart. "I was...I felt, I just wouldn't know what to do."

"It's a lonely existence when you want someone so badly that everything and everyone else means literally nothing to you. I was empty and nothing mattered. My insides were twisted in knots. Not to mention the distance I lived from Marda wreaked havoc on me. You're aware of the negative effects you felt growing up. You feel as if you're being pulled by something out in the world but you don't seem to know what. You feel connected but incomplete. Jai told me some Coesen go mad if they don't do an initial bonding period with their ward in the first few years. Me, I became belligerent, short tempered, and a drunk because our abilities never had a chance to sync properly.

"I hated everyone and everything but most of all I hated Marda for not wanting me. During my self-destructive phase, my father had the pleasure of witnessing the new me on several occasions before he passed away. I didn't shed one tear for him. I regret that. I regret what I'd become."

Maiden Hall Plantation
July 1826

Marda ignored Jai, who was standing on a crate and looking out of the small rectangular window in the cellar, which was also a storage area and their bedroom. It was dark outside but no light was needed to know who it was out there screaming drunken curses one moment then pleading for death the next.

Jai lowered her head and sighed as she stepped down from the crate. "He's out there again, this is the third time this month," she said to Marda. She walked over to her bed and pulled the blanket up over Selene's shoulders. Jai's daughter was two now, with the fair complexion and hair texture of her white father but the beauty and grace of her negro mother.

"I was wrong to allow this," Jai said as she lowered to the bedding. "We should have released him when you still had the power to do it yourself."

"Should I have?" Marda whispered angrily. "We are bound to *them*. It seems only fair to have one of them bound to me." She lay her head down and tried to block out Caleb's tirades.

Marda didn't find joy in Caleb's suffering. She even thought of releasing him that first year but she knew that she couldn't. She had to think of Jai and Selene. They all needed his protection and Caleb could keep them together. He could encourage his brother to not sell them off like cattle.

When Caleb abandoned his infatuation, she planned to convince him to send them home. He could free them. Then, and only then, would she release him.

"Go to sleep Jai," she whispered, "As always, we have a full day's work tomorrow."

Fredrick dropped Caleb onto the bed like he had so many times before. He removed his brother's boots and waistcoat and threw them to the floor.

"Sir?" A small voice came from the cottage doorway.

Fredrick continued removing Caleb's clothing, except for his breeches. "Jai, it's best that I do this. I rather not have you girls around him when he's like this." He didn't look up. "Go on back to sleep."

"Shush," Caleb slurred as he sat up, "you'll wake my owners." He lifted his wobbling finger to his mouth.

Fredrick leaned back as the smell of alcohol and cheap perfume hit him. He lifted his hand and covered Caleb's face, pushing him back on the pillow. Caleb frowned but fell back with no resistance.

"Thank you, but have your leave," he said, looking at Jai. Fredrick saw her confusion. He'd thanked her. Slaves were never thanked. But she recovered and slowly backed out of the cottage.

Caleb stirred with awareness but made no move to sit up.

"It is late in the day, Caleb," Fredrick kicked the end of the bed. "Rise up."

Caleb brought his hand up over his face. He lifted his heavy head up enough to look at Fredrick who was seated in a chair at the foot of the bed. Caleb moaned, "Please brother, spare me."

Fredrick kicked the bed again, this time with more force. "You've slept for two days passed. Get up," he said louder.

Caleb grimaced as he pushed up on his elbows. It took him longer to sit up on the side of the bed. When he was stable, he looked over at his older brother then submerged his face in the basin of water on a table beside his bed. He toweled his face and bare chest dry then picked up a few pieces of meat from a plate next to the basin.

"What is so dire?" Caleb asked, as he chewed.

"I'm taking mother home," Fredrick said. "We depart in a few hours."

Caleb gave no indication that the news of his mother's impending departure affected him. He continued to eat from the plate.

"What's happened to you, brother? You drink and keep company with the lowest assortment of loose women and scoundrels. The few times you've graced us with your company, you are drunken and bloodied from the fighting you do. I am told you boxed several men at a time, and for what?

Pennies." Fredrick sighed. "Uncle has told mother of your partying. That you reside and associate with Watkins and his sort. Scoundrels you should not acquaint yourself with."

"Have you considered that I am the sort of man they should not acquaint themselves with, dear brother?" Caleb lifted a glass to his mouth.

"Clearly you've no care of our mother's well-being." Fredrick stood. He walked over to the cottage door and opened it. He gently ushered Marda inside, who walked in with her head down. Fredrick closed the door and followed her. He pointed over to the bed for her to sit. Marda sat down on the very edge, on the other side of Caleb.

Caleb's entire body tensed when he smelled her sweet floral scent. He fisted his hands until his knuckles turned white but he didn't turn to look at her.

"Jai and her child will accompany us to France. Marda will remain." Fredrick pulled some papers from his breast pocket and flung them on the bed behind Caleb.

Caleb ground his teeth together as he felt for the papers. He refused to turn around to look at Marda or his brother, who for the first time in his dull predictable life had done something shocking. He peered at the documents.

It was papers concerning Marda. Marda, the girl of his dreams, now woman of his nightmares. The woman he tried to drink from his mind was now his property. He read the papers over and over again.

"What game do you play?"

"She is yours now, Caleb. Do with her what you will." Fredrick made his way to the cottage door.

"What do you mean, she is mine?" Caleb stood, and in the blink of an eye crossed the length of the cottage and grabbed his brother's arm. He whipped Fredrick around to face him.

"I have a theory, you see. I think that your behavior is the direct result of what you desire and can't have. I know you care for her, Caleb. I've always known. We all do. Why do you think father refused to sell her to Mr. Potts, Lord Havers, and all the others who offered much more than what's fair? You know that Mr. Potts was planning to breed her with Zeus, his biggest and hardest working slave, as a gift to bear offspring. Lord Havers…well, his intentions were much more unsavory. Father flat-out refused their generous offers, often because of you and mother. So, brother…she is yours." Fredrick grunted out. "Now let go of my arm."

Caleb knew exactly why Lord Havers wanted Marda. He was the proprietor of a brothel and Marda would have made him richer. He heard the man say those exact words to his father at one of his mother's dinner parties one evening. It took all he was not to clobber the hell out of the old bastard.

"Are you that heartless? You are no better than them. What would you have me do? Take her screaming to my bed and in a few months' time, she bears a child I cannot claim as my own? In a few years, I marry an upstanding white woman who bears me children as well, but they can call me father but Marda's young cannot!" Caleb yelled. "Is this the life you want to condemn her to?"

Fredrick tried to pry Caleb's hand off him. "If that is what will calm the storm in your mind and bring my brother back to what's left of the family who loves him, then yes, it is."

Caleb dropped his hold on Fredrick's arm as he stared at Fredrick, wide eyed and stunned.

What have I done to my family?

Fredrick pulled the door open. "No need for farewells. I had them escorted to the docks this morn. You had important business to attend but you will send correspondence as soon as you can. Your wealth is great, try not to squander it all." Fredrick sighed. "We hope to see you soon, Caleb." Fredrick left, leaving Caleb standing by the door.

The children.

He felt a wave of hopelessness overtake him. He leaned on the door jamb with his hand over his eyes, blocking out the sun. Selene, Jai's daughter, and William, Fredrick's son, were dear to him. To not be able to say goodbye to them and his mother, or even the judgmental Abigail, his sister by marriage, was a painful blow.

Caleb felt his anger rise as he moved to confront his brother and show him exactly what made him a sure bet during his boxing matches. But he froze when he heard Marda stir behind him. He wanted to tell her to be gone by the time he returned.

He didn't mean to turn around and look at her, but when he did, Caleb stumbled back into the open door. Marda was standing naked next to the bed. One of her arms was stretched across her small perfect breasts. The nipples were hidden but the pressure of her arm pushed the flesh below them to swell. Her other arm was stretched the length of her torso, her hand covering the hair over her sex. When his burning eyes trailed back up to her face, Caleb's heart almost stopped because when their eyes met, Marda slowly let her arms fall away and displayed her slender yet shapely body.

Dear God, she is magnificent.

Marda stood bare for him to see. Her hair was uncovered and freely flowed down her back but several strands fell over her shoulder. Caleb took scores of women to his bed but none equaled Marda.

No…you hate her, he reminded himself.

With new determination, Caleb crossed the room and covered Marda with the blanket from his bed before she could blink. He could tell his movements frightened her because he felt her fear like the blast of a cannon to his chest. In all the years as her Protector, he never felt such raw emotion. It was so strong it caused him to stumble forward.

Marda reached out to steady him. "I do not fear you, but seeing you move that fast…" She paused and lowered her head. "Forgive me, I did not mean to speak." She let go of his arms and moved back.

"Forgive you? Marda, you speak when *you* choose." Caleb turned his head to look away as he bent to retrieve the blanket that fell when he stumbled. He continued to look away as he placed it around her again. "…and I do not own you."

"I *am* yours, sir."

His body immediately reacted to her declaration. Caleb looked at Marda's face. There was nothing in her eyes. No fire, no passion, no desire that would have him believe she wanted him. Marda was clearly acting on orders.

"Use my name please, not *sir*," Caleb spat. He wanted her away from him. She could go away with his family. Living without her love was his cruel reality but to have her offer herself because she was ordered to was unbearable. He turned his head toward the door and twisted his body to follow but…he heard the blanket hit the floor again. Damn his super-sensitive hearing.

Caleb stilled when Marda took a step toward him. They were inches apart now. He could feel her body heat against his skin.

"Caleb," she said softly.

He closed his eyes when he heard her sing the two syllables that made up his name. Speaking was something Marda didn't do often. Everyone thought her mute. The only one she spoke to was Jai…and him.

The times she spoke to him, she never said his name. Her pronunciation and her soft tone warmed him in a way he didn't expect.

"You torment me," Caleb hissed. He balled his fists tightly. "Can you not see? It is immoral, what I want of you, Marda."

"Have you quenched your desire for me with all the women you have taken to your bed?"

Marda pressed her breasts against his bare back and wrapped her arms around his chiseled chest. Caleb shivered when they touched. Lost in her warmth, he allowed his fingers to trace her arm before he realized what he was doing.

Caleb turned around and grabbed her wrist tightly. "You mock my pain," he said angrily. He threw her to the bed.

Marda fell back, and before she could sit up, Caleb was on top of her. He felt the dizzying effect that alerted him of her fright but he ignored it. Doing so caused him a great deal of pain that shot through his head but he locked it down, growling because his need for her was even more painful.

The physical evidence of Caleb's need for Marda angered him so much that he didn't even notice that she lay still under him and wasn't struggling. Using one hand to hold both her wrists above her head, he buried his face in her neck and breathed in her scent as he separated her legs with his own.

Crazed, he pushed down his breeches, gripped his shaft, and sighed as he rubbed it through her wetness. Caleb pushed inside her. The pleasure he felt was so foreign, so amazing, that a moan came from a place so deep inside, he didn't recognize it as his own.

Marda cried out as Caleb ripped through her innocence. She lay unmoving as he set into a rhythm. Throaty moans and hissing escaped his lips that pressed against her neck, causing her body to shiver beneath him. The discomfort was paled by the intense pleasure that rippled from her core and moved throughout her entire body.

One of Caleb's hands restrained both of hers above her head, while the other ran down her hip to support her raised leg so he could bury himself deeper. She almost blacked out as her body tightened around him. Her mind and body felt like she was going to explode, and when he started whispering words she couldn't understand, something grabbed hold of her.

The sensation was something so foreign, so amazing that she closed her eyes tight. Her body tensed and a strangled cry poured from her. Caleb whispered something else then his breathing came quicker, louder, until his body stiffened. A guttural growl escaped him as pressure built then he released inside her.

Several heartbeats later, Caleb rolled off her. With his back to her, he lay silent.

Marda's arms ached but the pain was nothing compared to her need to touch him. She wanted to touch him.

Her plan was in jeopardy. The moment she discovered Master Fredrick meant to leave her, she plotted. For her plan to work, Caleb had to want her desperately. Only, there was a problem. Marda didn't think she could lie to herself about her feelings for him. Not now.

Caleb peeled his eyes open as the toll of the work bell sounded for the plantation. It was morning but the sun had yet to rise.

Beside him, or rather nestled in his arms with her face inches from his, Marda slept soundly. He took in her face as her skin shimmered bronze in the flickering candlelight. Caleb felt the urge to kiss her full sweet lips but he restrained himself.

He slowly slid his arm from underneath Marda's neck but as he did, her eyes opened. They looked at each other for a few seconds before Marda lifted so he could move. Caleb shifted and sat on the side of the bed.

"I should not have touched you. If there was some way I could…" He lowered his head in his hands. Caleb jumped to his feet then quickly dressed.

"My intent was not to mock your pain," Marda said hoarsely. "I only meant to end it."

Caleb opened the cottage door without looking back. "I am sorry. Much more than my inept words may reflect. I do love you…"

He was gone before she could respond.

The Present

"I was no better than Shaw, really," Caleb said. "She deserved to be handled with love and patience but instead I treated her like one of my whores. The one person I loved the most in my miserable existence and I treated her like I did."

Caleb looked down. After all these years, he still had no answer for why he let selfish desires override his common sense.

"I felt so much guilt that I couldn't face Marda. But having her didn't free her hold over me like Fredrick believed, either. It only fueled my need to make her mine all the more. I wanted things I could not have. I wanted to marry her. I wanted her to carry my young, to be a family. But laws were in place to prevent that sort of thing." He paused. "That did nothing to deter me. I had a plan. Get myself right, earn Marda's forgiveness, then do whatever I had to do to win her love."

The vibrating of his phone on the table briefly pulled Caleb's attention from his story. He reached for the annoying device and noted the fourth call from an unknown number. His brows creased.

"You can't just stop there. And, Jesus…what a relic." Tristan frowned.

Caleb retracted his hand, leaving the phone where it lay. He looked at it again then back to Tristan. "Being who Marda needed wasn't as easy as I thought it would be."

City of Dominion

Caleb looked over his shoulder at Jack and Ben. The two men standing in front of the door didn't seem ready to move. Mr. Watkins paid them well because they didn't frighten easily. Shame.

Bill Marshall, the owner of The Broken Nail Tavern, the establishment they were in, sat quietly behind his desk. He flinched when Caleb cleared his throat then adjusted in his seat nervously.

Clearing his throat was all Caleb could do to mask the discomfort he felt from ignoring Marda's summons. Her mental summoning was continuous since he left her in the cottage three days past. The first day he ignored her summons, he felt a slight irritation in the back of his head. But with each passing day, the irritation mounted until it was agonizing.

Somehow, Caleb could determine the seriousness between a simple summoning versus her being in danger. Jai told him that a Protector can ignore a summons but the urge to respond will grow more urgent over time.

"It makes me nervous when people stand." Mr. Watkins said from the chair he strategically placed next to Bill's desk. The candy he was chewing made his words slur a bit but they were clear enough. "Have a seat son, so we can discuss this. Make sure you're making the right decision," Watkins said then smiled as he leered at Caleb.

Watkins' cold calculating stare broke many men but Caleb wasn't moved.

"I am confident this is the right decision, for me, Mr. Watkins," Caleb said, as he remained on his feet. "At present, I have to ask you to excuse me. I have somewhere to be."

Caleb wanted to get to the Magistrate before returning to Maiden Hall. He turned to leave but the men blocking the door didn't move. Caleb moved forward anyway.

Mr. Watkins exhaled loudly but gave no order to his men to move. He bit into his candy, chewed and swallowed before he spoke. "Do you realize the amount of money you can make?"

Caleb knew Mr. Watkins was only concerned about the money that could be made.

Stopping just in front of Jake and Ben, who continued to block the doorway, Caleb gave them a lazy grin. When he was fighting for Mr. Watkins, he had little interest in getting to know the two. Caleb kept himself soothed with whiskey and female companionship most days so socializing around with these two wasn't a high priority.

"Money has never been a concern of mine, Mr. Watkins," Caleb said without looking back. He would give them a few more seconds to move.

Watkins sat forward. "I don't want to keep you, *Mr. Scott,* so I'll be brief. This endeavor of ours has been very profitable for you, me, and Bill here."

Caleb looked over his shoulder in time to see Bill's eyes widened and cheeks flame with embarrassment.

"To turn away from this right now would be…foolhardy. Being as your older brother has inherited your father's wealth, working for me will allow you to live off your own salary."

Caleb turned to face Mr. Watkins.

Watkins continued, "To liberate yourself, if you will. I myself am put out that you've decided something that affects us all," he spread his arms out, "on your own. Now that doesn't seem fair." Watkins smiled as he placed his hands together then placed them in his lap.

It was customary for the first son to inherit a father's fortune and land, but to have a charlatan such as Watkins assume to know his economic state was disturbing and offensive. To be honest, Caleb never gave the man's character a second thought before now. Fighting was what Caleb enjoyed and it was of no consequence who brokered the matches. But there was always something unsettling about Watkins.

Sober enough to see the real Watkins for the first time, Caleb could honestly say that the man was a parasite. His fancy dress and artificial manners were a means to deceive and hide his true nature.

"As I said *Mr. Watkins,* acquiring money means nothing if you already have it."

Watkins sneered, "You have nothing. Your father was a practical man. He would have left all he owned to his elder son. You, his disappointment, were left with nothing."

The Scotts were loving, fair, and very wealthy. He and his brother were each left with a fortune of their own. Enough money to burn. Caleb shrugged, knowing the truth. He shifted most of his weight on his left foot and placed his hands in his pockets.

Mr. Watkins reluctantly waved his hand. His men moved away from the door.

As Caleb walked down the long hall, leaving the office behind him, he heard what sounded like a fist slamming on a desk. Then he heard Watkins speak, so he walked slow.

"No one quits on me," Watkins hissed.

"I think we should leave it alone," Bill said, his voice weak as usual. "There's something about this kid that's not right."

"I would expect that from a spineless oaf like you Bill. The boy needs to be taught a lesson," Watkins sneered.

You should listen to Bill, Caleb thought, as he continued down the hall.

Maiden Hall Plantation

Marda listened as she cleaned the floor.

"That boy done lost his mind." Tempie said to Barkly, as she handed him a piece of sweet bread. She sat down across from him at the small wooden table in the kitchen.

"I'd say the fever touched him hard," Barkly said as he bit a piece off the of bread and chewed.

Five days had passed since Caleb made love to her and left her alone in the cottage. Despite her summons, he hadn't returned.

"Lawd only knows, Master Fredrick probably turning in his grave." Tempie shook her head but she had a jolly smile on her round face. "Tell me Barkly, what the man say?"

Marda listened more intently now as her hand slowly made little circles on the wood floor.

"Well dat white fella come and rings dat der bell this afternoon, fer all us ta come in. I was in da stables tendin' to da horses when I heard it. It kinda took me by surprise cause'n we just went back out in dem fields seeing as mid-day break had been just a hour befo."

Barkly stuffed the remaining bread in his mouth but continued his story. "He say his name and tell all ta listen up. He call out a list a names, all being field folk and most bein' up in age. We scared, not knowing why this white fella telling dem to step out, but dey do. One of dem fella pull em to the side while the other fella keep talking ta us who left over. But I see that other fella hand dem workers a paper. The fella talking to the rest of us say we gonna be paid fer our work. He say young Mr. Scott need all us to remain till the crop come in then he gone let us buy our freedom wit some of the monies he be given us."

"Lawd…you sure you heard right?" Tempie asked.

"All us can't believe we hear him right, Tempie. We just lose our words. Then we hear Norma call out ta da lawd, sang young masta Scott's name over and over. Some of them fall to the dirt crying like dey's being flogged, saying da young master's name too. All start ta sang him praise."

"What else he says?" Tempie asked anxiously. "Did he say nothin bout us?" She motioned to Marda without turning away from Barkly.

"He just tells us to get back ta work. I tell ya, Tempie, we go back wit a hop n a step," he said laughing heartily. "Ya shoulda seen dem overseers faces when dem fine dressed white men start talking to 'em. I wish my momma wuz here ta see it. No," he laughed louder, "I wish Shaw was here ta sees it all. We got freedom."

Marda grabbed the bucket of water by the handle and pushed to her feet. The day was so full of excitement that neither Tempie nor Barkly noticed her as she walked by them and out the side door to dump the dirty water.

As she stepped into the darkness she wondered what was going to happen to her. If Caleb meant to free them all like everyone was saying, she had no place to go. Jai was headed to England and Marda had no idea of how to get to her home from here.

Several scenarios crossed her mind when a scent in the air caught her attention. When she breathed in deeper to get a better whiff of the scent, panic overtook her. Marda ran the length of the side of the mansion and looked the distance to the cotton fields. Dark smoke rose into the twilight sky like clouds on fire.

"The fields," Marda called out. "The fields afire!"

Barkly ran outside but just stared at her for a long moment with a stunned expression on his aged face. Marda saw the exact moment Barkly smelled the smoke because his face contorted with fear before he started for the fields without saying a word. Tempie stood in the kitchen doorway screaming prayers as tears rolled down her face.

"Get back here gal," Tempie yelled as Marda took off for the fields. "Lawd, she gone kill herself."

"**Caleb**!" Marda screamed as she ran toward the fields.

Caleb felt Marda's panic explode inside him. The intensity of it was like nothing he ever felt before. It caused him to dismount from his horse just twelve miles from Maiden Hall. Then he heard her desperate summons inside his head. This one was wholly different from the others.

A powerful need to go to Marda overwhelmed Caleb. He slapped his mount on the backside and it took off in the direction of Maiden Hall. Caleb started running full speed knowing that he'd get there faster on foot.

He ran through the woods to avoid travelers on the road, though no one would be able to make him out. It took him only minutes to reach the borders of the estate. Caleb stopped briefly only to see his fields aflame.

His first thought was Marda. Though her anxiety still pulsed through him but it wasn't immediate. So, he took a moment to soak in the utter chaos that lay before him. Barkly and a few hands gathered others and livestock, moving them away from the blaze. Slaves and whites worked together on the bucket lines to extinguish the flames.

Caleb marched as close as he could to the borders of the field. He held his arm up to block the flame that licked at his flesh as he looked into the smoke-filled aisles.

Is everyone out and safe?

He called out several times as he choked from the smoke, prepared to go in the flames if need be.

"Ya have ta move back, masta Scott suh," a boy called out from a few yards away. He threw the water from his bucket into the fire tube. One man pumped the lever while others held the hose as water sprayed over the fields.

Caleb was standing next to the boy in a flash, which made the kid stumble back toward the flames. Caleb grabbed the boy's arm and pulled him to safety. The boy's face was dirty but mostly red from the heat. Caleb knew immediately he was one of Shaw's bastard sons.

"Was everyone clear of the fields?" Caleb asked.

Chapter Twenty

Speeding eighteen wheelers ripped by the set gas pumps that sat disturbingly close to the road. Only a narrow sidewalk and a cement parking bumper protected the user from being road kill. If the need arose for a person to use the facilities, get gas, or snacks, most would avoid the hazardous dinosaurs of creepy gas station.

But Caleb wasn't like most people. The little store was the only place for miles that sold some foods and it offered him a measure of peace and distraction. Plus, it allowed him privacy. His reason for being here now: Tristan.

Caleb thought he and the kid understood each other now, but last night Tristan attempted to escape again. It was the kid's first attempt in weeks but it didn't surprise Caleb. He knew Tristan would keep trying.

He expected it.

What he didn't expect was how the new injections were affecting Tristan. He was stronger than he ever was. He moved faster, and processed his surroundings quicker. It was amazing to witness Tristan's transformation, but Caleb also knew that it was too soon to completely place his trust in the new serum.

Right now, the serum held Death's Door at bay for four weeks. But just like it happened with the old serum, Tristan's mutated DNA could adapt and the length of time required between injections could lessen, or the serum could become ineffective at any time.

If Tristan succeeded in his escape he might have been killed by something as simple as a bee sting if he became suddenly weak. Clearly, Tristan didn't care; even though he'd been warned, he still made the attempt.

Whoever wants the kid dead will succeed if Tristan doesn't take his life and training seriously.

Caleb knew firsthand how painful it can be to not have the ones you love with you, but Tristan needed to consider the bigger picture.

He leaned against an out-of-service gas pump and dialed. "Richard," Caleb said into the receiver, "it's me."

"I want one of my men to accompany you on this one," Richard said.

"No," Caleb said, "but I appreciate your concern."

"I don't think you understand," Richard told him.

Caleb laughed to himself. There were times that Richard asked for Caleb's help on sensitive military missions, missions where there was little hope of any of his men returning alive. Caleb got the job done and saved the lives of Richard's men on several occasions, thus catapulting Richard's special branch into legend and heightening his career in the military.

"Uncle, you're personally vested in this one. I have to say it worries me some," Richard said.

Caleb hated when his nephew called him uncle. Especially because Caleb hadn't physically aged past the age of twenty-six and Richard, a distant nephew, was now dyeing the gray out of his head and beard.

"This Zuri, he's like you?" Richard asked after a moment of silence.

Richard knew little to nothing of the Coesen, but Caleb did divulge his own secrets and abilities. What little Richard did know was due to an incident in Budapest that involved a man with special abilities. That man killed members of a prominent family but was holding the children hostage.

Richard called on Caleb, who completed the mission before the Coesen Guard was sent in to suppress the situation.

"The less you know," Caleb said quietly.

"Right," Richard agreed, "but my soldier is good. He can be of use if you need him. It will make me feel better. He's the one who traced the bullet for you. His orders are to hold back unless needed."

Caleb understood his nephew's concern. His power did get away from him, once. "I know you worry I will lose control. Say I do, how is your soldier going to stop me?"

"His orders aren't to stop you," Richard said then paused, "they are to clean up if there's an incident."

"You mean he's to cover up my mess," Caleb said.

Richard didn't respond but that was exactly what he meant. Caleb was family. They knew each other for over twenty years. Up until now, Richard wasn't able to help him, but now he had the opportunity.

"Whatever helps you sleep at night." Caleb sighed. Neither spoke for a few seconds.

"New Orleans, huh?" Richard broke the silence. "How long since you were there?"

Caleb closed his eyes. Marda and a smiling young boy with warm sand-toned skin and blue eyes invaded his thoughts.

"A long time," Caleb said before hanging up the receiver.

Caleb dialed another number. When the person on the other end picked up, Caleb spoke. "This is Mark calling on behalf of the preservation of historical-."

The person on the other end hung up, understanding the message loud and clear.

Tristan heard her approach way before she stepped into the clearing, walked to the front door, and opened it. He knew her scent but his mind could be playing tricks on him again so he didn't get up. The same faint fragrance, honeysuckle and sunshine, filled the cabin a few weeks ago but she wasn't there.

She couldn't be.

Footsteps suggested a small human female entered the cabin but he just lay in his bed gazing up at the wood beams that made up the ceiling. His mind was going to break at some point.

Why not now?

Even if there was someone in the cabin, there was no reason to get up anyway. He was confined to his room, again. Having tried to escape again and ultimately failing, Tristan's prison had shrunk *again* as Caleb restricted his movement to his room once more.

It's been two since his recent attempt and Caleb still won't speak a word to him. No more story, no training, not even a call to dinner. Caleb didn't even give him the "I'm doing this for you, can't you see that" speech parents gave their kids.

Caleb wasn't his father but the dick sure as hell treated him like a child and it was pretty clear that big daddy was displeased.

The footsteps stopped so Tristan sat up. Was his mind finally splintering? Because each day away from Cianne, Nadia, and Aidan felt like it.

Tristan listened, hearing nothing. *Get up.*

He cursed as he got to his feet and pulled his bedroom door open. There, by the sofa, was Zeta with an uncomfortable look on her face. Tristan's eyes grew big with excitement, and the corners of his mouth turned up to reveal a long-forgotten smile.

"Zeta!" Tristan moved forward with his arms open but he hesitated just before his foot crossed his bedroom's threshold because of the tingling that began under the ankle device. He backed up, remembering his restriction.

As he looked at Zeta, who didn't move, it dawned on him. There was no excitement or relief on her face. She wasn't here to take him home. She knew of his detainment.

The smile on Tristan's face fell but he continued to hold his arms out as he tried to think. He couldn't show his anger, that wouldn't help and it wouldn't get him home.

Tristan quickly pointed to his ankle. "Sort of can't leave my room. Been punished," he said with a smile, but added a shrug.

Zeta looked nervous as she glanced at the device, though she seemed to relax. She raised her head then smiled at him. She moved at a Protector's speed into his open arms. "How are you feeling?" she asked when they separated.

Tristan bit down his frustration, accusations, and anger, and responded. "Tired from all the training and healthy food. I feel like I'm going to die if I don't get something greasy to eat. But overall, I'm alive, right?" He backed up to look her over. "Wow, you look great!"

Zeta shyly turned her head as she scratched the nape of her neck and blushed.

She's just a girl, Tristan said to himself. *Like any other girl.*

Fireworks went off in Tristan's head. Zeta *was* just a girl. Who might be capable of freeing him of the anklet. If she could, was he prepared to do what it took to get her to free him?

He moved off to the side to allow her entry. "Come on in," he said.

Zeta peeked inside the room and Tristan noticed her attention fell on the full-size bed for more than a few seconds.

"Uh," Zeta stuttered, "there's no place to sit in there." Her voice sounded strained. Then she took in a deep breath. "Turn around," she told him.

He did what she said, knowing then that she was capable of extending his reach. *But can she remove it?*

Tristan lifted his leg so that Zeta wouldn't have to get to her knees to get to his ankle cuff. He didn't look back at what she was doing because there was no use. He watched Caleb adjust the cuff several times and he still wasn't able to extend the range or remove it. As a matter of fact, every time he touched it for more than a second he was shocked, literally.

He figured it recognized prints or DNA. Whatever the case, he knew now that Zeta could program it.

Done with the device, Zeta stood and Tristan lowered his leg. "There," she said, "now you can go as far as the front door again."

Tristan took a careful step over his bedroom's threshold before accepting that he wouldn't get fried again. He followed Zeta into the living area.

The two talked for hours. Tristan did all he could not to ask any questions about Cianne. The children were who he focused on. Zeta filled him in on all their milestones and achievements. He found out that they'd moved to Vivian's mansion but Zeta really didn't go into detail about why, and Tristan decided not to push it. By dinner time they had spoken about everything other than why she was there; how she was a part of it; and Cianne's life without him.

"I'm starving," she said, stood then stretched. "What have you got in the form of food?"

Tristan forced himself to laugh. "Nothing satisfying," he said blankly. "I've got an idea. Say you go out and get us something edible."

"I don't think so, Tristan," Zeta said right away.

"What is it going to hurt if you go out and bring it back? You know I can't leave." He motioned to the anklet. "All I want is a burger and a beer. Honestly," he said with a smile, "I can't run off while you're gone."

Zeta looked at him, unconvinced.

"You can put me back in the room if you like. I just want some real food. I don't even need a beer. I want to celebrate seeing you."

Tristan smiled.

Zeta looked as if she was going to agree but she shook her head. "We're going to have to find something here."

He cursed silently as she went to the kitchen and looked in the refrigerator. When she returned to the sofa she had chips, dip, and wine. They ate, drank, laughed, and talked well into the night.

Finally, Zeta brought up his wife. "You haven't asked me about Cianne," Zeta said as she lifted the glass to her lips and drank.

Tristan's smile faded as he looked at Zeta. He sighed then spoke. "I've had a lot of time to think about Cianne and me." He took a sip of his wine and swallowed. "I wonder if our lives would be simpler if I decided to stay away."

Zeta peered into his eyes as he spoke. He held her gaze long enough for her to look away. Clearly, she was uncomfortable about him looking at her. She tried to stand but fell back, giving Tristan the opportunity to assist her. He quickly steadied Zeta, holding her closer than he needed to.

How much wine did they drink?

"You've had a bit more than you can handle," he told her. She looked up and Tristan stared into her fog-induced gaze. He held her petite wobbly frame up, then with no effort he lifted her and carried her to Caleb's bedroom. Tristan placed Zeta on the bed, covered her up with a sheet and kissed her forehead. "Goodnight Zeta."

As he walked to his room, Tristan thought about what he was planning to do. For the first time in a long time, he hated himself.

Caleb took his time walking through the mass of celebrating strangers. The streets were filled with people celebrating one of the many festivals New Orleans hosted. It seemed they always had something to celebrate here.

The scents and people seemed to change over time but the ambiance seemed to remain since he was here last. Caleb cleared his mind of all the memories he had of this place, but they seemed on the verge of a comeback. A whiff of her scent, the sound of his laughter, they slammed into Caleb but he steeled his mind and buried his pain deeper.

To anyone who may have noticed him, it looked as if he was taking a relaxing midnight stroll. His shoulders were hunched over; his hands were in his pockets, and his gaze floated from people to objects with little interest. It wasn't until he came to the storefront he was looking for that he became alert.

Azazel's Gift shop was printed on the sign that hung above the door. The building was located on the corner, in a row of quaint side street shops beside an empty lot. Caleb could have passed the store entrance, went to the café across the street, and watched it for a few but he didn't want to spend any more time in the city than he had to. Plus, he wasn't the wait and see type.

The bell above the door rang as he opened the door and entered the store. He took no notice of the occult trinkets that lined the shelves and tables throughout the establishment. None of that interested him. All he wanted was to find the man named Zuri.

It looked as if the store was empty but Caleb slowly walked over to the door behind the counter anyway. He opened the door which led to stairs to a second story room. The room was trashed. It looked as if someone had left in a hurry. Furniture was turned over and items broken.

Caleb followed the sound of a phone's busy signal, finding the phone under a few pieces of paper. He pressed redial. The line rang a few times then transferred to a fax machine. He hung up.

Upset that he was too late, Caleb left the shop and headed to the other address Richard sent him. It was in an old industrial park outside of town. He drove past the unmanned security post and into the complex that housed five large windowed warehouses. Caleb drove to the one addressed 4215-C. He noted there were cars parked in front of the building, so he might get the answers he needed.

He was also aware of the sniper perched on the roof of the adjacent building.

Caleb sensed no aggression from the sniper so he sent the sniper a mental question and received an answer instantly; it was a name—Richard Scott.

Richard had no idea that the soldier on his Special Forces team was a Coesen.

Caleb could have dug deeper into the sniper's young mind or, with a thought, be on the rooftop right beside him but Zuri was his target tonight. Not some young Coesen who most likely was ordered to seek out "Big Bad Caleb's" relatives to smoke him out. He'd deal with the kid when the kid made a move on him.

Caleb saw no reason to prolong the situation so he walked in through the side door of the warehouse, deciding on a straightforward approach. The two men that were watching the door from inside looked at him, both frowning in amazement. With a wave of Caleb's hand, the men fell to the ground before either of them could react.

In the center of the virtually empty warehouse was a large rug with a sizable desk, several chairs, file cabinets, and a coat rack. It was a little office sitting in a room of vast emptiness. Several other men who didn't notice Caleb yet were gathered in and around the large rug. It could have been because they were occupied with watching the beating of the man who was tied to the chair in the center.

Caleb continued to walk quietly to the edge of the rug. "Excuse me," he interrupted, "I have an appointment with Zuri. If you could let him know I'm here."

All the men turned to look at him, all except an older man who sat behind the wooden desk and was busy mixing something in his hands. Caleb instantly knew this was the man he was looking for, Zuri.

The men shifted, and when they did Caleb saw a familiar face. Well it *had* been familiar before all the bruises and blood distorted his features.

"I see you had an appointment too," Caleb chuckled as he regarded the prisoner.

It seemed to take a lot of effort but Perkins raised his head. "Nope," Perkins breathed. His head hung down but his eyes were fixed on Caleb. "But they fitted me in."

The man closest to Perkins punched him hard across the jaw. Perkins grinned, cursed, then spit out a mouthful of blood.

With another wave of Caleb's hand, the two men who moved toward him flew back as if they were kicked in the abdomen. Their weightless bodies parted on either side of the desk where Zuri sat, and hit the wall far behind him.

Zuri didn't look up. He continued to work as his other men advanced on Caleb.

With his target in sight and making no moves to leave, Caleb decided to have a little workout, a release of frustration… He gave each man a good beating before he ended their lives. Zuri didn't even flinch as Caleb killed off his men one by one. It wasn't until Caleb broke the neck of the man who stood beside Perkins that Zuri sighed then leaned back in his chair.

"I was hoping we'd meet one day, under different circumstances of course," Zuri said as he stared at Caleb. "I've heard so much about you Mr. Scott."

Caleb heard Zuri but didn't acknowledge him. His attention was locked on Perkins who was slumped over in the chair. He heard a faint heartbeat and the intake and exhaling of air. Perkins lifted his head slightly, as if signaling he was still alive, but let it fall back down.

"There can be only two reasons why you're here," Zuri continued. "The first would be you admire my work and maybe you wanted to meet me or…you want information."

Caleb looked into the old man's dark eyes. Could anyone be more arrogant?

Well…I can be.

And what was with the Witchdoctor get up?

"Never heard of you until a few days ago." Caleb walked at a lazy pace toward the desk.

"If you had, you wouldn't have come here." Zuri smiled. *Yup…a real arrogant piece of work.*

"Why is that?" Caleb asked as he grabbed for the old man. He held Zuri's necklace in his hands but the man's body was gone. On the floor, were the old man's undergarments, a purple dress and other jewelry. Caleb dropped the necklace. He looked around the room but didn't see the old man anywhere.

Okay, the disappearing act wasn't unexpected, but the fact that Caleb couldn't even sense the old bastard was… Caleb frowned. *What is the word? Oh yeah, perplexing.*

As Caleb backed away from the desk, Zuri appeared in front of him. He was stark naked and holding a syringe. Caleb sighed, his tolerance waning. He made no attempt to reach for Zuri when he appeared but the old man disappeared again.

At that moment, Caleb was thinking of how disappointed the old guy was going to be when he realized that shit had no effect on him. But a familiar sound from a good distance away reached him, the sound of breaking glass followed, then there was the sound of impact. Caleb cursed as he whirled around in time to see Zuri fall to the floor. The bullet seemed to have hit him in the shoulder.

Still, he didn't sense the old man disappear or reappear. Was there something messing with his instinct in this place? He looked up at the only broken window and used his exceptional sight. Richard's soldier was useful after all.

Seconds later Caleb followed the trajectory of another bullet coming from the same direction. It hit the front leg of the chair Perkins sat in, causing Perkins to fall forward, narrowly escaping a bullet from the enemy that was meant for his head. One of the men who was guarding the door had come too and shot at Perkins.

As Perkins fell to the floor, the man who shot at him hit the floor at the same time, a perfect shot between the eyes.

The Coesen *was* useful.

Caleb bent over to get Zuri, who seemed unable to use his disappearing act with a bullet in his shoulder, but Zuri had other plans. He took the syringe he still held in his hand and jammed it into his own neck. Caleb tried to stop him but as soon as the needle penetrated Zuri's dark skin, the liquid contents released into his body.

Zuri shook violently for several seconds before his body went still.

Caleb cursed as he stood and kicked Zuri's body several times. The last kick sent the body flying across the room and into the far wall.

He heard movement. Caleb looked over his shoulder to a man who pointed a gun at him.

The other guy who guarded the door.

Caleb, still fuming that Zuri had killed himself, didn't move. He just watched the nervous man with the gun pointed at him.

Richard was right, he was too emotionally attached. He needed to calm down or he would kill this guy and this damn trip to this godforsaken place would be for nothing.

Caleb decided it was better that he didn't touch the guy so he looked up at the windows, knowing the sniper was watching. "The knees," he said.

The man pointing the gun at Caleb screamed. He buckled when his left knee shattered but before he could fall to the floor another bullet came through the window and shattered his other knee.

The henchman screamed in agony as he rolled on the floor.

Another shot hit the knot of the rope that secured Perkins to the chair. Perkins slowly wiggled free.

It only took a few minutes of torture for Caleb to accept that the henchman knew nothing of the assassination of Vivian Harper or the attempted murder of Tristan. Zuri took his secrets to his grave, leaving both Perkins and Caleb empty handed.

"Thank your friend for me," Perkins looked up at the roof top. He held on to Caleb as they walked to the car.

Caleb looked up. A figure dressed from head to toe in all gray, resembling the color of the buildings, stood. Caleb opened the car door and helped Perkins inside. When he looked back up, the sniper was gone.

Azazel's Gift Shop is no more, the Soldier made his thoughts known to Caleb.

As Caleb drove away, building 4215-C exploded in flames. He had to admit, soldier boy was good at cleaning up.

Tristan woke to find Zeta in the kitchen pouring coffee. He stopped inside his door briefly and looked down at his anklet cuff. A wave of nausea came over him as he anticipated the tingle that preceded the shock, but nothing happened. Then he remembered, Zeta extended his leash.

He bit back his anxiety and focused on his plan. "How's your head?"

"I'm good," Zeta said. She smiled, exposing perfect white teeth. "No side effects really."

She sipped the hot liquid in her cup but Tristan felt her eyes follow him as he sat on the sofa. He smiled at her when he turned her way. Zeta quickly turned around.

This might go more smoothly than I thought, Tristan said to himself when she joined him on the sofa.

"So, what is he paying you to babysit?" Tristan asked.

Zeta didn't respond. Her attention was focused on the bruise marks on his arm. He pulled down his bunched-up sleeve.

"Does it hurt?" she asked as she moved closer. She pulled up his sleeve and touched the bruises. "The poison, I mean," she said.

Tristan waited until she looked up at him. He thought he would milk this, but when their eyes met he could see the hurt in Zeta's eyes, the compassion. He did a mental shake of his head and thought of Cianne and his children. He would do what he had to do to get home.

"Nothing I can't handle," he said softly, leaning forward slowly, stopping only inches before their lips touched.

Zeta moved the rest of the way, touching her lips to his. Tristan closed his eyes and pulled her close. He tried to imagine Cianne but his mind wouldn't give him ease with this task, so he reverted to his wild days and focused on making Zeta believe. When he slipped his tongue in her mouth, she moaned and went limp in his arms. He felt her hand moving over his chest, pulling him closer as if they could melt together. Then her body tensed. Next thing he knew she was breaking their contact and jumping to her feet.

Tristan grabbed her arm. "We can leave this place Zeta. Be together, just the two of us if you want. We can go anywhere in the world," he said as he kept a grip on her wrist. "But we need to leave before Caleb returns."

Zeta seemed confused.

"Please Zeta," he begged as he looked to his leg.

"If I want?" Zeta asked.

"What?" Tristan frowned.

"If *I* want," she repeated louder. "All I have to do is remove that little device around your ankle, right?" Zeta yanked her arm free.

He could see the anger well up in her as her eyes watered over. Before he could say anything, she was in Caleb's room. He heard her lock the door.

"Shit!" Tristan yelled. He kicked the coffee table across the room causing it to hit the wall and fall into several pieces.

Tristan knocked on the bedroom door every hour to no avail. Zeta didn't answer, and worse, she didn't reply when he spoke.

Around midnight he knocked on the door again. Zeta didn't answer but he knew she wouldn't.

"I'm sorry," was all he said before he went back to his room.

Chapter Twenty-One

Caleb used his arm to brace Perkins as he made a sharp right onto Riverside Drive. He looked at his badly beaten passenger, knowing the Coesen needed medical attention or he wasn't going to survive the night. As if to confirm his assessment, Perkins coughed and blood sprayed over the passenger side window and door.

"You need a doctor," Caleb said. He'd been driving for over an hour, trying to put as much distance between him and New Orleans as he could. "I know someone in Biloxi." Caleb merged onto Interstate 110 South.

Sometime later, Caleb drove down a dark street and pulled into a parking pad that grass had grown over long ago. He looked at an adjacent house that seemed out of place. It was a three-story home with clean siding and a new roof. It looked like it was an office and a home at one time but was just a home now.

The neighboring homes on either side of the renovated house were ranch style homes that were in great disrepair, although they both seemed to be occupied.

Caleb carried Perkins to the side door of the out-of-place home where he knew the clinic entrance was located, and knocked hard five times. A minute or so later, he heard the familiar sound of a friend's voice from behind the door.

"Randall?" the woman gasped. Caleb nodded and she slowly pulled the door open. "What are you doing here?" Her eyes moved from Caleb to Perkins, who lay still over Caleb's shoulder. "What's going on?" she asked drowsily.

"I need your help, Silvia," Caleb said calmly.

Silvia closed the door behind her. She didn't look at the man she once considered her friend as she moved around him and over to the cabinet. It's been six years since she last saw Randall. That last day they met for lunch like they did so many times before. They talked and ate just as they always did. Nothing special happened, just two friends in the hospital café, though their friendship did raise some eyebrows.

At the time, Silvia was a doctor and the wife of the great Nathan Franks, who was the head of the surgery department and a force to be reckoned with. He was an arrogant, nasty man who accepted no excuses from any of his employees or coworkers. His demeanor and Silvia's quiet nature limited her from making many friends. The only person who didn't fear her husband was Randall Smith, a janitor who happened to speak to a lonely woman who looked like she needed a kind word, he later told her.

"Your friend will be fine but I don't think he should be moved. You can see him now," Silvia told him. It took three hours to get the beaten man stable. She walked over to a cabinet, looking over at Randall as she placed some items in inside. "You look younger," she said under her breath, "but it's you," she said, staring for a moment before turning back to the cabinet.

"It's me. How are you, Silvia?" he asked.

"Right now, or are you asking about the last six years?" She picked up what she needed and turned around. She looked straight ahead so she didn't have to see his face.

"My intent wasn't to hurt you, Silvia."

"You had intentions, Randall? You mean to tell me you actually planned to not hurt me? I suppose leaving with not even a goodbye or a, hey Silvia I don't think our…" She choked on her tears. "Friendship is beneficial to me any longer but I'm too much of a shithead to tell you face to face."

"It wasn't like that," he said. He moved to the edge of the chair he sat in. "You were starting to-"

"To what Randall? Feel something for you? God forbid anyone in the world ever have feelings for Randall Smith." She couldn't hold back the tears as she walked by him.

"I believe your God has forbade that a long time ago," he said.

God, she was a fool. She wanted to kick herself for being so emotional. Especially because he seemed so unfazed by the way his absence, or his resurfacing, affected her.

"You should know my name isn't really Randall. It's Caleb Scott."

"Oh great," she said then smiled bitterly as she turned and looked at him with contempt, "you're a shithead *and* a liar." Silvia bundled the items in her arms as she walked out of the side door that led outside, leaving him alone in the clinic lobby.

Caleb tapped on the door that said Exam Room 1, unmoved by the conversation. He didn't wait for Perkins to say come in. He entered the room and pulled a chair up to the side of the bed. Perkins lay still at first as if he was sleeping but he let his head fall to the side to look at Caleb.

"You didn't kill her, did you?" Perkins slurred. His lips were unnaturally swollen and had a deep cut that ran through the center.

Caleb felt his jaw tick as the sudden urge to snap Perkins' neck pulsed through him. He took some air into his lungs, his movements so calculated and subtle that no one would be able to ascertain his irritation. He was an expert at hiding his emotions but over the years he hadn't had to hide them. He virtually buried them so deep that he didn't have to.

Now emotion, and feelings he long thought were dead were again surfacing. He heard Richard in his head again, *"You are personally vested."*

He was.

Caleb swallowed a curse as he pulled a cloth from his pocket. He unfolded the cloth and held up what he showed Zeta to gain her loyalty.

Perkins looked at the familiar necklace that dangled from Caleb's hand. He focused on the clear marquise shaped stone with a thin platinum band that wrapped around it two full times. Perkins sighed. When he spoke again it was with more difficulty. "Do you know who did it?"

Caleb placed the necklace around his own neck. "Don't talk, just think of what you want me to hear and I will hear you," he told Perkins. Perkins shook his head. "As for your question," Caleb said, "No, I don't but I will. My search led me to Zuri. I gather yours did too?"

"Yes," Perkins thought. His right eye closed due to reflexes as he thought the word. The left eye was beaten closed. It seemed that Zuri's men were partial to that side of his face. *"It took me seven weeks to track him down; to end up with nothing."* He sighed.

Caleb was also upset about the outcome. The henchman he questioned was just a stooge. He knew nothing and just took orders blindly like a minion should. "Zuri killed himself to protect someone," Caleb said. He looked Perkins over. "You don't have to listen to me but I think it's best if you stay here a while, let Dr. Franks look after you until you're on your feet. If someone's looking, they won't find you here."

Perkins hissed in a breath through his swollen lips. "Soahn Harper trusted you, so I will trust you as well."

◉

The Cabin

Tristan stepped out of his room and into the kitchen with a smile on his face. Zeta hadn't left the room for a day and a half, despite his apologies and all his begging. He was an emotional wreck because of what he did. So, when he heard movement in the kitchen he thought that she finally forgave him, but it wasn't Zeta in the kitchen.

"You can wipe that smile from your face," Caleb said. "The fact that you couldn't tell from my footsteps who it was in this kitchen is pathetic."

Tristan winced.

"I hope you didn't do anything stupid to the girl," Caleb said, giving him a hard stare. Then he dug in a brown paper bag and pulled out two more items and placed them in the cabinet.

Tristan leaned back on the wall outside his bedroom but didn't speak.

"I never understood it when a man says he has no idea that a woman has feelings for him." Caleb turned and looked at him.

Tristan lifted his hanging head, confused by Caleb's comment. Then it was clear to him. Zeta was so upset with him because she actually felt more for him than just sexual attraction. To her, that kiss was probably a slap in the face and not a harmless attempt to get free. As he looked over at Caleb, his shame turned into anger. The bastard knew how Zeta felt.

"You're to blame for all of this," Tristan said bitterly. "If I was home with my wife and children, I wouldn't have hurt her."

Caleb said nothing. His smug devil-may-care attitude was pissing Tristan off. Frustrated and angry, he roared his emotions to the ceiling. He was so loud the beams shook.

Caleb looked over at him. A flicker of interest covered the man's face for a moment then it was a mask of stoicism. "If you refocus that power and use that emotion you're feeling as a base, no one will be your equal."

Tristan was tired, tired of it all. "What do I have to do to prove that I am no longer the weak link you think I am?"

Caleb unloaded the rest of the groceries. "When nothing can stop you from walking out that door, you can leave."

Finally, a clear answer.

If that was all it took, then fine, Tristan pushed off the wall and walked over to the front door and opened it. He knew his limit was the threshold but he was determined to cross it. He raised his foot up and over the doorsill, overlooking the familiar tingling climbing up his leg. His body stiffened as electricity began to course through him. He leaned forward. Tristan clinched his fist and leaned his head back as his body pulsed with more pain.

He didn't know how long he stood with one foot out of the door and the other foot in but he knew it was a new record as he felt himself losing consciousness. Tristan pulled his foot inside. He looked over at Caleb, who was now seated on the sofa eating fruit.

Tristan smiled. He didn't pass out. He never lasted over thirty seconds. "I'm not going to be here too much longer," he said confidently, so you might want to finish up that story of yours."

Caleb raised a brow. He liked the kid more and more as the days passed. "Right," he chuckled, as he recalled where he left off in his life story. "Small patches of the fields were still smoldering when the sun came up and my neighbors, who'd come to help, began to take their leave. There was nothing more anyone could do.

"Eighty percent of the crop was destroyed. No one knew for sure who was responsible though several men were seen riding away from Maiden Hall after the fire started. But I knew, and I was determined to make them pay."

"And, Marda?" Tristan plopped down in the chair next to the sofa.

Caleb could see the electric charge had exhausted him but Tristan would never admit it. Although he could tell the little stunt did drain him, Caleb was impressed.

"Marda was safe." He sighed with relief as if reliving that day again. "When the fire began she and some of the suckling women gathered the children in the safety of the chapel.

◉

Maiden Hall Plantation
Early morning after the blaze of 1826
The sound of the bell that alerted the slaves to begin their work would not be heard as it had been for over twenty years. The overseer's call would not be heard either. The once-bustling plantation looked as if it had been abandoned. Most everyone was inside the dwellings, tired from fighting the fire, tending wounds, or helping with the young, animal and humans alike. Some of the slave quarters burned when the fire spread but most still stood.

Alone, Caleb walked the fields, noting the damage. He stood looking out over what was left of his crop in disbelief and shock when movement to his left caught his attention. Caleb moved faster than he should have, crossing the distance in a flash. He was able to make out her scent, even over the rotted stench of cindering fields.

"You should not be out. Those men may still be on the property," he said to Marda as he stood over her bent form.

Marda looked up at him. On his face, his emotions lay bare for all to see. His anger, his hurt. She looked at what was left of the plants then looked at him as if she wanted to…as if she was sad for him.

"You never asked me what my gift is," she said, looking down at her hands. Marda slowly placed them flat on the healthy grass just beyond the fire's reach. She closed her eyes and exhaled.

Confused, Caleb watched her. Nothing happened at first then he saw what looked like seedlings crawl up from the charred ground. The seedlings turned into leaves in a matter of seconds. Then blossoms appeared, then an open boll. Twenty-five weeks of nature happened in under a minute.

"How?" Caleb asked, astonished by what he just witnessed. It was as if all he'd come to know as a Protector never happened and the Coesen world was new.

"I can bring it all back for you." She closed her eyes again and an entire row of mature cotton sprang up from the once burnt ground. "I am what my people call an Engron. I am able to will the growth of living things." She opened her eyes and looked at him.

Caleb's attention was on the row of cotton that was just right for the picking. "Make it go away," he demanded when he looked at her. His face hardened and his eyes were fierce.

"I can fix it all, *for you*, Caleb."

Marda placed her other hand on the mound of dirt to her left but Caleb kneeled down in front of her. He grabbed her left hand and pulled it away from the mound.

"You must hear me. What you can do, what you have made possible for me, is miraculous," he told her, "but it's something we need to keep hidden. People do not accept what they choose not to understand. If this crop returns after so many have seen it burn, someone will be held responsible for what will be viewed as witchery, instead of a miracle. Return it as it was, Marda. Return it now."

As they stared intensely at each other, Marda slowly slid her hand from his and placed it back on the mound of dirt where the cotton stalks were growing. She reversed the process so the plush cotton was instantly returned to burnt twigs then ash.

"Now, I have much to do and little time to do it, so if you could return to the house and gather what you hold dear." He stood then pulled Marda to her feet.

It took only a few minutes for Marda to reappear, carrying a sack. Caleb wasn't privy to what the sack contained but he would bet she carried the two books his mother gave her soon after she arrived at Maiden Hall.

Caleb waited outside in a horse-drawn wagon. When Marda slowly approached, he got down and took her sack. He helped her up in the wagon and placed her sack beside her. He signaled for the horse to go after taking a seat next to the sack.

Neither of them spoke as the horse galloped to their destination. Caleb didn't tell Marda where they were going and she didn't ask. Instead she rocked with the wagon in silence, looking over at him in the large hat he wore every so often.

Once within city limits, Caleb felt the fear that rose in Marda trickle over him but he didn't stop. Minutes later, he pulled the wagon on the side of a building with a sign that read Scott's General Store.

Inside one of the rooms over the store that Caleb used when he stayed with his uncle, he sat Marda on the bed. "You rest here. I will not be gone long," Caleb said to her.

He turned to his uncle, who waited just outside the door. Caleb hurried out of the room, pulling his uncle with him before shutting the door.

"What is going on Caleb?" his uncle asked.

Caleb rushed down the stairs. His uncle followed close behind. They moved through the empty store to the back room. Only then did he stop and turn toward his uncle. "Watkins sent his men to torch the crops last night."

"Is everyone ok?"

"There were a few injuries but everyone lives." Caleb pulled the door open but turned back and grabbed his relation by the shoulders. "I need her safe, Uncle. You are the only person here that I trust. Promise me you will send her to my mother in London if I should not return."

His Uncle nodded. "Tell no one I was here." His Uncle nodded again. Caleb relaxed then gave a nod of his own before he left the way he'd come.

He was outside of Broken Nail Tavern a few minutes later. Being Sunday, the place was closed but Caleb had no problem slipping inside. None of the usual goons stood outside of Bill's office so Caleb pushed the door open with no resistance.

Inside, lying with his upper body sprawled out on his desk with a dangerously low bottle of whiskey inches from his hands, was Bill. Caleb strode over to the desk, gripped Bill's hair in his fist and raised the inebriated man's head so they were eye to eye.

"I told 'em not ta do it," Bill slurred as he focused on Caleb. "That you ain't right."

Caleb let go of his hold on Bill's head and watched it sway until Bill gained some sort of control. "I warned 'em. You ain't right boy," he repeated.

It was true. Caleb heard Bill Marshall tell Watkins on several occasions to "steer clear of that boy". At first Caleb thought the man's constant obstruction was due to him being of a fine home and his gentleman status but later realized that Bill feared him. After each seemingly unwinnable victory, Bill was always watching. Caleb was certain Bill knew nothing, but the man sensed enough to always place money on him to win.

…and Caleb always won.

"Is he home?" Caleb pressed.

Bill fell back, rocking the chair on its back legs before stabilizing himself. The entire time his eyes stayed glued to Caleb. "My mother's mother, she was Cherokee and spoke of dark spirits. Boy, you have the darkest spirit I've ever seen in a man."

Caleb was astonished that Bill thought his spirit was darker than Watkins', a double-dealing murderer who would slit his own parents' throats for a nickel. He mentally shrugged. "Then you know to not deny me."

Bill nodded and the movement almost knocked him off the chair. "Then," he said, then sighed, "the unlucky bastard is indeed at his home."

Before Bill could finish, Caleb was gone.

The two-story brick house was located on the outskirts of town in an affluent neighborhood with big townhouses and large plots of grass located in the front and sometimes in the rear of the homes. The sun was higher by the time Caleb got there but neither of the two fireplaces in the home smoked.

All the homes on the Exeter Street were in the midst of their morning bustle while only one room was lit up at the Watkins home. Caleb had been inside the office many times and knew that on Sundays, Watkins gave his slaves the morning to themselves while he conducted his business.

Again, no one saw him as he entered the residence. Casually, he walked through the kitchen, past the servant's rooms to a small entry hall that led to the office. Caleb heard the conversation from inside the closed room as soon as he entered the townhouse but now he was close enough to distinguish that there were four voices. It would have been easier to match the voices to the person if he wasn't drunk most of the time when in the presence of the men he now stalked.

What he did know was, Watkins was inside. Wherever the boss was, Jack and Ben were. So, he had the identity of three of the men. The fourth voice was a bit of a mystery. Caleb pushed the door open.

"Mr. Scott," Watkins said then smiled. "What do I owe the pleasure?"

Caleb moved his gaze over the interior of the room, resting briefly on the newcomer in Watkins' company. He saw Ned only a time or two but didn't know him like he knew the other three.

"The little matter of my fields burning," Caleb said as he entered the room.

Knowing your opponent was the first lesson he learned. He walked slowly over to stand in front of Watkins' desk, sweeping a glance at each man. He was compounding information such as, Ben carried two guns and a large knife. Jack carried one gun, a thick metal pole, and a thin wire for strangling his victims. Watkins didn't carry any weapons, other than his forked tongue. Ned was a fighter.

"Yes…well, that was unfortunate. I am sure you are relieved that it wasn't the Manor that went up in flames instead." Watkins smiled like he was holding a winning hand.

Caleb narrowed his eyes and balled his fist at the threat as a flood of adrenalin pumped through his veins. Ben tensed and Jack reached into his pocket; preparing his strangling wire, was Caleb's guess. Ned and Watkins didn't move.

"I can offer my protection against those kinds of mishaps, for you and your family, if you should decide to come to work for me again."

Ben must have been holding his breath because he exhaled when Caleb relaxed. The tension in Jack's hands released as well.

"If you offer your protection for me and mine, then who will be protecting you?" Caleb asked as he moved with blinding speed to Ben's side then to Jack's back. Caleb was suddenly back in front of Watkins' desk, the spot he was in before he moved, with a look of pure hatred on his face. Ben's and Jack's bodies were slumped to the floor where they stood.

One punch to Ben's heart and it stopped cold. Strangling Jack would have been poetic but Caleb wasn't in the mood to play with them.

Ned raised his gun at the same moment Caleb turned and rushed him. Ned flinched as he clumsily pulled the trigger of the gun he pressed into Caleb's shoulder.

Damn, that burned.

But the pain was bearable. Caleb grabbed the warm barrel of the gun, snatched it free and tossed it before he slammed his head into Ned's face so hard his teeth ached from the sound of the cracking bone.

Caleb lowered his head and listened for any sounds outside of the office. The only sound he heard was the drumming of Watkins' heart and the short intake of the man's breath.

"I came here with the intent to appeal to your humanity. You are void of even the smallest amount. I was willing to overlook it and your blatant disregard for my property, and permit you to live," Caleb said, looking over his shoulder. He let Ned's body fall from his grasp as he turned and made his way to the desk. "But you threatened my family."

Watkins, frozen by the events that unfolded, was frantically pushing away from the desk. Sweat covered his brow and his heart rate sped up. "What…what the hell are you?"

"To you…I am death." Caleb smiled, as he moved forward.

Caleb climbed the stairs with silent speed even though the ride from Maidan Hall had the injury to his shoulder aching. He shouldn't have come, but the pain in his chest ached more. As he stood with his hand on the knob he reminded himself that this was a bad idea. The woman on the other side of the door would be better off without him.

The night he killed Watkins and his men he told himself that he would let her go. He was a murderer, and Bill Marshall aimed to prove it by hiring a lawman named Benton. Caleb spoke with Benton two days past and it seemed he managed to convince the man he had no information to help solve the murders, but Caleb needed to be careful.

Being careful meant not going to Marda.

After he murdered those men, he went back to Maiden Hall and sent word to his Uncle to purchase Marda passage to London.

Caleb just got word that she didn't accept. He planned to stay away until she came to her senses but his resolve weakened with each passing day.

Until…

Caleb opened the door without making a sound but Marda must have sensed his presence because she whipped her head around and stared at him. *God.* Her long hair flowed freely down her back like black silk. Her sleep gown was thin enough to see her comely figure beneath. Her face glowed with an ease he never saw before.

When their eyes met, Marda threw the book she held to the floor, jumped off the bed, then wrapped her arms around his waist and lowered her head on his chest. Taken off guard, Caleb wrestled with the idea of embracing her but felt it was useless to fight one's heart.

He slid his arm around her waist, brushing his hand over her hair and bracing her back with his other hand. Caleb didn't know why she ran to him but with her soft body pressed against his, he didn't care.

"You're bleeding." Marda gasped as she pulled away.

Caleb was reluctant to let her out of his arms but he forced himself on her enough. She took his hand in hers. His chest tightened from the casual contact as she led him over to the bed and had him sit.

"Please, sir," she said as she wet the cloth in the basin near the bed, "Undo your garments."

Caleb unbuttoned then shrugged out of his carrier's bag, waistcoat, and shirt. When Marda turned to face him, her eyes inspected his naked chest thoroughly, invoking his body's natural response to such attention.

He shifted to hide his engorged appendage.

"I'm fine, really," he said. But when she began to undo the bloody bandage Barkly placed over the bullet wound, he bit down on his tongue and forced a moan. No, he wasn't beyond faking discomfort for the pleasure of her touch.

"Did they do this to you?"

She didn't look up when she asked the question, which made him sigh with frustration. Her tone let nothing slip and he needed to see her expression to gauge his next move, but her hair hid her face.

He was about to answer her question when her hand caressed his shoulder. The gentle touch made his shaft twitch and took his breath away, making it impossible to respond verbally. Caleb managed a nod.

"Will they be able to hurt anyone else?" Marda lifted her head then. Those soft brown eyes of hers were waiting for his response.

Caleb knew what she asked and he wanted to lie, to tell her that they still lived, but when he opened his mouth he simply said, "No."

To his amazement, she blinked then gave him a solemn smile of understanding. It was as if she knew he didn't want their deaths but felt it had to be done.

"May I?" she asked as her hand continued to caress his shoulder.

Caleb's brows furrowed.

She looked at his wound. "May I, stop the bleeding."

"Yes," he said without hesitation. He wanted her to know he trusted her with his life.

"Because we were separated and didn't sync well, you're not healing as you should." Marda smiled at him before placing her lips to his wounded shoulder.

The sudden feel of her soft lips on his sensitive skin sent a shock through him like nothing he ever felt. Pleasure and pain ripped through his body at the same time as his wound merged closed. It was the very definition of what he endured since realizing he was lost in love with her.

After the burn of her kiss subsided, Caleb leaned back he said, "I did not know your lips could heal."

"They cannot," she said, smiling seductively.

They were only inches apart but he fought the urge to close the distance and suck her bottom lip into his mouth.

"I can regenerate the living tissue, but the pain and soreness of the injury will continue through the natural stages of healing. Though, because you are my Protector, the process will be much quicker than that of an average man. My lips have no more power than my hands," she said sucking in the bottom one briefly. "I just chose to use them instead."

Caleb wondered if it should bother him that she was attracted to him sexually. It was clear the night he took her, she wanted his body just as much as he wanted hers. But he selfishly wanted more and it seemed she wanted only the physical. Sex was what men always wanted, the physical. Should he be offended that she wanted to use him in the same way?

Can I live with that?

No, he couldn't.

"Why are you not on the ship?"

She sat back on her knees gazing back up at him. Her innocence, beauty, and gentleness overwhelmed him to the point of insanity.

"I go where you go, sir. I am yours," Marda said, confused.

Caleb closed his eyes briefly, in an attempt to calm himself. Given the chance, would he urge her to stay with him? "Marda," he reached for his bag, "you are your own person. I have set all the others free. The ones who chose to stay on at Maiden Hall will be paid a wage, secretly of course. They have been given their papers. I hold yours." Caleb pulled carefully folded papers from his bag. He reached for her hand and placed the papers in them.

Marda looked down at the papers she held in her hand. Finally, she held her freedom in her hands. When she looked back at Caleb, she couldn't stop the moisture building in her eyes. She expected to shed tears of happiness once this day came.

Only her tears weren't from being deliriously happy. Her tears were from her heart that was now shattering in a million pieces. Shattering because she was free of the man she just recently realized she loved.

Chapter Twenty-Two

City of New Orleans 1826

Every evening, since arriving in New Orleans almost two full months ago, Marda ate alone. When she sat down at the table that could comfortably seat ten, in the richly decorated dining room, there was no reason for her to think this night would be any different.

Dressed in a long white newly purchased cotton nightdress that originally had a high lace neckline that she unstitched and redesigned to her liking, she ate quietly until she heard the front door being unlocked.

Marda got up from the table and hurried to the kitchen, returning to the table with a warmed plate of food and a glass. As she readied his place at the table she tracked his steps in her mind, having seen him act them out on several occasions. She imagined that he was removing his coverings and was now making his way to the dining room. When he physically entered the dining room, she was placing his silverware next to his plate at the head of the table.

He walked around the table to where she sat and grabbed the back of her chair. Marda looked at him as he waved his hand over her seat. She walked over and sat down in her seat as he instructed. She wanted to ask him where he was the last three days but she didn't. She came here with him of her own free will and that meant she wouldn't make demands of his time.

The home he bought was beautiful and so were all the clothing and jewelry, but it wasn't her. Marda felt the women here wore too many layers, the sleeves were too puffy and the fabric wasn't breathable. Seeing free people of color, the Creole people, and the whites doing business with each other like their skin color meant nothing was refreshing. But none of it made her happy.

Caleb didn't sit at the head of the table where Marda placed his dish. Once he scooted her chair under the table, he sat beside her. Formalities always bothered him. So much so that he once told himself that when he became a man, he would do away with such etiquette when in the comfort of his own home, unless he was entertaining of course.

"Has Lisette retired for the evening?"

"I had no use for her today," Marda said quietly as she moved her food around her dish.

Caleb stared at Marda for a moment. When she didn't look at him, he lowered his head to meet her eyes. "Marda, I pay Lisette to mind your needs but you have to allow her to do so." He looked over her nightdress. "Do you dislike the clothing I had commissioned for you?" Then he asked, "Marda, do you not like it here?"

Marda looked up at him. "I am not sure what it is you wish me to say, sir."

"I wish you to speak your mind, Marda. Tell me what I must do to make you happy."

"I feel lost here. Is this dwelling, the new garments, Lisette and Pierre, all to appease me?" Marda whispered, "I can never be happy here—"

"Forgive me, Marda," Caleb cut her off. He pulled her chair from under the table and was on his knees with his head lowered on her lap before she noticed he moved. "I had wished that time would soften you. That you would grow to love me. That by leaving Maiden Hall we would have a chance at a life together. My selfish heart wants to hold you hostage but my mind screams a logic I can no longer ignore. I have tried to let you go but I do not think I can live without you."

Marda's eyes glossed over. Her chest rose and fell with every breath she took as she raised her hand over his head, but lowered it without touching him. "When I was taken from my home I was determined to only speak the language of my people. I hated this country and everyone with pale skin until your mother."

She smiled when he looked up at her. "Then you came. With you, I wanted to talk. To say something to you, and I waited for the day you spoke to me again. But when you did, my anger with my situation prevented me from doing so. I did not know it then, but that day you put your lips to my hand was the day my heart tied to you. But I cannot be happy here if you are not here with me…Caleb."

Caleb repeated what she just said to him in his head twice before clearing his throat to speak. "You want *me*?" he asked.

She nodded.

Elated, he placed his hands on either side of Marda's face. He moved in to kiss her but stopped and pulled back when the familiar sensation rolled through him. All the air in the room seemed to thicken.

Caleb's eyes widened. "But, you are afraid?"

"I fear what will become of us. In this place, it is common for a white man to share a bed and keep his Creole or woman of color comfortable. I fear that if I give you my heart that one day you will one day marry and abandon me. You haven't lain with me again. I fear you have another and that the fire you once felt for me has burned away."

Caleb took Marda's hands in his and laughed. "My God, Marda, you must know how greatly I hunger for you. I stay away because I struggle to leash that hunger. You need not fear any of those things. I have not known any other woman since the day I lay with you. I vowed to love and honor you as my wife. That is why I brought you here, to make a life with you where we can be together. I was only waiting for you to show a sign that you want me as I want you." He waited until his words sunk in. When he saw the light in her eyes, Caleb kissed Marda's lips with a fierce possessiveness.

Marda weaved her fingers through his hair and returned the kiss with all the passion he gave her. She was breathless when he broke away. "I vow to love and honor you and to make the time you spend here enjoyable."

Caleb shook his head. "I will have no other home or woman anywhere else. I will reside here with you." The way of it was common here, but should a problem arise he would handle it. "You are mine and I am yours. I will die before I let *anyone* ever take you from me, Marda. I promise you that."

Present Day

Caleb sighed. His mood was shifting, but he couldn't help that if he told his story the way it happened. "Later that same night, I asked Marda if she wanted me to take her home. I told her that I would stay with her no matter where we were."

Caleb closed his eyes.

"She told me that she had forfeited her right to be with her people. When I asked her what she meant, all she said was that she was not the same girl she once was and her life was now on a different path. A path that she believed led her to me." He sat back and exhaled as he looked up at the ceiling.

When Caleb lowered his head back down he felt hollow, empty.

"Looking back, I should have asked her more questions about her people. But the truth was, I didn't care about them or anything else for that matter. All I cared about was her. We were happy," Caleb sighed. "For a few years, I was happy."

New Orléans 1830

Caleb patted then rubbed his hand over the boy's tightly curled golden hair. "Samuel, dire à ta mère à que le repas était parfait."

"You cook well mamma," Samuel said. His bottom was half on the chair and half off as his foot swung anxiously back and forth. He looked at Caleb with his large blue eyes. "May I now, papa?" he asked excitedly.

Caleb looked at his son then through the window to the courtyard where two boys about the same age waited, both bubbling over with the same energy Samuel was trying to contain.

"You may," Caleb said, then laughed after making his son wait another agonizing minute.

"Do not leave the courtyard Samuel," Marda said as she frowned at Caleb.

Caleb always gave in, making him favored in their son's eyes. He stood and began helping Lisette gather the dinner dishes. The feisty Haitian cut her eyes at him, placed the dishes she had in her hands back on the table and said something under her breath before throwing her hands in the air and going into the kitchen. Caleb laughed again, this time louder, as he called out his apologies.

"I told you she hates it when we help," Marda whispered. "She is already ill tempered due to me preparing the meals." Marda turned, exposing her small bulging belly.

Caleb came around the table and took one of her hands and brought it to his mouth. "I can meet Lanier some other time. You can read to me tonight. Perhaps one of those fairy tales you love so much."

"It makes no sense you missing an engagement. I will be fine, Caleb." She placed her hand on his chest, smoothing out his shirt. "Lisette will be in her quarters if I need her. I will be fine."

Later that night Caleb entered his home feeling more joy than a man should be allowed. Marda's love gave him purpose. Then she gave birth to Samuel, which made life perfect.

Caleb made his way to his son's room. The boy was asleep with his fingers tightly grasping a carved horse that resembled

Caleb's steed. Caleb gently removed the wooden horse Pierre had carved from his son's hand. He placed the horse on the side table then kissed his son goodnight. He would make sure to give Pierre his gratitude for such a gift. Maybe even a raise in wage.

He cracked his son's door then silently made his way to his own room. He quickly undressed then slid into bed with Marda, placing his arm protectively over her stomach, which held Samuel's soon to be baby sister or brother. Within minutes he was sound asleep.

Caleb slept peacefully, the way a man does when he has no worries. His life was not the way of a seasoned Protector. So, when five men entered his home, he didn't hear what his ears would have picked up if he was properly trained. He did not wake until he felt a waterfall of fear wash over him.

"Marda," Caleb called as he got to his feet. A brief glance around the room told him she was not there. It took him only a second to get down the stairs and in the sitting room, only to freeze in confusion as he looked around the room.

In his home were four smartly dressed black men with their eyes fixed on him. Caleb ignored their scrutiny and used that moment to search the room for Marda. She sat on the sofa with her back to him so he couldn't see her tears but he knew the sound of her cries. What he did see was that each of the strangers had a mark branded on their necks. The same mark that Jai and Marda also had.

"Marda?" he called to her but no one moved.

The man standing over Marda huffed as he glanced at Caleb, but continued speaking to her. His language was foreign to Caleb but it sounded as if this person had authority over Marda…and the others. As the man spoke, his steely eyes moved to Caleb several times. When he was finished speaking he gestured to Caleb with a closed fist.

This can't be good.

Marda stood and turned to face Caleb but turned back to look at the man. She called him Arie, and spoke in the same foreign tongue. She was begging. Caleb stood silent as Arie's hard eyes bore into Marda until the weight of his stare seemed to be too much and she looked away to face him.

She was so upset that Caleb was having a time trying to understand her. Caleb took a step toward his wife but one of the men blocked his path. Without hesitation Caleb pushed the man out of his way, launching the stranger across the room and into some furniture.

Each of the men turned to look at Arie, who shouted what sounded like a command.

Mistake.

One of the men moved faster than Caleb could track, landing blows that Caleb couldn't stop, let alone see. Before he knew it, he was on the floor, blood spilling from somewhere on his head and into his eye.

Two of the men grabbed him under his arms and raised him up.

Marda ran to him as he virtually hung forward with the men supporting his weight. She wiped the blood from his eyes and mouth with her night shirt and kissed his face several times before Arie spoke again.

Marda held onto Caleb's face but turned her head to look at Arie, "Jai is dead. She died several years earlier, protecting me." Her gaze swept back to Caleb, imploring him to keep her lie. Caleb gave her a discrete nod. When Arie frowned then looked away, she spoke again. "I used my magic so they found me. A man called Bill sent them here." Her eyes grew sad as her tears continued to fall. "If we go with them," she said sobbing, "my brother has sworn that no harm will come to you."

Caleb's head felt heavy but he managed to shake it. *No!* his mind screamed. *What is happening?* Shocked and confused, he tried to wiggle his arms free of his captors' grip. But he was unable to shake them.

Finding his voice, he began to scream out the word "No!" But no one paid attention. Once he realized he wasn't able to get the man's attention he focused on Marda. "Don't do this!" he yelled, "Don't leave me!" He repeated his pleas even as Marda covered her mouth and stood. "Take me with you!" he screamed to Arie. But the man only regarded him coldly.

"Papa?"

Samuel.

Caleb whipped his head around to see another of the men carrying Samuel into the room. "Samuel, tout va bien." He looked at Marda, "Please my love, don't."

She didn't respond in words but her sobbing became more and more frantic. And as she reached for a sleep dazed Samuel, she was close to hysterical.

The man who carried Samuel waited for Arie to nod before he placed the boy on the floor next to his mother. But Samuel didn't go to Marda. Instead the boy ran to Caleb, wrapping his arms around his father's neck.

"Ecoutez votre mère." Caleb told Samuel. "Listen to your mother," Caleb said again in English as he kissed his son repeatedly. Samuel rubbed his now wet eyes and sobbed as Marda pulled him away and walked toward Arie.

"I. Will. Come. For. Them." Caleb said angrily, making sure Arie got every word.

Caleb saw hate and intent grow in Arie's eyes but there was nothing he could do other than brace himself. He watched helplessly as Arie raised his hands toward him. He waited for whatever came as he glanced over at his family.

He saw the decision in Marda's eyes and fought with all his might to break free.

Marda spun to shield him as she embraced Samuel to her chest, taking the blast in her back. The force in which she was hit, with whatever it was that hit her, was so great that the repercussions knocked Caleb and the two men holding him to the floor.

Shaken and in immense pain, Caleb managed to crawl over to Marda and Samuel. She was still clutching their son in her arms when he rolled her over.

"No…no," he said as he shook them. He gently touched Samuel's hot face but kept his eyes on Marda. "Please…Marda," he begged as he rubbed her protruding belly.

An agonizing scream erupted from his gut and out of his mouth as tears trailed down his face. His attention moved to the little arm that fell limply away from Marda's neck. Caleb covered his mouth with his hand, keeping his shocked pain inside as he focused on his son.

"Samuel," he cried as he pulled his boy from Marda's death grip. "Samuel, please God not my son!" he screamed as he clutched the motionless body to his chest.

Caleb didn't hear it when the man named Arie told the two men to restrain him, but when they pried Samuel from his arms he was face to face with the men who just murdered his family. He struggled for a while but it didn't do any good. His strength and speed expired the moment Marda had. Grief-stricken and numb, Caleb looked at his enemy with fire in his eyes and a promise in his heart.

"Marda chose her fate," Arie said in English and lacking remorse. "Leaving me to choose yours." He looked at his companions and spoke in his native language again.

What he said translated to, "Hang the devil from his tree."

Present Day

Tristan sat on the edge of his chair. He sighed, wiping his hand over his face. He couldn't believe what he just heard. But somehow, he knew it was true.

"I was hung from the tree in the courtyard. A fitting death for the son of a planter, I suppose." Caleb stared off, focusing on the sky. "Or it would have been if Lisette hadn't come to me. You see, to the Coesen warriors she was a slave who needed to be freed, not my employee. Lisette did leave but she returned with my friend Lenier, and a few others. I don't have to tell you, Arie and his band of brothers were nowhere to be found at that point. They murdered my family and disappeared and I wasn't able to do a damn thing to stop them."

"I didn't know something so horrible happened. I just…I'm sorry."

A dull ache built in Tristan's chest as he listened to Caleb recount the final moments of his wife and son's life. The ache was now a throbbing pain.

"I don't know what to say. They were trained Guards," Tristan whispered. "But, Marda was his own sister. Why would he—"

"For weeks, that's all I asked myself. Why would he murder his own sister, his nephew, our unborn child? Jai tried to explain it all to me later when Fredrick brought her to New Orleans after they received Lenier's letter. The consensus around the city was that I was targeted because of some situation I mishandled badly during my days in Dominion. No one except Jai knew that this in fact was my first lesson in Coesen justice.

"Arie had spent years searching for Marda and Jai, only to find that his sister, a princess of his tribe, had willingly given herself to one of the devils who had enslaved them. He was to take her to stand before their King but when they discovered that I was also her Protector... As you know, it is a death sentence for any Protector and Coesen who should fall in love.

"But Arie had given Marda a choice. She could take me to her father which would mean a death sentence or she could go with them willingly and I would be spared. Marda decided to save me. She agreed to go but had asked her brother to spare our children's lives; that they were still Coesen. Because I was a Middling and would be once more when her sentence was carried out, Arie agreed to Marda's last request. To let me and Samuel and our unborn baby live, but…it didn't work out that way." Caleb exhaled as he stood.

Tristan didn't say anything as Caleb walked to his room and shut the door. He closed his eyes and tried to picture his family as they were when he last saw them. His memory was fading. Not of them, but of the clear image he once had of them. He remembered events, clothing, Cianne's hair and the way she smelled, but it was just a shadow image now.

It was as if he was eating his favorite food but wasn't able to taste it.

The desire to get home just hit crucial. Tristan got up, went to the front door and stuck his foot out over the threshold. He held it there until the pain was so bad that he felt himself passing out.

He pulled his foot in back, breathed, then waited until his heart stopped pounding. Then he raised his foot over the threshold again. He repeated this over dozen times, extending his resolve on each try before his body succumbed and his eyes fluttered closed.

Chapter Twenty-Three

Ark Mansion
September

Cianne jerked to a sitting position on the bed as her chest visibly rose and fell. Her body was wet with perspiration and she could hear every breath she took as she fought for clarity. The imagery was so real to her that she couldn't tell if it was a nightmare or reality.

I'm falling apart, she thought as she wiped her hair from her forehead.

"Are you alright?"

Whodai's deep seductive tone sent a shiver through Cianne. "I'm fine," she sighed. Conscious of his presence now, Cianne pulled up the neckline of her damp night-shirt but it did little to hide her breasts through the thin cotton. She pulled up her sheet. "Do you ever sleep?"

"Another nightmare about Tristan?" Whodai asked. He got up from the chair then strolled across the room toward her.

Cianne saw the worry on Whodai's face and felt the weight of her guilt again. She reached out and took his hand, pulled the sheets back and attempted to tug him down beside her as she scooted over to give him room to slide in next to her. "If you're going to stay in here all night, like you have all week," she said rolling her eyes, "you may as well sleep in the bed and not that uncomfortable chair."

Whodai eased his hand free before he returned the sheets the way they were then lay on top of them.

Cianne tucked her hands under her head as she lay facing Whodai. She yawned and her eyes felt heavy. She opened and closed them a few times but tried to mentally shake herself awake. When she noticed Whodai was focused intently on her she said softly, "I don't mean to be such a pain."

"You're not a pain. You're my friend," Whodai told her, matching her tone. He reached out and peeled a long strand of damp hair from her face, letting it fall to her shoulder.

"Best friends," Cianne said as she yawned. She mumbled a few words, with the intent to talk through the night.

Whodai watched as Cianne fought to stay awake. His gaze traveled over her coal arched brows and long lashes that emitted shadows over her rose-tinted cheeks. Her nose was perfectly centered and her lips were full, pouty, a peach tint that promised the taste of heaven. The smooth skin of her neck led to her average sized breasts that were pushed together, creating a tantalizing cleavage.

He groaned a curse and shifted his body.

Being this close to Cianne, watching over her this past week was too much for any man to bear. He wanted a taste. He deserved that at least.

A test then, he told himself.

She was sleepy and stressed, that made for low defenses. If it didn't work, he'd play it off. The fact that she was exhausted…she would believe anything right now.

With his mind made up, Whodai decided he did want to taste Cianne. He inched closer to her and spoke. **"Cianne, you want me to kiss you goodnight."**

Cianne didn't move immediately, like most who heard the tune of a Wheddler; the command hung in the air for a few seconds. He figured it was the recipient's brain trying to fight for control. When she blinked and her eyes opened, with that aware yet hazy glow, he knew the order had been received.

She moved forward and placed her lips on his mouth.

Whodai cupped the back of Cianne's head with his hand and rejoiced when she opened her mouth for him. Lost in a moment of heated passion, he inched closer and moved his other hand down her back to rest on her hip.

Dare I try for more… The thought instantly died when Cianne broke away.

Whodai moved back and peered at her confused face. He quickly kissed Cianne on her forehead, though her swollen lips called to him. "Goodnight, Cianne."

Cianne, still appearing confused, smiled. "Thank you for putting up with me, Whodai. Goodnight." She lowered her head back on her pillow then closed her eyes.

Whodai sighed with relief as he watched Cianne sleep like he did every night since arriving at Ark Mansion. Only tonight, he lay beside her with the realization of two things. His Wheedling worked on her for the first time. He tried so many times before and only succeeded in giving her a headache.

His second realization—he didn't just want Cianne to be his wife. He wanted Cianne to love him of her own free will.

Zeta arrived at Ark Mansion shortly after eight am. She hadn't seen Cianne or the twins in more than thirty days. She missed them but she wasn't too comfortable with Cianne knowing how she felt about Tristan. Add on that she knew he was alive and safe, and her guilty conscience was eating at her. Keeping Tristan hidden was keeping him safe but Zeta wasn't sure she could hold on to the information once in front of her friend.

Damn Caleb for involving me in all this.

Instead of going to the house, she headed for the Guard headquarters which was a separate building just beyond the main gate.

"Zeta," Kim exclaimed as Zeta walked into the eating area "We were so worried about you." Kim jumped to her feet and pulled Zeta into a bear hug.

Not yet comfortable with Kim or the way she liked to hug, Zeta tried to back up, but being a Protector, Kim was quick. American born, Kim was in her mid-twenties, had a round face, long plaits on either side of her head, and a pierced left brow. Everyone called her Southern Belle because of her drawl, warm hugs, and unbeknownst to her…the big breasts she sported around.

When Cassius assigned Kim and the two other Protectors to the young Royals after Vivian's death, Zeta was upset about not being offered the job. She felt that she was best qualified, and due to her relationship with Cianne and Tristan, the lateral move would have been seamless. Cassius apparently thought otherwise.

Maybe Cassius bypassed her because of her feelings for Tristan.

"Uh, why were you worried?" Zeta inquired as Kim released her.

"Oh gosh, you don't know do you, sugar?" Kim grabbed Zeta by the hands and pulled her over to the small table. "So much has happened since you've been away. About a week after you left, someone broke into the house in Arizona. Felix, the one from Trinidad who was assigned along with me and Jacobi, he was killed. It was a freaky kill too. That's why we moved the family to Ark Mansion. It's more of a fortress than a cozy house…ya know."

That's why they moved?

"Who killed him?" Zeta asked.

"Honestly, no one really knows," Kim said. "But I saw Whodai shortly after it happened and he looked downright shaken."

"Really?" Zeta asked. *Whodai shaken.* Zeta would have paid to see that.

"Yup, but things have been just as crazy here. The alarms are being tripped at least three times a week but Cassius feels this is the best place to protect the Royals." Kim looked up as she put her finger to her chin, then said, "But things have sort of calmed down a bit."

"Where is Cassius now?" Zeta needed to know what she could do to help.

Kim shrugged. "Last I heard, he was investigating a lead on Caleb. No one really knows where he is or when he's coming back. Whodai is in charge." Kim quickly interpreted the look on Zeta's face. "I know right, but he hasn't been all that bad. He basically lets us do our jobs without imposing his all-mighty will."

Zeta raised both brows, "Really?"

"I suppose all the time he's spending with our Soahn has softened him a bit. They're inseparable you know." Kim smiled. She was about to say something else but stood up and lowered her head instead.

Zeta automatically did the same when she looked over her shoulder and saw Whodai standing inside the doorway.

"Kim, don't you have some place to be?" Whodai said.

How long has he been standing there? Should it irritate me that I didn't hear him open the door or enter the room? Yes, it should, Zeta decided.

She watched as Kim hurried out of the room without looking back.

"Excuse me," Zeta said to Whodai as she attempted to slide by him to exit the room.

"Just a moment," Whodai said, blocking her way.

The door was slightly open but Zeta still knocked. When she heard Cianne's voice telling her to come in, she almost turned to leave. But she didn't. Instead, she stepped into the brightly lit room and noted that all the curtains were pulled back to let in the natural light.

Soahn Vivian once told her that was what the room was designed for, exposure to natural light.

"Just sit it here please," Cianne said in her soft tone.

Zeta walked over to the seating area that faced a large sliding door and looked over the balcony to a large grassy field. The high back chair hid most of Cianne's body except for the hand she extended to motion to the table beside her. Zeta walked around the quaint seating area for two and gazed at her friend.

Cianne, clearly not expecting her, dropped her cell phone. Zeta quickly caught it before it hit the floor.

"Zeta!" Cianne screamed out with joy.

Zeta stiffened as Cianne jumped up and hugged her tightly, her guilt chastising her very existence. "How have you been?" Zeta asked. She held Cianne just as tightly. The embrace lasted so long that Zeta wondered if she was afraid to let go and actually face her friend, knowing what she knew.

"I'm well," Cianne muttered.

When they separated, Cianne's smile seemed to be pasted on, suggesting she wasn't well at all, but Zeta said nothing.

"We've missed you, the children and I. Sit, tell me about your vacation."

Zeta followed suit and sat after Cianne did. She glanced at the cell phone she caught before handing it back to Cianne. On the screen was a picture of Tristan. He was smiling of course.

I'm not a true friend.

Zeta couldn't look at Cianne. She instead looked out the window into the clear sky as she took a deep breath. She had to be careful of what she thought and said. Being away from Cianne for even a few days, one could miss knowing about any newly developed or enhanced abilities.

When she turned back to Cianne she managed a smile, "I'd rather hear about what's been going on with you and the children. Is Nadia walking yet?"

"She is," Cianne said with real excitement.

Cianne began sharing all the cute little things the twins did over the past month. As Zeta listened she couldn't help but notice how tired her friend looked. Cianne's hair was loose, but it had a ponytail dent from frequent use of hair ties. Her skin looked pale and the skin under her eyes was darkened. Plus, she kept looking around the room every few minutes.

Zeta felt saddened by all of this. If Cianne knew the truth about Tristan, then… No, she couldn't tell. Vivian trusted Caleb and so would she. She had to believe in the plan.

With her mindset reinforced, Zeta said, "I've missed them so much. I'd like to see them before I leave."

A worried look appeared on Cianne's face. "You're already planning to leave?"

"I've been reassigned. I leave tonight." It wasn't a full out lie. She was reassigned but the Royal she now guarded gave her leave. They currently resided in a Safe Zone.

"No," Cianne whined, "you must stay with us. I'll talk to Cassius."

"Please don't." Zeta shook her head. "I want to go." It was clear to Zeta that Whodai didn't want her around because he wouldn't have had her assigned to a family moving to a safe zone. She would go but she would find out why he wanted her gone.

Cianne eyes glossed over as she looked away. "Oh, ok."

A long silence followed before Zeta spoke again. "Are you getting enough sleep, Cianne?" Zeta touched her hand.

Cianne scrunched her nose up then shook her head. She was on the brink of tears when Zeta revealed she wanted to leave. With the recent question, Cianne couldn't seem to hold them in any longer.

"It was his birthday you know, the third of this month."

It had been over thirty days since Zeta last saw Tristan as well. She was still upset about the stunt he pulled on her. But now, now she understood why he did it. She cursed herself for not remembering. She slipped from the chair and kneeled in front of Cianne, then pulled her friend into her arms.

"I didn't even remember. My damn cell phone reminder kept going off...and yeah." Cianne sighed as she eased out of Zeta's hold. She placed her phone on the table between them. "I don't sleep too well these days. I'm afraid to close my eyes because when I do...I see him."

"Don't you want to see him again, even if it's in a dream?" Zeta asked softly.

"It's not like you think." Cianne wiped her tears with the back of her hand. "They're not dreams, they're nightmares. In every one, Tristan is hurting me. Either he's stabbing, drowning, shooting, or smothering me. Whatever the device, I always end up dying in his arms."

Zeta was initially speechless. All she did was look at Cianne for a few minutes, until it soaked in. "Have you told anyone about these nightmares?"

"Only you," Cianne said then sniffled. "We're forever connected you and I. We've loved and lost him together," she whimpered.

Zeta sat back on her heels. It was a bad idea, her coming here.

"Do you think he," Cianne hiccupped, "forgives me?"

Zeta eyes grew wide. "Who?"

Cianne didn't say his name. "If he's dead like they all say, do you think the dead can forgive...or am I fucked?"

Zeta was about to respond but she heard a knock on the door. Cianne wiped her eyes with her nightshirt sleeve and jumped to her feet just as the door opened. She pointed to the table.

"Is there anything else I can get you ma'am?" the maid asked as she placed what looked like a smoothie on the table.

Cianne shook her head no.

The maid, someone Zeta didn't know, looked her way. "You ma'am?"

"No thank you." Zeta watched the maid walk out of the room. When she turned back to answer Cianne's question,

Cianne was already closing the bathroom door a few feet away.

Zeta sat in a daze inside the bright room, the sun beaming on her as if demanding something of her. She hadn't decided if she was going to keep Caleb's secret when she arrived, and now after speaking to Cianne, things were even more confusing. Telling Cianne that Tristan still lived may get him killed in the end. Not telling may result in Cianne's insanity.

When the bathroom door slowly opened, Zeta turned around. Cianne stood in the doorway with a large pair of scissors in her hand.

"Cianne," Zeta yelled, getting to her feet. "What have you done?"

Chapter Twenty-Four
Continent of Africa Gedgi Territory

The crowd's applause was deafening and it took several minutes to stop before Chandra spoke into the microphone again. "The Arkean bloodline has run dry and the last of the great queens has been laid to rest. I will not allow a Middling raised hybrid destroy what our ancestors have worked so hard to preserve," she said then paused as clapping ensued. "Are you prepared to do what you have to do, because I am!" she yelled.

Screams of support dwarfed the applause as Chandra raised her fist in the air and smiled. She waved to the crowd before moving out of the spotlight and off the stage.

"Cassius," Chandra said. She walked over to the corner of the stage where he stood and gave him a quick hug. "Have you come to your senses?" She led the way down the platform stairs and into a small gathering of people. They met up with Chandra's Protector, who led the way to a waiting vehicle.

"I just need a few minutes of your time," Cassius said as he walked with her. When Chandra stopped beside her car, he did too.

"You haven't come to your senses." Chandra raised a brow and said, "And you're not alone, are you?" She looked around.

"Soahn Brenna left for the hotel shortly after your speech began. She would like you to join her."

◉

When Chandra walked into the suite, Brenna stood, acknowledging her. Chandra took a seat across from Brenna after nodding. She looked past Langley, who sat in a single chair near the window, as if he wasn't in the room.

"You look well, Brenna." Chandra lifted the drink Cassius sat in front of her. When he sat down next to her she smiled. Chandra looked over her shoulder at Victor, who gave her a nod. She offered him a nod in response then watched him leave the suite to join Brenna's Protector in the hallway.

"Do you have any idea what you're doing, Chandra?" Brenna scooted to the edge of her seat, her expression very serious. "Are you completely mad?"

"I wonder the same about you, my friend. Considering the circumstances involving your appointment as Soahn, you of all people should understand how dangerous the girl is." Chandra accused.

Like Chandra, Brenna had been affected by Cianne's existence. Deni, Brenna's mother, was called upon when the child's powers manifested. Cianne, then known as Zaria, was unable to handle such power. Deni and the other four, which included Vivian, Chandra, and Eldra, suppressed the child's abilities but the process weakened them all. Deni never fully recovered. Brenna was in her twenties when she inherited her place as the Quende Soahn and one of The Four.

"You blame Cianne for the sins of her father and things she had no control of. Her coming was foretold and we have been appointed to counsel her so that she can reach her full potential. To become sovereign of our people." Brenna placed her hand over her chest. "I beg you sister, stop this sedition."

"Cianne cares nothing for our people or our culture and she has no reason to pretend now that Vivian is gone." Chandra looked away. Suddenly her attention moved from Brenna to focus on Langley. "You seem to have a lapse in judgment, Brenna. You know how I feel about outsiders."

"Engraved on his skin is the same mark you and Cassius bear, the mark of the Quende Tribe." Brenna looked at the mark on Langley's neck then back to Chandra. "Which means, in his veins runs the blood of *our* people. Vivian accepted him as one of our own and we should too. To not accept him is to debate our very existence and the Source's gift to our people."

"*Humph,*" Chandra breathed. She cut her eyes at Langley again before returning her attention to Brenna.

If Langley felt anything during the exchange, his temperament or expression didn't change to reflect it.

"I'm sorry, sister," Chandra said then sighed as she turned to Brenna, "but I've made up my mind about this."

"And just what does that entail?" Brenna stared into Chandra's eyes.

Chandra grabbed the back of the sofa, digging her nails into the cushion. She narrowed her eyes as her head slightly shook. The two women's eyes were fixed on each other as if no one else was in the room. Slowly Chandra's hand rose to her head.

"You will not learn my plans like this, Brenna," Chandra hissed through clenched teeth. "I have prepared all my life to withstand Scanners. Even one as powerful as you."

Brenna continued to try to invade Chandra's mind but was unable to get anything. She had to stop or risk draining her ability on one of the Four.

Chandra smiled when the pressure let up. "You shouldn't try that again."

"You leave me no choice, Chandra. If you proceed with this, you will be waging war. If there is something, anything I can do to prevent that, I will."

"You can stop this right now. All you and Eldra need to do is rid our lives of the devil called Caleb…and his offspring and her children," Chandra demanded.

Brenna gasped. "Have you changed so much, Chandra? Is life so meaningless to you that you would kill an innocent, and children? You know, when Tristan disappeared I was reluctant to believe that you had anything to do with it, but now I can't be so sure."

Chandra looked over at Langley with disgust. "The Breed will tell you I speak the truth when I say I gave no order to harm your Middling king. But know that if you aren't with me," she said, eyeing Cassius now, "then you're all against me." Chandra stood and walked toward the door. She left the room without saying another word.

Langley looked over at Brenna who was waiting for him to speak. "She has no intention of ending this," he said.

Brenna sat back on the sofa wearing the look of defeat across her face. She failed to convince Chandra that peace was best for their people. She was so upset that she didn't see Cassius run over to the window or that her Protector, Riley, had come into the room shouting orders.

"We need to leave," Cassius grabbed Brenna by the arm and pulled her to her feet. He looked at Langley and Riley and said, "Shoot to wound, not to kill. These men are still our brothers."

Mid-September
Missing four months

Tristan sat on the porch steps looking out into the forest. He rested his elbows on the step behind him and closed his eyes. He let his head fall back so that the sun's warmth covered his face. There was a breeze blowing but it wasn't cold. It was a lovely September morning. The date? Tristan didn't know.

"Tell me, what do you hear?" Caleb asked him.

Tristan took in an exaggerated deep breath then exhaled. He turned his head and opened his eyes to look at Caleb who sat on the porch chair by the window. He had to squint to keep the sun out. "The same things you hear." Tristan turned his head up again and basked in the sun.

"Is there something else, something new, in the background that you didn't hear before you got here?" Caleb leaned forward.

Tristan sat up. He looked around slowly then peered at Caleb. "Birds, the winds blowing the leaves, maybe a cricket or two," he said. "Nothing I don't hear every day. Why, what should I be hearing?"

Caleb sat back. He lifted his feet up on a crate that sat in front of him.

"This has to do with what you did to my ears, huh?" Tristan continued to look at Caleb. After a while he realized Caleb wasn't going to answer him. He shook his head then returned to the laid-back position he was in before Caleb interrupted him. "I was hoping you'd continue your story today," he said finally.

"I think we can take a day off from storytelling."

Tristan sat up and turned around so he could see Caleb without stretching. "You are kidding, right?" Tristan grimaced at Caleb's confusion. "You went to your room after telling your story and didn't surface until this morning."

Caleb went over what felt like the last few hours in his head. He slept most of the time and occasionally lay awake in his bed looking at the walls, but in no way did he spend days in his room.

He didn't look at Tristan, who glowered at him with a look that most people gave the insane. The telling of Marda's and Samuel's passing nearly broke him but Caleb supposed he should finish what he started. Besides, Tristan was showing great improvement in his training and should be rewarded.

A deal was a deal, and he always kept his word.

Maybe when he was done his blasted story, Tristan could focus on what he had to do.

"Alright. After my family died, I had nothing to live for. Days ran together with me lying in "our" bed. Some nights I would crawl to Samuel's room because I was too weak to stand. I'd sit there in a corner until Fredrick helped me back to my room. After a few weeks, it was decided that I should be taken back to London, but I couldn't let that happen.

"The night Fredrick came to inform me of his plans, I was already gone. Something inside me had rose to the surface and it would drive me for the next two years."

Tristan whispered, "Revenge."

"I wouldn't rest until I had it. I was owed four lives and I was willing to do whatever it took to claim my due. Arie was at the top of my shit list. But without my Protector's strength and speed it would be suicide. Only, I didn't care. I would take Arie's life or forfeit my own in the process. So, I boarded the first ship that left port to the continent of Africa. My plan, stay there until I found him.

"I drew Marda's birthmark on a piece of paper and hired a native named Modat to travel with me. Modat seemed to be one of the few not wary of me or the mark I showed. He was just as young as I was and just as fearless. We went from one village to the next showing anyone who was curious the mark I had carved. No one seemed to recognize it or would admit they did.

"Two long years passed with no sign of Arie or any other Coesen. The deeper into the terrain, the less tolerable the native people became of my presence. I was a white man that most saw as a slave trader. Some of the villages we entered, the people yelled angrily at me as they waved their fists. Other villages, the villagers wouldn't even allow me to enter at all. So Modat entered and questioned whoever would listen. Then, one day Modat was told of a village that held natives who were…unusual. We set out to find this village. One night, while we slept, we were ambushed."

Continent of Africa
Circa 1830

There was no use struggling. The rope that was wrapped around Caleb's wrists and feet was so tight he wasn't able to feel his fingers or toes. Flat on the dirt floor, his arms were stretched above his head and fixed to some kind of hook in the ground. His feet were hooked in the same manner, stretching him to the point where he wasn't able to move a muscle. The only part of his body he could move was his head but even that movement was limited.

With his eyes wide open, he tried to focus on the first image he saw but the blood running from the cut above his right eye made it difficult. He turned his head to the side so that his lips were scarcely touching the skin on his arm. His gaze rested on Modat, his guide, restrained the same way he was.

"Modat," Caleb called. He repeated this several times before Modat grunted. "Where are we?"

Modat said some words in his native tongue that Caleb didn't understand. After taking a few deep breaths, his guide spoke again. "I do not know my friend."

"Can you get free?" Caleb struggled to see Modat, hindered by the way he was tied and the angle his friend was beside him. Modat grunted several curses in his language then said "no" in English.

Caleb looked around, digging his head in the dirt to see as much as he could. They were in a hut. It was round with one opening that was covered with a long cloth. The place was virtually bare. In fact, Caleb saw nothing in the space that would suggest that any of the natives that captured him and his guide actually used this particular hut.

"I didn't get a look at any one of their necks, Modat. Did you see the mark?"

Before Modat answered, the cloth covering the entrance was pulled back and four tribesmen entered the hut. One of them was dressed in ornate clothing that included a large headdress. Both Caleb and Modat lifted their heads as much as they could to get a good look at their captors but neither could see much.

Modat called out but the tribesmen ignored him. Modat began shouting. That did get one of the men's attention because he lifted his foot and came down hard on Modat's face.

"Stop, he did nothing," Caleb shouted but no one paid him any mind. He looked helplessly over at an unconscious Modat.

When the men started to talk amongst themselves, he strained his head up again to see if he could interpret anything. Caleb silently watched as they stood close by, speaking and making hand gestures toward him and his unconscious guide. Then they cut Modat's bonds and lifted his limp body. As one of the men bent over to look at Caleb, he focused on the tribesman's neck where there was no mark.

This was not the village he was looking for.

Caleb let that sink in as he watched the men carry Modat out of view. At some point Modat awakened and began to scream. Caleb squeezed his eyes closed as he listened to the struggle but could do nothing. He tensed as Modat's screams became loud shrill cries for help. The cries stopped but were replaced by the sound of loud gurgling followed by a loud thud that caused some dust to rise from the ground and cloud over Caleb's head.

Then there was silence.

The quiet didn't last long. The men began conversing once more as Caleb's anger rose. He made this journey for nothing. He wasn't going to get the revenge he sought, and a man he called a friend was most likely dead. He roared his frustrations, silencing the conversation in the hut.

A command was given and Caleb was cut from the posts that held him to the ground. With his hands and feet still bound tightly he was lifted by his captors and dragged across the floor, leaving lines in the dirt from his heels. His limbs hung limply due to the strain that was inflicted by the ropes. Caleb let the men carry him without struggling. He didn't open his eyes until he felt his foot drag over what his eyes confirmed to be Modat's body.

Caleb tensed but he still did not resist. It wasn't until he was placed in front of a brown shell-like object that looked to be as tall as he was or taller, that anxiety set in. He was going to die, a fact that he had come to terms with mere minutes ago, but in what way?

The object looked solid, and was covered with knots that resembled those on trees and curved lines that made it seem rough, like scales. But when they brushed his body against it he realized the object was smooth and gave the appearance that it was wet but it wasn't. Overall, it looked like a large, very old, disfigured tree stump, minus the leaves and branches.

Caleb watched in silent horror as an opening appeared and a long thin transparent yellowish appendage or tentacle reached out. The thing moved like smoke wafting through the air toward him, light and graceful.

Instinctively, Caleb attempted to move back but there was a man on either side of him securing his arms, and one man behind him with a firm grip on his hair to secure him. His eyes widened as the appendage floated closer to his face. Only a few inches separated him and the smoky haze as it moved around his head.

No one in the hut made a sound and nothing moved but the thing for what seemed like forever, then Caleb's breathing became labored. His eyes rolled back in his head and his body began to shake.

"My food usually begs for their life. Aren't you going to beg for yours? No...I suspect you won't. You are not like the others."

"Leave my head!" Caleb yelled. But the thing continued doing whatever it was that caused Caleb's head to feel like it was being pounded with a hammer.

"I've been waiting for someone like you. Someone to free me."

The men released their grip on Caleb and backed away when his body began to shake more rapidly. Suddenly the cocoon cracked open and a gust of wind blew throughout the hut. An airy figure appeared, with long horns that resembled those of an antelope, a narrow face that had wide eyes, and a long slender body.

Its smoky form hovered in front of Caleb for a moment, then just as quickly as it left its protective cocoon the entity fused with Caleb.

"Whit debil!" a tribesman he assumed to be the spiritual leader of the tribe shook his staff.

Present Day

It asked my permission to bind to me. All I could think of at the time was how badly I wanted Arie. It read me you see." Caleb rubbed the back of his neck.

"What the hell was it?" Tristan gasped. He sat on the porch now, using the crate in front of Caleb as a chair.

"I don't know," Caleb admitted. "Once it entered me everything shut down. I know how this is going to sound but I swear I felt nothing, heard nothing, and I saw nothing. Then, as if something jump-started me, I was back. My body rebooted. Only, I couldn't catch my breath. My lungs burned as I tried desperately to suck in air to breathe. I was suffocating. *We* were suffocating.

Central Africa

part 2

"Kill him!" the leader yelled.

As he struggled for air, Caleb heard and somehow understood the words the man in the headdress yelled. His eyes were open but everything went black when the "thing" fused with him. Now, with another threat of death, he needed air desperately to protect himself.

"Take his heart now."

From what Caleb now understood, the man barking the orders was the spiritual leader of the Bressi tribe. He gave the order to kill a second time as he shook his staff at his tribesmen.

Their language wasn't all Caleb understood now. He knew things too. He knew that for generations the Bressi offered many of their tribesmen and anyone else they came across as a sacrifice to their cocooned god they found and brought to their village long ago.

The Bressi lived unconquered among the local tribes for all these years because of their god and Caleb soon understood that they would not allow him to take their deity away.

Still reeling from the merge, Caleb didn't realize that one of the men had driven a spear through his chest until he raised his hand to clutch his throat and brushed over the wood spear. Just as he made the discovery and grasped the wood so it couldn't be buried deeper, another of the men came up from behind and wrapped his forearm around Caleb's neck, pulling him hard to the ground.

The spear, still lodged in Caleb's chest, ripped through more flesh as both Caleb and the man who drove the spear into him continued to hold on to it. Still gasping for air like a fish out of water, Caleb took one of his hands off the spear and pushed the man holding the other end in the chest as hard as he could.

To Caleb's surprise, the man flew into the air and through the roof of the hut as his scream trailed off in the distance.

Caleb could allow himself only seconds to be in awe of what he did because he was still suffocating. The spiritual leader and a third man, the youngest of the four who helped carry prisoners to the cocoon, watched everything unfold in a frightened trance. They both backed out of the hut.

Caleb gripped the spear and pulled it out of his chest, spilling blood that seemed too light, all over him and the ground. Refusing to let go of his neck, the man squeezed tighter and arched his back. With more ease than seemingly possible, Caleb pried the large arm from around his neck and was finally able to take a deep breath.

The sound of the man's wrist bone snapping didn't even register with Caleb, nor did the gut wrenching scream from the man's mouth that followed. Caleb was only concerned about the hole in his chest as he scrambled, slipping on his own blood, over to the cocoon.

Leaning back against the hard metal-like shelter that he originally thought was wood, he placed his hand over his wound. A blood and dirt-mud mixture dripped through his fingers, to his leg, then to the ground. Startled by a sudden movement in front of him, Caleb pushed back, digging his heels in the dirt as he raised his hands up at the man racing toward him with some kind of ax.

Wanting, wishing, or willing the man to halt, Caleb didn't know which he did, but the man stopped. Seeing someone running full speed at him then seeing them come to a full stop without slowing, like there was an unseen wall blocking their progression, scared the hell out him. It seemed to frighten him more than the thought of what the man planned to do to him.

Breathing now, but with immense pain, Caleb dropped his hands and again placed one over his chest. To his surprise the man dropped as well, his head held at an awkward angle. His neck was broken from the force that stopped him.

Caleb, expended, closed his eyes. An image of Marda and Samuel dying was what he saw. "I cannot expire now," he called out to no one in particular. His anger forced his pain aside as he clenched his chest. "Not until he pays for the wrong he's done to me."

Present Day

Caleb took a deep breath before he went on. "That was the first time I healed myself." He fisted his hands so tightly his knuckles turned white. "I've had a lot of time to consider what "it" was and why "it" chose me. Pithos…that was the name I gave it because it never gave me one—"

"Like Pandora's box," Tristan interrupted.

Caleb agreed by nodding his head. "Pithos never again communicated with me aside from that day. What Pithos was I didn't know; I still don't but I know how it makes me feel. Invincible, fearless, and callous with no regard for anything or anyone, not even myself.

"Why Pithos chose me, that's easy. I was the perfect vessel. My body was strong due to the reconditioning I endured during the cycling or transition to become a Protector. To my knowledge, no non-Coesen has ever survived the transition other than me, and of course, you.

"The right host was vital but the hate that consumed me and the fact that I really didn't care if I took another breath was apparently what Pithos needed. I gather that the cocoon was protecting it for a very long time. How long, I can't say but I'm pretty sure it wasn't able to survive outside of its cocoon without a vessel. The Bressi were the only ones who could answer any questions about Pithos' origins."

Caleb sighed.

Central Africa
part 3

Healed and barely alert, Caleb emerged from the hut. He paid no attention to the frightened villagers who backed away from him, creating an aisle but avoiding his gaze as he made his way to the border of the village. Everyone was afraid they might suffer the same fate as the two who died by his hands.

Outside the village, Caleb fell to his knees by a bed of water. He began to cough violently over the water until he expelled a bitter dark fluid from his mouth. After coughing up what remained in his belly, he rinsed his hands then cupped some water into his mouth.

Quenched and clear of the blood on his face, he sat down on a large boulder.

With his breathing better than normal, he took a moment to think. Not about what just happened or the dead friend he traveled with the last two years, whose body he had to step over to exit the hut.

No, he thought about how he would find Arie.

In that moment, the moment he thought of his enemy, a feeling overcame him. Caleb felt an overwhelming urge pulling him southwest. It was a strong source of power that beckoned him, or rather, called to the thing that was now housed inside of him.

Why he was being led to his desired destination didn't matter to Caleb. He knew the source of the power was Marda's people. They wielded great power, a power that no other humans possessed.

Caleb got to his feet. He staggered forward as he took in the landscape. After getting his footing, he began to jog then slowly accelerated into a run. To his surprise, he was fast again. Not Protector fast but infinitely faster.

He sprinted over dry plains and lush landscapes for who knows how long until he came to a chasm from which a cataract waterfall fell. Hidden behind the water was a small entrance to a cavern that Caleb's newly acquired vision permitted him to see with ease.

Without thinking, he began to climb down on pure instinct only, not once considering his own safety. Every move he made was quick and precise as he drew closer to the power source and Arie.

The entrance was clearly man-made but inside the cave was pitch black. Caleb's eyes adjusted as he walked along a slippery path that followed a wide stream of fast flowing water from the falls. He increased his speed gradually the further he went on. After walking for miles, light filtered ahead through a narrow opening.

Stepping through, Caleb stood on a rigid ledge where the cave opened, allowing the water to plunge a couple hundred feet into a pool. On the shore, several people stood looking up at him. Another two were climbing up the sharp rugged cliff toward him.

Caleb knew he was in the right place as he watched the men climb with ease, grace, and speed. The two men moved like spiders. When they reached Caleb, one of the men jumped to the ledge.

The man looked much older than Caleb and he bore a mark that was similar in size and shape as Marda's but it was in a different position. His stare was intense but Caleb didn't quake.

Instead, he took note of the people that stood by the water's edge. *They must be the first line of defense*, Caleb thought. There were both men and women but he didn't see Arie.

"I am here for Arie." Caleb said as he slowly looked from the people standing below him to the man standing beside him.

The man looked at Caleb a few seconds more before he turned around and yelled words Caleb understood down at the people below. They were getting permission. Caleb had no issue with waiting but he would fight his way to Arie if they didn't let him in.

A woman below took off in the direction of a wooded area. When she returned a short time later everyone was still in the same position, waiting patiently. She called up to the man who stood next to Caleb.

"He awaits you. Do you need help getting down?" the man asked. His English was very good.

When Caleb first looked at the man standing beside him, he only glanced at him to make sure he wasn't Arie. But when the man spoke, Caleb looked at him again. He saw this man before, at his home.

"You offer me help now?" Caleb said through clenched teeth. He then leaped off the ledge, falling very close to the side of the cliff. Halfway down, he grabbed a small protruding section of rock with one hand. Then, turning so he faced the people below who watched him with curiosity, shock, and suspicion, he let go, landing near the edge of the pond on his feet.

As Caleb began to walk, the Coesen who waited by the pond flanked him on either side while the two men, who took a little longer to descend the cliff, fell in behind them. The group led Caleb into a grove of large trees that were all the same size and evenly spaced as if nature had no hand in how they came to be arranged. On the other side of the grove was a large village.

They walked until they came to a large empty area. Standing on the far side were several people who gave off the vibe that they were important. Among them was Arie. Caleb's jaw ticked. He set his eyes on his enemy as he and the guards closed the distance.

"I am Garwa. You have traveled a great distance to find my kingdom, stranger. It is a place that is almost impossible to find. Why have you come?"

Caleb turned his piercing gaze from Arie to the old man who spoke. He was dressed no differently from the others, tightly fitted tops with loose bottoms, only he wore a thin gold band around his head and a large stone hung from his neck.

"I have business with Arie."

Garwa didn't seem surprised, but the woman who stood next to him was. She frowned, "I am Mina, first wife. What is this about?"

Caleb looked to Mina and instantly saw the resemblance. His posture almost faltered as his pain surfaced. Caleb pushed what heartache he had aside and willed his anger to the forefront.

"He feels he has been wronged mother," a young girl who held Mina's hand said.

Caleb looked at the child. No older than eight, the girl stared at him with her lovely brown eyes.

"He wants revenge for lives lost when our sister passed over." She looked at Arie, then to her mother. "An unborn son and a small boy with sand tinted skin, his and Marda's young." The girl pointed to Caleb.

Several onlookers gasped. Mina dropped to her knees and screamed out. Some of the women near them tried to console her as she sobbed openly.

You look just like her, Caleb thought.

"*My sister and I share the same mother and father,*" the girl said.

Caleb focused on the girl but said nothing while she continued to talk in his head.

"*The wives were not aware of the children,*" she said looking at the women who surrounded Mina. "*My sister, Marda was the first born and would have succeeded father. Your son would have been next in the line of kings.*" Her tone suggested she was sad.

Garwa continued to just look at Caleb. There was no emotion on his aged face. Caleb didn't consider Garwa;

instead he looked down at the women, forgetting his mission. He focused on a woman who wrapped her arms around Mina.

"That is Sele, my half-brother's birth mother." The girl looked over at Arie. *"She is also second wife to Garwa and birth mother to Arie."*

"Is what your sister says true, Arie? Did you… Did you judge the innocent?" Sele asked as she held Mina.

Arie did not respond as he stared at Caleb.

"Marda was of me and I mourn her as you do." Garwa looked at his wives as they cried. "But what has happened cannot be undone." He concentrated on Caleb. "My daughter chose to forfeit her life when she took you as her mate. That is our law, Middling," he said. "You survived but you do not see this as a gift, instead you come here to welcome death."

Caleb heard Garwa but was looking at the girl who continued to stare at him. She looked so much like his Marda when she was a child. She welcomed his gaze with a sorrow in her young eyes, but her look soon turned suspicious.

Her eyes grew wide and she cried out, "He carries a powerful evil inside him."

With that Caleb launched himself at Arie. To his dismay, Arie was pulled aside and his Protector took his place, hitting Caleb with such force that he sailed into the air and fell hard to the ground. Caleb was stunned but not hurt. He stood and looked at his opponent. It was the same man who offered him assistance a few minutes ago, the same man who held his son in New Orleans.

Some of the people backed away while some, possible the soldiers of the tribe, stepped forward. Caleb took no notice of their formations. He walked toward Arie's Protector in an unhurried pace. The Protector quickly closed the distance, running at Caleb with blinding speed. The guy was fast but, Caleb was faster.

Caleb reached for the warrior's right arm, twisted him around so that their backs were touching. With his free hand, Caleb reached behind him, grabbed his opponents chin, and twisted his neck with such speed and power that the man slid to the ground, dead. Caleb then turned around to see the shocked faces of all the spectators. He stepped over the Protector he just killed and slowly began to close the space between him and Arie.

Arie lifted his hand. A blast of force hit Caleb in the chest, throwing him into a structure a few feet away. "Go for shelter!" Arie yelled at the females as Caleb crawled from the rubble.

"That should have killed him," Garwa said in disbelief. He backed away.

Within seconds, Caleb was up and on his intended path again. As he came closer, Protectors attacked him from all sides. With a wave of his hand they all stopped, frozen in place. Caleb didn't want them. He wanted Arie.

Again, Arie raised his hand only this time Caleb spun. The blast missed him and was headed for an onlooker when Mina stood. She quickly raised her hand, creating an invisible barrier between the onlooker and the blast. The blast hit the barrier and dissolved.

Arie unsuccessfully tried to hit Caleb again with his blast, but just as before, Caleb moved from its path and grabbed Arie by his neck, lifting him in the air. Heat pulsed down his arm into his fingers, burning Arie's neck. He smiled with satisfaction as Arie's cries filled his ears.

With revenge a heartbeat away, Caleb couldn't help looking to the girl who looked so much like his Marda. His fractured mind wanted to tell her he was doing what he promised, that he was getting revenge for them, but he suddenly felt light headed. Caleb peered once again at Arie before everything went black.

Caleb blinked a number of times before he was able to keep his eyes open. He lay on the ground staring out at nothing for over a minute before he dug his fingers into the soil beneath him and pushed himself up and to his knees. His movements were slow due to his stiff, sore muscles and an inability to focus his vision.

As he got to his feet, Caleb looked around the once lively village that was unnervingly quiet. He didn't hear any people, animals, or insects. The only sound he could hear was the sound of the water in the distance.

Suddenly dropping to his knees, Caleb cried out, pressing his temples as an intense pain ricocheted through his head. When the pain subsided just a few moments later, his vision was clearer than it had ever been but what he saw caused him to gasp in shock. He closed his eyes and turned his head away.

Caleb slowly opened his eyes again. Horrified, he looked around at the dozens of lifeless bodies that littered the ground. He crawled over to the closest body and rolled it over. It was Arie. He searched the body but there were no visible signs of trauma.

He looked around again at the bodies. Men, women, and children lay dead all around him.

"I did this." Caleb sat back in disbelief. "So many innocent lives lost because of my need for revenge." Somehow, he knew.

It didn't take long for Caleb to search the entire village. Nothing survived. Pets, livestock, insects, even the trees suffered the same fate. As Caleb climbed the cliff the image of the little girl and her big brown eyes came to him. Then it dawned on him; he didn't see the girl among the dead.

Present Day

"**I** found myself standing at the top of the large waterfall that hid the opening to the Quende village." Caleb closed his eyes, hoping to dissolve the memories he suppressed so long ago. "Feeling sadness and regret, I jumped to rid the world of the monster I'd become." He took a deep breath before looking over at Tristan who blankly stared back at him.

"As I lay broken and in severe pain, thinking that I was breathing my last breath from my blood-filled lungs, I prayed that God would allow me to see my family in heaven before the demons of hell swallowed me. I woke several hours later. My bones seemed stronger, the damage reversed. Healed but mentally broken, I was certain of two things. Pithos was not going to let me die as long as he inhabited my body."

"What was the second thing?"

"That God doesn't exist," Caleb said plainly.

Tristan turned from him and peered into the forest. Caleb thought that maybe he should have kept that god comment to himself, knowing that Tristan came from a religious background. Caleb shrugged as he watched Tristan lean forward to pick up a branch that lay next to the crate in front of him. The kid peeled back the layers of bark from the branch like a banana. Caleb wondered if Tristan was imagining that the branch was him.

"I prepared myself for several reactions that you might have. Your silence was not one of them."

"I'm sorry to disappoint." Tristan broke off a small piece of the branch and threw it to the ground.

"It's a lot to take in. Knowing the type of man you are, I applaud your restraint. I'm sure you want my head," Caleb said.

"My silence isn't in response to anger. I'm silent because I'm ashamed. If my family…" Tristan grimaced then said, "I'm not sure I would feel the guilt you do." He threw the rest of the branch away, got to his feet and walked to the other side of the porch. "I don't know." Tristan sat down on a chair next to Caleb on the porch.

"What happened to me was no excuse for what I did. Innocent people died. Women and children, who will never know the joy of life or the pain of loss, died because I needed revenge." Caleb sighed. "And the worse of it was that I had no idea of what or how I did it. So, I went back to the Bressi village to find out what Pithos was and how to free myself of it.

"The destruction I unleashed on the Quende tribe extended for miles beyond their hidden village. All that flew had fallen from the skies. Death was extended to any land animals or burrowing pests as well. I walked for hours before the first sign of life appeared.

"When I finally made it back to the Bressi village, it was as if I was caught in a nightmare. Everyone, just like the Quende village, was dead. I felt sick and had to run to the stream to wet my face, maybe take a drink…and that's when I saw it. The black bile I'd thrown up had eaten through the rocks and gotten into their water.

"I was responsible for the massacre of two tribes, and their ghosts will haunt me for a lifetime," Caleb said, "or three." He sighed. "I've gone over it a million times and only one thing could have saved my family. Fate brought Marda and me together but I allowed us to be ripped apart when I let pity stay my hand. In that deciding moment, my crossroads, I failed. That night in Dominion, I should have killed Bill."

Tristan looked down, his expression one of concentration, then he looked up. "Was there anything that could tell you what Pithos was?" Tristan asked.

"The cocoon was gone; it had dissolved. In the rubble, I found a small piece of material, a type of metal for which I've never been able to find a classification. I would eventually use that metal to make two rings." Caleb pulled a long chain from under his shirt. Two rings dangled from it.

"There was nothing for me to do then. I later realized that my search wasn't to kill Arie, it was to provoke him to kill me. With dying no longer an option, and believe me when I tell you it's not, I could do nothing except exist. Only that wasn't as easy as it sounds.

"The Coesen hunted me relentlessly. They knew I was the one responsible for the deaths of over two hundred Quende and they wanted my head. I had to break ties with my family to keep them safe.

"The years passed with the Coesen discovering my whereabouts from time to time. Some by chance and other times I actually think they located me using some special ability. I did my best to limit their casualties as I got away but I wasn't always successful. As the years changed, the Sovereigns changed as well. Most of them were humane but some not so much. They all wanted the same thing, me dead. Depending on the Sovereign, the importance to apprehend me varied. The ones who gave orders to relentlessly pursue me did so with no care for the lives lost."

Caleb smoothed his hands over the armrest of his chair. "It didn't take long for me to realize I wasn't aging, and that presented a whole new problem for me. I could never get comfortable with any place or anyone. So, every five years I left whatever town I was in, doing my best to never return. I'm sure you can guess that maintaining a connection with my family became harder and harder until I stopped communicating with them all together."

He shrugged. "I traveled the world learning my abilities slowly, perfecting each over time, never allowing myself to feel anything for the people I came across. I began to see people as supporting actors in my own private hell. It was easy to disconnect, or at least that's what I told myself until about twenty years ago."

Chapter Twenty-Five

French countryside
February, Twenty years ago

"**W**ell, Turner," Sophie teased as she wiped the bar down, "Brigitte hasn't been able to sink her claws into you yet, has she?" She winked her eye when he looked up.

"Not from a lack of trying, I'd say," Alain said before putting the beer bottle to his lips. "You could do worse. A young man like you needs a girl to warm his bed."

"Mind yours, you old busy body." Sophie waved her cloth at Alain. "He doesn't need a girl like *that*." She leaned over the bar and met Turner's gaze.

His brilliant green eyes smiled back at her.

"No man needs a girl like that, fast and forward. You wait 'til you find a nice girl, Turner. A girl who you can be proud of. Leave girls like Brigitte to the undesirables and the drunks." She gave Alain a dirty look.

Turner chuckled as he continued to unload the crates of liquor. He loved her concern but didn't want her to worry. "Not really looking to settling down right now," he said as he placed the bottles on the shelves.

"No one said you had to settle down." Alain chuckled.

"Drink up you rotten pervert, before you wear out your welcome." Sophie walked to the other end of the bar where

Turner stocked the shelves. On the way, she lightly tapped the bottle Alain lifted to his mouth, causing beer to spill.

"Ah." Alain smiled as some beer dripped from his chin. "You want me don't cha, Sophie? No use playing hard to get, now." Alain said the rest to Sophie in French as a way to keep it private.

"English," Sophie snarled as she stepped into the rear of the pub. "In my place we speak English when Americans are around," she called from the back.

Turner felt a sting in his throat. It was a constant lately, a tell-tale sign of how much he cared for the woman. His mother made certain he knew French, not to mention now there was no language he could not read, understand, or speak. For some reason, he wanted to tell Sophie. But that wouldn't be smart. He leaned on the bar and placed another beer in front of Alain.

"You shouldn't provoke her. I won't always be here to save your ass, you know."

"Ah," Alain agreed, "but she's so cute when she's mad."

Turner stood. "Yeah," he said as he turned around. He went back to the crate and began stacking again.

For the first time in a very long time the thought of leaving a place saddened him. It was two years ago that Caleb first entered the pub and introduced himself as Turner Reed. In that little time, he managed to start caring for Sophie, who owned the rustic pub in a small rural village. Sophie went out of her way to make him feel at home. She gave him a room, a job, and her friendship without asking for anything in return. She was a kind and lovely widow who made him care again.

"Like me *mad*, huh?" Sophie cut her eyes. She made her way around the bar. "Don't pay your tab today and you'll see me mad." She placed a bowl of peanuts on one of the tables, turning around when she heard the bell over the door jingle. "Not open just yet," she called out.

Before she could tell the patrons to come back later, Caleb pulled her to the floor. He rolled Sophie over so that his body covered hers as small arrow shaped objects were propelled toward them, hitting the tables, wall, and bar.

He looked up just as several of the spikes hit Alain in the back and head. With Alain's back to the door and his drink to his lips he had no time to take cover. Alain slumped over the bar, dying instantly.

Using one of the tables as a shield, Caleb held Sophie close as the stranger stepped further into the pub. A second round of spikes flew out in every direction.

"Don't move." Caleb said as he held a frantic Sophie by the shoulders. He shook her and held her face. "Please Sophie," he said in French calmly. "Don't move."

She nodded.

Caleb moved. Before the man had a chance to send out a third wave, Caleb grabbed him by the back of the neck, forcing him to the floor and causing him to spill a handful of round metal balls. As Caleb applied pressure to the man's neck, a woman dressed in dark gray came through the door. She didn't hesitate as she kicked Caleb in the back of his knee. When Caleb bowed forward the woman kicked him in his side. The kick was hard enough to catapult him across the room. At the same time, the man waved his hand over some of the metal balls that lay on the floor in front of him. The balls rose in the air, formed into sharp pointy arrows, then soared at Caleb as he fell onto some tables and chairs.

Sophie stood up and screamed when she saw the spikes stab into Caleb's chest. The man looked over at her, grinned then waved his hand, throwing several spikes in her direction. They were thrown with such force that her body was thrown several feet back.

When the intruders turned away from Sophie, their faces showed their surprise to find Caleb right in front of them. Floating around Caleb were the spikes that impaled him seconds ago, dripping with his blood and at his command. Moving quicker than either of them could track, Caleb whisked the spikes at the man, pinning him to the wall behind him, leaving the man's major organs untouched.

A loud horrific scream came from the man, filling the pub. Caleb ignored it.

The woman stepped up to attack but Caleb raised his hand, stopping her in her tracks. Unable to move as her body compressed in on itself, she had no choice but to look Caleb directly in his eyes as a red hue began to overtake their natural green-blue color.

She was afraid, he could sense it. *She should be.*

Her pretty face contorted as her pain increased. She tried to speak but her wind pipe was already crushed. Only soft moans came from her mouth now. Blood slowly drained from her ears, mouth, and eyes as Caleb turned his attention to Sophie who lay in her own blood.

He squeezed his eyes shut. *How could I let this happen to you?*

Heartbroken but thinking clearly when he turned around, the red in Caleb's eyes faded.

Still fixed to the wall, the man moved a few of his fingers, commanding the balls that remained on the floor to rise. As they transformed into spikes he shot them at Caleb. With a slight wave of Caleb's hand, all the spikes fell to the floor except two. Caleb turned the spikes so that the pointy ends faced the stranger. Releasing his hold on the woman who continued to bleed out, and allowing her body to drop, Caleb walked over to the man who hung on the wall. The two remaining spikes floated beside him.

When he reached the man, Caleb willed the spikes inches from the man's brown eyes that stared at him with disgust. "Your name?" Caleb asked.

The man grimaced or smiled, Caleb couldn't tell which, so he moved the spikes closer to the man's eyes.

"Sergio. My name is Sergio," he said, raising his chin as the spikes inched closer.

Caleb willed the spikes to stop.

"How did you find me, Sergio?" Caleb asked. "And before you answer know that you *are* going to die. How painful your death will be is up to you."

Sergio seemed to think, then he did smile. With a jolt, he pulled himself free from the wall and into the spikes that waited.

With only the clothing on his body, Caleb left the pub with a purpose. He left the bodies of Sophie and Alain undisturbed. The bodies of the two Coesen Guards, he left only a pile of ashes for the Senior Guard to find. Caleb knew that the two he killed were only scouts who were most likely overconfident and didn't wait for the rest of their unit.

He could stick around and kill the twenty or so Guards who were coming, but what would that solve? *Nothing*, he told himself as he hurried down a large grassy hill. They will keep coming unless he convinced them otherwise.

When he entered the broken-down barn, he uncovered an old dusty vehicle. Caleb sat in the driver's seat and transformed his appearance to that of Alain. He ignored the pain; he was used to it by now.

A perfect replica of his recently deceased friend stared back at him from the rear-view mirror. Normally he would have chosen someone random but he needed DNA to duplicate a person. Alain's happened to be available.

Caleb made it to town in record time. As Alain, Caleb walked along the busy streets without worry. It wouldn't take long to find a Coesen. Even though they were spread out over the globe, France was the epicenter of their civilization for the last twenty or so years due to the new education campus that the current Sovereign, Vivian Harper, constructed. The new campus dwarfed the other two so there would be no problem finding a Coesen civilian, one who could be frightened into giving him the information he needed.

Letting his instinct guide him, Caleb turned the corner. Across the street stood a Coesen rife with power, someone he would be comfortable torturing. The man apparently sensed Caleb too, and their gazes locked on each other. He looked to be in his late fifties or early sixties, with long salt and pepper dreads that fell over his chest. His slacks and shirt were nice but basic. Everything about him said unassuming, but this man was far from that.

The Coesen raised a brow at him then turned around and slowly walked away.

To say that Caleb was curious was an understatement. Having no problem sensing Coesen, Caleb knew they had virtually no way of sensing him, unless they had one of those damn stones, then it would alert them of an enemy. But even then, there would be no way for them to know who the enemy was in a crowded area.

The sun was setting as Caleb entered the Coesen's home through a high window. Inside he walked down a short hallway, glancing into two open rooms before making his way toward an open sitting room. The Coesen was in the kitchen minutes before, moving around what sounded like pots. But as Caleb stepped into the sitting area, the man was seated in a recliner with a cup and a saucer in his hands.

The guy was actually smiling.

"Your coffee has gotten cold," the Coesen said as he placed his cup on the table in front of him. Caleb returned the man's smile with a cold stare. "I am Marcel. I have information that I am willing to give you. So, the torture won't be necessary. If you would—"

"Really?" Caleb interrupted.

Marcel sat back, looking a bit put off. "In order for me to help you, Caleb, our time together needs to be pleasant. You can trust that what I tell you will be the truth."

Caleb walked into the room and took a seat. He wasn't worried about this being a trap because he was confident no one could trap him. He would sense any others in the vicinity. Plus, there was also something about Marcel that intrigued him. So, he was going to play along.

"I'm assuming you know me, which brings a question to mind," Caleb said then paused, "why would you give me anything, especially if you know what I intend to do?"

"To saves lives of course," Marcel simply said with a smile. "You are intent on getting information and you're willing to kill for it. I can give you what you want and no one gets hurt. Win, win on all sides, wouldn't you agree?" He didn't wait for a reply, "Good, then let us get to it. I am a Time Weaver. One of only two living Coesen who are capable of weaving into the future. Recently, I was asked to weave into a young woman's future to ease a mother's worries. That young woman is the very one you seek. Her name is Kayla Harper, Sovereign Vivian Harper's only child."

Caleb sat forward. He thought he'd have to begin his search again–find someone without the crazies, but Marcel was exactly who he needed. "You've seen it then? So, my plan works."

Marcel continued, "I've seen what could happen. That path did not include my assistance, but when I made the decision to help you I saw a different path, a path that will bring about peace." He took a labored breath. "I want you to understand that if you decide right now to give up this course of action you are now headed toward, things may still possibly improve for you. But if you are determined," he paused to reach for his coffee, "then there are some things I can help you with. What will it be?"

"You can see the future, right?" Caleb taunted. "You tell me."

Marcel nodded slightly then held out a small colorless stone in his hand. "Very well, this is a Veilex, my Veilex. Its purpose is to warn its owner of the presence of someone who would do them harm, when that someone is close enough to do said harm. How it does this is unique to each wearer. Mine gives off a bright blinding glow that only I can see. Originally a piece of one large stone, it was fashioned into gem-like pieces that are given to Royals, those who serve in the Guard, and those of us who are deemed important enough.

"It only works for its owner and no one else, unless freely given to another. If stolen or the owner dies before bequeathing it to another, the stone turns into a useless black rock, losing its power forever." Marcel moved forward in the chair and held out his hand.

Caleb held out his hand.

"It has one other use. If two people who both carry a Veilex stone intend harm to the other, neither stone will give off a warning. The stones remain neutral; neither wearer has the advantage." Marcel dropped the stone into Caleb's hand. He then closed Caleb's hand over it, leaving his hand on top. "I give this Veilex to you."

A bright light shone through the open crevices of their hands and slowly faded as Marcel pulled his hand away. "Kayla attends Claremont University." He stood and walked over to a bookcase. Marcel ripped a piece of paper from a pad then slowly returned to his chair.

Caleb realized that Marcel moved much slower than he had earlier. In fact, as Caleb looked at him, Marcel seemed to look pale, almost sickly.

"It is in North America. You will find the address on this paper." Marcel handed the small piece of paper to Caleb. "Everything will go smoothly as long as you follow your instincts."

"And this stone," Caleb asked, opening his hand, "will what, hide me?"

"The Veilex won't hide you, Caleb. All it will do is make any other Veilex stones in the area ignore or not recognize the threat you impose. You will be able to interact with Kayla without her, or the secret security detail her mother placed around her, becoming suspicious of you. Your description is well known, but with the stones not responding you will be regarded as just another Middling with a likeness to Caleb Scott. Young men with blond hair and green eyes are common enough, and there are no surviving images of you; you've made certain of that. And none who've meant you harm has ever lived to tell about it."

Caleb stood. He looked down for a moment then back at Marcel who appeared to look even worse than he did a few moments ago. "And you?" he asked.

Marcel laughed weakly. "You needn't worry about me."

"What happens to you for helping me?"

Marcel squinted as he looked up at Caleb. "My safety will not be an issue." Marcel took another labored breath. "Permit me to give you a piece of advice Mr. Turner," he said, grinning. "There will come a time when someone you care about asks you about all the bad things you've done in your long life. Don't just tell her, show her."

What did he see?

Caleb frowned but nodded as he looked into Marcel's glossed-over eyes. He saw that look many times. It was when he saw it long ago as he watched his brother Fredrick die, that he deciphered it. It was the look of a man who knew his death was coming.

"Is there something I can do for you?"

With a wave of his hand, Marcel dismissed Caleb's offer. "You can leave me to my fate."

Caleb did as Marcel asked.

Marcel got to his feet once he knew he was alone. He used his wall to lean on as he made his way to one of the back rooms in the newly-rented space. Once in the room, Marcel sat on the edge of the bed and lifted the receiver of the phone on the nightstand. After dialing an assortment of numbers, he put the phone to his ear and listened as it rang.

"Hello, dear friend," he said into the receiver. Not giving the person on the other end a moment to respond he quickly continued. "My theory was correct. A weaver gifted enough to travel forward must never do so or they will suffer the same outcome I have. No, please listen to me, Vivian," he said, "I don't have much time. One day you will question everything you've lived and fought for. It will all be alright if you trust your heart. It will guide you in the right direction." With those words, Marcel fell over onto the floor, dropping the phone receiver next to his head. He was weak and tired but also content. His life had meaning. He was born for a reason. As he closed his tired eyes, hearing his dear friend screaming his name through his phone receiver, he knew he was dying for something with great meaning.

Chapter Twenty-Six

Present Day
September 27th

Caleb waited a few hours before entering the clinic to see if he could will the person out but it didn't work. "You're being watched," he announced.

Perkins spun around as he yelled, "My God!" He tried to catch the toothbrush that dropped from his hand but it fell through his fingers. He cursed.

Standing beside him now, Caleb caught the toothbrush before it hit the floor then held it out for Perkins to take. Looking surprised, Perkins reached for the toothbrush.

"Did you know?" Caleb asked.

"No!" Perkins placed the toothbrush on the edge of the sink. He rinsed his mouth out before walking out of the bathroom and into the room that had Exam Room 1 over the doorway. "How long you think they've been watching me?"

Caleb followed but didn't go inside the room. He stood in the doorway. "I'd say the entire time you've been here. One person, but I'm having a tough time tracking him." Caleb wouldn't divulge how weird it was that he couldn't track the person.

Perkins went to a chair that sat in a corner and began to struggle with slipping his foot into one of his shoes. Once done he started on the opposite foot. "I've endangered her." With both shoes on, he checked his gun for bullets before placing it in his holster. Then he lowered his head and sighed.

Was I ever that weak?

If he was, Caleb was sure he wouldn't wear it for all to see. "There aren't any obstacles keeping him from getting to you, if that is the goal." Caleb turned around before the lobby door opened. "Good morning Silvia."

She looked surprised to see him too.

He was surprised to still see the subtle glimmer of affection in her eyes before she lowered them.

"Morning," she said, sounding nervous and slightly irritated. "Are you going to make a habit of dropping by…" She paused, then said, "Unannounced?"

She was angry. Unrequited love had a way of pissing a person off. Silvia needed closure. Without it, her anger would continue to fester. Unless…unless there was someone else.

"My being here bothers you," Caleb said. He watched her hurry past him to help Perkins sit on the bed. He heard her ordering Perkins to relax but he spoke over her anyway. "I didn't consider how my surfacing would affect you."

As she pulled off one of Perkin's shoes she turned her head to look at Caleb who stood behind her. "Your surfacing, as you call it, was a surprise but that's all it is, Caleb. It is Caleb?" she said mockingly. She pulled the other shoe off. "I just prefer you to give me notice when you want to visit my patient. Now, as for you," she told Perkins, "it is much too soon for you to leave. Your body hasn't fully healed, so whatever it is you feel you need to do can wait." She helped Perkins take his gun holster off. She placed the holster with the gun inside the nightstand and closed the drawer. "I don't care for guns and I don't permit them in my home or clinic, but because you are an officer of the law I will make an exception."

Caleb moved to the side as Silvia passed him again. "She's right." Caleb said when he was sure she was gone.

"There's nothing you can do in the state you're in." Caleb turned to leave.

"Staying here puts Silvia in danger," Perkins said then grimaced.

"Silvia isn't in any danger and neither are you." He said when he turned back.

"How can you be so sure?"

Caleb walked into the room and over to the egress window. On the sill was a small metal pin. He held it up. "Because of this," he said.

"Where did that come from?" Perkins looked at the shiny object in Caleb's hand.

Ignoring Perkins, Caleb walked to the lobby door quickly. "I won't be coming back. If you should need to get in contact with me, Bannerman would be the man to contact."

"Bannerman?" Perkins whispered.

Caleb left through the lobby door before Perkins could ask anything else. He got inside his car and flipped open his phone. He tapped each number and a few seconds the line began to ring.

"The job is done Richard. You can call your soldier home."

"Hello. I'm good and you," Richard said bitterly. "As for the soldier you speak of, he's MIA and off the grid."

"He made contact. He left one of those little pins you give to your special team members. I can't seem to get a fix on him though, and I don't like it. Tell me all you know about him."

Richard sighed.

"This isn't a request from one of those diplomats you bullshit regularly. It's me, and unless you can convince me otherwise, I will hunt and kill him."

"His name is Cipher Shawn, age twenty-three. His team calls him Shadow. Cipher's grandmother, a Native American, raised him on a reservation. In high school, he joined the ROTC. When his grandmother died, he enlisted in the army where his talents were noticed almost immediately. He impressed me so I recruited him for the Link Project four years ago. Cipher is highly intelligent and virtually unmatched in every challenge we gave him. Like you, when he is given a job nothing else exists, other than that command. Unlike you, when the job is done he is just a regular young man who does the things young men do, video games, girls, friends. Hangs out with a rowdy bunch, has gotten himself in a few bar fights but nothing too serious."

"His parents?" Caleb asked.

"Father unknown, the mother died of a drug overdose when he was seven. Look Caleb, aside from you he is the best soldier I know. I don't know why Cipher has decided to stick to you but I can tell you that whatever the reason he will see it to the end. He won't be easy to hunt or kill."

Tristan didn't expect to see Zeta when he woke, but her movements were unmistakable. Caleb's steps were soft yet solid and confident, the movements of someone who was familiar with his surroundings and had no fear. Zeta's steps were light but hesitant, cautious like a Protector.

When he opened his door, she was sitting on the sofa with her back to him. He wanted to hug her, to promise to never test their friendship ever again, but he figured it was too soon to attempt. He would just have to be satisfied that she was out here, and not locked in Caleb's room.

Tristan moved forward without even glancing down at his ankle cuff, and that's when the smell coming from the kitchen registered. Rather than walk or jog over to the kitchen table the way an excited Middling would have, Tristan moved with such speed that the bag the smell was coming from rolled from the gush of wind. Tristan caught the bag as it rolled with one hand and the photo that was underneath it with his other hand.

He clutched the image as his eyes scanned every detail. "They're so big," he said then laughed. Nadia was smiling, sitting on a patch of grass, as Aidan stood over her with a flower. "Tell me about them." He sat down at the table.

Zeta walked into the kitchen and sat across from him. "They're both very smart. Aidan takes care of Nadia like a big brother should. I have to work hard to get him to smile but he almost never cries. He likes being read to and has a calming effect on his sister. Nadia is bubbly and full of laughter. She hates sitting still, loves apple slices but hates her hair in her face."

Tristan lowered his head. "And my Ci, how is she?"

"Tired," Zeta said. "She insists on doing everything for them herself. The only time she gets any rest is when your parents visit."

He placed the photo on the table. Still looking down at it, he cleared his throat. "Thank you, Zeta. I don't deserve your friendship after what I did, let alone this. It means more than you will ever know."

Zeta stood and went to the refrigerator. He could see that her attempt to hold in her tears failed when she used the back of her hand to wipe them away. "Don't thank me yet," she said, sounding hoarse, "you haven't tried the burger." Zeta pulled out a beer and closed the refrigerator door. She placed the cold beer next to Tristan's arm and walked back to the living room.

When Tristan looked over at her, she held a magazine close to her face. He smiled as he unfolded the paper bag and pulled the aluminum-wrapped burger out. He smiled even bigger as he chewed the first bite. Not because the burger was good, although it was. Tristan smiled because in that moment he was determined to be home before his children's first birthday.

October 1ˢᵗ

Whodai watched the bubbles float slowly through the air above Nadia's reach as she sat on the grass below, reaching and swatting without reward. He laughed at her determination as he kneeled closer to her and blew a stream of bubbles in front of her. He then turned and blew some bubbles in Aidan's direction.

"There you go big guy," Whodai said. He watched Aidan swat at the bubbles with both of his little hands.

Being around the twins wasn't bad at all. He couldn't shake the fact that if things had gone the way they should have, they would be his kids. Cianne would be his wife and they would be ruling the Coesen together, then the world.

He looked over at Cianne who was helping Nadia stand by holding her up by her hands. He smiled when they made eye contact. Cianne smiled back.

"You have some visitors, Soahn," the butler called from the patio.

Cianne's smile widened as she lifted Nadia onto her hip and hurried over to Cassius and gave him a big hug. As Whodai walked over with Aidan to greet Cassius, he saw his sister step onto the patio.

Trying to disguise his irritation as surprise, Whodai forced a grin when he reached the interlopers. "Nice of you to return old man," he said to Cassius as he shook his hand. "Raya, it's always nice to see my big sister." He hugged her tightly.

Whodai loved his sister but they were like night and day. She didn't seem to know him at all. Even his mother, who was consumed with duty, saw the darkness in him early on. His mother did her best to control him and he did his best to let his dear old mother believe that she succeeded.

"Is mother inside?" he asked.

Raya was being groomed to become leader of the Bode. When Raya accepted to be their mother's successor, she basically signed over her freedom from that moment on. Pity that all her dedication was for nothing. When he had Cianne, he planned to rule without a council.

"Royal Brenna has accompanied us as well," Raya told him. She focused on her brother's hand, the one that held on to Aidan's tiny hand.

Maybe she does see the darkness in me.

When she looked up at him, she was smiling.

No…she is just being a woman.

"Something has happened?" Cianne asked with concern.

Whodai saw the fear in her eyes as she took Aidan's free hand and pulled him near. "Don't worry, I will protect you and the children," he assured her.

"You can both calm yourselves." Raya reached for Nadia. "Everyone is waiting in the study. I'll care for the children." She moved Nadia to her hip and took Aidan's hand from Cianne. "Come little people," she urged, "Auntie Raya will get you a snack."

Cassius ushered Whodai and Cianne to the study without saying a word to let them know the reason for the sudden meeting. *Why is he being so tight lipped*? Whodai didn't like not being in the know.

As they entered the room everyone stood. He and Cassius remained standing until all the greetings were over and each royal was seated. He took a seat next to Cassius and looked to his mother for some sign of what was going on. She gave away nothing as usual. *A fucking statue*. It figured.

"We apologize for the intrusion, Soahn Cianne, but we felt that with all that has developed, it was necessary to request an audience," Brenna said, sounding formal. "Civil War is looming. Chandra has been rallying supporters to her cause, and Eldra and I feel that there is a possibility that you may be able to prevent this uprising and save the lives of so many."

"What can I do?" Cianne asked hesitantly, looking to both women.

"Cianne," Eldra said softly. "I realize that this isn't the life you imagined for yourself. You have lost so much in the last couple of years. Many women would have given up but you haven't. Why?"

Cianne's eyes glossed over, but she was done with crying. No tears would fall from her eyes. "I want to but…"

"But your children need you," Eldra finished. "And you've held on through all the suffering to be there for them. The love you feel for your children, Vivian felt for you. But she also felt that same love and devotion for our people. Brenna and I do as well. Even Chandra, as foolish as she is, feels that she is protecting our people. But I fear she will bring about our destruction which will no doubt spill over into the lives of unsuspecting Middlings."

No, they can't ask this of me.

"You want me to become your Sovereign," Cianne said. "Even if I wanted to I'd just be a figure, a puppet. I know nothing about your culture or your laws, some of which I've already broken."

"You are the Halo. In time, you will be much more than just our Sovereign," Eldra said with a confidence that paled the sincerity that Vivian showed when she told Cianne the same thing.

"Becoming what you were meant to be is all we want of you. Your mother's gift to you was to allow you to be raised as a Middling. I did not see it then but that decision allowed you to learn compassion, humility, and the ability to forgive, things we have lost over the centuries," Brenna said. "We can teach each other."

"That is not all we've come to ask of you." Eldra seemed saddened by her words. "A gesture is needed from you, to prove to those who doubt your sincerity."

"What sort of gesture?" Whodai spoke up. "Why would she have to prove herself? She's the Halo. You're both backing her. Isn't that enough?"

The three women looked over at Whodai as if they forgot he was in the room. For the first time since she knew him, Cianne saw anger distort his handsome face. Even Cassius must have felt the tension coming from Whodai, because he stiffened next to him.

Whodai asked his question again. "What kind of gesture?"

Cianne could see his mother's irritation with his probing. She had that "I speak, you listen" look about her.

"What we ask of you may seem insensitive but we've thought it out thoroughly. Know that this is in no way easy for us to ask." Brenna rubbed her hands together in her lap. "We ask that you accept the Tandot victor as your mate."

Cianne gasped. She slanted her head, disbelieving what she heard because surely, she must have heard wrong. "Um...I." She cleared her throat.

"This isn't right," Whodai stood. "She shouldn't have to prove anything to anyone."

"Whodai please," Brenna said as she motioned for him to sit.

Whodai looked to Cassius pleadingly. When Cassius only nodded, he looked at his mother. "You can't ask her to do this. Even if she agrees to what you ask, it doesn't mean the threat of war will go away."

"No," Eldra said, "but shouldn't we do all we can to prevent it?"

Whodai bent down in front of Cianne and placed his hands over hers as she unconsciously scratched at her jeans. "You don't have to do this. We can find another way."

Cianne frowned. *Why is he so angry*? She looked at the doorway.

Whodai gave her hand a slight tug. "Fight, if we have to. Many will stand with us."

"And many will die," Brenna said plainly.

Cianne stared into Whodai's simmering brown eyes. She couldn't let any more people get hurt because of her. She dropped her shoulders. "If I do all you ask," she said, as she turned to Eldra, "do you think it will really save lives?"

Whodai pulled his hands away as he stood. "It is too soon. Vous ne pouvez pas demander cela a elle," he pleaded.

"He said that we should not demand this of you." Brenna translated when she saw the confusion on Cianne's face.

"I understood him," Cianne said, still confused, "I just don't understand why you're so angry." she said looking at Whodai.

Whodai seemed to struggle with his response as he looked at her. He glanced over at Cassius who looked pained for some reason. Then he stalked out of the study without saying a word.

Eldra focused on her again. "Accept your rightful place, Cianne. Be the leader Vivian and Kayla knew you could be. Be who you were born to be." Eldra stood. "Now if you'll all excuse me." She silently left the room.

Cianne hunched over, and placing her forehead in her palms, she sighed. "And all I have to do is give myself to a man I don't love." She said more to herself than to anyone in particular.

Brenna crossed the room at some point and was kneeling in front of Cianne. She placed a perfectly manicured hand on Cianne's leg. "At least you two are friends. That will allow things to go more smoothly. Most don't meet their mate until the day of the bonding ritual."

Cianne jerked her head up, her face blanched and her eyes wide.

Brenna face lit with understanding. "I see. You didn't know."

Whodai heard his mother getting to her feet after he stormed out of the study. No doubt to follow him.

"Whodai," she called. "What is this all about?"

Stopping just inside the Great Room, Whodai turned to face his mother. "This is not the way to go about this."

"Cianne needs to take her place as Sovereign. Why shouldn't it be now?"

Her tone warned him to tread lightly. Whodai looked down. Eldra had an intimidating effect on him since he could remember. He hated the weakness she brought out in him. "I just think that—"

Eldra's eyes narrowed. "You are not concerned with her taking her place as Sovereign, are you? No, that's not it, is it?" Eldra grabbed his chin and held his face steady as she looked into his eyes.

He tried to pull away but it was too late. She was already pulling his fear to the surface to read and he could do nothing to stop her.

"You've never told her. Why Whodai, why have you kept this a secret?" Eldra loosened her grip, allowing him to pull away. "You want more time. Time, for her to…fall in love with you," she shook her head, giving him a look of revulsion. "Did you believe you could win her heart? You have feelings for her?" She chuckled. "You listen to me," she said, following his gaze with her own until he looked at her. "If she will have you, together you will lead and unite our people again. Love is not a requirement." Eldra turned and began to walk away.

"Do you speak from experience?" he sneered.

Eldra stopped and gave him a sideways glance that made him flinch but he stood his ground. "As a matter of fact," she told him, "I do."

All my planning and sacrifice could go up in smoke all because of my mother, he thought as he entered his room. The same room Vivian gave him when he was a small boy.

For the first time since Vivian's death, Whodai cursed her very existence.

Why didn't you explain it all to Cianne?

It was her responsibility to educate her granddaughter in their ways. Her death wasn't personal to him, but right now he was angry enough to stomp on her ashes.

Whodai looked at his reflection in the mirror on the chest of drawers.

Why didn't I tell her? It never seemed like the right time.

He swatted a small vase off the corner of the chest. The vase hit the floor and shattered into small pieces. That self-righteous husband of hers didn't tell her either. Though, he had to respect Tristan for not telling, even after their little encounter…the very same encounter that resulted in a few broken ribs for the fucker.

Tristan didn't know who he was messing with. He had the rest of his afterlife in hell to think on it.

A light tap at his door pulled Whodai back to the here and now. *Fuck off,* was what he thought as he crossed the room. *Is it too much to ask for a damn minute alone to sulk?*

He didn't expect to see Cianne when he pulled his door open. Their eyes met long enough for him to see the confusion on her face before she looked away.

"You lied to me." Cianne side-stepped him to get inside his room.

"I didn't lie to you," he said, leaving his door open. "I told you that I was in love with someone who found someone else before I could tell her how I felt. Your grandmother's plan was to introduce you to me, then gradually introduce you to our customs. The night we arrived at your home not only did I find out you had been kidnapped, I found out that you already had someone. There was no point in telling you later that I loved you. That I had for a very long time."

Damn. She looked annoyed.

Cianne sat on the end of his bed. "How could you love me? We never even met before that day in the garden."

Whodai walked over to his nightstand and pulled out a thin billfold. Sitting down a few inches from her, he pulled two 5x7 photos from the billfold and handed them to her. On one of the photos, Cianne was about eleven years old. She wore a yellow sun dress with a big white flower covering the lower half. Her long hair was in two long braids and her hands were clasped behind her back.

The other picture was a fairly recent photo of her during her junior year. Her long beautiful loosely curled hair was pulled over one shoulder and rested a few inches past her breast. She wore an off the shoulders gray shirt that made the green color of her eyes stand out vividly.

"Where did you get these?"

"Vivian. There is another, in my home in London." He watched her as she looked over the photos. When she stood he reached for her but then pulled his hand back, closing it into a fist. He mashed his fist into his bed. "You don't understand," he said. "As a child, my first memories are of people complimenting my mother about what a perfect candidate I was. It is an honor to be considered for the Tandot competition so she groomed me.

"Every second of my day was dedicated to my studies and training. Very early on, the other entries and I realized that this competition was different from the rest. And when our Sovereign, your grandmother, began appearing at some of the testing, we knew for certain. She took an immediate interest in me, Cianne. Maybe because of my mother, I don't know." He stood. "You can't imagine the honor I felt, my family felt, because of me. Vivian couldn't interfere with the process but she did something that drove me even harder."

He walked over to Cianne, then moved around her to face her. "I was thirteen when she gave me the first picture." He remembered the exact day because he just eliminated two more candidates. His mother actually smiled at him that day. "I never told anyone I had it. Not even my mother. I used to stare at you for hours. You were so beautiful, so perfect."

Cianne looked up from the photos. Her expression was one of curiosity. Curiosity was good.

"Soon after she gave me the photo, Vivian began sharing things about you with me. Like how smart you were and the things you liked. It drove me in a way you couldn't imagine. When I was sixteen I defeated seven of the remaining competitors. By then I was already in love with you."

"You were in love with an idea," Cianne told him. "Believe me, I know how strong loving someone from afar can be but it's not real."

"Maybe." He took her hand that held the photos. "But then I got to know you."

Cianne pulled her hand away and took a few steps back, shaking her head, "I can't think straight. Everything…this is so epically wrong." The photos toggled on her fingertips before they fell to the floor.

Whodai stepped over the pictures. "That day we met in the garden, you felt something. I know you did." He mirrored the head movements she made to avoid him, making sure his eyes were locked with hers. "I felt it too."

Cianne pulled away, backing up, but he moved with her. "Why are you saying these things? We're friends," she said.

"**Accept me Cianne**." His words sounded normal enough but they were laced with determination and authority. A thickness coated the air and he knew she heard the magnitude of power in his words.

He watched Cianne squeeze her eyes shut then press her right hand to her temple. Tapping her head repeatedly, she opened her eyes. He almost backed away from her when he noticed the thin red line that trimmed her lovely green-blue irises.

"You spoke up for me downstairs. You were upset when they said I should be with…" she said, motioning to him, "you."

She was angry and all it did was turn him on. He knew she wouldn't be like the others he took to his bed. Yes, she was gentle, maybe even innocent, but push her into a corner and she literally saw red.

"I don't just want you to couple with me," Whodai dared to say. "An exceptional match is what every Coesen is taught to hope for. We couple to keep our race pure and strong. To love, that is rare. I think that's why Vivian gave me the photos. She wanted you to be with someone who loved you," he said, looking into her heat-filled eyes. "**And I want you to love me**."

Cianne grabbed her head with both hands as if buckling under the pressure of his words. She squeezed her eyes closed and her breaths came out short. Then, she straightened to her full height. With her eyes fixed on him, it seemed as if she was going to smile. As if his command worked.

Relishing his victory, Whodai stepped up to Cianne, ready to kiss those luscious lips of hers. But the expression that came over her face gave him pause.

"I can't love you the way you want me to." She moved past him. "That kind of love disappeared when he did."

"Shit," Whodai cursed. He wanted to run after her but he didn't. Never did he think to use his power to make her love him. He wanted her to come to him freely but he was getting desperate. He cursed again as he slammed his door shut.

He used his full power on Cianne and she shook it off like it was a pesky headache. Things weren't going as quickly as he wanted, and he was losing the ground he already gained. But, he loved a challenge. He loved Cianne's strength, and most of all, he loved her.

Whodai smiled. This setback wouldn't stop him. Quit? Hell…he was just getting started. But his next move would have to wait because now he had to feed the raging hormones his future wife had unintentionally set ablaze.

Another disposable beauty would do just fine.

Chapter Twenty-Seven

Caleb slid a bottled water across the table to Tristan. He smiled inside because the kid was working his ass off. The determination Tristan fought with…it was awe inspiring. His dedication…Caleb knew no match. His skill was exceptional. But the kid was missing one thing…the same thing Caleb lacked when he was about his age.

That cutthroat ruthlessness that determined a win or a loss.

"So," Tristan said after he gulped down his water, "Did I earn the rest of your story?"

Caleb shook his head. Yeah, he liked the kid. A lot. "I'm in America…"

Twenty years earlier
March

Weather didn't impact Caleb's life much but for the average man it was a chilly day. He hadn't felt the discomforting chill of a winter or the scorching heat of summer for a very long time. The organism inside him regulated his body temperature automatically. It was something he and the Coesen had in common.

He glanced over at the man standing next to him at the intersection, wearing a thin jacket, smoking a cigarette, and totally oblivious to the cold. Even though it wasn't obvious,

Caleb knew he was being thoroughly examined by the Coesen beside him.

Caleb slid his hand inside his jean pocket to feel the Veilex stone once more, to make sure it was still there. He then pulled his hand out and casually looked at his watch. The Coesen next to him flicked the cigarette to the ground then smashed it with his shoe.

The Veilex stone worked just as Marcel said it would. And it didn't take long for it to come into play either. So, when Caleb began his journey back to the states he was prepared to kill whoever got in his way.

He wasn't fully convinced that Marcel wanted to aid him, and he questioned whether the man really knew what he intended to do. There were a few tense moments and questioning looks but no Coesen approached him while he carried the Veilex. So, Caleb started to accept that the old guy spoke the truth about the stone.

Today was the real test. Caleb entered the bookstore in disguise at first but as himself on four occasions without incident. *Why go in undisguised*? He wasn't ready to admit it himself but on that first day he entered the bookstore and stood in Kayla's aisle to purchase some random periodical, he felt something when he peered into her lovely dark eyes. Something he hadn't felt in a long time. Interest. With one look, his interest was piqued.

…and when she giggled after her coworker bumped into her and whispered in her ear, her sweet carefree voice quickened his pulse.

He watched Kayla for almost two weeks, committing her routine to memory so when he grabbed her it would be at the most opportune time.

Only, he had every opportunity to take her, yet he didn't. Now, he stood at an intersection waiting for the Coesen who stood next to him to make a move.

Caleb looked at the traffic going by then took a step back from the curb and waited for the traffic light to turn green so he could cross. He wondered if there was a picture of him circulating out there amongst the Guard. Well, maybe not a picture, but a sketch was possible. He didn't know.

"Excuse me," the Coesen finally said, "you look really familiar. What's your name?"

Caleb frowned. "Believe me, I'm not that guy," he said, forcing a grin. "But I know a guy if you're into that kind of thing."

The man grabbed him by the arm and pulled him away from the intersection and over to a run-down brick wall. Caleb raised his hands as if surrendering when the man grabbed him by his jacket and pushed him into the wall. He dug his nails in his palms, trying hard not to resist when the man patted his pockets then pulled his wallet out and looked at his id.

"You've been hanging around here a lot, Turner," the Coesen said.

Caleb pushed off the wall and reached for his wallet but the Coesen shoved it into his chest, causing him to stumble a few steps to maintain his balance. A small group of college students took notice but continued to pass them by. The Coesen watched as Caleb checked his wallet.

"Look man, I just like the coffee," he said, trying his best to sound scared. The alias he set up must have been convincing enough because the Royal Guards allowed him to be in Kayla's presence, but his frequent visits to the bookstore seemed to put them on alert. As they should be.

After allowing Caleb to straighten up, the Coesen pulled out another cigarette and lit it, then he locked his eyes with Caleb's. "Why are you really hanging out here?"

Caleb knew the Coesen was using some sort of ability but he felt nothing. Usually when the Coesen tried to use their mind reading on him, he felt a tingling sensation that was harmless but irritating. If this guy wasn't trying to read his mind, then the words he spoke were being analyzed.

"There's this girl." The words just came out.

The Coesen laughed.

One of the students who passed by a few minutes earlier must have been concerned because she stood across the street with an officer and was pointing at them. Caleb looked at the police, then to the man in front of him.

"You're wasting your time, fella," the Coesen said, laughing again as he walked away. He was blended in with the crowd by the time the officer reached Caleb.

The police officer wasn't completely satisfied with Caleb's explanation of what happened. All he saw was a big black man bullying a white guy, possibly a student. After another firm assurance from Caleb, the officer realized there was nothing more he could do.

As Caleb walked toward the bookstore he thought about how bad that could have gone with the Coesen if he had lost it. Good thing he didn't.

Pulling the door to the bookstore open, Caleb hesitated as doubt inched its way into his mind. *Shit*. What was he doing? Take the girl…force a face to face confrontation with the great Sovereign Vivian, and slit her daughter's neck while the mother watched. The bitch took from him and he was going to take from her. Then after, he planned to kill the Sovereign slowly. Feel her fragile bones break under his hands.

A dark need rose in him at the thought of bringing the head of the Coesen down.

As Caleb made his way to the periodicals his gaze fell on Kayla, who stood behind her regular register. When she saw him…her face lit up in the most beautiful smile. For a moment, Caleb didn't know how to react, but then his lips spread and the darkness clawing to the surface fell away.

Just like that, the game changed.

He pulled a chair out at a small round table and attempted to read, but his focus was on Kayla Harper. He discovered he liked listening to her alluring voice. From time to time, he looked up to watch her move about the shop. Kayla's shoulder length coal black hair, brows, and lashes, were a stark contrast to her warm cinnamon-toned skin, and he couldn't help wondering how it would feel to run his fingers through it. Her high cheek bones angled into an adorable chin. Her straight nose and dark eyes were perfect. At about five foot seven, her long limbs and elegant features could have her working any runway. Her steps were graceful and concise, the way you would expect royalty to walk.

"You can't sit in here."

Caleb didn't know why but he looked up. He spotted a guy wearing a shirt and tie who stood over a young woman sitting a few tables away.

"I'm not bothering anybody," the woman said to Shirt and Tie. She looked to be in her late teens, and wore a pair of shorts and an oversized windbreaker. Her right cheek had a two or three days old bruise that she shielded with her stringy hair.

Caleb scooted his chair back to intervene but Kayla was moving toward the table carrying a tray. She placed the tray in front of the young woman. "I'm sorry I took so long."

The woman seemed confused at first, then she saw Kayla's raised brows. "Uh…thank you."

Kayla smiled as she turned to the shirt and tie. "She said she was a little tired, so I told her if she sat I'd bring her coffee, sandwich, and change to her table." Kayla placed a few dollars and coins on the tray without looking away from the man.

The man gave Kayla a disbelieving look but Ray, per the name tag, came walking up to the table with some cream and sugar. Ray handed them to the woman. "Sorry, I couldn't find the flavor cream you asked for. I hope plain is fine."

"It's fine." The woman smiled big but avoided looking at Shirt and Tie.

A voice rang out. "Jim!" Rochelle, another of Kayla's coworkers, yelled from a register. "You think you could get your electronic girlfriend we normal people," she said, throwing quotes in the air, "call a cash register, to work? Aren't you the captain of this ship?"

Jim, aka Shirt and Tie, huffed with a look of disgusted defeat before letting his eyes fall back to Kayla. He gave her a disapproving glance before walking away. Ray followed their manager but not before holding his hand behind his back and giving Kayla a thumbs-up.

Caleb noticed the woman wasted no time. She dug into the food as if it was her last meal.

"I told you that you can't come in here when Jim is here Claudia, remember." Kayla said softly when she moved closer to the woman. "...and slow down, before you choke." She leaned forward to inspect the bruise.

"I fell," Claudia blurted out. "Hey, I didn't mean you trouble."

Kayla watched her with concern for a few moments before slipping a twenty-dollar bill on the tray. "You're no trouble. I'll get you some cookies." She started to walk away but stopped. "Claudia, you can crash at my room if you want."

Caleb noticed that Claudia tensed.

"Uh...no, thanks though," Claudia said quickly.

Caleb watched Kayla shake her head as she walked away. He continued to listen as Kayla walked behind the counter, retrieved a couple of cookies, and returned to Claudia's table.

Kayla sighed as she placed the cookies on Claudia's tray. She made her way back to the counter where she was sorting items. She wasn't one to meddle but if she saw one more bruise on Claudia's body, she was going to sic the Guard on that asshole boyfriend of hers.

"Tell me you noticed this time," Rochelle squealed. "Girl, he was checking you out." She got close enough that, for Kayla, the baby powder scented oil she wore overrode every other scent in the café/bookstore.

Kayla gave Rochelle a little push. With her friend, personal space was an issue. It irked Kayla when space invaders breached hers but Rochelle seemed oblivious or ignored the subtle hints so now they've graduated to the physical.

Rochelle rolled her eyes as she nudged Kayla back.

"Stop reading into things," Ray said, coming toward them. "He ain't said nothing to neither of ya'll. It's a book store, maybe he's just here to read."

"Not." Rochelle dismissed Ray with a raised hand, displaying all four fingers and a thumb. "His fine ass has been checking my girl out every day this week. Believe me, he's not here to read."

Kayla placed two more bookmarks onto the spinning caddy then looked over at the guy in question. She did notice him the first time he came into the store a week ago and every day after. He was the kind of guy everyone noticed. He was tall, about six feet three inches, with short dirty blond hair and fair skin. But it was his cyan eyes that struck her silly. He was gorgeous.

It was clear he had no clue how gorgeous. He didn't seem to notice all the females who watched him. A few of whom decided to start hanging out "reading" in the store like he did.

Kayla realized she was staring. For goodness sakes, she was no better than them. Turning away, she rotated the caddy and placed several more bookmarks in the allotted hooks. Absently, she looked at the clear Veilex stone clasped in her bracelet. A necessary gift from her mother when she decided to come to Claremont, if she wanted to leave the safety and protection of her people. There was no reaction from the stone to the stranger's presence.

Why do I keep checking?

"He's here to read," she said as she let her eyes fall on him again. She and her friends watched the guy pick up a book and read the back.

Caleb felt her eyes on him again but this time, unlike the other times, he looked up. Rochelle and Ray looked away but Kayla didn't. They held each other's gaze until she turned her attention to a customer who stepped up to her register.

He smiled. She was beautiful, confident, and somehow, she demanded his interest.

With the book in hand, Caleb made his way to Kayla's register even though the other lines were empty. He didn't even decide what he planned on doing about her until the woman in front of him took her bag and strolled away.

"Thank you and have a nice day," Kayla told the woman.

Then her eyes fell on him, again. He felt her gaze studying him, sizing him up, then she cleared her throat.

"Is that all?" she asked, as she reached for the book.

Caleb didn't want to risk touching her just yet so he slid the book across the counter toward her. She turned the book to see the title then looked up at him again with a raised brow.

"So, it's going to be a book today?" Kayla asked.

"You've been paying attention to what I purchase?" He grinned but Kayla didn't reply, she just smiled as she rang up the book. As Caleb handed her the money he didn't let go when she tried to take it. "Kayla," he said, "would you like to go out with me sometime?"

"Uh hmm." Rochelle smiled as she and Ray watched them with no shame.

As he held onto one end of the twenty-dollar bill, Caleb saw Kayla's eyes brighten then dim.

"I can't," she said softly.

He let go of the money and she quickly gave him his change. Confused, Caleb nodded then collected his change and left the store. He was a block away before he slowed enough for Rochelle to catch up with him.

The baby-faced girl stopped in front of him, breathing heavy and waving her hand at him with nails the exact same color as her hair. Several of her many long thick black and red braids hung over her shoulder and past her waist.

They looked heavy.

"Hey," she called, panting, "me and a few friends are gonna be kicking it at my crib in a couple weeks. I thought you might want to come."

"I don't think I'll be in town then."

His plans for Kayla changed drastically. There was no way he could kill her now. But what the hell came over him in that damn store?

Why did I ask her out? What the hell?

He needed to leave tonight.

As he turned away, Rochelle cried out, "Kayla will be there." As he started walking she added, "She doesn't have a boyfriend. It's just that her mother is always tripping. She likes you, I can tell." Rochelle handed him a folded piece of paper. "Come, it'll be chill."

Chapter Twenty-Eight

Caleb was from a simpler time and though he enjoyed some of the modern conveniences, he couldn't get used to what people called music these days. To him music from the past few decades was a complete setback. Lately it's gotten infinitely worse.

He pinched the bridge of his nose then moved his index finger and thumb over his closed lids as the music drummed so loudly that he felt it in his chest. Caleb placed the beer to his lips and took a long swig.

As far away from the speakers as he could get, Caleb still wasn't far enough. He leaned on the fence as he stared out of the yard and ignored the half dozen girls who hovered nearby, waiting for him to notice them. As he looked over the dark alley and viewed another row of townhomes, he laughed to himself.

As a nation, the United States had grown. They classified slave descendants as African Americans now. He liked the new classification better and though the conditions for people of color seemed vastly improved, he knew that the core of the nation was still averse to change. But, some were open.

The party seemed to reflect diversity. Hispanics, Caucasians, Asians, they were all represented here. During the past hour and a half, he was approached by a girl from each of those ethnicities and, dare he say it, they all tried to "get with him". He hated the slang too.

"Not your scene?"

Her voice drifted effortlessly through the noise and chatter to his ears. Caleb looked over his shoulder to see Kayla standing behind him. "Not really," he told her.

Having stepped beside him, she said, "You haven't been in the store since you asked me out."

A few guys yelling at each other briefly caught her attention. Caleb used that time to really look at her. It was dark but it didn't matter with his excellent vision. She wore a black lace choker which accentuated her delicate neck and urged her audience to look lower. The keyhole neckline of the long sleeve black bodysuit she wore and the way the fabric clung to her upper body, showing all her curves, teased him. Loose-fitting jeans hung just low enough to see the bodysuit's beginning descent into a region of her body that his mind should not travel.

Ashamed of his own thoughts, Caleb forced his gaze to travel up to her stunning face only to see dark, smoldering eyes staring back at him.

She raised her sculpted brow and stretched her full glossed lips into an accusing grin.

Caught, he could only smile as he maintained eye contact and raised the beer to his mouth.

Kayla watched him put the bottle to his lips and wondered when a guy swallowing became so damn sexy. Speaking of sexy, even the way he moved, every action regardless of how basic, was remarkable. And the way he checked her out just now, it made her blood boil. She wanted his penetrating gaze all over her and waited patiently for his eyes to find hers.

"Are you here with someone?" She was certain that if his date witnessed how he just caressed her entire body with his eyes, he was leaving alone.

When he pulled the beer away from his mouth his tongue slid out and licked across his bottom lip. *Wow*. Kayla's heart sped up. He leaned in, so close that she felt his warm breath on her neck.

"I came here to see you," he said in her ear. "Can we go somewhere quiet and talk?"

He didn't move away so there was little space between them when she turned her head and said, "I barely know you. I don't even know your name. Besides, I'm not here to hook up. I'm here at Claremont to get an education and you would definitely be a distraction."

Despite her discouraging words, Kayla saw their closeness as an opportunity. She inhaled his cologne, savoring the mixture of his natural scent and the earthy fragrance, before she moved away from him and walked back toward the house.

Her gorgeous customer followed. He wasn't directly behind her but he was close enough for her to know he was there. She placed the paper cup she was holding in an overflowing waste basket as she made her way up the rusted metal stairs, opened the screen door, and stepped into the full-on Party! Squeezing through the crowded kitchen sort of stalled her sexy exit but hey, he was going to have to navigate through all the people too.

When Kayla reached the dining room, she glanced around to realize she lost him.

Good, I think.

She moved forward again, taking a much-needed breath but it was caught in her throat when fingers wrapped around her wrist. "You really don't want to be touching me," she said angrily to the jerk who was brave enough to grab hold of her.

"I do," her bookstore guy answered.

Damn it all to hell, she blushed.

"And, my name is Turner." He brushed over the top of her knuckles with his thumb then tightened his grip on her hand.

Kayla felt a warm sensation trail up her fingers and caress her palm, then it shot up her arm until the warmth coursed through her entire body.

What the…?

Her legs almost buckled under her but he was right there to brace her with his own body.

"You alright?" he asked. His face was laced with concern.

Oh, yeah, she felt great. Whatever happened when he touched her was over now but it ROCKED.

Kayla saw his confusion but before she could reply, Danielle grabbed her free hand and pulled her through the crowd. Kayla gripped Turner's hand and was giddy when she realized he didn't need encouragement to come with her. They came to a halt at the front door where she and Danielle collided, but Turner was able to stop gracefully with no contact.

"That hooch has gone tribal," Danielle said as she grabbed Kayla's shoulders and turned her around. "Now she *knows* those things need maximum support."

Kayla gasped when she saw Rochelle wilding out in the center of a dance circle of intoxicated college boys. Her breasts bounced freely with no support under the thin shirt she wore. All Kayla could do was shake her head. She turned to Danielle and said, "I'm bouncing, so you need to babysit."

Danielle all but drooled when she noticed Turner. Her mouth widened into a toothy grin then she looked over to her drunken roommate, Rochelle, still dancing. "Any room for a third? I'll make it interesting," she said to Kayla but her eyes were on Turner.

Kayla turned to Turner. He mouthed the word "no".

Good boy, Kayla thought as she led the way to the front door. "He's shy," she told Danielle over her shoulder.

As Kayla and Turner stepped outside, they heard Danielle call out, "You've missed out on a life altering experience."

"No doubt," Turner said then laughed but continued to follow.

Kayla giggled as she led Turner down the porch stairs. Out front, people talked and drank but were spread out comfortably. She led him to a couple talking on the steps of another townhouse, two doors down the street.

"Need a quiet place, Ray," she said with urgency.

Ray waved his hand toward the front door of the stoop where he and a random chick sat. She was apparently his latest conquest, and this one looked extravagant. Knowing Ray, Kayla wondered what he was doing talking to a girl who resembled a walking mannequin. Ray, part white and part Asian, hated label whores with a passion and yet, here he was talking to the likely co-founder of label whores united.

"Thanks," she said as she led Turner into Ray's place.

"No problem," Ray said, not even looking at her.

Caleb felt some kind of energy pass from him to her when he slid his hand into hers back at the party. He felt her shiver, and he thought he hurt her, but she didn't pull away. And to ease his short-lived panic, she tightened her fingers around his hand and just looked at him.

As he followed her through her friend's house, Caleb half expected to see her Guards waiting for him. No telling what she actually felt from that jolt of power he unintentionally allowed to slip through.

The surge of power was forgotten as Kayla dropped his hand and moved ahead of him, disappearing behind a wall. She flicked the light switch on the wall then looked over her shoulder at him. It wasn't a seductive look but it called to him in the same way.

Caleb followed her to a small two-seat sofa in a corner of the room. Glancing around, he realized this was some kind of game room or a common room for gaming and entertaining.

"So," Kayla said. She sat down on the sofa and pulled him down next to her. "This is quiet," she said as she looked around, "so let's talk."

Caleb smiled. "You've heard it all, haven't you?"

"Just about," she admitted. "Do you have something new?"

Caleb held her gaze. "I don't think what I say now matters. You already know how far you're going to let me get."

He noticed her hand rubbing the stone on her bracelet. Then, without a word, Kayla moved closer to him. She braced her hand on the cushion between them, leaned in, and placed her lips on his.

The kiss was soft, sensual, and sudden. So sudden, initially Caleb pulled back but he moved forward to taste the sweetness of her lips. He palmed the back of her neck and used his thumb to stroke her cheek.

Caleb kissed her until she needed air. As Kayla took deep breaths while staring at him, he chuckled.

"What's so funny?" Kayla cut her eyes at him. "Isn't this what you wanted?"

Caleb actually laughed. "A quiet place to talk is what I wanted."

The truth was, he was laughing at himself. He couldn't believe how this *girl* was affecting him. He was older than her mother's mother. He was most likely older than the city they were in, yet here he was wishing he didn't pull away. He felt ridiculous for being here with her at all.

"Isn't that guy talk for 'let's go someplace so I can put my hand down your pants'?"

"Is that what you're used to?" he asked.

Shit. From the look on her face he knew he just embarrassed her.

Kayla stood but he grabbed her wrist and pulled her back down. "That's a shame because you are such a beautiful, smart, and compassionate young lady who deserves nothing but the most untainted form of love a man can offer."

"How could you know that?"

"When I first saw you smile, I knew everything I needed to know about you."

Kayla sat back. "That's upsetting because I know nothing about you. Well, except for that you're kind of old fashioned and talk like a senior citizen."

"My parents were old fashioned, I guess it stuck." Caleb couldn't be honest but he didn't want to lie either.

"Were?"

"They're gone. It's just me now."

"I'm sorry. Do you have other family?" She seemed genuine.

Caleb was flattered by her concern. "I have one or two living relatives but I don't know them yet."

Kayla seemed to consider his response but shook her head and frowned. "I don't usually do this. It's just that you are so… Anyway, I just thought that we could have, I don't know, a fling," she told him.

"A fling?" Caleb repeated. "Have you had many of those?"

"What? No. It's just, my family is sort of old fashioned too, Turner," she said. She nibbled on her bottom lip then stood. "I should go."

Caleb wasn't sure why but he felt that if he let her leave, he would never see her again. He jumped to his feet. "You don't want something permanent, so I suggest we start out as friends," he said as he followed her.

Kayla shook her head. When she reached the door, she pulled it open. As they exited the house, she said, "I have enough friends."

Caleb didn't respond right away. He followed a few steps behind her as she walked to her car that was parallel parked across the street. He waited until she was seated before bending inside the open door to kiss her. He kissed her with so much passion that he hoped she felt what could be.

When he pulled back, Kayla touched her chest as she watched him with hooded eyes.

"I don't plan on being just a friend for too long." Caleb closed the door to her car.

May

Caleb didn't know why he wasn't able to get Kayla or her question out of his head. He hadn't communicated with anyone in his family for a very long time. He kept track of them but he felt they would be safer if he didn't engage. Yet, now he stared at his childhood home, knowing he wasn't alone.

Maiden Hall was newly restored. The mansion remained, but everything else that would suggest that it was once a plantation was replaced with lush greenery and gardens. His cottage was now some kind of large shed.

Throughout the years, not once did he feel the need to visit this place. Caleb kept his distance. The memories were still raw. But as he stood next to his tree looking over the lake where he watched her swim so many times as a boy, he felt a peace he hadn't felt in a long time.

"Can I help you?"

Caleb threw the rock in his hand into the lake. "Just looking at the old place," he said without turning around.

"I got a call from the grounds keeper, said someone was hanging around the property. I'll tell you the same thing I tell everyone who comes out here," the man said. "This place isn't for sale. There is no amount you can offer so don't waste your time." The man stepped closer. "If you want something in the area, the neighboring land, across the lake, is for sale."

"You sound like him," Caleb said quietly. "Even look like him a bit." He turned to face the young man, who looked at him and took a step back. Caleb learned a lot about Richard Scott, a college student who kept Maiden Hall pristine over the past couple of years. The young man loved history, and had a particular interest in a family tale of his ancestor who fell in love with a slave. "I've never had a desire to meet any of you, but I made sure that I always knew where all of you were. It wasn't anything personal. I didn't think I could bear it, I guess. But you Richard, I find interesting enough to warrant a proper introduction."

Richard took another step back, still looking confused. Caleb smiled as he came closer. "I am Caleb Scott, the brother of Fredrick Scott and second son of Henry and Catherine Scott. But you've figured that out already, haven't you?"

Kayla didn't see the exact moment Turner slipped into the bookstore but she had a clear view of him as he took a seat at a table that faced her register. He playfully winked at her then picked up a magazine from a nearby rack and began to aimlessly flip through the pages.

A wink, she thought as she rang up another customer. *The nerve*. Yeah, he left a message with Rochelle telling her that he was going away for a few days but he was away for more than a week without a word. No, she had no claim on him. Anytime they hung out, they acted like friends. She *was* the one who said they should be friends and nothing more. But…

Kayla was so busy thinking about Turner that she didn't see the little girl who was staring at her, waiting for her change. *Great*, now she couldn't even do her job. *What the heck*?

"Do you see this ho?" Rochelle whispered. She stepped in front of Kayla with her lips twisted in a frown.

Kayla leaned to the side to see a woman talking to Turner. It was the same woman who approached her a few weeks ago, after Turner left the store. Kayla never forgot a face and the buxom brunette with her smoky gray eyes and mini, mini skirt was hard to forget. That day, the woman asked if Turner and she were seeing each other. Kayla told her the truth, they weren't.

So here the woman was, pulling a chair out and sitting down at Turner's table. And why not, Turner was gorgeous. When the woman extended her long legs out in front of him with those screw me hooker heels on, Kayla bit her lip hard enough to draw blood.

Who cares?

Kayla shook her head then focused her attention back on her work. Well, she *tried* to focus on her work, at least. Only, when she heard laughter coming from the table she bit her lip again.

Rochelle stomped her feet. "Girl, go get your man."

"He's not my man," Kayla said through clenched teeth.

Rochelle rolled her eyes at Kayla then turned back to watch Turner. "Oh, no this hussy didn't do a laughing hair flip."

"Get a grip, Roe," Kayla sneered. "Turner's a free agent."

Ray appeared at the counter. Where he came from, Kayla didn't know. "And it seems like he has a solid offer on the table," Ray announced as he peered over at the table where Turner sat.

Rochelle smacked Ray on the shoulder hard enough to draw the attention of a few customers who stood nearby.

"Ooh, but I like it when you get all physical and shit," Ray said to Rochelle as he raised his finger. "Know that I can take it but I also like to dish it out."

Rochelle cringed. "Gross."

Kayla laughed as she watched her friends' playful banter but her smile vanished as she glanced over to Turner and his new friend. The woman was leaning into him now, and his eyes were fixed on her large breasts instead of her eyes.

That. Is. It! She'd seen enough.

Kayla typed in several numbers on her register then went to her supervisor and lied, though she was really feeling sick. Thirty minutes later she was opening her dorm apartment door, armed with some much-needed supplies. Pecan swirls, mint chip ice cream, and a Slurpee were essentials for sulking in the pinnacle of "piss-tivity".

"What's wrong?"

Kayla cried out as she whipped around, dropping her shopping bag but holding on to her Slurpee. "How do you know where I lived?" she asked as she watched Turner bend to pick up the bag. She took a few steps back, almost falling through her door that was slightly open, but Turner steadied her. Pulling away from him, she peered down the long empty hallway.

Did they see him?

Flashing a winning smile, Turner asked, "What, is it a secret?"

She had to be careful not to let her Guards find out about Turner. The ones her mother didn't think she knew about. The ones who drove away any guy she showed any interested in. That was why she didn't want Turner to know where she lived or have her phone number. He had to call Rochelle and leave her a message.

"Nothing's wrong," she almost shouted as she snatched her bag from him. Kayla stepped inside her room and went to close the door, but he placed his foot in the way.

When she reopened the door, he sighed as he looked up at the ceiling. He removed his foot and turned to walk away. "Alright."

"I guess I won't see you for another two weeks," she said venomously.

Turner turned back. He peered at her with such intensity that she backed away as he moved forward until he was inside the apartment with her. The door closed behind him and he locked it, causing her to frown.

"Friends, Kayla. As my friend for the past couple of months, you're not privy to how I spend my time when I'm not with you. Or who I spend it with." He moved closer and she move back. "That is the way you want it and I respect that but you can't have it both ways."

Her eyes narrowed and her blood heated as he closed in on her. There was nowhere else to go as her back made contact with the small kitchen counter.

Caleb was confused. He kept his feelings for her bottled up just to be near her without causing problems for either of them. He only met up with her at her job, parties, or at neutral places where he treated her like he treated the rest of her gang. It was her call.

"Get out!" Kayla yelled at him. "Go call that girl who is aching for your attention."

Caleb moved closer. Her anger was misplaced and he didn't like games. At least not the kind she was playing. He saw Kayla reach behind her back but didn't think she was hostile until something silver flew at him. When he angled his head, the fork missed him and lodged into the door behind him.

She covered her mouth, seeming to realize what she just did.

This was ridiculous. She was a temperamental child and he was a grown ass man.

Caleb turned around and unlocked the door. He was done with it all. His original plan was ruined the moment he laid eyes on her. And with all the time he spent around her over the past month or so, he couldn't bring himself to hurt her in any way.

That meant that she could never know what or who he really was.

He needed to leave and never lay eyes on her again. That was exactly what he was doing, but before he could open the door, Kayla was holding him around the waist with her head buried in his back.

"Do you like her?" she murmured.

Caleb rested his head on the door. His breaths were short and staggered. His blood bubbled beneath her touch. "You can't do this," he hoarsely told her. He gently pulled her arms away and turned to face her. Holding her face in his hands he said, "It's like a tug of war with you. You want us to only be friends but you look at me in a way that makes me think there might be something more. Or you'll give me more attention when you see that someone else is interested in me, but not too much. Just enough for you to keep me under your spell. Why the games, Kayla? Do you think this is fun for me? That I am just some idiot you can lead around on a leash?" he asked angrily.

His jaw tightened. Never before did he want so badly to shake some sense into a woman.

Kayla grabbed his wrists and pulled his hands away from her face. The next thing that happened, Caleb wasn't prepared for.

Kayla pushed up on her toes and kissed him. His strength wavered as she forced him against the door. Her hands found his belt and she quickly unbuckled it. Undoing his jean buttons, she smoothly moved her hand inside his pants.

With a jolt, his entire body awakened. *Control*, he thought as his desires threatened to overcome him.

"I can't," Caleb whispered over her lips. He grudgingly pulled her hand out of his jeans.

Kayla snatched her hand from his then turned her back on him as he buttoned his jeans and buckled his belt. "Why the hell can't you?" she yelled. "I know you want me in that way."

"I do but I won't accept just that part of you. I want all of you, Kayla." Caleb touched her shoulder but she quickly moved away.

"So, you have to possess every woman you make love to."

"Yes, I do. But don't confuse the act of making love with sex. The women I have sex with are not important to me. You are, and what I don't want right now is for you to have some meaningless night with me so you can satisfy some jealous itch." Caleb sighed. He walked over to her and laid his hand on her cheek. "I don't know how I can make you understand that I have no interest in anyone but you. Stop fighting what you know you feel and give us a chance."

Caleb traced his thumb over her lips. He could smell her blood from her biting them. It made him angry that she would inflict pain on herself, no matter how insignificant the damage. The need to kiss her overwhelmed his senses, so he gave in.

Kayla resisted at first but soon she returned his kiss.

Chapter Twenty-Nine

About a year later

Kayla entered the fifth story one-room apartment hoping Turner was home. She closed and locked the door behind her, determined to wait. She dropped her handbag on the floor then took a seat on his couch. Looking around then rubbing her hands on her knees, her eyes darted to the front door several times.

She stood and pulled off the jacket she borrowed from Rochelle, then threw it over the back of the couch without considering how wet it was. Her sneakers were the next to come off. She used her feet to pull off her shoes and left them where they dropped. The glasses and the wig came off next.

The apartment was clean and everything was put in a specific place, but Kayla had something on her mind today which made the pristine condition of Turner's apartment the least of her worries. She lay down, resting her head on the arm of the couch and stared at the ceiling. She bit on her lip as she thought of the past year.

How wonderful everything had been for her lately. How she loved Turner more than life itself. How she didn't want to lose him. She'd fallen for him even though she tried so hard not to. But he made it so easy, didn't he?

He was exactly what she needed.

Turner was kind, gentle, understanding and accepting, and he very seldom questioned her about her life before him, which was refreshing because she would have had to lie to him. She didn't want to lie to him if she could help it.

He didn't even complain about her cloak and dagger behavior when they had to avoid her Guards; he accepted her explanation of her mother being quite strict. For fear of his questions, Kayla never asked him questions about his family or life before her either.

It was as if their lives didn't exist until they met each other.

Turner did introduce her to his nephew, Richard. She and Turner spent Christmas with Richard at their family estate. It was just them—Richard's parents passed away two years earlier, making Turner his only living relative. She had a wonderful time at Christmas break with her two hosts for the weekend. All that was missing was a nice girl for Richard.

Kayla yawned but kept her eyes wide open. There was no time for sleep. She needed to see Turner. To speak to him before she lost her nerve, which was fading with every heartbeat. With Joe and Dana, her guardians, more thoroughly watching every move she made lately, it was becoming harder to get away and spend time with him.

She readjusted herself on the sofa. Her eyelids closed and reopened a number of times before they became too heavy for her to keep open.

Caleb wiped the rain from his face as he slowly climbed the ten flights of stairs to his studio apartment. Earlier today, while on campus, he felt a presence unlike anything he ever known. He hunted and found the source easily enough, possibly because the young man wanted to be found.

The boy wanted his help but Caleb sent him on his way. Now Kayla was in his apartment.

Caleb made no noise as he opened his door. He picked her bag up off the floor and placed it on the coffee table before he sat on the edge of the sofa beside her. Leaning down, he kissed her gently, causing her to stir. Kayla slowly wrapped her arms around his neck and drew him into a more passionate kiss.

Caleb gently pulled her hands from around his neck. He broke from the kiss with a few pecks to her lips and cheeks.

"Please Turner," she begged. Kayla tried to pull him closer but Caleb shook his head no, then kissed her on the nose. "This isn't the time to be old fashioned. Trust me," she whispered as she attempted to pull him down a second time.

Caleb resisted as he had every day for almost a year. They were intimate in other ways but he refused to cross that line with her. Not yet anyway.

He looked into her eyes and frowned. "Something's wrong."

Of course, something was wrong, he told himself. He was in love with a woman who knew nothing about his past and how she was involved. He was her enemy who had every intention of killing her when he first found her.

Kayla sat up and scooted back so they were further apart. "I've been keeping something from you," she said.

Caleb knew everything would come to a head at some point but hoped he would have more time. The oxygen in the room seemed to become heated as his lungs burned with all his secrets. All he could do was listen.

"I'm sorry about earlier. I know you can't just run away with me." She said nothing for several seconds then continued, "I have to leave soon. A marriage has been arranged for me. I have to leave for home," she said then sighed, "we can never see each other again."

"You had someone waiting for you?" Caleb asked, angry and confused. He felt as if his ribs were constricting over his heart. Breathing was a chore.

"No, Turner, it's nothing like that," Kayla said. "It's an arranged marriage. I've never met the man but I did know that it was going to happen at some point. I just didn't know it would be this soon." She touched his face. "I never meant for us to happen, to fall in love with you, but I did."

Caleb stood. The Coesen practiced arranged marriages. That explained a lot. "Is this what you want, to marry a stranger?" Sighing, Caleb couldn't bring himself to tell her not to do it. To stay with him, marry him.

Marriage was always on his mind even though it was unlikely. He didn't make love to her in all these months because not only was he old fashioned, but in some recess of his mind, Caleb saw a future for them.

The hurt on her face answered his question. "What I want isn't important. I made a promise to Vivian, I mean, to my mother. She allowed me to come here against her better judgment. She's..." Kayla looked down before continuing. "She's Royalty and so am I. All I wanted was a few years of freedom. I didn't plan this. Do you hate me?"

"I could never hate you, Kayla." Caleb stood up then walked over to his bed and sat down. He could take her away, like he originally planned, but he would have to tell her who he was and that wasn't an option.

He fell back on the bed, looking up at the ceiling. There was nothing he could do. She was going to marry another man and he could do nothing about it. He closed his eyes tight as the realization set in that there was no workable solution. Losing her, the very person who made him feel alive again, to another man was worse than losing her in death. The thought of knowing she was out there somewhere but he could not have her, made him crazy.

Her hand was what he felt first then the rest of her slid beside him. She cuddled into him as he turned and held her tight. Her sobbing, the only sound that could be heard in the apartment, tortured him because there was nothing he could do to fix this. So, he did the only thing he could do, he held her in his arms as she cried herself to sleep.

They slept the entire night away in each other's arms. Caleb was the first to wake. He didn't move for fear he would wake her. Last night, as he listened to her cry, he decided that when the time came, he would not stop her from leaving, with promises or declarations of his love. He would let her go without a fight but she was going with his heart. He inhaled her scent, a light airy fragrance, as he took time to appreciate her beauty.

When Kayla stirred, Caleb slowly closed his eyes.

Kayla woke with a groan. There would be no dramatics this morning, no more tears. So, when she realized Turner was still asleep, she slowly slid from his grasp and crept to the front door. She turned back to look at him one last time.

He loved her; she knew it even though he never told her. It was probably because he knew that love wasn't enough. She took his key from her ring and placed it on his coffee table then opened the front door.

"Goodbye," she whispered, closing the door behind her

Caleb lay on his bed looking from the ceiling to the wall then to the ceiling again. There was no solution. They couldn't be together.

After another twenty minutes or so, he jumped in the shower. Frustrated and heartbroken he closed his eyes and let the warm water washed over him.

Of all the modern advances of the world there was one that Caleb appreciated above all others and that was indoor plumbing. He loved all kinds of modern transportation, the oven, and the nylon bristled toothbrush, but indoor plumbing was something he could never live without again.

Caleb wondered if he would be able to live without Kayla.

He washed much slower than he usually did, then got dressed. Reaching under his bed, Caleb pulled out a large duffle bag and packed. It was time to leave town.

Worse off than when he arrived, Caleb no longer had Kayla and now he had no way to stop her mother from hunting him or hurting the people around him.

Why didn't I tell her how I feel? Would it have made a difference?

Caleb sat down on the edge of his bed. He knew he truly loved her, he knew before Christmas. Yet, he never actually said the words, "I love you". Those three words didn't fully express what he really felt for her.

The emptiness of his future without her weighed heavily on Caleb. He wanted to throw something, to break something. He wanted to lose control.

Caleb lowered his head in his hands and took several deep breaths. He must not ever lose control. "Not ever again," he whispered.

He should have left that very first day. He should have never come here. He should have realized something was afoul when that old Dread offered to help him. The Dread saw this, seen his heartache, his pain. If this was a way to punish him, make him suffer…well, the Coesen succeeded.

Caleb finished packing the duffle bag and was zippering it when he felt a familiar presence in his building. Throwing the duffle over his shoulder, he dropped it on the floor and opened the front door just as Rochelle was about to knock.

"Kayla sent me," Rochelle said. She peered at him with red watery eyes.

From crying with Kayla, he surmised.

Caleb opened the door wider to let her in but Rochelle made no attempt to enter.

"She wants you to meet her in the campus courtyard in an hour. She'll be on the stone bench by the tall bushes."

Washington State
About a year later

Kayla was with the man she loved and life with him was all she dreamed it would be. Only, she didn't feel complete and she didn't seem able to shake it. As she lay on the sofa with the remote in her hand, she tilted her head up and began staring up at the vaulted ceiling.

"Feeling alright?" Turner asked.

Kayla angled her head around and smiled as Turner closed the door. "I didn't think you would be back so soon. You, just missed Mrs. Deeds." Kayla placed the remote on the table and sat up as Caleb sat down on the edge of the sofa next to her. "What's in the bag?"

He pulled a bag from behind his back and held it out to her. Kayla grabbed the bag and opened it. She pulled a smaller bag with Mike-n-Ike candies and cashews out. Frowning, Kayla looked from the bag to him.

"I overheard you talking to the woman on the first floor this morning." Turner slowly pulled her feet up on his lap as he sat back. "She seems nice; maybe we should invite her and that musician boyfriend of hers to dinner."

"You know we can't, Turner. Not if you want us to remain together. We can't get too close to anyone. I told you before," she placed the bag on the table. "My mother is a very powerful woman, and even though I know that I've married an amazing, loving, and gentle man, she will never allow us to be together."

Kayla decided the less he knew about her mother and the Coesen, the better. Though she couldn't help but wonder if he would have made the same choice if he knew what they were hiding from.

She looked to Turner's hand as he moved it in small circles over her round belly. "I know what you're trying to do and I appreciate it. But we have to keep to ourselves. Once Mrs. Deeds delivers our baby, we must leave this place. We've been here way too long. I would be lying if I said that I didn't miss my family and friends, but I accepted the consequences when I emptied my bank account and ran off with you."

Turner slid down beside her on the sofa. It took longer for her to maneuver herself so that she was facing him with her being seven months pregnant, but she managed. As they lay face to face, Kayla thought the extra work it took to turn over was worth it when she looked into his handsome face. She ran her fingers through Turner's dyed dark brown hair and looked into his now brown eyes. His readiness to change his appearance and move to a city on the west coast showed Kayla how much he loved her even though he rarely spoke of his feelings.

Turner was hers. He was her lover, her husband, and her child's father. She sighed with delight as she gazed at him.

"You miss the blonde hair and green-blue eyes, the old me?" he asked softly.

"I love you." Kayla kissed him. "With brown hair and eyes, you're still gorgeous. Besides, *this* lighter color and cut isn't exactly me."

Caleb absently rubbed his head, touching Kayla's hand as he did. He didn't dye his hair or purchased contacts like she did. He changed his appearance the way he always did, with only a thought. It would be nothing to change back to his blond locks and original eye color.

Caleb took a deep breath. "Kayla," he said, "You've sacrificed so much to be with me. You deserve to know everything about me. I am——."

"No," Kayla interrupted. She laid her hand over his cheek. "There are things about me I haven't told you, and to be honest, I can't tell you. So please let's leave our pasts where they belong, in the past. I love you so much it hurts. I actually feel an aching in my chest when I think of losing *this*…you…us. Let's just keep things the way they are." Kayla held his gaze.

Caleb closed his eyes. When he opened them, he could have them back to their original hue. She would know instantly that he wasn't who she thought. She would know he wasn't a Middling.

"I…" he said then sighed, "I don't want to lose you either." Kayla rested her head on his shoulder. Opening his eyes slowly, Caleb revealed the chestnut brown.

Well into the night, Caleb grew more on edge. He sat on their bed watching Kayla sleep as he thought of a way to tell her who he really was. He knew what the truth could do but she deserved to know who she was in love with.

By morning he made up his mind. For her and their child's safety, he would tell her after the baby arrived. Whatever she decided, he would accept.

Caleb pushed his past out of his mind. He made Kayla his special homemade recipe of blueberry pancakes. It was the only breakfast foods she could keep down now. As she ate he washed the dishes.

"How's our finances?" Kayla asked.

He sighed. Caleb knew she worried about money and he hated it but couldn't tell her that they were filthy rich. That would need an explanation.

"Our finances are fine," he said. "You shouldn't give it another thought."

"I just feel that you should take the money. I want to contribute."

"Finances are something we don't have to worry about. You're my wife and I will always take care of you and our baby," Caleb told her. She wouldn't believe him; he knew this but there was no way he was taking a dime from her.

Kayla looked down at the metal band that was on her ring finger. She ran her finger over the thin red strip that circled it. Her wedding day had been so…well…so simple. A justice of the peace and two witnesses were the whole of their wedding guests. But even though it wasn't the wedding she had always dreamed of having, she would always remember it as one of the best days of her life.

After breakfast, Turner got Kayla a few pillows so she could watch television comfortably then went for a morning run. Kayla took her vitamins and was just about to sit and watch her favorite program when she heard a knock at the door.

"Who is it?" she called out as she got to her feet. Kayla walked over to the door and looked through the peep hole. Seeing a man in a police uniform on the other side of the door, Kayla opened it. "Yes?" she asked.

"Good morning," the officer said. "There have been a few disturbances in the neighborhood and we think the perpetrators may be some local kids. If I could come in and show you a few pictures, I like to see if you recognize any of them."

Kayla looked at the officer's friendly pale face, then looked him over. "I really don't know any of the kids in the neighborhood," she said.

A low distorted voice came from the officer's radio on his waist. "One moment," he said to her then lifted the radio up to his lips and turned his back to her.

This officer wasn't a Coesen, he was Caucasian and his red hair and brown eyes told her he wasn't a Child of Jai. But, Kayla looked at his neck anyway and saw no birthmark. When the officer turned back to face her, he pulled a few sheets of paper from his pocket.

"It will only take a few minutes. Just give these pictures a quick once over and I'll be out of your hair. I promise," he smiled.

Kayla returned the smile as she back away, opening the door wider for the officer to step inside. When she closed the door, she was grabbed from behind. The officer covered her mouth with one hand and with the other pulled her hair up and away from her neck.

Holding his hand over her mouth, the officer lifted his radio to his mouth and spoke. "It's her," he said. "Tell them I'll have her in my cruiser at the corner of…"

Kayla shook with fear. *They found me.*

"Negative," the voice on the radio said. "You are to detain her there and wait. They will come to you with the money for the unharmed girl."

No.

Kayla grabbed his hand but couldn't pull it away to scream. She kicked at his legs and feet but the officer held her tight. Through her panic, she remembered something she learned in a self-defense class. She relaxed her body, as if she'd fainted. When the officer took his hand from her mouth to catch her limp body from falling, Kayla scratched at his face. She dropped to her knees but quickly got to her feet; then Kayla screamed.

Before Kayla could reach the door, it swung open and then closed. "Turner?" She froze where she stood. The look on his face frightened her so much that she took a step back, but she remembered the officer behind her who was reaching out to grab her, so she moved to the side to avoid him.

Kayla wasn't completely out of the officer's grasp but he didn't get to lay a finger on her because Turner was between them so quickly that Kayla almost fell again from the shock of what she was seeing. Truth is, she didn't see much of anything. Turner was by the door one moment then in front of the officer the next.

"Who sent you?" Turner asked the officer. The man was on one knee trying to brace the arm that Turner gripped.

"I don't know," the officer cried out. It was clear he was in excruciating pain. "My partner and I were approached by a man who offered us a lot of money to keep an eye out for a runaway matching her description. Her hair and eyes are different but it's her."

Turner tightened his hold, raising the officer to his feet. "I swear. He never gave his name, just a picture." Turner pulled a photo from the officer's pocket then tossed him across the room and into a bookcase with no effort. The officer crumpled to the floor, unconscious. Turner studied the photo briefly then looked to her.

Kayla's face reflected her panic as she backed away when Turner approached. "But you probably are a Coesen..." She shook her head as she continued to back away. "Stop!" She held up her hand. "Stop right there. Just stop!" she yelled. Kayla took a few more steps back before hitting a dining room chair.

Turner stopped.

"You could have had a birthmark. You don't cover it with anything," she thought aloud, looking away. "So, you had it removed somehow. Not that it's possible, but you're smart." Kayla looked at him. "You had it removed, right?" She was almost begging him to agree.

"No, Kayla," Turner said softly. "I'm not a Coesen."

As she watched his eyes turn from brown to their natural green-blue color and his hair become blond once again, Kayla tilted her head in disbelief. "Caleb? But...you're not real. Caleb...is a boogie man, just a story our parents tell to scare us." She leaned forward. "You're not...evil." Kayla stepped closer. "You aren't a monster."

Caleb crossed the space between them and pulled her into his arms. Still confused but comforted by his familiar touch, she wrapped her arms around him. "You're him, aren't you? You killed all those people." Kayla pulled away. "I've heard stories, but I want to hear it from you."

Kayla saw pain in his eyes, something she never saw before. She also saw the love he felt for her.

But this is Caleb.

She felt her chest constrict, and tried to pull her hand away but he held her hand firmly.

In a blink of an eye, Kayla found herself surrounded by the dark of night. She heard a voice, and at the same time, the glow from the moon brightened her surroundings. There was a boy in a tree. He had the most beautifully odd green-blue...

Caleb?

Kayla stood so close that young Caleb should have seen her but he acted as if she wasn't there. *This is a Time-weave.*

She didn't conjure this one but she knew she was in the past…a place she didn't exist in. *But how?* Caleb…he was doing this, and it was perfect. She could smell the scents that surrounded her and tasted the air. She was hot and felt muggy from the summer's heat. He wasn't just presenting his life to her. He was allowing her to experience it.

Kayla heard another voice. She focused on Caleb and a beautiful young girl who swam in a lake. She felt his every emotion as she witnessed that night and each night after. At times, Kayla felt overwhelmed but she couldn't stop now. Not when she was finally seeing who he really was.

Except…

Kayla gasped in horror as she watched the night Marda and Samuel, his son, died. She cried with him and felt his pain as he locked himself away in his room. She watched as Fredrick and Jai tried to comfort him. Kayla was there to see his pain turn to anger. She knew the moment he made the decision to die by seeking out her people. She saw when he and his guide were brought to a strange village then everything went black.

The next thing Kayla saw was Caleb, stronger and more confident. He was different. He had a power he didn't have before. Kayla watched as he entered the Coesen village. She saw the compassion in his eyes when he looked at Marda's little sister, Oma.

Oma?

She saw everything that happened that day in the village, and she wept for the dead.

Kayla witnessed as Caleb moved through his long life of solitude. She saw how lonely and depressed he was. And how Caleb repeatedly put himself in situations that should have killed him, situations a person who valued life would have avoided. But as years became decades, Kayla began to see Caleb's anger disappear.

He was a man who just wanted to just be left alone, only her people continued to hunt him. He killed indiscriminately whenever attacked. Then, she saw a familiar face. She stood in the flat that belonged to Marcel, her teacher and friend as he and Caleb discussed…*her*.

Why?

As she watched the two men talk everything suddenly became much slower. The lifetime that flashed before her eyes was slowing to a crawl. Kayla stood in Marcel's flat watching him and Caleb plan, wondering if the connection to Caleb was breaking. She almost cried in frustration but then Marcel turned from the ongoing act of Caleb's memories and looked at her.

"I was hoping to see you again, Kayla. There is little time my dear, so listen closely," Marcel told her as he left his seat beside Caleb in the memory and walked toward her.

Kayla didn't believe it but it was happening. A shadow of a dead man was communicating with her inside a weave of time, he was weaving within a time weave. This was unheard of, and dangerous. A weaver cannot talk to anyone they witness in a Time-weave. A weaver was only able to view and bear witness. But, this *was* Marcel, and as she stood there she knew this was actually happening because he was the very best.

"If you stay with Caleb, you and your unborn daughter will die, and Caleb will never rest until the entire Coesen bloodline is wiped from this planet to avenge you both. You must leave him and take *his* wedding band. The blood that flows around his band, your blood, is a way for him to find you no matter where you are or the distance."

"I can't. I love him, Marcel." She rubbed her belly. "I cannot take his child from him," She said as she stood straighter.

"Then she will die." Marcel turned and walked back to the chair he sat in. He looked over at her again and smiled. "You must be strong for your daughter, Kayla."

Kayla would have crumbled to her knees if she could. Her heart was breaking but she had to be strong. What Marcel told her, she figured Caleb didn't know or he would not have shown her any of this.

Once Marcel sat back down, time sped up again. Her old teacher was again talking to Caleb. Nothing seemed to suggest that what she just experienced even happened, so Kayla continued to watch Caleb's life play out. After the memories of their meeting, courtship and marriage flashed in front of her, Caleb broke the connection and pulled her back.

Kayla looked at Caleb. He was her husband, her best friend, her lover. He was her everything. "Do you prefer Caleb or Turner?" she asked. He peered at her with sadness in his eyes that seemed to lift a bit when she spoke.

"Caleb," he told her, then said, "Kayla, I swear the person that I was is gone. You've inspired me since the moment I laid eyes on you. I don't want to hurt anyone. I just want me and you to be together. I've never lied to you…except for telling you my name was Turner. I use Turner because it was my mother's father's name."

Kayla just looked at him without saying a word. She glanced over to the wall clock. The screening of his life had taken only minutes. Kayla spun around and headed for the bedroom. She grabbed a duffle bag and began filling it with some of her clothing and some of the things they bought for the baby. Caleb watched her with defeat on his face.

Looking over her shoulder she spoke, "We need to get out of here fast. I'm sure they're close." She tossed him a bag. "I know you have another place we can go. Someplace secluded, no people, an island maybe?"

Caleb stood unmoving, speechless.

"I'm in love with you, Turner…Caleb, and I feel the love you have for me. You never tell me how you feel and now I know that it hurts you to even admit it to yourself that you love me, but I see it every time I look into your eyes. I believe in us and nothing you've done is going to change that." She crossed the room and kissed him with all the passion she felt for him. "So please, Caleb," she said as they parted, "we need to run."

"They're already here," he said plainly. "It's too late to run."

Kayla looked around him and into the living room. She saw no one but she knew he was telling the truth. She bit her bottom lip as she tried to think. "You still have the Veilex." She pulled his sleeve up to reveal a bracelet. She hadn't been able to tell before but knew now that it was made with a Veilex stone. "If you change your eyes and hair back to brown they will think you're a Middling."

As she made the suggestion Caleb was making the change.

"Kayla Harper," a voice called from the living room. "Our sovereign would like your audience."

Kayla's face burned but she knew it was actually a shade paler. Her mother, Vivian Harper, Sovereign of all Coesen, made the journey to bring her home. She took a deep breath as she took Caleb's hand. They slowly walked out of their bedroom and into the living room.

Vivian and Cassius were the first faces she saw as she entered. She looked at Caleb and suddenly wished that she told him to be calm. When he nodded, she gave him a surprised look.

Did he hear me?

She always felt he was someone special, someone strong, and intelligent, and he was also very handsome, someone she should be honored to have in her life. Only she didn't know how special he really was.

Kayla thought, *I love you.* Without pause, she heard Caleb inside her head.

I love you more, Kayla.

Her eyes widened adoringly as she looked from his creased eyebrows to his tightened jawbone, but movement beside her caused Kayla to look away from him. Two of the Coesen Guard were picking up the unconscious officer and carrying him from the apartment.

Vivian looked at Caleb then to Kayla's hand that rested inside his. Her expression changed from anger to a look of helplessness but only for a moment. She spoke with her usual confidence and poise. "This is my fault. I made a grave error in allowing you to come to this place. If you come back willingly, I give you my word that your friend will not be harmed. What does he know?"

"He knows nothing," Kayla said quickly. She lied to her mother before but this lie was treasonous. She felt Caleb tighten his grip around her hand.

Stay. Calm, she willed to him.

Vivian looked to Cassius. "Have the boy's memory wiped." She then turned cold eyes to Kayla. "Then wipe hers."

"I can't allow that," Caleb said. "I won't let you forget me," he declared as he looked at her.

Kayla squeezed his hand again as Vivian and Cassius looked at him. Then Cassius looked at one of the six guards that were scattered throughout the room, the one closest to Caleb.

"Please don't do anything to give yourself away." She begged Caleb as she felt his hand stiffen. She let her hand slide out of his and walked toward Cassius and her mother. Kayla noticed that her mother continued to stare at Caleb as the guard grabbed him by the shoulder. Another guard stepped forward and took her by the arm.

Caleb watched as the Guard led Kayla across the room. It was happening again. They were taking his love away from him, again. *His life*. He wanted to stop them but couldn't risk it.

Images of Marda and Samuel dying in his arms replayed in Caleb's mind. His bones felt heavy, unmovable. He closed his eyes as he tried to breathe through his panic.

He couldn't let it happen again. He wouldn't provoke them. He would let them take her without incident then he would find her and make her remember him. Her blood lined his ring. She thought it was sweet that he wanted them to keep a part of each other with them always. But that wasn't why he suggested it. The ring's special metal, metal he recovered from the cocoon, worked as a beacon when introduced to blood. As long as he had his wedding ring, he would find her no matter where they took her.

Kayla and the Guard had just about reached Vivian and Cassius when she doubled over. A sharp pain ran down the center of her belly causing her to cry out and cup the lower part of her abdomen.

Without an ounce of compassion, the Guard yanked her back to a standing position and pushed her forward. Kayla whipped her head back. She could see the anger in Caleb's eyes. Before she could say a word, Cassius pulled her out of the way. The Guard who had hold of her arm was falling to the floor and Caleb was standing over him.

Everyone in the room froze. Vivian held Kayla back as she screamed and struggled desperately to free herself. She needed to get to Caleb. Everyone in the room focused on him in disbelief. Everyone except for Vivian, because while she held her daughter so closely, Vivian's hand rested around the protruding belly that the oversized t-shirt was hiding.

"Let her come to me," Caleb ordered.

"And you are?" Cassius asked.

Caleb turned his gaze to Cassius. "I am the person who will not hesitate to kill all of you," he said, as his gaze passed over everyone in the room, but rested on Vivian, "if you don't let her come to me."

Kayla heard what Caleb said, but she was looking at her mother who was blankly staring at her. Vivian then glared at Caleb and back to Kayla again.

"You're pregnant," Vivian said. Her words sounded more like an accusation than shock. Kayla attempted to pull away from her mother's hold but at the moment Vivian was as strong as Cassius. Her empathic ability allowed her to draw from the abilities of any Coesen within a certain distance. The nature of her ability and the particular distance was a well-guarded secret, and the latter, Kayla didn't know. Vivian was a Silo, a very rare Coesen.

"Let me go to him," Kayla begged, but Vivian held her tighter.

Everything imploded when Caleb took a step toward her. Kayla watched as all the Guardsmen attacked Caleb, who moved quicker than they probably ever seen anyone move. None of them touched Caleb as they swung limbs and weapons at him from all angles, some in unison. It looked like an elaborate dance but it wasn't. They were all fighting and Caleb was winning. He was outnumbered but it didn't matter, and to make things worse, it was beginning to look as though he was playing with them. Then it dawned on her. Caleb wasn't playing. He didn't want to hurt them.

Cassius, who was watching beside Vivian, took off his suit jacket and pulled two very sharp daggers with marbled handles from a holster that was fitted in his vest. He waited until Caleb threw another of his men across the room like a sack of feathers before facing off. Crouched in his attack stance, Cassius challenged Caleb.

Caleb watched the impressively built man as they circled each other. "You have some skill with the blade?" Caleb asked. The man didn't respond but Caleb could see he was skilled by his movements.

That hate glowing in his eyes is going to be his downfall, Caleb thought as the man nodded then lunged.

The warrior sliced the air with dexterity but missed his target with every thrust. Caleb smiled as the frustration the man felt boiled over and he expressed it with a loud growl. With the next series of swings, Caleb easily disarmed him of one of the blades.

Caleb looked at the beautiful knife before throwing it with great force at the man's leg. The blade embedded into his upper thigh, prompting a muffled grunt.

When Caleb turned his attention back to Kayla something hard with a lot of force slammed into the side of his face. Stumbling a few steps back, he touched his mouth and looked up.

"You bleed," Vivian snorted, looking at his lip.

"Caleb," Kayla cried, holding her stomach. He watched her grimace as she fell to her knees.

"Not again. NEVER AGAIN." Caleb was about to go to her when he felt a sharp pain running along his back. The impact caused him to fall forward. As he fell, he saw the Warrior with his blade.

Vivian gave him no time to recover. She moved in, positioning her foot to come down hard over his head but Caleb sent a gust of air toward her that pushed her back. He got to his feet so fast that the force of his movement startled both Vivian and her Warrior. Caleb raised his hand as a couple of recovered Guardsmen came at him. Both men flew back, landing hard, one on the floor the other hit the edge of a chair.

Caleb narrowed his eyes as his breathing quickened. He looked at the Warrior, who stomped toward him again. Caleb held his hand out in front of the man, stopping him where he stood. Unhurried, Caleb closed his strained fingers into a fist. He ignored the gut retching screams as the Warrior's skin began to compress in on itself.

Without turning from the Warrior, Caleb raised his other hand, freezing Vivian's advancement. With a wave of his hand, he raised Vivian from the floor and pinned her to the wall. Kayla screamed but he didn't hear her cries. He didn't hear anything.

Kayla saw fear in her mother's eyes for the first time in her life. She had to help her. Fighting her pain, Kayla stood and stumbled over to Caleb. The closer she got the more she felt a foreboding sense of totality.

Directly in front of Caleb, she touched his face but he didn't acknowledge her. "Your eyes," she breathed. His eyes were vacant with a red strip pulsing around the iris as he stared past her and at Vivian.

"Get out of here," Vivian grunted through clenched teeth.

Kayla somehow heard her mother over Cassius' screams. She didn't know the extent of her mother's pain but she knew it was bad. Kayla shook her head "no" to her mother's order as tears ran down her face.

She stroked Caleb's cheek then leaned forward on her toes and said in his ear, "You have to stop, Caleb. Leave them. We have to go."

She sobbed as another pain pulsed through her belly. Kayla's slight form shook as she leaned into Caleb. She rested her head on his chest as she continued to beg him to stop. When she realized her words were falling on deaf ears, Kayla stroke his cheek.

"I love you so much," she said, repeating it several times.

Caleb didn't so much as blink. The red band in his eyes grew as he slowly killed the people she loved.

Caleb heard a loud blast then felt what can only be described as a horrible pain. He closed his eyes tight. It felt as if a bomb had gone off in his head. He rocked back, then clutched his head with both hands. The sound of hollow screams filtered through his clouded haze, giving him something to focus on.

He smelled blood.

Caleb pried his eyes open and at first all he saw was light. He rubbed his eye with his palm but that only made his vision worse. He blinked, then focused on his hand that he held in front of his face.

Blood…his blood. He knew because it wasn't dark red but rather a lighter shade.

How? What?

Caleb stumbled a few steps back to take in the room. His gaze fell Vivian, then the man who wielded those awesome blades. They lay on the floor, writhing in pain.

As they should be, he thought, then he grabbed his head as his pain amplified. They tried to take his family. His baby. *Kayla.*

Caleb lowered his head, feeling as if he was moving in slow motion. Kayla, she stood in front of him. He smiled. She seemed unharmed. He needed to get them away safely.

He tried to move but felt himself tilt back as he looked into her eyes.

Fear? It was fear he saw reflected in them. *Fear of me*?

Confused, Caleb tried to move forward. That was when his gaze fell to the gun Kayla held, pointed at him. His brows scrunched as confusion washed over him but he couldn't think. His head ached so damn bad.

Kayla sobbed louder when he raised his hand to his right temple. He rubbed his head, feeling the stickiness. He brought his hand in front of his face again. Blood, it was his blood. It was running freely down the side of his head.

Caleb stumbled back, using the ceiling-to-floor-glass window to support him.

Kayla moaned as she looked into Caleb's beautiful eyes. She had to be strong.

Be Strong. Kayla told herself as she gripped the handle of the gun and moved toward him. Her finger trembled over the trigger.

"I love you. I'm so sorry," she cried as she placed the gun to his chest, directly over his heart.

"Kayla?" Caleb said as their eyes met.

Before he could say another word, she pulled the trigger and a second shot rang out from the officer's gun. The force pushed Caleb through the glass window, over the ledge, and into the icy waters that waited several stories below.

Kayla screamed as she dropped to her knees, looking out of the shattered window. When she felt the gun being pulled from her hands, Kayla didn't fight it. She didn't fight when she was gently lifted up into someone's arms. All she could do was mutter his name. It wasn't until a hand reached for the ring in her hand that Kayla reacted.

"Don't you touch his ring," she hissed.

Kayla managed to pull it from his finger after the first shot. She took off her own ring which was an exact match to his, other than size, then slid his on her finger. Kayla then slid her own ring on to hold his in place. The ring was the only thing she would ever be able to offer her daughter, from a father she would never know.

Chapter Thirty

Tristan still wasn't able to get the image of Kayla, who was pregnant with Cianne, pointing a gun at the man she was supposed to love, since hearing about it three days ago. He couldn't understand how she could do what she did. Even more, he couldn't understand how Caleb seemed to still love her.

"You're not focused!" Caleb shouted. He shot an arrow at Tristan from a few yards away.

Tristan leaned out of the way but not quick enough. The arrow grazed his arm.

"You can't protect yourself or the people you love if you're not focused at all times." Caleb shot three more arrows. "I know this more than anyone. Take heed."

Tristan dodged the first two arrows but caught the third and launched it back at Caleb's face. Caleb took a step to his right just before the arrow hit him. It burrowed into the tree behind him.

Tristan didn't give Caleb time to reload. He closed the distance, grabbed the arrow from the tree and stabbed Caleb in the shoulder.

"Are *you* focused?" Tristan grinned. His celebration didn't last long.

Caleb grabbed Tristan's wrist, the one that still grasped the arrow that was planted in his shoulder. Without making a sound, as if pain didn't register for him, Caleb bent Tristan's wrist, snapping the arrow's shaft but leaving the head still in his shoulder. Elbowing Tristan hard in the face, Caleb threw him into a tree several feet away. Before Tristan could breathe, Caleb was next to him with the bloodied arrowhead pointed at his neck. After several tense seconds, Caleb lowered the arrow and walked away.

"I'm ready," Tristan called out.

Caleb turned around and stared at him. "Yeah, you think so?"

Tristan caught up to Caleb. "I'm stronger and faster, and I've been able to hold you off. Even injuring you at times. That means I'm ready for whatever's out there."

"You've improved, Tristan," Caleb agreed. "And the fact that you have been able to scratch me is impressive but you're not ready."

Tristan cursed. "Just tell me what you want me to do. I'll do it," he pleaded, "anything to get back to them."

Caleb lowered his head then looked back at Tristan. "I hope so."

"What the hell does that mean?"

Caleb grimaced. "You don't think I get it do you. Do you think I don't know how hard it is to be away from the woman you love, from your child? When Kayla shot me, when she left me, she broke my heart. It broke my spirit. So much that I didn't drag myself from that icy water for hours. I let her get away. I tried to convince myself that I didn't love her. When I finally got back to our apartment, looked upon all her things, my feelings for her came flooding back. I found myself going through her clothing, smelling everything that held her scent. For the next seventeen years, I searched for her, for my child.

"Then one day as I sat in the kitchen in one of my apartments on the east coast, I heard a news story on the television. You see, I paid close attention to the news and any events that didn't seem normal, for any sign of them. There was news about a kidnapping and how you saved a young girl named Cianne. Only that wasn't what drew my attention. It was the dead dogs that brought me to her."

"And you came to our little town, began dropping bodies, and here we are," Tristan said with a smirk.

"It wasn't that simple, but yes. I cleaned up a few pieces of trash in your little town."

"All in the name of love," Tristan sang. He placed his hands over his heart mockingly. A mild wind blew through the trees around them as they stood in the small clearing. "Let me get this straight. Your wife shoots you and takes your child then disappears, and you still love her."

Caleb looked away.

Tristan could not believe it. "She may have loved you once but she put a gun to your fucking head and shot you. She ran away with your child. You never saw her again and didn't see Cianne until last year."

"Love is sacrifice!" Caleb yelled, causing Tristan to back up several steps.

He never witnessed this side of Caleb before. He never saw the man so emotional, and now he was visibly angry.

Caleb's temples pulsed but he closed his eyes and took a deep breath. "Love is doing what you have to do to protect the ones you love. Even if it means losing yourself. Kayla had her reasons for what she did but I know she loved me." He laughed as his eyes took on a faraway look, "I saw it every time I looked into her eyes."

"Love isn't that complicated. People and their fears make it complicated." Tristan moved next to Caleb, who was looking off into the distance as if he heard something. "If you love someone and they love you with the same intensity and passion, there's nothing that can stop you from being together…but you."

"If that were true, if that is what you believe," Caleb said, smiling devilishly, "then why are you here and the woman you love is—"

Tristan didn't allow Caleb to finish. The words he spoke were like acid in Tristan's veins and they were burning through him. Tristan attacked but Caleb was ready and able to block several of the blows. Only, Tristan continued his attack and at some point, he knocked Caleb to the ground.

Caleb got to his feet quickly, retaliating with several debilitating blows that connected with Tristan's body.

Tristan coughed, spitting blood from his mouth to the ground. When he looked up at Caleb, Tristan smiled, exposing bloody teeth as he advanced. The two matched blow for blow until Tristan caught Caleb in the throat and wrapped his arms around Caleb's neck, squeezing it tightly. Caleb raised his knee, connecting with Tristan's face. At the same time, two blades came at them from high in the trees.

Caleb spun free of Tristan's hold. He avoided a kick to the head as he reached up and grabbed one of the knives out of the air by the handle. Caleb flipped the knife so he was holding the blade and flung it back into the forest in the direction it had come.

Just as Caleb was throwing the knife he caught, Tristan caught the second knife. When Caleb turned to face him, Tristan struck with a direct swipe from left to right.

Caleb gasped as his throat was opened. Tristan gave him no time to react as he buried the knife deep into Caleb's chest. Caleb grabbed at his neck with both hands as he sent a mental message to the man in the tree to not interfere further.

What Caleb saw in Tristan's eyes was exactly what he needed to see. He also noted the look on the boy's face as he backed away. It was cold, emotionless, deadly.

Caleb laughed but it sounded more like a raspy gurgle, causing more blood to flow from his neck.

Tristan jumped up and kicked the knife deeper into Caleb's chest, knocking him on his back.

A faint swooshing sound came from the direction the knives had come. It was the sound of bullets being fired. Caleb watched as Tristan skillfully avoided every bullet with ease as he darted deeper into the forest and away from where he lay watching.

When Tristan crossed the invisible barrier without even twitching as the shock of the device on his ankle activated, Caleb smiled.

He coughed up blood as he rolled to all fours. Grabbing the handle of the knife that stuck out of his chest, he pulled.

"Are you badly hurt?" The voice was quiet but sounded concerned.

Caleb looked over at the man dressed in some kind of ninja like outfit, completely covered in an oddly colored camouflage from head to toe. He heard when the guy walked up but he had a suspicion that it was only because the man wanted to be heard.

Healed, with only the fresh blood stains on his shirt and pants to show there'd been an incident, Caleb stood. "No," he said handing the trespasser the knife, "this belongs to you." Caleb pulled off the bloody shirt, exposing no damage at all to his body.

"Neat trick," the man said. He peered at Caleb's chest for a second longer then turned his head in the direction Tristan ran. "I can bring him back."

"How long have you been out here?" Caleb started walking toward his cabin. Once inside he went to the kitchen sink, wet a towel, and wiped the blood off his face and neck.

"Ever since you came back from Louisiana. I've been hanging back, mostly so you wouldn't sense me but the sound of this particular "discussion" you two were having seemed…different," the young man said. He stood just inside the doorway but didn't enter the cabin. "I lost you after the warehouse job but I knew if I stuck to Perkins you would show up at some point."

"It's Cipher, right?"

The man nodded.

Caleb placed the towel on the counter and pulled two bottled waters from the fridge and held one up. Cipher nodded again so Caleb waved him inside then tossed the water to him.

"You are a very patient man, Cipher. Enlisting in the military, then cozying up to Richard all these years just to get to me. That must have been time-consuming for a young man." Caleb pointed his bottle at Cipher's face. "Assuming you're as young as your voice suggests."

Cipher gripped the fabric of his mask at the back of his neck but hesitated. Then, in a swift motion, he pulled the mask off. He slowly raised his head and looked at Caleb, revealing eyes so gray they almost looked white.

He looked to be between the ages of twenty to twenty-five, his tawny skin color, coal black hair, and Native American features suggested that he was of mixed ethnicity.

"A Coesen mongrel," Caleb said then smiled. Cipher didn't seem insulted. "I've never actually met one as old as you before, aside from my daughter that is." Caleb looked Cipher over.

Coesen carried out their punishment of breaking the law swiftly, that this man lived was extraordinary. The offspring from a Coesen/Middling union was never allowed to live. From what he knew, the Coesen parent was also killed for their crime. No one was exempt as far as he knew, except for Kayla and Cianne.

"You're in a pretty good mood for a guy who just pulled a knife from his chest. Do you mind if I ask who that was who bested the both of us?"

"That," Caleb said, then chuckled, "is my student who just graduated. He's also my son-in-law."

Cipher's face paled. "I…I didn't know." He lowered his head. "I didn't recognize him," he explained.

No…the beard and long hair may have had something to do with that.

Caleb pulled a chair out from under the dining table and sat down. He motioned for Cipher to come in and sit but Cipher didn't move. "Believe me, Tristan doesn't take himself that seriously and you shouldn't either. Have a seat."

"I better not," Cipher said, squeezing his mask in his hands. "I'm to stay out of sight unless you need me." He cleared his throat then looked away. "I thought you needed help," he said as he turned around to leave.

Caleb frowned. "The mission Richard assigned to you ended at the warehouse. You should return back to base to get new orders." Caleb kicked his shoes off and wiggled his toes. He didn't care for shoes much, never had.

"I'm here on someone else's orders," Cipher said as he stepped out of the opened door.

"Whose?" Caleb called out. But Cipher was already gone. As Caleb sipped his water he heard a response in his head.

"*My father's,*" Cipher transferred to him.

"Your father?"

Caleb wiped his face with his hand. *Who's his father?*

Tristan didn't know where his family was. Cianne's phone was disconnected and their house looked like it was empty for months. He also didn't know who else was working with Caleb to keep him hidden. That meant he couldn't just walk around town asking questions.

No, he didn't think his father-in-law was the evil man he once thought he was, but the man was hell bent on torturing him. He wasn't going back to that jail of a cabin he ran from three day ago.

There was also the situation with someone wanting him dead. To keep his family and friends safe, Tristan had to keep his distance. No way was he shining a spotlight on them. So, Tristan needed help from someone he didn't normally socialize with.

It didn't take long for Tristan to decide who was going to help him.

As he breached the unfamiliar home, he used his abilities to confirm that the man he was here to see was alone. Only one heartbeat was present. Tristan made his way to the upstairs bedroom, opened the door, and stepped inside. He didn't like to be indebted to anyone and he knew that if he went this route, he would owe the man who slept soundly just a few feet away.

Sighing, Tristan slammed the bedroom door.

The startled man rolled over, aimed, then sprayed the bedroom door and the wall with a hail of bullets. His startled expression was priceless.

Thank goodness for silencers.

"*Pssst*," Tristan whispered in the man's ear. He easily moved from the target zone and was at the man's side. Tristan grabbed the gun before the man could fire again and waited for recognition to set in. To speed it along, he brushed the hair that fell loose from his ponytail away from his eyes and smiled.

It didn't take long.

The man tilted his head up to take in Tristan. Grunting, he swung his legs over the edge of his bed and sat up. "What the hell are you doing in my house?" he asked with irritation.

Not long ago, this shady businessman was instrumental in helping Tristan discover that a man named Edgar Patton was behind Cianne's kidnapping. Tristan still felt indebted to the man but they would never be friends.

Tristan placed the gun down on the nightstand so it was just within the man's reach for good measure. "I need your help, again." He watched Lo push off the bed and walk over to the chair. Little of Lo's appearance had changed since their last meeting.

Lo rubbed his eyes and sighed. "How can I benefit from helping a dead man? You know you're dead, right? Been dead for almost six months."

Tristan gave him a sardonic grin and a shrug. "Not dead, just detained," he said. "I need some rest, clothes, and something to eat, not necessarily in that order."

Showered and dressed, Tristan jogged down the stairs. He could smell something delicious when he was in the bathroom. Though he could survive longer than the average man without food, he still hungered and it had been a while since he ate.

Tristan heard Lo speaking in a hushed tone as he made his way toward the kitchen but when he entered, Lo didn't have a phone to his ear.

"Thanks," Tristan said, as he took a seat at the round glass table that seated only four. He glanced at Lo's hand that moved to the handle of his gun that rested on the counter top beside the stove.

Lo's rigid body relaxed after a few seconds. His hand fell away from the gun and he hung his head over the countertop where two bowls sat. "You can't keep sneaking up on a man like me. It's not good for your health." Lo lifted the bowls, walked to the table, and sat across from Tristan. He slid one of the bowls across the table. "That doesn't look like any tether I've ever seen. Was it a ransom?" Lo asked.

Tristan looked up from the bowl of chili to Lo, who was looking down. He followed Lo's gaze to his ankle. He forgot about the bracelet. He wore it for so long that it was almost a part of him. Tristan winced then slid the chair back, bent over, and used both his hands to pull the contraption off. He laid the mangled metal on the table then started eating again. He didn't want to talk about the bracelet, or the reason behind his abduction. All he wanted was to find Cianne and the children.

"I just need some time to think and a little sleep. I'll go after that." Tristan looked up.

Lo was staring at him with his brows crinkled. "How the hell did you do that?"

Tristan regarded the mangled metal on the table. "It wasn't as durable as it looked." He put the last spoon of chili in his mouth and swallowed. "Any more?" he asked. "Been kind of on the move for a few days, didn't have time to stop and eat."

Lo just stared at him for a moment before pushing his bowl over.

"Thank you," Tristan said again, but this time with more sincerity in his voice. He put the spoon in the chili but stopped. "You mind if I ask, what the L O stands for in KEYLO?"

"Lowell," the man said. Lo, or Lowell, stood. He walked over to the refrigerator and took out a beer. He placed it on the table next to Tristan then sat back down. For a moment, neither of them spoke but it didn't take long before the low buzz of Lo's cell phone broke the silence.

"My ride is here," Lo said. He placed a set of keys on the table. Next to the keys he set down a small stack of hundred-dollar bills. "No one knows you're here so you can stay as long as you need to. There's a car in the garage. You can leave it anywhere, just make sure that the keys are in the glove compartment." Lo made for the entryway.

Tristan looked over his shoulder. "I only needed a few hours and this," he said, motioning to the food. "Why are you offering me more?"

"Let's just say that I've been locked down before, didn't like it." Lo shrugged. "If there is anything else you need that you can't think of right now, I left my number by the phone."

"Thank you," Tristan said as he stood, "I won't forget this."

"I won't let you," Lo smirked.

Seconds later Tristan heard the door close and a vehicle pull off.

Tristan tossed and turned for hours before falling asleep in the early hours of the morning. When he woke, a full twenty-four hours had passed. He shaved then dressed in the most inconspicuous clothing he could find, a hooded gray sweat shirt, white t-shirt, and black sweat pants. Tristan put the money Lo left him in his pocket, locked up the house, then got into the car with a plan.

His father had to know where Cianne was.

As Tristan drove to Houston, thoughts of Cianne became clearer, more vivid to him. His mental picture of her faded after the first month of separation. He desperately tried to cling to memories of their time together, focusing on her sparkling eyes, her scent, or her beautiful face. Yet, no matter how he tried, every image of her ran like watercolors until there was nothing but a canvas of faded memories.

How was it that he couldn't remember her face when all others appeared so clear in his mind?

It doesn't matter, he told himself as he pulled into the parking structure. Her face was clear to him now, and soon Cianne will be in his arms.

Tristan pulled his hood over his head to shadow his face. He easily avoided the security cameras and the security staff at the front desk to get to the stairwell. To avoid the cameras in the stairwell he swiftly scaled the railings and darted through the doorway when he reached the forty-third floor. Getting into his father's office unseen was impossible for him three years ago, but now it was just a series of well-timed stealthy movements and he was in.

The office was pretentiously decorated and unnecessarily spacious. Tristan smiled as he sat down at his father's desk and glanced at the calendar that said it was Tuesday, October the 4th. He relaxed, knowing that his father wouldn't be in the office today.

His father was a creature of habit if nothing else.

As Tristan looked over the rest of the desk's surface, he shook his head. The entire office resembled one of those staged rentals. Nothing personal, not even a single picture of his grandkids. The bigger question was, why did Tristan expect anything different now, because he was presumed dead?

He shook the sting of his long-term hang-ups and started flipping through the Rolodex. Just as he came to the card with Cianne's name, he heard a familiar voice on the other side of the door. He quickly read the address, closed the Rolodex, then crossed the width of the office and hid behind one of the walls that divided the sitting area from the office. He stilled, slowing his vitals to a crawl.

His father and a man whose voice Tristan didn't recognize entered the office. Standing at an angle behind the wall, he could clearly see the images of his father sitting at his desk and the man who stood beside him reflected in the glass window but he was sure he couldn't be seen. His father looked tired, the same, but tired.

Tristan shut down any worries he could conjure about his father's stresses and health before they started. He needed to focus on getting out of the office unnoticed.

As Tristan listened for an opportunity to escape, he felt an odd tingling sensation climb up his spine. He closed his eyes and shook his head, attempting to rid himself of the mild irritation but it continued.

Tristan shook his head again but this time when he opened his eyes, he saw his father's display case that sat under a large flat screen television. On the display were several framed pictures. One was a photo of him and Cianne on their wedding day, with his parents on either side of them. Another was a photo of Tristan holding the twins. All the rest of the photos were either of his mother or the twins.

Tristan wanted to smile or even feel some sort of happiness that his father actually felt proud enough to put his family on display, but the tingling in the back of his neck was becoming a bit distracting. If experiencing the annoying tingling wasn't enough, Tristan couldn't help but stare at the man who took a seat on the other side of his father's desk. He looked familiar.

When realization hit, Tristan didn't think before he stepped from behind the wall and advanced using his speed.

He gripped the back of the man's neck and tossed him across the room. The man hit the dividing wall, breaking off the corner, then landed face down on the coffee table, smashing it to pieces.

Mr. Bertram stood, but before he could react to the intruder his companion was not only on his feet but was moving with such speed that he could hardly make out what was happening. "What the hell is going on?" he called out.

Alexander didn't respond. He was attacking the hooded person, but by the looks of it he was no match. It looked as if the hooded man landed several punishing blows but Leslie wasn't certain. They moved too fast. Too damn fast.

When Alexander was tossed away like a rag doll the second time, the hooded man asked, "Why are you here?"

Leslie was in the process of lifting his phone to call security but stopped. He heard the tone through the receiver but didn't press any buttons.

Leslie leaned forward. "Tristan?" he murmured as he loosely held the phone to his cheek.

He glanced at Alexander, who was on his feet again. Leslie watched as Alexander dropped to one knee in front of the hooded man, then lowered his head.

What the hell?

Leslie focused on the intruder and was about to demand he remove his hood but the person sighed then slid the hood off his head and turned to face him. Leslie dropped the phone then sank down in his seat.

Tristan wanted to go to his father but he turned his attention back to the Coesen. "I don't want your allegiance. I want to know why are you here."

"I am Tykel Alexander. I have been assigned to shield your parents," the man answered. He waited on one knee. "If I may?" Alexander asked.

Tristan nodded, allowing Tykel to get to his feet. He would have to deal with his father's questions about the Coesen pledging his allegiance by taking a knee, but he kept his senses on alert. Tristan walked over to his father, took the phone out of his hand, and placed it back on the receiver. His father just stared at him.

Rubbing the back of his neck, Tristan said, "I'm sorry that you and mom had to go through all this. I promise—" He didn't get to finish what he was wanted to say because his father stood and pulled him into a tight embrace.

"I don't know what's going on… And frankly, I don't care. I'm just happy you're standing here." Mr. Bertram pulled back and held Tristan at arm's length. "You *are* here aren't you?"

"Yes," Tristan said as he raised a brow. He was even more confused when his father pulled him into another tight hug.

"So…let me recap. You married into a family that has the ability to do things that people—*regular people*—can not. You also have acquired some of these abilities but now someone wants you dead," Mr. Bertram said. He lifted the glass of watered-downed vodka to his lips and took a hearty drink then sucked in some air. "For the last few months, while everyone thought you were dead you were training to do what you demonstrated here in this very office, with Alexander no less, who happens to have the same gifts and who has been working here for almost a year just to provide me with protection."

Tristan and his father talked through the night. Against his better judgment, he explained everything. He knew the consequences but he wasn't the blind follower he used to be.

"Basically," Tristan acknowledged. He rubbed the back of his head. "What I've told you must never be repeated, not even to mom." Tristan's hard gaze bore into his father's eyes.

"The less she knows, the safer she'll be. And dad, no one must know I'm alive yet. The person who tried to kill me must think that they've succeeded, at least for now."

Mr. Bertram sat back in his seat. He sighed. "*Ahhh…* You weren't here to see me. You were looking for something and only revealed yourself because you thought I was in danger."

"I need to know where they are," Tristan said, then looked down in shame.

"I understand," Mr. Baxter nodded. "You wanted to see your wife and children first. I would have done the same thing."

The buzz of the desk phone made both men turn to the office door. "Mr. Bertram," Alexander announced, "Mrs. Bertram is on her way up."

Mr. Bertram jumped up from the sofa and rushed over to his desk. He pressed a button on the phone. "I'll come out to meet her. Thank you."

His father glanced at him and smiled before opening the door and quickly shutting it behind him. A few seconds later the door open and Tykel stepped inside. With a close cut and a freshly trimmed goatee, he was a nicely dressed man who was about ten years younger than Tristan's father and looked like he was used to the finer things in life.

Tykel bowed when Tristan stood. "Who do you report to?" Tristan asked.

"Forgive me," Tykel said, "but I was told that I can only tell you who originally assigned me to your parents."

"Alright, who originally assigned you then?"

"Sovereign Vivian, sir," Tykel said. "She said that if you should ever find out I was assigned, that I should say, remember what she said the day she cut the thorns off the roses."

Tristan knew the day well. It was the day he first met Langley who rode him from the police station to meet with Vivian. She said that he should look at her as family.

"She always protected her family," Tykel said.

"Thank you."

"You're very welcome, sir," Tykel said.

Tristan and Tykel stared at each other. Tristan trusted his father but he didn't know anything about Tykel other than he had Vivian's trust. Was that enough? No, it wasn't. Tristan took a step toward the man with every intention to end his life when the office door burst open.

His eyes fell on his lovely mother who had a smile as big as Arizona plastered on her face. Tristan looked at his father and frowned. At least he had the sense to look ashamed.

"I never stopped praying." his mother smiled as she hurried to him. She kissed him on the face. "I never stopped praying."

Chapter Thirty-One

October 5th

Tristan clenched and unclenched his jaw as he scaled the fifteen-foot stone wall that surrounded Ark Mansion. Just as his feet touched the ground he saw a guard coming his way. Tristan crouched and backed into the shadow of a large evergreen, keeping completely still so he didn't trip the motion sensor he knew were in the ground. The shape and size of a silver dollar, the green discs were virtually undetectable except for an almost inaudible sound they made, giving off their location to only the most sensitive ears.

Apparently, it emitted a sound the Guard couldn't hear because when the infrared light scanned him, Tristan noticed the Guard tense as he searched for the device. He watched as the Guard's eyes moved rapidly over the lawn, searching for the device as he continued to walk by.

Not waiting until the Guard was out of sight, but when he was only a few feet away with his back to him, Tristan stood and moved through the maze of sensors, avoiding setting them off. He moved very fast and very quietly, stopping when he saw the large wall of windows. It was a room he only been in once before, during Vivian's Fasen ceremony when the windows were shattered during a fight. He and Cianne left for home before the wall of windows were replaced.

In the calm of night, Tristan stood just steps away from his family. Only a window separated them. He felt…nervous.

As a drop of rain hit his shoulder, he looked up to the sky. Tristan closed his eyes just as the rain began to moderately fall, washing over his face.

He only had to reach for the handle, to step inside and let her know he was there.

To let her know that he suffered without her touch all this time. That he suffered even more in these last few moments was enough to move him forward, but his feet felt like cement. His heart raced and his mind clouded.

Maybe Caleb was right. Maybe he wasn't enough. Hell, he couldn't even bring himself to kill Tykel.

No. He was hers and she was his.

Just when Tristan reached for the knob, the room lit up and Cianne stepped inside. Still dressed in black with a hood over his head, he watched her enter the room without fear of her seeing him. He just wanted to look at her first. To see her.

Tristan held his breath as he watched Cianne pour water into a glass. Her hair was shorter, and her skin was paler but she was still breathtaking. His legs twitched. His body didn't want to waste another moment admiring her.

"I'm sorry."

Whodai? What is he sorry about?

Tristan remained in place on the patio as he watched Whodai enter the room. He looked to Cianne who seemed angry. She turned away from Whodai who walked over to her. What was Whodai sorry about and why did Cianne seem so affected?

"Please, Whodai. I'm too tired to do this right now. I need to time to think," Cianne told Whodai. Cianne tried to walk past Whodai but he grabbed her arm.

Tristan stepped forward but stilled as he watched Cianne turn and look at Whodai's hand on her arm. Whodai instantly let go of her and raised his hands in a defensive gesture. Tristan clenched his jaw but stayed still.

"Just hear me out," Whodai begged.

Cianne looked up at the ceiling then back to Whodai.

Whodai continued, "I won't presume to know what you are feeling. All I know is that if you allow me to, I can ease your worries and your fears. If you say yes," he said as he took her left hand in his and kneeled on one knee.

Tristan tensed. He cursed as Whodai pulled a ring from his pocket. He saw tears in Cianne's eyes but couldn't determine what she was feeling by her expression.

The rain picked up

"I promise that I will make everything right again. Marry me, Cianne?"

Drenched from the falling rain, Tristan just stared at Cianne and Whodai. His heart was beating double time as he waited for her response. He wanted to go to her, to shut this shit down but…

Tell him no. Tell him you're waiting for me.

When Cianne didn't immediately respond, Tristan frowned. He could go to her. But he stood there in the dark cold and rainy night, waiting for her answer.

Cianne nodded.

Tristan closed his eyes and dropped his head.

Cianne covered Whodai's hand with hers before he could slide her wedding and engagement rings off her finger to put his engagement ring on. He gave her an apologetic look then sort of smiled as if he understood before he placed his engagement ring in the palm of her hand.

When she closed her hand over the ring, Cianne lifted her head and looked out of the wall of windows. She felt Tristan. The pull of him was so strong that she couldn't hold in her tears this time.

Lightning flashed, illuminating the outside for a moment and showing her there was nothing out there.

You're certifiable, she said to herself.

Cianne opened her hand and glanced at her new engagement ring, then to Whodai.

Tristan exhaled as he slowly pulled his hood off his head, exposing his face. Rain dripped from his clothing to the floor as he stood over the crib. They were so big. He felt pride lace around his heartbreak. He wanted to hold them. To tell them he loved them and that he wished things were different. That he wanted more than anything to be a loving husband to their mother and the best father in the world to them but sometimes in life, you don't get what you want.

Lessons Whodai would teach them now.

"I'm sorry," Tristan whispered. "I have to leave again." Tristan used his sleeve to wipe his eyes, forgetting it was already wet. "Mommy," his voice cracked. He pinched the bridge of his nose. "Mommy and I have some things we need to work out, but we love you both so very much."

He gently lifted a sleeping Nadia and kissed her forehead then placed her back in the crib. Tristan then lifted Aiden. Aiden opened his eyes and smiled. Tristan laughed as he cradled his son in his arms. When he felt Aiden's hand on his face, he felt the same love he had when he held his son for the first time.

"Take care of your mom."

Cianne burst through the door to the nursery and saw that both children were in one crib again. Aiden stood in the crib, using one hand to hold on to the railing while the other hand was extended out toward the open balcony doors as he wailed. Nadia was seated next to her brother. She was reaching toward the open door as well.

She hurried across the room and over to the door. Cianne stepped onto the balcony and glanced from right to left before going back inside and locking the door.

"What is it?" Whodai asked. He lifted Nadia out of her crib.

"I don't know," Cianne admitted. She picked Aiden up but he struggled to get out of her arms. She felt helpless as she patted his bottom lovingly. "What's the matter sweetheart?" She looked at the balcony then to Whodai. "He never cries." She touched Nadia's red face, offering her daughter comfort, but just like with Aidan, she was unsuccessful. "I think I should call Dr. Bannerman."

"I'll call." Whodai placed a sobbing Nadia in her crib and left the room.

Cianne could do nothing but rub Nadia's back as she kissed Aiden's head while he screamed.

Tristan was blocks away when he yelled, "What do you want from me?"

"You can't just leave things like this," Caleb said. He fell in step with Tristan. "They need you." He placed his hand on Tristan's shoulder.

Tristan smacked Caleb's hand away then pushed him as hard as he could. The push should have launched Caleb in the air but it only caused him to take a few steps back.

Tired of Caleb, of it all, Tristan threw his hands in the air as he continued on his way. "She doesn't need me. She has him."

"She—,"

"She wants him," Tristan yelled, cutting Caleb off.

"You still don't understand," Caleb said.

Tristan stopped, rubbed his head. then looked Caleb in the eyes. "No," he shouted. "I guess I don't. Enlighten me."

"She needs you. You're the only person who can help her. The only one who can stop her. When she was held captive at the abandoned school, you saw the way she killed those dogs. You saw her at the house when she saw me restraining you. She attacked me with that same rage. You've seen her eyes.

She can't control it like I can. You are the one she loves and only you can bring her back to the light. You are her Protector."

"You said it yourself, she doesn't need my protection." Tristan turned his back to Caleb. "She wants *him*!" he screamed at the top of his lungs. "FUCK!" he yelled, then took off running.

"The world needs you to protect them from the darkness that sleeps inside her!" Caleb yelled.

To be continued in…

The Battle of the Halo

Excerpt Below (Unedited)

Head on over to my website www.SheaSwainWrites.com for Upcoming Releases,
Character Dream-casting
And sign up for my Newsletter
THANK YOU
Please consider leaving a review!

The Battle for the Halo

SHEA SWAIN

SHEA SWAIN

Prologue

The attractive anchorwoman did mouth exercises as she silently counted down from ten with the new guy who did the countdown to live. She beamed for the camera a second later when they both reached, one.

"Good morning viewers. This is your host, Stacy Crain," Stacy said from the plush cream sofa located on the newly remodeled interview stage. She looked to her co-host and smiled.

"I'm Russell Dumas."

"And this is Coesen News Today," they said in unison.

Russell brandished a dazzling white smile. It was stunning against his dark skin tone. "Today, we are diverting from our standard show because it's a very exciting time for us all."

"You are so right, Russ," Stacy confirmed then inhaled deeply. She fanned herself with one hand, placed the other over her breasts, and dramatically batted her eyelashes. "Grab a pen and a calendar people, and prepare to Save the Date."

Russell chuckled at his co-anchor's excitement. "Sovereign Cianne Bertram and Royal Whodai Tam have chosen a date for their mating ceremony."

"I'm so excited, Russ. It seemed only yesterday that rumors of Royal Whodai's involvement in a secret Tandot when he was just a boy were leaked to the public. For years, he managed to avoid questions from the press about the mystery bride whose hand he won."

Russell nodded in agreement.

"I, for one, am glad he will have his happily ever after," Stacy continued, but her smile suddenly transformed into a straight lipped grimace of concern. "All of our viewers are aware of the rollercoaster that our succeeding Sovereign has been through this past year, but let us recap.

"Whispers of the existence of our Halo has always circulated throughout our history," Russ picked up, "but CNT brought you an exclusive broadcast. We were told by our beloved departed Sovereign, Vivian Harper, that the Halo did indeed exist."

Both news anchors turned their heads to face the monitor as video footage from that recorded show, featuring Sovereign Vivian speaking to both anchors, replaced the station's logo on the wall of screens.

Vivian's hair was loosely curled and fell over her shoulders. The station's stylist decided it would give her an approachable look, something her tightly pulled back ponytail bun didn't accomplish. She was dressed in a delicate designer pale mint top, a gray jacket, and slacks to maintain a sense of professionalism. In the video, Vivian spoke of the reasons her grandchild was hidden from the Coesen people.

When the clip was done, the screen switched seamlessly back to the logo.

"I remember that day like it was yesterday, Stacy." Russell stared at the camera. "We received tons of responses after that broadcast, a good amount proclaiming the Halo's uncovering to be a hoax or propaganda, but in the following months the unbelievers were transformed into believers."

"Yes, they were, Russell. Soahn Harper provided not only photos of Cianne Baxter, but to everyone's surprise, she granted access to the beautiful princess in an unprecedented display of total disclosure."

Stacy's expression grew morose. "We rejoiced when Soahn Baxter married her high school sweetheart and the father of our very first set of Royal twins, Tristan Bertram."

"We mourned with her when we lost our esteemed Sovereign Harper," Russell said, then held his chin up then sighed, "and again after the tragic accident that claimed the life of our White Lion, Tristan."

Stacy shook her head. Then she offered her audience her most sincere look. "Like our new Sovereign, we must hold our heads up high and look to the bright days ahead."

"And it doesn't hurt to do so while looking a million bucks either. I will say it here, Sovereign Bertram is one of the most beautiful, yet gracious women I've ever had the pleasure of meeting."

"She truly is, Russ," Stacy said in agreement with a nod. She took a deep breath of reflection then said, "Well, let us make this union one of cheer."

Chapter

Norway
The Present, May 6th
Missing over 11 months

Cipher launched from one rooftop to another, undeterred by the snow and ice that covered them, and landed solid on the balls of his feet. He gracefully slid just a few inches, and while still in motion he crouched down, pushed a button on the device in his ear, and pushed the hood of his white camouflage suit off his head.

"Should I engage?" Cipher asked in a low whisper.

"Are you sure he's still there?" Caleb questioned.

It was up to Cipher to find Tristan Bertram, the White Lion and rightful mate to the Halo. He could find anyone anywhere. Being a half-breed or Breed, it was expected that if he had any abilities at all, they would be greatly muted. Cipher's abilities were substantial in every way. He wielded a multitude of heightened senses and other gifts that overshadowed some of the strongest full-blooded Coesen.

Well, all but three. He suspected he wouldn't hold a candle to the Halo. Plus, Caleb Scott, who wasn't a Coesen, was a bit of an enigma. One minute, Cipher felt they were evenly matched, but then Caleb did something well beyond Cipher's capabilities.

He wondered if Caleb liked to keep him guessing.

Cipher also found it difficult to track Soahn Tristan Bertram. Every time he had a bead on him, the man disappeared before he was able to make contact. Cipher wasn't sure how Tristan kept one step ahead of him but he welcomed the challenge.

"I am certain." Cipher stealthily reached for the edge of the roof then pushed off with his feet, dangled, then dropped to the snow-covered ground four stories down with a soft crunch. He listened while Caleb spoke to someone on his end.

"We don't know how he's been able to detect you yet. It would probably be best if you put some distance between you and him or you'll be hunting him down again," Caleb instructed.

Yeah, I should steer clear, Cipher thought.

"Besides, the last time you encountered each other, you were trying to gut him with a blade," Caleb said.

Cipher thought back to when he first laid eyes on Tristan Bertram at Caleb's cabin. With no knowledge of Tristan's identity, Cipher's main objective was to keep Caleb safe. That day he felt Tristan was a threat to his objective and he reacted. To his surprise, Tristan not only dodged his attack but responded in turn, by throwing one of Cipher's knives back at him. It took all of Cipher's skill to avoid his own blade.

That happened months ago and now he was in this winter wonderland tracking his King.

"I have someone else in mind but I need you ready if he runs again," Caleb said, then disconnected.

I'll be ready.

Later that night
Zeta peered at the nondescript building. The only reason she knew it was a pub were the sign above the door and the roar

from the patrons that echoed into the white haze outside where she stood.

The Ice Cave, per the ice-covered sign, was a basic one-story structure at the edge of what the residents referred to as a town. Several other buildings littered the landscape but were just as basic. Most looked as if they doubled as businesses and homes.

Conversation in the native language stalled as Zeta pushed opened the heavy door. The patrons ogled her as she stood in the doorway and scanned her surroundings. It could be because of the lightweight wool coat and pink pom-pom hat she wore. Her attire wasn't the kind of gear the residents wore in this frigid climate but she wasn't like them.

Zeta scanned the curious faces, finding who she was searching for instantly. Of course, the man sat at the bar in the darkest corner, alone. She could tell by the way he ignored her entrance that this man wasn't like the locals either.

After closing the bone chilling cold out by shutting the door, Zeta stomped her snow-covered legs free of the caked-on white powder. The patrons, mostly men, seemed to settle back into their usual habits, dismissing her presence or purpose.

Zeta appreciated the privacy as she made her way to the large bar in the rear of the building. She settled near the loner, leaving only the space of a stool between them. The bartender, a husky man with large hands and thick curly hair, looked at her with a questioning glare.

"Anything that'll warm me up," she told him, speaking his language as a native would.

The bartender raised a brow as he gave her a good once over. He then frowned. Zeta recognized that look. She reached inside the breast of her coat and pulled out a thin wallet. She flipped it open as the Bartender leaned over the counter toward her. He peered at the well-crafted fake ID for a few seconds, looked at her again, then shrugged.

"Anything to eat?" he grunted.

Zeta shook her head. She watched the barkeep walk away then turned her attention to the sole reason she was in this place. As she regarded him, she realized he hadn't spoken a word or moved a muscle since her entrance.

It wasn't humanly possible to be that still.

As if on cue, the man coughed, shifted in his seat, then lifted his glass up to his thickly bearded face. She assumed he somehow managed to find his lips because she saw his throat moving.

Zeta offered him a silent greeting, a nod, but she couldn't tell if he saw her because of the dark glasses that framed his face. The beard and sunglasses covered so much of him that she still wasn't sure if this was Tristan.

The bearded man didn't acknowledge her greeting but he did silently drink the remainder of the dark liquid inside his mug. When he was done, he slowly pulled money from his pocket and placed it on the well-worn wooden bar.

Zeta watched him out the corners of her eyes. His hair was long, which made it difficult to see his face, and he wore loose fitting clothing that left everything to the imagination. Yet, she determined that he was the right height.

As the man lifted his jacket and swung it around his back, the bartender placed Zeta's drink in front of her. She nodded at the bartender then looked over at the bearded man. "I'm looking for a friend of mine who I think came through here," she said to him as he continued to wrap up. "I was wondering if you might know him."

The bearded man didn't so much as glance at her as he finished putting on his winter coverings.

"Jack don't do much talking." A man seated at a table behind her offered. He stood and made his way over to where she sat.

Jack, is it?

Zeta flicked the nosy stranger a glance. She noticed his appreciative glare when she initially walked inside the establishment. It was times like these that she wished she looked less pixie and more Amazonian.

The stranger, a sloppy-muscular man with a neater beard than her target and at least two feet taller than her, stepped up behind Jack. "Do ya, Jack?" He patted Jack's back hard enough to drive him forward.

It would take more than that to unbalance Tristan, Zeta thought as she watched the bearded man, Jack, right himself.

"Sam, you leave Jack be now. I don't want none of your shit tonight." The bartender's gaze fell on Zeta. "Leave the girl be too."

"Thanks," Zeta told the bartender, "but I don't think *Sam* is going to be any trouble tonight. Are you, Sam?" Zeta looked at him.

Sam flashed her a coy smile.

Jack moved around Sam without acknowledging her interest in him while Zeta's new husky admirer slid up between the stool she sat on and the one next to her. Her focus remained on Jack, and when she moved to get up a heavy hand pressed down on her shoulder. Zeta didn't hesitate or look at Sam when she grabbed hold of his hand and twisted it.

Sam shrieked as he tried to relieve the pain in his arm by turning in the direction of his twisted wrist. The move caused Zeta to apply more pressure, ultimately driving Sam to his knees. Every patron in the pub watched as he screamed out in agony. Every patron except Jack, because he was on his way toward the door.

Still watching Jack's back as he moved further away, Zeta raised her leg and placed her foot inches from Sam's nose. "Do we have a problem, Sam?" Zeta asked, peering at the door that Jack left through and slowly closed behind him.

The Bartender snickered when Sam only grimaced.

His failure to answer in a timely manner was a mistake. Zeta moved her foot so fast that no one in the bar saw what happened, but they did hear Sam screech. Sam's broken nose spouted blood that drizzled onto the old wooden floor.

Zeta turned her full attention to Sam. "Do we have a problem?"

"No problem," Sam panted out. When Zeta released his hand, Sam cursed as he fell against the side panel of the bar, rubbing his uninjured but sore arm.

Zeta moved as slow as she could manage to the door. She pulled on the door handle and stepped into the frigid night air.

Bearded Jack was gone.

She spun on her heels and pushed the bar door open and strolled back inside. Zeta walked up to the bar and placed a fifty-dollar bill next to the glass meant for her.

She turned to leave when the bartender cleared his throat. Zeta stopped and looked back over her shoulder, ignoring the patron's whispers about her.

"Your ID says you're from America," the bartender said in English. Zeta nodded. "I rarely get to practice my English. Anyway, uh…Jack, the fella who just left. That's not his name but it's what we call him cause he only drinks Jack Daniels," the bartender said, as he slid the bill off the bar and placed in his pocket. "He hardly comes around here, and when he does it ain't for conversation. I sense he's a good fella, just had some bad luck." The bartender shrugged. "Guess we all had our share. He stays at Elmer's old cabin. If you head north toward the mountains, you'll eventually see it."

"Thank you."

The bartender looked down at Sam and chuckled. "No young lady, thank you." He laughed louder as she walked away.

Excerpt's End
Read on for more excerpts

SHEA SWAIN

CHAINED
to the
DEVIL'S SON

PROLOGUE

SUMMER OF 1976

*The sound of the gunshot was deafening
as it shattered the calm night.*

They were driving to Alabama. Had been driving for a long
time when Evelyn's mother, Pearl, asked her father, Harland,
to stop at a motel they were approaching. Only her father
didn't stop. He continued driving so long after her mother's
request that even the signs to direct them to food and fuel grew
scarce. With nothing to occupy her mind, Eve fell asleep.

When Eve woke, her mother was urging her father not to
pull onto a dirt road that looked deserted but for the beat-up
mailbox that stood out like a beacon off the main road. They
were just going to ask for directions or maybe use the phone;
at least that was what her father said.

Eve listened quietly as her parents' debated what to do.
Whether to knock on the rundown farmhouse door or to
chance driving further because they were clearly lost. Her
mother spoke of her unease. Having been raised in the South,
she warned them that they needed to be ever cautious.

Harland was of a different breed. He had been raised
among gentler white folk who seemed more apt to spear you
with words rather than a sharp knife. He believed in the power

of words, wholeheartedly. Harland Jones also believed that most people were well-meaning organisms who when given the facts were reprogrammable, at least that's what he often said.

Eve's father ended up winning the debate on whether to knock on the old farmhouse door or not. Eve fought a grin when she saw the handsome smile he always flashed when he won an argument. It was rare for her father to win one against her mother, who was a thinker by trade. He even offered Eve a wink as he gracefully slid from their vehicle and climbed the cracked stairs. He walked with that same grace before knocking on the tattered screen door.

Eve could barely see the girl who opened the door, and for a moment, it seemed as if the girl was going to allow her father to use their phone. Then, Eve heard someone yelling from inside the house. She tensed when a fuming man with stringy dark hair shoved the girl out of the way and pulled the screen door open wider. The man began yelling at Eve's father, who held up his hands in defense and seemed to speak calmly, which was his way.

Eve couldn't make out what was being said, so she rolled down the car window. The word 'nigger' was said a number of times by the man. She heard that word before, but it didn't have the sting it had on this man's lips. Eve's father must have felt the same because instead of arguing with the crazy-eyed man, he just shook his head and turned around.

Eve didn't even hear when her mother got out of the car, but she did and was ushering her husband down the porch stairs and toward the car. Her parents' slow trek back to the car didn't hold Eve's attention. Instead, she looked back to the door of the house, only to find that the angry man had disappeared back inside.

Eve settled back in her seat but kept her eyes on the dark house. She wanted her parents' to move faster. She had a bad feeling in the pit of her stomach and wanted to get away from this house as fast as they could. Her heart sped up as she silently willed them to move faster, to run if possible. The walkway wasn't paved and her mother was wearing heels. So while they tried to maneuver over the pebbles, neither her father nor her mother saw the angry man stepping back into the doorway with the long gun in his hands.

Eve did, and she screamed for her parents' to turn around. She screamed for them to run, but there was no time for either of them to react before the man took aim. Eve watched in horror as her father's chest exploded outward. She held her breath as her father slowly dropped to his knees. She saw the shock on his face and the sorrow in his gaze as he locked eyes with her briefly before falling to his back.

Mommy! Eve's panicked gaze immediately sought out her mother as she prayed that what she was witnessing from her family's car was just a nightmare.

Eve's ears rang from the loud blast, but she heard her mother scream as she frantically tried to stop the bleeding from her husband's chest wound. Wide-eyed with terror, Eve's young mind tried to process why this was happening. Shaking with fear, Eve watched through teary eyes as the girl from the house came to the doorway again. The girl was screaming and pointing when a boy rushed out of the darkened doorway and ran toward the man who now towered over her mother with the gun still in his hands.

"Mommy!" Eve shouted to her mother. Her mother didn't answer as she cried out for him, her father. Eve watched helplessly as the man raised the gun and slammed the handle down on her mother's head.

Jason Ray Shaw, aka Junior, tried to ignore being shaken awake, but it was useless because Sadie Shaw was determined. He groaned then rolled over and opened his eyes to see his sister's beautiful but worried face looking down at him. Though she was five years older at seventeen, she relied on him for a good deal of support. Clearly his sister needed him right now. She was crying, her brows were pinched, she looked freaked, and she was shaking him as if he was still asleep.

"Wake up, Junior. Dad…doing bad, bad," she said as she continued to shake him.

With a curse that would make a saint's ears bleed, Junior moved Sadie aside, slid out of bed, and pulled on his worn jeans then his socks as best he could. Sadie said a bunch of words but she wasn't making any sense, her crying jumbled everything. *God, my life is shit.* Not because of Sadie. She was his special girl. The doctors said retarded, but to him she was just plain special and he loved her just the way she was.

No, Sadie wasn't the problem.

As Junior followed Sadie out of his room he heard the tell-tale signs that his father was drunk again. The sounds of shotgun blasts were a constant here at home sweet home. The neighbor's dog was probably on their property again, and his sauced father was trying to shoot the damned thing... again. Seeing no reason to rush but wide awake now, Junior ranked Sadie's frantic pulls and urging low as he made his way through the hallway and down the stairs to the first floor of the house. It was only when he heard screams that he stopped dead in his tracks.

"Help them," Sadie cried as she pulled at his arm.

A second later, Junior was shoving Sadie behind him and running for the front door with no idea what awaited him. He pushed through the open doorway and stopped to take in the scene before him.

He saw… Junior blinked then blinked again. "What have you done?" Junior yelled. Cefus Shaw swung around with the gun aimed at him. Junior held up his hands and took a step back. "Pop?" Junior said softly.

Cefus' eyes were absent of any recognition or humanity. Junior saw this side of his father before. He endured many beatings that followed his father's drinking and this, what he saw, was that look. Junior gazed pleadingly into those hard, unsympathetic eyes enough in his short life to know that there would be no compassion. Would this be the night the old man ended it all for him? As he did often in times like this, Junior thought of his sweet, innocent sister.

Sadie was the only person in this world that Junior cared about. If he took anything his father ever said to heart it was, 'Blood boy'; the old coot would say 'it's all you got in this world.'

"Pop," Junior said again, cautiously.

As if jarred awake, Cefus lowered the shotgun a few inches, now aiming at Junior's chest instead of his head. Recognition flashed in Cefus' light glazed-over eyes before he blinked. "What the hell you doing sneaking up on me, boy," Cefus hissed before turning back around. With his father's focus away from him, Junior took a calming breath then looked past his father.

A woman was lying beside a man who had a huge hole in his chest. Junior immediately felt sick as pain and empathy slammed into him for the strangers. *Cefus done did it now*, he thought as he took a measured step closer. Junior was turning his gaze on Cefus when he saw *her* out the corner of his eye.

In a station wagon that had one of those wheeled storage moving containers attached to it was a girl. Her face was streaked with tears. Her eyes were pinned on the man and woman lying unmoving on the ground. Her mouth was wide as her screams filled the night. He hadn't heard her until now.

How did he not hear her?

Cefus heard her, and he was about to shut her up, permanently.

Junior moved; later he would wonder what propelled him to do it, but there was no time to dissect his actions now. He ran down the gravel walk as fast as he could, blocking Cefus' view and the barrel of the shotgun that he aimed at the car window where the girl was howling.

"Get the fuck out of the way, boy, for I fill you with holes." Cefus' words were slow but not slurred. That bastard wasn't as drunk as Junior originally thought. His father was a hell of a shot which explained why he actually was able to hit that man dead center in the first place. Cefus being sober…

"You need to think right now, Pop," Junior said. He shook his head when he noticed Sadie coming out of the front door. Sadie understood and quickly went back inside. "If you shoot that shotgun one more time, the Wilsons will have the law out here again. How you gone explain this," Junior motioned to the dead man. He only heard one shot so he assumed the woman may still be alive. "These aren't dogs, Pop."

"The hell they ain't," Cefus said, motioning with the barrel for Junior to move out of the way. "Niggers and dogs are one in the same. Now move your ass, boy."

"Sheriff Gifford won't be able to sweep this under his hat if you harm the girl. She's not a man, Pop. They won't see her as a threat like they might her parents'." Junior realized the girl had gone silent, but he couldn't check on her just yet. He was trying to reason with a man of many faces, and both their lives were on the line. The drunk, the punisher, the racist, on rare occasions the apologetic father, and now the murderer was staring at Junior as if he were a stranger.

Junior heard the gun cock. *Will he really shoot me?* The thought to appeal to the father in Cefus, the father he had never been, popped in Junior's head. "I'm your son, your blood." Cefus actually grinned, and that grin said none of that mattered. "You say that's all we got is each other, Pop."

That got Cefus to slowly lower the shotgun with a sigh. He stood there with his eyes on the girl in the car then he looked down at the woman lying at his feet. Cefus seemed to think for a moment then his eyes lit up. Junior's stomach churned because that look was one of his father's scariest, and by the way, Cefus was peering down at the woman's thighs, exposed by the rising hem of the dress she wore…

Junior could almost see the cogs in Cefus' depraved head turning. It was then that Junior realized that he should have let Cefus kill the woman and the terrified girl. That would have been more humane because now he and Sadie weren't the only prisoners of Cefus Shaw.

Excerpt End

Available Now

Read on for excerpt of Chained to the Devil's Son

INVIDIOUS *Betrayal*

SHEA SWAIN

Prologue

April 8th, 2012

Ian Howl cradled the delicate, unconscious, girl in his arms as he swiftly made his way through the maze of a mansion to get to the garage. Her head rested on his chest and his arms supported her back and legs as he held her close. The swell of her feminine curves against his body felt all too consuming; the warmth of her skin was like a sweet yet biting burn. Tapping down on his ill-placed desires, Ian forced himself to focus on the present: their escape.

He ignored the hulking guard that sat in the security room who called to him as he rushed by. Turning a corner, Ian glanced over his shoulder to see if he was being followed. He hoped for a confrontation-free getaway, but the odds were against them.

Gently, he lowered the arm that cradled the girl's legs so that they slowly slide down his body until he balanced her on the balls of her feet. Holding her close to his chest, he placed his thumb to the security scanner on the wall. He vaguely thought of her bare feet touching the cold floor, but it was something he couldn't help right now. He needed to get her out of there and a chill was the least of his worries.

Three heartbeats later, the door that lead to the massive garage swung open with an air-locked *swoosh* that brought his hope soaring to new heights. They were almost free.

Ian noticed his car was blocked in, so he grabbed a random set of car keys from the wall hook and pressed the door unlock button. The headlights of a beautiful Porsche flashed, but the vehicle was in the rear of the garage and several cars surrounded it. The third set of keys he tried unlocked a luxury sedan that wasn't blocked in and was close to the garage doors. Ian had eased the girl into the passenger seat of the sedan and was securing the seatbelt around her when he felt a heavy hand on his shoulder.

"Where do you think you're taking that car, kid?"

Ian turned his head around to see Brad... Or was it Brent? He didn't remember the guard's name, but Ian knew the guy was built like a defensive tackle. Striking first would surprise Brad/ Brent. So he grabbed the hand on his shoulder and pulled the guard into his elbow, targeting his large, beefy face. The guard stepped back, holding his gushing nose. Ian spun around; he thrust the base of his palm upward into the man's shocked, bloody, face causing him to stumble back again then fall to the floor. The guard didn't get back up.

"Please," the girl whispered.

Ian whipped his head around to see that she was still unconscious and strapped in the car. Rushing to the driver's side of the commandeered vehicle, he hopped inside and started the engine. The automatic doors to the parking garage opened when the car tripped the underground sensor and they barreled down the path toward the front gate of the property. Luckily there were still party guests inside because usually those sensors only allowed vehicles with an installed security plate placed under the hood to pass through without human intervention.

Again, the underground sensor allowed the vehicle to pass through. The large main gates had opened, but they were not in the clear yet.

Ian didn't floor the gas pedal until he was clear of his uncle's property. He wasn't being followed, but he continued to check the rearview mirror, knowing their absence would soon be reported.

The girl moaned, pulling his gaze from the road.

Her long dark brown hair was matted to her head, practically covering her delicate face, so he brushed some of it away. Bruises covered her body but her dry lips, puffy red eyes, and the darkening hand prints on her throat were the most obvious. She was in bad shape, and Ian feared that the thin sheet wasn't enough to keep her naked body warm.

"Help me," she moaned.

"I'm taking you to a hospital," Ian told her. He fought the bile that rose from his stomach. Disgust and shame assailed him, but right now he couldn't think of his role in what had happened to her. He had to get her medical help, but he didn't know Howard County, Maryland, all that well. The only time he even came to this part of Maryland was when he visited his uncle.

Ian brushed the back of his hand over her bruised cheek and was about to place it back on the steering wheel when her eyes popped open, jarring him a little.

She didn't move right away. She just looked at him with a hollowed gaze as if her mind had to reboot. Then those chestnut-brown orbs changed from confused to feral in a flash. Before he could react, she was screaming, "No hospital! No cops!" over and over as she kicked at him and pushed at the passenger door with her hands. Ian grabbed at her feet, but his hand slipped and she nailed him hard on the side of his head with her foot.

"All right, no hospitals!" Ian yelled her as he slammed his foot on the brake, causing the car to skid along the nearly empty road. The force of the sudden stop propelled her forward and the side of her head collided with the dashboard. Her body went limp.

"Shit!" he yelled as he slammed his hands on the steering wheel. Ian pulled the car off to the side of the road, took his cell phone out, and dialed his father's cell. The phone rang several times, then the voicemail picked up. He listened to his father's commanding voice, but he disconnected before the taped greeting ended.

"Damn it, Dad, this is important!"

Ian glanced up at the rearview mirror, peering out into the quiet darkness, lost in thought. The weight of his cell phone in his hand made him find his focus again. He turned the phone over in his hand twice before shutting off the power. Ian stared at the cell phone in his hand for a long moment as he unconsciously rubbed at a spot under his armpit.

"They will be looking for me, us."
He glanced at the girl then felt under his arm again. As long as she was with him, they would find her.

Excerpt End

Available Now

About the Author

Shea is a woman in love with the idea of love so it's no wonder she writes Romance Novels. The East Coast native is a romantic to her core and reads and watches anything with a love story. She especially likes binging on the Hallmark Channel around Christmas time.

She enjoys meeting people and chatting, collecting Barbie dolls, toys, and is addicted to The Sims games. Shea also loves music and has mentioned that she writes better when she has movie scores playing as white noise in the background.

This new and exciting author writes Adult Romance in the sub-genres of Contemporary, New Adult, Paranormal, Sci-Fi, and Erotica. Come…Taste A Sample.

Connect with Shea Swain

Website: www.Sheaswainwrites.com
Email: Sheaswainwrites@gmail.com

Coesen Definitions
Words in italics are defined

Coesen: In the *Ilterian* language, the word *Coesen* means the combination of two or more items, particles, or organisms. The Four Originals adopted the term for their classification that defines them as a race of human-hybrids who originated from a single tribe on the continent of Africa. Most are born with birthmarks behind their left ear. Each tribe has a variation of this mark that they are born with. Some *Coesen* are born with an ability. It is present at birth but doesn't manifest until the age of puberty. Most are born with a single ability. A very small percentage are born with two.

Breed: The child of a Coesen and *Middling* coupling. Most of these children do not carry the birthmark of a full blooded Coesen. The law on the books state that Coesen parent and Breed are to be sentenced to death, the human parent's mind is wiped cleaned. 98% of Breed children are born with no abilities but may still carry the birthmark. If they mate a Coesen, their children may or may not have abilities.

Child of Jai or Pet: Jai of the *Arkean* tribe conceived a Breed with a man named Shaw. Even after her descendants couple with only Coesens, each are born with the physical features of a Caucasian.

Middling: Term to define a human with no *Coesen* blood.

Protectors: A Coesen who is chosen by the *Source* and is infused with power during the *transition* stage to keep the Coesen's Ward safe. They sense when their ward is in danger and is able to locate them at all times. These Coesen are stronger and faster than any living entity on earth with exception of one person, *Caleb Scott.* In history only two Middlings have been chosen by the Source. It is believed that Middling aren't capable of surviving the transformation.

Transition: A Coesen abilities become active when they go through puberty. This process is called a Transition.

Transference: When a Coesen is chosen by the Source to be awarded the abilities to become a Protector.

The Halo: A Coesen whose prophecy states will bear a full halo birthmark and have all the abilities known to Coesen.

The Source: What the Coesen refer to the original source of power, *Lette*.

Royals: The bloodlines closely related to the Original Four. Only four generations are referred to as Royals.

Bodai: The Bodai were the original name and leaders of the nation that eventually become known as the Coesen.

Bresi: The Bresi was formed from the original Bodai who decided to opt out of the change when offered power by the *Original Four*. They isolated themselves for a very long time. Eventually they discover *Pythos*. They pray to his cocooned form as a deity.

Four Tribes: *Arkean, Bode, Gedgi, Quende*

CPA: Coesen Protection Agency, the overseeing security and policing branch for Coesen.

Tandot: A competition of strength, intelligence, and endurance, to win the right to mate a Royal. Only those who are considered perfect Coesen specimens are allowed to enter.

Old Age: The time of the gilded age when Coesen were obsessed with wealth, class, and breed. The rich were set apart as elites. Lineage and wealth dictated your place in society. It wasn't until compassion became fashionable that a new way of thinking was adopted and practiced by the Sovereign and most Coesen. Though, with change there is always the few who hold onto the ways of old.

Pula: Curse word, or derogatory name

Maatii: Three round challenge to become a Royal Guard. You cannot die in the dream-like state but you feel all the pain inflicted on you. The challenge is timed.

   The Village: The object is to fight your way through a village full of super beings that do not eat, sleep, or feel pain, in order to reach a pearl like sphere that each member needs to touch at the same time.

The Vortex: The object is for each member to cross a wet, slippery metallic pole over a swirling vortex to reach the pearl like sphere that is floating in the center without falling.

The Pride: The object is to get pass the pride of gigantic lions and lioness to reach the pearl-like orb which is guarded by an even bigger, White Lion.

If you should fail these tasks, you must reapply and do trials over…or settle to be a Sentry Guard

Cycling: The process in with a Coesen has been transferred to. These Coesen endures a physical change over a three-day period.

Rotation: Every Protector must enlist in the *Coesen Guard* for a time period of the service. They can choose the branch. The three branches are, the *Royal* (highest), the *Sentry* (detective Branch), or *Guard* (police branch)

Augur: A Coesen who can see the prophecies.

Fasen: Burial ceremony. The body is washed and cleaned by someone close to the deceased. Close family is in attendance when the body is burned. A viewing is held after the body is returned to ashes to show and offer respect to the surviving family.

Soahn: Term for Royal

Potentate: Sovereign's Mate, King.

Rootstone: The power unit of all *Keystones*.

Keystone: An object that denies or allows access to a protected area.

Veilex: A stone that will react to an enemy of the wearer.

Dregan: Coesen who for whatever reason do not agree with Coesen law. Although they consider themselves separate they follow the most important rules which is why they are permitted to live in peace. The name was taken from a Coesen who broke the law a long time ago.

Sodregs: Dregans who care nothing for the laws and break them without care. They are hunted and tried by the *Guard*.

Dardregs: Dregans who practice the *Dark Arts*. They follow no law and most are minions of Dregan, a Coesen Protector from long ago who fell in love with his ward. He eventually killed several Coesen.

Meriotia: Bonding or marriage ceremony that lasts three days.

The first is a celebration or *Gathering*.

The second day is the *Mating and Blooding ritual/wedding*.

The third day is the *Showering* in which gifts and well wishes are given.

Ilterian: The race of *Lette's* people that hail from a planet far from earth.

Ika: A medicine man or woman of the village.

Oracle: The seer or witch that foresees the future.

Jzerect: Black magic, forbidden.

CARD: Stands for Coesen Ability Registration Department, a specialized section of the Royal Guards. Coesen are required to register all abilities to this agency. Information is kept private unless legal, safety, medical, or employment requires to know the information.

Utopian Circus: A circus run by Coesen with Coesen performers.

Inhibitor Chip: A piece of tech that prevents the wearer from using their abilities.

Purist: Coesen who believe the Breed are an abomination.

Kytel: Group who are against Breed and prefer pure bloodlines.

Veris: The only way the Council of Four can meet face to face without fear of being exterminated in one swift move. In a sleep like state, very similar to the Maatii, each of the Four are ushered to a common room in an astral plane by the head of the Four. While in this mental state their physical bodies are vulnerable so they are housed in a secured room watched over by their Protector.

Hasa: A Coesen title of respect, used for someone who is a paternal protector, or progenitor.

Royal Guard: The justice branch concerning royals. They also handle treats, security, and keep the peace. The Sentry Guards report to them and they report to the Council of Four. They wear a brand, centered on the back of their right hand. A black circle surrounded by the beautifully scripted names of each tribe. A set of knives crossed at their hilts, starting at the wrist, while the blades encircled the script. The tips of the blades ended at the base of their middle finger.

Sentry Guard: The detective and policing branch of the Coesen. They investigate cases for their sector and manage the Coesen Guard. They report to the Royal Guards.

Coesen Guard: Policing branch of the Coesen who handle local cases. They report to the Sentry Guards.

Fading: The stage of becoming invisible before teleporting. The fade can be held as long as the necessary before actually teleporting.

Fader: Someone who can camouflage themselves into the objects around them to become invisible.

The Veris: The act of bringing the Four together on another plane of existence to meet and discuss business.

Monad: A single unit or entity. What the Coesen call the being inside Caleb.

Suma(s): Dry season or summer months.

Rising Sun: 1 day.

Abilities

There are different degrees of these power. The more powerful the Coesen the stronger the effects. Some of the abilities are rare. All abilities are not listed.

Siphon: Can recognize, search, draw the power and ability of another Coesen within range without causing the host harm or alarm. The stronger the Sipher, the longer the distance that they can siphon power. This is a very rare ability.

Empati: A Coesen who can sense power and get readings such as how clean your spirit is.

Engron: A Coesen who can accelerate the growth of living organisms or tissue.

Phantom: A Coesen who can enter your mind and make or produce images that seem real to the dreamer. The recipient will feel the effects as if what presented to them is reality.

Wheddler: A Coesen who can influence another with spoken words.

Time Weaver: A Coesen who can travel through to the past. They can witness events but they cannot interfere mostly because they have no form. People of the past will not be able to see or hear these Coesen. Over time only two Coesen were born with the ability to weave into the future. They both had the ability to be seen and heard, giving them the opportunity to change things.

Fyeah: A Coesen who can wield fire. Two types exist. Some can do it through touch and some can do it through thought.

Seer: A Coesen who can see the future.

Sooth or Truth Seer: A Coesen who can hear the ring of truth from words that are spoken.

Markers: A Coesen who can tattoo skin with only a touch.

Cleoma: A Coesen who can render a Coesen's ability void. This Coesen can make it so you cannot use your ability in their presence.

Toma: A Coesen who can see your inner most secrets, the things you even hide yourself. This is not like reading some one's thoughts, it's reading your desires and fears.

Feeler: A Coesen who senses someone's emotions and sometimes intent through objects they've come in contact with. Some Feelers are strong enough to sense the feeling in a room without touching an object.

Brander: A Coesen who can mark another with tattoo like art by touching a person's skin. The mark is permanent and can only be removed by the Brander or someone in that brander's bloodline.

Reader: A Coesen who can sense the abilities in others.
Scanner: A Coesen who can reach into someone's mind to find intent or goals. They can also see past offenses and evil they are guilty of.
Snare: The ability to wipe another's memories
Saik: This ability is similar to that of a Protector. One has speed, advanced hearing, and has great strength.
Senser: A Coesen who can make their target feel pain or pleasure. This ability can kill.

Places

West Hills High School: A school in Arizona.
Ridgeview Park: Local park near Cianne's home where she usually run for exercise.
Valley Estates: Residential middle-class neighborhood
Kennecott University: Educational institution
Dorchester Psychiatric Hospital: Bianca received her treatment
Northridge Hospital: Hospital where Tristan was discovered during the Cycling
John Hopkins Hospital: Real Hospital in Baltimore Maryland
Wingate University Hospital: Hospital where the twins were born.
Ark Manor: Vivian's Canadian Home
Azazel's Gift Shop: New Orleans
Gering Academy: School for Coesen Three locations, Texas, Europe, and Canada with a small location on the Continent of Africa
Hammonds Drugstore: Local old-style pharmacy. Where Tranae works.

The Broken Nail Tavern: Bill's establishment and front for Watkins

The Man Cave: The bar and grill where Tristan goes while on the run

Koves Glenn: California USA. Koves choice in Coesen. Kove Glenn is a community that Vivian set up for Coesen who fall in love with Middlings. The middling must sign a gag order in blood once they are welcomed into community. They know of the power the Coesens wield and must keep it secret. The Coesen is stripped of their abilities. Any offspring must be registered but it is assumed that they will not have any abilities.

Shoppers Row: Shopping district located in Koves Glenn

The Descent of the Halo

SHEA SWAIN

www.ingramcontent.com/pod-product-compliance
Lightning Source LLC
Chambersburg PA
CBHW060609100726
47907CB00006B/1556